PAPER

DOLL

LINA

PAPER DOLL LINA

a novel

ROBYN LUCAS

LAKE UNION
PUBLISHING

Published by Lake Union Publishing, Seattle

www.apub.com

Amazon, the Amazon logo, and Lake Union Publishing are trademarks of Amazon.com, Inc., or its affiliates.

ISBN-13: 9781542030151
ISBN-10: 1542030153

Cover illustration by Sylvia Pericles

Title treatment by Faceout Studio, Amanda Hudson

Printed in the United States of America

*For everyone who has had to shrink themselves to fit
into another person's life
To Hannah & Charlie: you make me smile,
you make me sing
&
Kala, Thea, Sara*

Don't make yourself smaller and apologize for existing by saying "I don't know" and "I'm sorry" when you didn't do anything wrong. Trust what you know. Take up space. Be yourself. Step into your power and live your life.

—*Dr. Ayana Jamieson, from*
"A Note of Encouragement," 2019

CHAPTER 1

Whoever coined the term "calm before the storm" was very misguided. There wasn't a damn thing calm about anticipating disaster.

The only thing that kept Lina Henry from losing it while she waited for her name to be called was the one-size-too-small Spanx bodysuit well hidden beneath her sapphire-blue wrap dress. It'd taken her a while to pull on, tucking in jiggly bits and wriggle dancing into the unforgiving spandex to a slew of curse words. The girdle's firm pressure hugged from her chest to her thighs, forcing her to take slow, deliberate breaths. It reminded her of the twenty-pound weighted blanket back at home she'd crawl under on her most unbearable days . . . which seemed to happen more often recently.

Now, in the ice-cold studio foyer, to the early nineties soft pop playing a little louder than a hum, with a perfectly beat Fenty face, a fresh blowout, and her curves tamed and snatched in all the right places, Lina prayed like hell she wouldn't sweat it all out.

"Henry family, right?" Vivian, the production assistant, greeted Lina and her children, Mimi and Danny, near the security desk. The model-thin Asian woman sported a neat ponytail and oversize round glasses that would've looked absolutely ridiculous on Lina. She gave them all a once-over and made a note on her clipboard. Lina was sure she'd caught a nod of approval, like Vivian was saying: *I was right to book your cute kids.*

"I'm so glad you guys were able to make it on such short notice," Vivian said, handing them each a badge.

Lina could pull this off. She could do this. She flashed her best smile at Vivian and heard her husband's voice in her head: *I'd hate for you to get the kids' hopes up, again. Remember when . . .* When she'd promised to take them to their very first television interview a month earlier but canceled at the last minute. The crushed looks on her kids' faces flitted across her mind, snatching the little confidence she was faking. She'd only canceled to keep the peace after David had nitpicked at it the entire week, grunting and rolling his eyes whenever one of them mentioned it.

"Should the kids even be on TV?" he'd asked during dinner when she'd first shared the news.

"Is their little project even worth all the buzz they were getting, or was it because they're kids?" he'd mumbled while brushing his teeth the next night.

"Is this going to be like Scouts, where we'll end up doing most of the work?" he'd asked Lina when he'd called to remind her to pick up his dry cleaning.

"They don't need another distraction. Church and school are enough," he'd declared before jumping on a call the morning of, followed by, "Yeah, I'm pretty sure they'll just embarrass themselves when the cameras come on, anyway."

Having the kids embarrass themselves had been the last thing Lina'd wanted. Before she knew it, she'd sent the cancellation email, with an apology and half-hearted excuse about school. The kids had been heartbroken because they'd told all their friends, so David had whisked them off for ice cream and a movie after firmly placing the blame on her for letting them down. She'd sulked at home, watching the news broadcast a cooking segment to replace what would've been the kids' segment—their time to shine and show the world just how incredible they were.

Was she doing the same thing David had done with the ice cream by taking them to Los Angeles?

Lina opened her mouth to thank Vivian for the opportunity, but words tangled in her sandpaper throat. Had she made the right decision? An awkward pause stabbed the air. One. Two. Three seconds . . . Lina was certain Vivian was second-guessing herself now and could see disappointment flicker across her face like a scrolling announcement sign: BIG MISTAKE. SHE'S A TOTAL FLAKE AND I'M GETTING FIRED OVER THIS BOOKING BECAUSE HER KIDS ARE PROBABLY JUST AS FLAKY. Panic rose from Lina's gut, twisting and turning her insides. She swallowed hard, hoping to push it back down.

Not now. Not now. Not now.

Danny spoke up. "Thanks for having us. This is so cool. When do we go on? Can we get Sophia's autograph?"

Vivian smirked, slashed something else on her clipboard, and motioned for them to follow her. "So here's the deal," she said over her shoulder as they wound around the maze of hallways. "We're shooting a double today, and the greenroom is for our special guest, so you guys will be in our secondary waiting area." She ticked off the show's expectations and rules, Lina and the kids on her heels until her words strung together and jumbled in Lina's head.

They'll embarrass themselves, and it'll be your fault. Lina's husband's voice pulsed along with the timpani beating in her ears.

What if the kids messed up big-time? What if this was all a bad idea? What if Mimi and Danny screwed up and hated her for letting them take such a massive leap, even though they'd begged her once again for the opportunity to share their creation? A dumb, empty smile slid across Lina's face, masking the anxious tears that were building. Her heart didn't know whether to speed up for a marathon or slow to rest. She low-key felt like she was having a heart attack and did her best to hide it all as she kissed her kids and wished them luck before Vivian led them away. Her mind raced through everything she should've told them: *Remember to breathe, Mimi. Danny, don't be too much of a clown. Don't forget to smile. Speak up and have fun.*

3

It took only a few steps in either direction to pace the length of the spartan waiting area. A minifridge filled with juices and water bottles occupied one corner, a few slotted plastic chairs—the type that looked like they'd pinch the backs of Lina's thighs—sat here and there, and a television hung on the wall in front of her. It was slightly off-center and grew more crooked the longer she stared. She was beginning to think they'd relegated her to a storage closet.

After her seventeenth trip across the room, the television's screen flickered to life. There were so many faces in the stadium seating but just a small fraction of the people who'd be watching her kids when the show aired. She swallowed whatever saliva she could manage, reminding herself this wasn't Mimi and Danny's first time being interviewed. They'd cut their teeth by doing the school news and Zoom interviews.

But this was *The Sophia Show*—the number one talk show in the country.

She gave all her attention to the television screen. The live audience cheered and laughed at one of the producers' instructions. They waved into the camera, and the lights brightened, illuminating the stage—the stage her kids would either sink or swim on—and she couldn't throw them a life raft. She braced herself against one of the chairs, breathless. The producer began his countdown for the filming to commence. A hushed silence fell over the crowd, their excitement raw and electric in anticipation.

"Five. Four. Three. Two." The small man pointed to the audience and mouthed, "And we're rolling." Cheering swelled into thunderous applause, summoning the show's host. Sophia, of her eponymous hit daytime show, appeared—all hips and hair—at the last row in time with her theme music. She gyrated down the aisles, pumping her fists to the techno beats, her ample cleavage testing the buttons of her shirt.

Lina said a silent prayer for that kind of industrial strength, her front teeth now worrying the lipstick off her bottom lip. "You got this, kids. You're so much stronger than me. You're going to be amazing," she whispered, hoping her words would find their way into Mimi's and Danny's ears.

"Happy hump day!" Sophia announced, her full face bright and her voice sure. She immediately launched into a monologue highlighting the top pop culture gossip.

A curious jealousy niggled Lina. How was Sophia so confident? Lina had always struggled to make eye contact with most people, even the checkout person in the grocery store. Oftentimes, she'd pop her earbuds in without music to keep from having to people. It made her feel invisible, relegated to the background. Lina took another look at Sophia and drew her shoulders back and her chin up, trying to leech some confidence for herself.

"I have some very special guests today." Sophia clasped her hands at her waist.

Lina's knees weakened.

"Coming all the way from Atlanta, Georgia, are a pair of teen siblings who created something extraordinary. Please help me welcome Mimi and Danny Henry."

Lina squeezed her eyes shut and whispered to her daughter's psyche, "Please don't fall. Please don't fall. Please don't fall." Slowly, she opened one eye, then the next in enough time to witness Mimi gracefully take her last stride and give Sophia a firm handshake. Danny followed closely behind, fist-bumping Sophia in lieu of a handshake. They both waved at the audience and settled into their seats.

Oh my God, this is really happening.

"So you guys created this neat little website together. Tell me more about it," Sophia said.

Danny cleared his throat and ran his fingers through his tight, dark-brown curls. He shot a mischievous grin at the camera. "I play basketball," he began.

Lina leaned in closer to the screen, her breath bated.

"I love basketball, but it's hard to train and stay motivated when we don't have practice. I complained to my sister. We came up with a cool solution that will help student athletes with their workouts in the off-season." Danny flashed a brilliant white-toothed grin at the audience, and they cheered.

Sophia turned to Mimi. "So he complained to you, and you two brainstormed for a solution?"

Mimi nodded timidly. The hot, bright lights picked up just enough of Mimi's sun-kissed, reddish highlights to complement the subtle makeup the show had chosen for her rich brown skin. Lina willed her to speak up.

Mimi seemed to catch herself. She cleared her throat. "Pretty much. We were like, why isn't there a place for this? Everyone has a cell phone."

"That would be the first thing I'd think of too." Sophia smirked at the audience. Lina couldn't help but giggle.

"I started posting workout videos online, and my friends left comments," Danny added. "They kept me motivated, you know?"

"So we just took that concept and made it a little bigger." Mimi tucked a piece of hair behind her ear. "Kids can post exercise videos for their particular sport; then they have to log in at least three times a week to check in for accountability."

"That way they earn points to post more videos," Danny said.

"Did both of you make it, or did your parents hire someone?"

Mimi pursed her lips. She closed her eyes, inhaling deeply. Lina breathed along, using whatever mom sense she had in an effort to draw out Mimi's discomfort.

"Actually, Mimi did most of it. Hashtag Black girls code," Danny said.

"That's impressive. How did you go about it?" Sophia asked her.

Danny elbowed Mimi slightly.

"Well," Mimi said, taking her cue, "I'd already taken some Java and HTML classes and whatnot in school and at summer camps, so it wasn't that hard."

"You lost me, kid. I can barely turn my phone on, let alone build a social media website," Sophia said.

"We started last spring and began beta testing this past fall," Danny said.

"I'm not impressed or anything." Sophia winked into the camera, adjusting herself in the white leather chair. "I take it you guys are supposed to be in school today?"

"I'm missing a chemistry test," Mimi said.

"Hi, Ms. Bennett!" Danny waved into the camera, all teeth and cheeks. "Can I get some extra credit?"

Sophia waved as well. "Ms. Bennett, these kids totally deserve extra credit. How about you give them all As for the rest of the year?"

Mimi's shoulders relaxed a little at that request. So did Lina's.

It hit her then, just how long she'd been stressing about the show. Her anxiety had skyrocketed into overdrive the instant she'd received Vivian's email the week prior.

They did it!

Relief coursed through her. Tension slowly unfurled from her core, radiating out in long ribbons to her fingertips. Lina's breath matched her heartbeat, easing from frenzied jackhammering to calm, slow palpitations. She'd been worried for nothing, but then again, she usually worried about everything. Worrying *was* her love language, according to her all-knowing husband. With that thought, she shook her head, feeling the muscles in her neck pull. What she needed was a good stretch to loosen up before the kids returned.

Rolling her shoulders, she tilted her head from side to side. The muscles along her spine tingled in anticipation as she gently leaned over, lowering her head to her knees. Ligaments and tendons lengthened, making her vertebrae pop out a thanks. Hair curtaining her face, Lina closed her eyes, exhaling. She deepened her stretch. A heavy groan escaped her mouth, carrying her anxiety off with it. She'd needed this all day—all week, for that matter.

She was going to be okay.

Danny and Mimi were going to be okay.

Everything was going to work out.

Everything was going to be perfect when they returned to Atlanta.

David would be cool with everything.

Everything was—

"Oh, I'm so sorry," a man's voice said from behind, startling her.

Lina yanked herself back together, snapping her head up a little too quickly. The dizziness was instantaneous. She stumbled backward a bit, fuzzy black spots clouding her vision. The man's hands were on her back before she could protest.

He guided her over to a chair, grabbing a juice from the nearby fridge. "This should help."

"I'm okay," Lina said, her brain Jell-O. She sealed her eyes shut for a few moments to stop the spinning.

"You sure? Want me to call someone?"

"No. It's okay," she mumbled. It hadn't been the first time she'd moved a little too quickly and almost fainted. It wouldn't be her last. She just needed some time to get back to herself before the kids returned. "Straightened too fast. I'm totally fine. It happens." Lina gave the guy a thumbs-up. "Feeling better already."

"Okay," he said.

Lina sensed him crouch down in front of her, his palms raised to either grope her or catch her—she wasn't quite sure. *Great, he's either caring or a creep.* Lina slowly opened her eyes.

Damn.

Knots instantly returned to her stomach, but for a whole different reason now. Noah Attoh, as in Noah freaking-superfamous-actor-also-known-as-the-superhero-named-Vengeance Attoh was gazing back at her, concern pinching his handsome features.

"Better?" Noah Attoh looked exactly like he did on television, only taller. His rich, dark-mahogany skin radiated, and his signature salt-and-pepper five-o'clock beard rose when he smiled at her.

Lina nodded, afraid of further embarrassing herself. She suddenly felt like a complete idiot for being so extra. Of course this was how she'd meet anyone important. She could almost hear her husband's voice: *Seriously, Lina?*

Noah motioned to the chair beside her. "Mind?" Hints of sandal-wood teased her nose when he sat.

How do people even talk to celebrities, anyway? Stupid. Stupid. Stupid. Stupid. Wanting to salvage whatever dignity she had left and maybe even get him to mention the kids' site on-air, she mustered a drop of confidence, finger combed her hair back into place, and motioned to the television as Danny said something else to make the audience laugh. "My kids."

"Yeah? I overheard the staff talking about them," Noah said.

She could totally adult for Mimi's and Danny's sakes. "All good things, hopefully," Lina said, pretending to have some level of chill.

"Definitely. Had to see for myself."

She raised an eyebrow at how genuine he sounded, pretty sure he was the "special guest" Vivian had mentioned. "You're the one in the superfancy greenroom," Lina blurted.

Noah held his chest, feigning injury. "You got me. But it wasn't set to precisely seventy-two degrees, and they didn't have any VOSS."

And there goes the kids' shout-out. She'd screwed up again. She should just leave, go hide in a bathroom until the kids' segment was over.

"That was a joke. It was fine," he said, glancing at the television. "I don't like a lot of fuss. It feels . . . it's very uncomfortable." He crossed his arms as Danny made another joke.

"He's such a clown," Lina said, snapping a photo of the kids on-screen. It was a great shot of them interacting with Sophia and would be perfect for their yearbook.

Danny quipped a response, working the crowd.

Noah laughed.

It was throaty and warm, like he appreciated Danny's sense of humor. She'd totally have to tell her son about it after the show. It would make Danny's entire year to know Vengeance thought he was funny. Her poor boy would freak out if she were to somehow get Vengeance to tweet about their site. But how would she bring it up? Images of cereal commercials, luxury watch ads, cologne, and sports gear flashed through her mind. Did he have a Twitter account? Her leg bounced as her mind climbed back on the hamster wheel of what-ifs.

"It's pretty cool how supportive you are," Noah said after a few minutes.

Lina shrugged, formulating a game plan. She'd pretend to be nonchalant about his fame and try to find a way to bring up Twitter. "Didn't really have a choice. They're pretty headstrong."

"No way would my parents have invested anything in me like this." He leaned closer to her and lowered his voice. "My dad was all, 'I got mine; now you go get yours,' and my mother had her own struggles."

His confession caught her off guard. "I am so sorry."

"It's okay." His brows knit a beat. "I . . . can't say I've ever told anyone that before."

"Your secret is safe with me," Lina said after Sophia asked another question.

"How old is he?" Noah asked.

"Fourteen."

"And your daughter?"

"Almost sixteen."

"I was nowhere near their maturity. I would've probably pissed my pants and ran offstage already."

Lina giggled at the thought, peeking back over at him to see if he was serious.

"True story: I must've been Danny's age when my chorus teacher forced me to sing in front of the class. I opened my mouth, and all of a sudden found myself standing in a puddle. Hid in the bathroom until school ended and faked sick for the rest of the week."

Lina snorted out a laugh, mortified at the thought.

"And"—Noah drew out the word, crossing his arms pensively— "here I am once again telling you something I've never told another soul."

"I think it's the tiny room," Lina said after some time. "Might make you feel like you're in confession or something." *Speaking of confession, do you ever confess anything via social media?*

"Probably, except I'm not Catholic."

"Then a therapist's office." *By the way, I've heard tweeting can be therapeutic.*

He tilted his head as if seriously considering it. "Maybe."

"If you keep it up, I'll have to start charging you."

He pretended to lock his mouth and throw away the key.

Is Noah Attoh a giant dork? Lina smiled, completely shocked at herself for interacting with someone like him. She was seriously owed some major adulting points. She'd continue to play cool and confident, then maybe ask what he thought about the kids' site. She opened her mouth, then closed it immediately. Who was she kidding? This wasn't her. She would never be confident and cool enough to ask a celebrity like him anything.

She picked at the polish on her nails. Noah checked his phone. Lina was sure he was as uncomfortable as she was.

She stood slowly, wiping her sweaty palms across her dress.

Noah gazed at her for a few moments, squinting as if he was about to ask a question. Instead, he pursed his lips and checked his phone again. It made her feel more awkward; she wasn't quite sure why. It wasn't like he owed her a full-blown conversation or anything. She wasn't anyone special and was pretty sure he could see through her fancy-dress and made-up-face facade for what she really was: nothing. If David knew she was thinking about asking a celebrity for a favor, he'd be so embarrassed for her. So embarrassed *by* her, actually.

She felt herself shrink and laser focused her attention on gathering her purse, trying to not so much as blink as the kids wrapped up their interview.

"You've got some pretty incredible kids there." Noah stood, offering his hand. She glanced over her shoulder to see if she was being filmed or something, because there was absolutely no way Noah Attoh would want to shake *her* hand. He was probably trying to be nice to the weird lady in the room.

Shoving her hand into his awkwardly, she wanted to be invisible. "Thanks, and, um, thanks for the chair," she said quickly and smacked the top of her head for her stupid word choice. "Helping me sit and the juice. Orange. It was orange because it was orange juice from, like, the fruit that's orange. It's an orange . . ."

"Yeah, probably from Florida, er, the orange juice, not the chair, um . . ."

"Or California, I guess." Why couldn't she stop talking already?

Noah laughed. "I'm, um, sorry for interrupting you again." He pocketed his phone, his forehead wrinkling when he smiled at her. "It was really great meeting you, Lina."

Lina checked out her hand after Noah left and blushed. She'd met Vengeance and couldn't wait to tell the kids all about it. Maybe they could find him and get an autograph or even a pic with him.

But who in the world would actually believe she'd met and had a conversation with freaking Vengeance, anyway? She hardly even believed it herself. He'd been so handsome and funny and . . . Lina replayed their interaction in her head while Mimi and Danny bounded into the tiny room, filling it to overflowing with pure exhilaration. With their babbling a hundred miles an hour, it was almost overwhelming. And yet a thought slipped through the chatter, even louder in her head.

"It was really great meeting you, Lina," Noah had said. How had he known her name?

CHAPTER 2

"C'mon, Mom, you totally promised." Danny made the saddest puppy eyes. In that instant, he reminded Lina of when he was a sweet little four-year-old boy eagerly anticipating a treat.

"You heard her; just do it. Geez," Mimi yelled from the bathroom in their junior suite, and the four-year-old version of Danny dissipated into the teenage boy in front of Lina—arms crossed, lips stuck a mile out, eyes narrowed in frustration.

Lina plucked out one of his earbuds and shot him one of her signature "don't try me" looks. "Not until you pack, charge all of your devices, and finish your lunch," she said, standing her ground. It was funny to Lina how her kids had a selective memory when she made a deal. All they remembered was her promise, not the contingencies for the deal to work.

Danny grumbled something. Lina raised an eyebrow, daring him to say it louder. He sighed, crossed the hotel room, then unpacked his various devices and cords.

They were finally back at the hotel.

Lina wholeheartedly regretted making a deal with the kids to hit the pool after sightseeing around Los Angeles for the last few hours. Could she at least get a nap first? A part of her wished they were still young enough that she could enforce nap time, but the kids were relentless in wanting to try out the hotel pool. She figured she could use the time to mentally prepare to return home despite all their internal clocks running three hours ahead. It was closer to their dinnertime and bedtime than pool time, but a deal was a deal. She hoped they broke their end so she could renege on hers.

Mimi sashayed out of the bathroom in a superadorable yellow bathing suit and checked herself out in the mirror beside the door. She tugged the bathing suit here and there and eventually rummaged through her bag for a swim shirt.

"Why'd you do that, Tater Tot? You looked so cute," Lina asked, already knowing the answer.

"Not a big deal." Mimi shrugged. Lina caught her stealing a glance into the mirror, her eyes trained a little too long on her ample cleavage. Lina wished there was more she could do to help her daughter, but Mimi had gone from training bra to Dolly Parton in less than a year. Last time they'd gone shopping, Mimi had filled out a solid DD cup. Mimi rolled her eyes in the mirror and stomped to the bathroom.

If they both kept it up, Lina might be in pajamas within the next hour or so. She was almost giddy at the thought. She held up her cell phone and announced, "If you're not packed and dressed in fifteen minutes, deal is off"; then she set her timer and collapsed into the nearest bed.

~

Lina was snatched from sleep by a blaring alarm fifteen minutes later. Her face was damp with slobber, and she could feel the ridges of the pillow imprinted on her cheek. She rolled onto her side, hoping to see the kids relaxing, but she wasn't so lucky. Both Danny and Mimi stood nearby, bathing suits on, goggles dangling from their necks, smirking. They shifted slightly so she could see their suitcases lined up at the door. *Ugh. Stupid deal.*

"Dang, Mom, you were knocked out," Mimi said.

Lina stretched like a lazy tabby cat. She would grab some coffee by the pool. Coffee and something sweet. Caffeine and sugar would keep her on her feet for another few hours.

"I'm up. Give me a few minutes." Lina yawned, shuffling to the bathroom. She needed to splash her face and throw on something comfortable enough to chill poolside.

She trailed behind the kids moments later, her iPad tucked under an arm and her swim cover-up hanging down her shoulder. It looked sort of chic, when in actuality it'd been an accident—she'd stepped into the light-blue cover-up instead of pulling it on, causing the button to pop off and the shoulder seam to split. Lina donned Mimi's ginormous sunglasses and pushed out her lips, pretending to be someone fancy and important as they stepped into the mirrored elevator.

"Mom, just stop." Mimi reached for her sunglasses.

Lina slid out of her way and leaned on the rail dramatically. "I don't know what you mean."

"Ohmigod, for real?" She laughed. "You do look cute, though. Here"—she handed Lina a tube of lip gloss—"try this."

Lina smeared on a healthy amount until her lips rivaled the mirror's shine, then noticed the elevator was going up instead of down. "Why are we going up?"

"I saw it online. There's a pool on the roof, and it looks so cool," Danny said.

"But there were signs in the lobby for one down there too." Lina peeled off the sunglasses.

"Mom, it's a pool on the roof. C'mon, please?" Mimi begged.

Before she could respond, the elevator stopped. The doors slid open to a spa-like foyer area. Mimi was the first to exit, and they navigated through the bar and restaurant area to the open veranda until finally reaching the massive pool. Lina felt like she'd been transported to a Tuscan villa for vacation. Textured plaster walls in varied hues of warm terra-cotta seamlessly dipped into honeyed concrete that hugged an infinity pool so blue it looked like the brilliant azure sky above fed into the water.

"It's so beautiful," Mimi said. Lina was as awestruck.

Danny, however, wheeled back like a man on a mission. He dashed toward the water, landing in a massive cannonball. Water sprayed everywhere. Lina checked to see if he'd splashed anyone, but the pool area was empty.

"I'm never leaving." He gulped a mouthful of pool water and blew it out in an arc like a water fountain.

"You are so gross," Mimi said, posing for a selfie. "This light is perfect. My friends are going to be so jealous." She snapped pics until water sprinkled on her phone from a very wet Danny leaning over her shoulder mid-photobomb. "You are so dead." She deposited her stuff in a cushioned lounger and chased after him into the pool.

A soft breeze played in Lina's hair, teasing it across her face and shading her eyes from the late-afternoon sun. Lina felt like she should pat herself on her back or order a trophy or something. Mimi and Danny had nailed their first national TV show, and now they were having fun. It'd turned out to be an absolutely perfect day.

She snapped a few photos of them and some more of the lush mountains hemming in the towering buildings that reflected the cloudless sky. It was their own little oasis. She took a long, cool drink of this moment and tucked it away for when she'd need it.

Her phone rang.

She glanced down at the screen, tightness returning to her body. It was her husband. Hesitating for a few moments, she declined the call, not quite ready to surrender her peace. An invitation to *The Sophia Show* had been such a major opportunity for the kids and their site. She hadn't wanted David's mind games again, so she'd never expressly told him they were going. She'd mentioned the show a few times in passing, and one night, after an unfulfilling quickie when he was a blink away from sleep, she'd said how she was taking the kids to LA. He'd mumbled, "That's nice," before rolling over and fading into a deep slumber. She'd tried to bring it up the following morning, but David had been in one of his moods, riding Danny over his grades and his lackluster basketball practices. It was going to be a quick trip anyway—two days—and she'd have a few weeks to break it to him before it even aired.

Her phone rang again.

She knew she'd better answer it. She hurried around the elegant mahogany bar and ducked into the adjacent restaurant for a quiet spot. Slipping into the first booth, she chewed the inside of her cheek, weighing her words.

"Hi, honey," Lina said in a cheerful voice, hoping he was in a good mood.

"Hey, checking on you guys. I called the house a ton of times, but no one's answering, and your location is off. What's going on?" David asked.

"Everything's good. Couldn't find the handset. Not sure what the kids did with it," she said quickly, hoping he'd forget about not being able to locate her cell phone. She kicked herself for not forwarding the landline calls. They'd been in such a rush to make it to the airport. "How's Boston? How's the conference?"

Laughter and noise rose from his end of the call. Where was he?

"Lots of snow." His voice was lighter than normal.

"I'm sorry." Guilt gnawed at her when she considered the kids were swimming just then. "Hey, I need to talk to you about something sort of important."

"Sure. What's going on?"

"Remember how the kids have been working on that website?" Lina said, but David mumbled something she couldn't quite make out. It sounded like he was talking to someone else.

"Yeah, website," he said after some time and then laughed heartily. It was such a foreign sound. Lina searched her memories for the last time she'd heard him so happy and came up empty. Sadness needled her.

"Know what? We can do this later. Just give me a call when you're back at the hotel," she said, but David resumed his conversation on the other end. She listened intently and caught bits and pieces. Her ears perked up when she heard him utter something that sounded a whole hell of a lot like "another whiskey sour" before one of his finest fake laughs; then he told someone he'd join them in a minute.

"Are you drinking again?" she asked.

"No. Why would you ask that?"

"Sounded like you just ordered a drink."

"And?" he said flatly.

"You're not supposed to be drinking."

"I'm not."

"But I heard—"

"I said I'm not."

She knew what she'd heard but also knew he'd keep denying it until they were fighting again if she pressed. "Sure," she said.

"Why do you always have to start?" He asked someone to hold his seat. "I'll be back late tomorrow night. Can you cook something other than chicken?"

"Sure."

"I'd better go."

The line went silent before "I love yous" were shared. It used to be so routine, telling him she loved him and receiving it back. *How could he start drinking again?* David had promised he wouldn't drink anymore after his DUI. She clenched her jaw until it hurt. She was tempted to call him back and throw LA in his face.

Instead, she texted him: I love you too.

The message bubble on her phone appeared—one, two, three dots. Hope gurgled in her chest; then the text bubble disappeared. She added a quick **You promised not to drink** before tossing her phone onto the table. It landed with a loud clunk. Her fingers ached to text fight with David because she knew what she'd heard—she wasn't imagining it.

She ran her hands through her hair, tugging a little at the roots, her frustration mounting at the ensuing drama that always followed David's drinking.

"Excuse me?"

Lina looked up to find a hotel employee standing at her table. "Yes?" she asked, unable to take her eyes off his impeccable eyebrows. She wondered what sort of witchcraft he had to use in order to get them so perfect.

"I'm going to have to ask you to leave," the employee said pointedly.

"I'm sorry, didn't know you guys were closed."

"To you we are." The man pursed his thin lips in satisfaction.

What the actual hell? Lina's skin prickled. She slowly rose from her seat, willing her legs to stay strong. "What is that supposed to mean?"

"The roof area is reserved for our platinum members. Somehow the elevator granted you and your"—he looked over his shoulder, scowling at Danny and Mimi in the pool—"children access when it should not have. The issue has been resolved."

She wanted to smack the smugness from his pixie-perfect face. Why was he being such an asshole? "Oh, come on. They're having fun. Can I buy a pass or something?"

"We don't sell passes. This isn't Disney . . . or the Oakland City Pool." He added the last bit under his breath.

The hairs on Lina's arms prickled.

"Please remove the children from the area. There is a family pool on the first floor. I'm pretty sure it's teeming with"—he sneered—"guests."

She'd dealt with assholes in Georgia before, being in an interracial marriage and all, but something about this situation threw her off. Had she not been expecting it in LA? "I need to see your manager."

He punched a few buttons on his cell phone. "Send security up, please."

"Are you serious? Security?" She hated how soft and weak her voice sounded in that moment. "I asked to speak to your manager."

"I'm not going to ask you again. You have five minutes to vacate the area."

Lina froze with anger, hurt, and rage. A shadow of tears clouded the backs of her eyes.

"There you are! I'm so glad you made it."

Lina glanced over her shoulder and gawked as Noah Attoh approached them.

"Is there a problem, Brad?" he asked, leveling his gaze at the guy, whose name tag clearly read: Lucien.

"N-no, Mr. Attoh. I was just—"

"Being rude," Lina said.

"I invited them. They're my guests."

She glanced at Noah, grateful, but trained her expression. "I didn't see you."

"Sorry." He pointed to a booth at the very back of the restaurant. "I was working. You know how I get when I'm in the zone."

She, in fact, did not know but was willing to play along.

"Do the kids look bored to you?" Noah asked.

She shrugged, unable to hide her confusion.

"Hey, Brad, how about you scrounge up a few of those floats for the kids."

"We don't allow floats."

Noah stared through him.

"B-but I'm sure I can find some."

"I'm thinking swans or maybe a poop emoji float. What do you think?" He turned to Lina.

"Poop emojis, definitely."

"Twenty minutes should be enough time to get some up here, right? Or should I speak to management?" Noah asked.

Lucien looked like he was making a little poop emoji himself. Lina bit the inside of her lip to keep from smiling.

"I'll see what I can do," he said.

"And whatever else they want. Why don't you go over there and get them set up in a cabana as well?" Noah said.

"Y-yes, Mr. Attoh." Lucien's voice was whisper thin. Lina tipped her head higher.

"Has Mama Tish arrived yet?"

Lucien checked his watch. "She'll be here in a few minutes."

"Great, please let her know I'm here," Noah said.

Lucien's face turned stark white when four large security guards bounded into the restaurant. Now it was Lina's turn to smirk.

CHAPTER 3

"I'm really sorry you had to experience that," Noah said.

A helpless dread filled Lina. She and her kids hadn't been seen as worthy enough to do something as simple as swim in a pool. Her mind hearkened back to similar experiences from her past. Growing up in a small suburb in upstate New York, she'd had her fair share of nasty slurs and contemptuous stares. It made her wince when she considered how Mimi and Danny had almost experienced something as disgusting. Lucien's blatant attack would've hushed the carefree, jovial voices that were now bouncing off every surface from the pool area to the bar, and finally back to the restaurant area, darkening an otherwise incredible experience for them.

Lina wasn't naive. Sooner rather than later she and David would have to give them both the talk about how to handle themselves during a traffic stop. As Black teenagers, hearing a racist comment or being followed throughout a store was bound to happen. She couldn't shield them forever, but she'd protect them as long as she damn well could.

"I can't believe that just happened," she said, watching Lucien lead the security guards back to the elevator.

"Me neither. I'm going to have a long talk with the owner," Noah said. "Are you okay?"

"Yeah, I'm good." Lina motioned in the kids' direction. "I'm just glad they didn't have to see any of that."

"I hear you." He clasped his hands over his head and exhaled heavily. An understanding passed between them—the shared pain, embarrassment, and helplessness left in racism's wake. It was like bumping an old wound, the sting a reminder of something larger, deeper.

"So should I bring my stuff over here?" he asked after a moment.

"You don't have to do anything. I'll go hang out with the kids. I've interrupted you enough."

He scratched his head, shooting her a boyish look. "Well, I did say you were my guest."

"Umm—"

"And Mama Tish's cooking is something you definitely do not want to miss."

Was she about to have a dinner with Vengeance? She felt all the blood rush to her face and for a second wondered what kind of drama she'd get from David if he found out she'd had a casual, nondate dinner with a man . . . with Noah Attoh.

Whiskey sour.

Since her husband was currently breaking his promise to her by drinking, why not? Mimi and Danny were having such a great time, and she had to keep up the charade of being Noah's guests, anyway. It was just dinner. She could use the time to find enough courage to ask him to post about the kids' site on his social media accounts.

Decision made, Lina tucked some hair behind her ear. "I mean, as long as it's not a bother."

"Not at all."

Lina fumbled with her phone, wanting to kick herself for being so clumsy as Noah guided her to a booth at the very back of the restaurant. She bit her lower lip hard in an attempt to kill the dorky smile that was now forming.

She was following Noah freaking Attoh.

She was going to have dinner with Vengeance.

She was going to get him to tweet about the kids' site.

Mimi and Danny's site was going to be a huge success, and she'd finally feel like a helpful mom, a useful mom . . . a *good* mom.

She began thinking of ways to bring it up as she slid into the booth. The tufted fabric was soft on the backs of her thighs. She couldn't help but run her hand over the seat and wonder if it was some sort of incredibly expensive suede.

"Hey," Noah said, taking his own seat. "I need to apologize for stooping to Lucien's level earlier."

Lina squinted.

"The poop emoji float." He waited until recognition crossed her face. "Yeah. No matter how terrible he was, I should've handled myself better." He tapped the table a few times. "The way he treated you, I guess I just wanted him to feel a piece of how he made you feel. But it still wasn't right . . . I've just never seen that side of Lucien before. I didn't know he was that kind of person."

"Do you live in the hotel or something?" Lina attempted to make light of the situation.

"I probably should." He snorted. "I usually stay here instead of my place when I'm only in town for a day or two."

Lina must've had a weird look on her face, because he immediately added, "LA traffic. Takes forever to get home, and it doesn't make sense if I'm only home for less than forty-eight hours. I hate wasting time."

She nodded as if she understood why someone would stay in a hotel when they had home nearby, but whatever.

"And Mama T really is something else."

"I sure am, baby." An older woman with a thick Caribbean accent appeared just shy of their table, her silver-white dreadlocks crowned with a crisp chef's hat. She was rail thin and walked with a boldness Lina was sure she'd never achieve.

Noah stood and hugged her gently. "I was just telling Lina about your cooking."

There it was again. She hadn't imagined it earlier. How had he known her name?

"Well, I hope you're hungry," Mama Tish said. "What do you want, honey?"

"No menus—she can make anything you want," Noah added.

"Oh, um, I'm not sure," Lina said, overwhelmed at the idea of making a decision. Chicken, steak, Mexican, seafood, breakfast, lunch, dinner . . . her head spun at all the possibilities. She gave Mama Tish a leading smile, hoping the old woman would give her some parameters to work within, but she didn't. The pressure to choose correctly weighed on Lina's shoulders.

Noah leaned on the table. "What are you in the mood for? First thing that comes to your mind?"

"Chicken and waffles," Lina said before thinking and immediately wanted to take it back, confident she sounded as ignorant as she felt.

Noah quirked his mouth to the side.

Lina couldn't meet Mama Tish's eyes. "I, um . . ." She fingered the edge of her cover-up, slouching in the seat a little, hoping it would open up and swallow her whole. "I, um, promised the kids Roscoe's earlier, but we haven't had the chance to try it." She bit her bottom lip, preparing to be chastised. She was so stupid for even bringing it up. Noah was probably used to dinners with ultraclassy women who ordered food that sounded more like Harry Potter spells: Époisses de Bourgogne, foie gras, boula boula with essence of whatever, deconstructed roulade with foraged truffles.

And this is how Lina ruins dinner. She could almost hear David's words just then: *I can't take you anywhere.*

She sucked in a deep breath, bracing herself for an onslaught.

Instead, Noah nodded and laughed like it was the funniest thing he'd heard all year. "Roscoe's is the best thing I've ever eaten in my life.

I'm sorry, Mama T," he added quickly. "I tried this place in Atlanta that boasted about their chicken and waffles, but it just wasn't the same. Mind if I copy you?"

Lina shook her head and peeked up at Mama Tish, who only winked at her.

"I like this one," the old woman said. "Has a mind of her own. Them your babies?"

Lina suddenly felt ten years old. "Yes, ma'am."

"They look like good kids. I'll make some waffles for them too."

"Oh, wow. Thank you so much."

"No bother, just take care of this one here." She pressed a bony finger into Noah's chest. Embarrassment crisscrossed his face.

"Oh, it's not like that," Noah and Lina said in unison.

Mama Tish grinned accusingly.

"Okay, okay, okay, Mama Tish," Noah said. "We've got some work to finish up, and I bet the kids are starving."

She patted his cheek. "I'll send the food up in a bit, my boy. How long are you staying?"

"Just tonight. Flying to New York in the morning, then Korea."

"Always coming and going so quickly."

"But I'll be back in a few weeks."

"Well, I'll be here. I'd better go." She reached for another hug before leaving.

"Hope I didn't insult her," Lina said as Noah settled back into his seat.

"Not at all. Mama Tish is cool, definitely not offended."

"You guys have a cute mother-son vibe."

He nodded slowly without adding anything further. Should Lina have said that, given what he'd shared about his mother's addiction? She never knew what to do or how to act. She finally understood why David had stopped dragging her to social events. *Awkward* and *embarrassing* had been the nicer words he'd used after the Governors Ball a few years back when she'd interjected unsolicited business advice to one of his clients. It'd been as if she'd broken an unspoken rule where wives remained smiling, silent trinkets, seen, not heard, unless sharing recipes or talking about their children.

Lina shook it off, powered on her iPad, and connected to the hotel's Wi-Fi to distract herself by searching for Noah Attoh's social media accounts.

Noah cleared his throat. "Lost my mom a few years ago and Mama T sort of adopted me. I'm sorry for making it weird, Lina."

"I'm so sorry to hear about your mother." She felt a slew of questions rise. "Can I ask you something?"

"Anything."

"How do you know my name? I never said it earlier."

"I can see how that's a little creepy." He chuckled.

"Level three on the creepiness scale."

"Saw it on one of the AP's papers." He looked like he'd been caught stealing a cookie. "I appreciate you agreeing to have dinner with me," he said after some time.

"Even if it's waffles?" Lina still felt a twinge of embarrassment at her choice.

"*Because* you wanted chicken and waffles! I'm so glad you didn't order a salad."

"You can't be serious."

"I've been in beast mode for the last four months, training for the next Vengeance installment. Haven't had so much as a cheat meal."

Lina couldn't wrap her head around that level of commitment. It'd taken her the last eighteen months of hard-ish work to lose sixty-five pounds, and she still had another thirty or so to make the goal weight she'd set with her therapist. She would've lost them faster had she had Noah's level of dedication, but she loved tacos and cupcakes too damned much, and the thought of black coffee sans sweetened creamer made her violent.

"Health is healing the body *and* the mind," Brenda, her therapist, would remind her every session. "We're working on your mind; you've gotta find peace with your body."

"Four months and not even one tiny cheat meal?" Lina asked.

"Sixteen weeks of lightly seasoned fish or lean chicken, steamed vegetables, and protein shakes," Noah said.

"I can totally order something else. Don't want to tempt you or mess up your routine or anything."

"A little temptation is good."

Lina pretended to look at something on her iPad as her cheeks flushed. She couldn't think of a clever retort and worried awkward silence would fill in the gap between them. She liked talking to him. To be honest, she liked the attention and couldn't remember the last time David had actually listened to her. "What were you working on before all of that drama?" she asked quickly, unable to find Noah's name followed by a blue check mark on Twitter.

"Trying to nail down distribution for an indie I directed a while ago."

"Sounds exciting."

"Not really. It's a bunch of rejections and lowballing. I'm grateful for the break." Noah closed his laptop and tucked his ballpoint pen into his leather notepad, then appraised her. "Tell me something."

"Sure, anything." Nothing on Instagram either. She opened her Facebook account.

"How do you do it?"

Lina tilted her head to the side. "Do what?"

"How are you so sure and carefree? Like, I would've never imagined ordering chicken and waffles if a chef came to my table, but here you are just living life. How do you do it?"

"I'm not sure if that was an insult or a compliment."

"Definitely a compliment. You're not trying to impress me. It's refreshing. Don't get that very often."

"Thanks, um . . . I'll take it as a compliment, but I'm not sure I have an answer for you." Lina pinched herself to keep from laughing. He'd had her pegged all wrong—she was just a woman who said all the wrong things, all the time. *Did you think first?* David's voice bit into her thoughts. She couldn't argue; she had no filter.

"It's just who I am, I guess," Lina added with a shrug.

"I'll keep that in mind." A satisfied smile crept across his face like he'd figured out the first in a series of ciphers. He made some small talk, leaning into the table more with each passing moment. Soon, Lina's iPad screen darkened and went into sleep mode.

They eventually settled into comfortable conversation while the sun finished its trail across the sky, painting it blue with pinkish-orange streaks, then deep orange, like the sky was on fire, and finally settling into a hazy purple so deep it would've been black if they weren't in the city.

Lights flickered on around them, giving their table an ethereal glow, like the night was magic, and maybe it was. Maybe there was a little magic keeping Lina chill and cool instead of goofy and awkward. She was amazed at how naturally their words ebbed and flowed, rolling from one side of the table to the next and back again. He'd mention some random subject, and she'd have a similar story to add. She'd laugh about something the kids had done, and he'd follow suit with an anecdote.

He didn't judge her.

He didn't criticize her.

He just let her . . . be. It was an unusual sensation Lina had trouble understanding. For the first time in a long while, she felt seen and heard, and she wanted more. She was just about to ask if he ever visited Atlanta when a server appeared with a stacked tray.

Noah shifted around his stuff, making room for the plates in antici-pation. It was as if nothing else mattered except for the food. Lina couldn't blame him. She was starving. Her stomach whined to be filled the very second the delectable plate was placed in front of her.

Vanilla and buttery scents mingled with the sweet, oily spices of the fried chicken. Lina's mouth watered. The server droned on about the chef's technique to enhance the southern style used on the chicken and how Mama Tish made it her own by incorporating some of the waffle batter to coat the wings. Noah gave the man his rapt attention, nodding and mm-hmming every other word.

Seeing the desperation in Noah's eyes, Lina felt compelled to send him a life raft. "Hey, Jonathan." She waved a little to get the server's attention. "Have the kids eaten yet?"

"Not yet. I was just about to bring up their plates."

"I think we're good here, for now. Would you mind bringing their food up?"

Noah mouthed, "Thank you."

"The kids have to be starving. Just bring up another bottle of water for me," Noah said.

"I'll take a water as well. Thank you," Lina added, holding her breath for Jonathan to leave so she could devour her food.

"I owe you for that," Noah said when Jonathan was out of earshot. "Thought he'd never stop."

"Yeah, you looked hopeless." She laughed. "Thought you were going to start crying."

"Another minute or two and you would've seen tears." Noah picked up his utensils and started in on his waffle. Lina watched, witnessing the stages of unadulterated joy ripple across his face.

"That good, huh?" Lina asked, then dived into her plate. Every single taste bud responded orgasmically. "Ohmigod, this is the best thing I've ever had in my life. I see why you live here. Like, I may never leave. Bet I can get a job washing dishes or something just to be close to Mama T's food."

"Aren't you glad you stayed?" Noah asked between bites of chicken.

"Like I said, I may never leave." Lina felt like she was having a purely religious experience as she bit into the chicken wing, hearing a satisfying crunch immediately followed by an explosion of spices, a little heat, and the sweet, earthy flavor of maple syrup. *How the hell did Mama T make this?* Lina wondered, taking another bite.

Before long, a satisfied exhaustion set in—the hallmark of amazing cooking. She wiped her mouth, wondering if she could fit any more food into her stomach as she looked down at her half-full plate.

"My trainer will have me doing burpees until I vomit if he ever finds out I ate this," Noah said, his waffle destroyed and his chicken bones picked clean. He eyed Lina's food.

She pushed her plate to him. "Have at it. I'm stuffed."

"Really?"

She giggled, watching him clean her plate as well. Why did it feel like they were old friends instead of having just met earlier that day? How had they developed a familiarity so quickly?

"Mom? Mom?" Mimi called.

Lina started. *Crap.* She'd forgotten that she was with Noah Attoh and not just some regular person.

"Hey, I'd better go. Don't want my kids freaking out if they see you." She gathered her stuff, saddened at the thought of having her evening come to an end, but what had she expected? And why hadn't she taken the time to ask about shouting out the kids' site?

Noah shifted to stand. "I wouldn't mind meeting them. They seem like great kids and maybe—"

"Mom?" Mimi's voice grew closer, and Lina's heart raced. It wasn't that the kids would embarrass her or cause a scene fangirling over him; she just didn't want to share him. She wanted to keep Noah all to herself: her one evening of laughter and . . . freedom. She felt lighter than she'd felt in years.

"It's okay. Thanks again for everything," she said.

"You're welcome, Lina. Have to admit this was one of the best evenings I've had in a while."

"You really need to get out more."

He held out a hand. "I'd say it was great meeting you, but that would be an understatement. It was . . ."

"Yeah, I'm glad we met."

Mimi called again.

"I'd better go," Lina said.

Noah tapped his cell phone screen a few times. Her phone sounded with an AirDropped file with his contact information.

"Just in case you'd like to keep in touch," Noah said sheepishly.

Lina glanced down at her phone in disbelief. She had Noah Attoh's phone number. He wanted to stay in touch with her. Noah freaking Attoh! She sent him her number, figuring if he really wanted to, he'd call her first. Otherwise, his offer was probably an empty gesture people like him used to make people like her feel special. And she did feel special . . . she just hoped the feeling would be enough wind in her sails to carry her through the next few weeks.

CHAPTER 4

Lina walked faster than her kids through the Hartsfield-Jackson Atlanta Airport when they landed the next afternoon. It was ridiculously busy for a Thursday this early in January due to the threat of ice. The city was slated to shut down the following day, a standard reaction to winter weather since southern states were so ill prepared. Lina was thankful they'd managed to make it back before the weather hit.

There was a sort of bouncy, lighter-than-air sensation to her gait. She felt sexy for the first time in at least a decade and was actually looking forward to seeing her husband. Maybe dinner with Noah Attoh had been exactly what she'd needed to jump-start her marriage again. She shot David a quick text message: Can't wait for you to come home. xoxo

She and David *had* been attracted to one another when they'd dated eighteen years earlier. A few years out of college, Lina had been a small business strategist, and David had been one of her clients. He'd worked as a financial adviser with dreams of starting his own firm. He'd shown up late for his second appointment with an apology scrawled across a box of Godiva chocolates. He'd been so disarmingly charming, it'd been hard to turn him down when he'd asked her to dinner. Dinner had quickly turned into breakfast, and before long they'd spent every waking hour together outside of work.

They could regain some of that.

Maybe not immediately, but she had to at least try. She had a plan: drop the kids off and run to the mall for some sexy lingerie. Once the kids were in bed, she'd be all flirty with him and initiate sex. It was always something he'd complained about—how she never wanted to have sex with him and how she never tried to excite him. She thought about how Noah had looked at her, like he'd actually peeked inside and appreciated what he'd seen. She imagined David looking at her like that: his eyebrows relaxed and interested, not furrowed with contempt for her; his eyes kind and focused only on her, instead of calculating and critical.

Butterflies thrilled in her gut. She could be happy again.

No, *they* could be happy again.

She carried out her plan, making sure to use her secret debit card— the one tied to the bank account she'd kept after she'd stopped working . . . or at least after she'd told David she'd stopped working. It was only a few consulting hours here and there, but it made her feel useful, especially now that the kids were older.

She'd used the money for things she didn't want David to complain about, like a therapist after her miscarriage two years ago and expenses she didn't want him to nitpick. While keeping her job and bank account from David riddled her with guilt, it was better than his reaction, and she'd tell him . . . eventually.

Nothing was going to ruin tonight for her.

It was late afternoon by the time she finally pulled her two-year-old Mercedes SUV into one of the bays of their three-car garage. David may have been a cheap bastard, but he still went overboard to impress everyone. Once inside, she hurried the kids to unpack, clean up, and complete their chores while she popped dinner in the oven.

Within seconds of setting the oven timer, Lina's brain went back into overdrive. Scenarios of how she'd tell David about LA—and how he'd react—played over and over in her head. Nausea, a familiar friend, returned to her gut. She considered not telling him at all—keeping it secret until *The Sophia Show* finally aired. She'd concoct a lie about how they'd filmed it here in Atlanta. But this wasn't like her job or bank account—it wasn't her secret alone. The kids were bound to tell David the truth; it was only a matter of time.

How was she going to show him their site wasn't like the other handful of ideas they've all had? Their website wasn't like Danny's attempts at soccer or baseball; Mimi's gymnastics, knitting, bookbinding, or basketball tries; or Lina's writing, sewing, singing in the choir, small group, or handbag resale fails. Mimi and Danny's website was something special. Their brilliant idea had the potential to be huge, had the potential to get them into any college they wanted, had the potential to give them more options than she'd ever had.

She just had to get David to see it as well. But knowing him, it would have to be successful before she told him. Her answer was simple: she had to do whatever she could to make sure their site succeeded so her husband wouldn't discourage the kids to the point of quitting.

Noah Attoh's number.

That was the solution—she'd text Noah Attoh and ask him to give their site a shout-out. One or two tweets from Vengeance would do the trick. Lina dug her phone from her back pocket, pulled up his contact information, and sent him a text message, hoping he'd in fact given her his real number.

Lina: Hi. It's Lina Henry. We met yesterday at the Sophia Show.

Lina: We had waffles.

Lina: And chicken.

Lina: I mean, waffles and chicken. Together. For dinner.

Lina: Mama Tish made them.

She read over her text messages and couldn't believe how completely stupid and psycho she sounded. She chewed the inside of her cheek. What was she doing?

Her phone chirped with a text message.

Noah: Hi Lina!

She felt herself blush. She leaned against the kitchen counter, the granite cool beneath her. In that moment, she wanted nothing more than her husband to desire her and make love to her like he used to. She needed him to want her. She needed him to make her feel like she was more than a frumpy wife and ever-exhausted mom. She needed him to make her feel seen like she did in this moment.

Lina: Thanks for dinner. I had a good time.

Noah: So did I. We should do it again sometime.

Lina: Sure.

Noah: Had to confess to my trainer this morning. 100 burpees.

Noah: Almost vomited.

Lina: Oh no! I'm sorry.

Noah: 110% worth it.

Noah: Did you make it back before the snow?

Lina: Why, yes, thanks for asking.

Noah: Not a stalker. Have some family and a house in Atlanta.

Lina: Oh, okay.

Lina: By any chance, have you checked out the kids' website?

Noah: I have! It's incredible!

Lina felt the rush of adrenaline surging through her and was on the cusp of asking about shouting the kids out when Mimi entered the kitchen.

"Is that Dad?" Mimi asked.

Lina fumbled with her phone. "Yeah. Yeah, your dad."

Mimi leaped up onto the counter and sat.

"What's up, Meems?"

Mimi shrugged, swinging her legs in long arcs. She had that exhausted-but-functioning-because-I-have-to look that accompanied flying across the country twice in as many days. Poor kid needed a hot bath, dinner, and bed ASAP.

"You okay?" Lina asked.

She shrugged again. "Dad isn't texting me back. Like, he always used to text me back, but he's been . . . I don't know. Different."

Different was a nice way of putting it, if *different* meant David had become more critical of their family while also pulling away from them.

Mimi tugged at a loose thread on her ripped jeans until the white strand gave way. She twisted it around her ring finger until the tip plumped and reddened, then unwound it. "I mean, I don't know, he hasn't been Dad. Know what I mean?"

Lina had sensed it too: David slowly disconnecting from the family and withdrawing into himself, into his work, into his church relationships, into everyone else except for the people who lived with him, who were suddenly not enough. Danny's grades had never been good enough, despite all As and Bs. Mimi's clothing choices had become questionable, despite them fitting her like any teen girl. Lina's everything had bothered him: her naturally curly hair—so she straightened it; her glasses—so she got surgery; her wardrobe—until he'd bought her a new one . . .

It'd become one less family dinner here, a snide remark there. One extra workweek in another city here, a biting text message there. Soon, family vacation was canceled or postponed because Lina had been too indecisive, and David had shown up less and less for any of the kids' activities because he'd been certain they were going to quit, and he didn't want to waste his time.

On the rare occasion, they'd find whispers of the David they knew when he'd come home in a flurry and whisk them all off on a weekend trip to Savannah, where they'd spend forty-eight hours doing nothing but laughing and having a good time. Or when he'd take a day off work and keep the kids home, where they'd all don matching pajamas and spend the entire day in Lina and David's bed, hanging out and watching silly movies. Or even sometimes when he'd crawl into their bed after a long workday and simply hold Lina close to his chest until he slept.

It'd felt like their bad days were bookended by good ones here and there.

Lina'd had an electrocardiogram days after her fortieth birthday. In the icy, dark room, as the technician crinkled the thin paper gown away from her chest, she'd imagined her family as the electric green line surging across the monitor; the sudden dips and sharp spikes along a seemingly mundane line were how her life felt. Straight line, then dip: David's in a mood, so everyone in the house pays the price. Straight line, then spike: Normal David is back and they're all happy.

Straight line, dip.

Straight line, spike.

Small dip.

Tiny spike.

Major dip.

Big spike.

Eventually, Lina'd attributed David's mood swings and distance to all the traveling he'd been doing and the stress he'd been under since being overlooked for partner last March. It'd been a major blow for him and had been on the heels of their last miscarriage. It'd felt like their family couldn't catch a break over the last few years: IVF round one, IVF round two, failure, success, success, miscarriage; David's DUI, David's demotion, David gets passed up for partner; David gets sent to work on new account in Boston.

Lina felt sorry for him when she looked at how hurt Mimi was and how much of the kids' lives he was missing. She tucked some of her daughter's hair behind her ear and pecked her forehead. "Your dad is just stressed about his job. He loves you guys. You know how your father is," she reassured Mimi . . . and herself as well.

"I guess."

"And he's probably rushing to get home before the storm hits. You saw how busy the airport was," Lina added, then remembered she needed to remind the kids not to say a word about *The Sophia*

Show until it aired. She had several weeks to work on making the site successful.

"Can you get Danny? I need to talk to you two about something."

"Hey, loser, get your butt down here. Mom needs you!" Mimi yelled at the top of her lungs.

Lina rolled her eyes, her ears ringing. "I could've done that."

"What do you want, Mom?" Danny called from his room upstairs.

"Your butt down here before I tell her what you're looking at online!" Mimi gave her mom a satisfied grin. Danny shuffled down to the kitchen, making sure to "accidentally" bump into his sister.

"Sup?" Danny said, joining her on the counter.

"We have perfectly working chairs, guys." Lina motioned to the tufted barstools she'd ordered as a Christmas gift for herself.

"But sitting up here annoys you," they said in perfect unison and giggled. It was amazing how quickly they could switch from insulting each other and fighting to being friendly.

Lina couldn't help but laugh too. She reminded the kids *The Sophia Show* was a surprise for their father and to keep it to themselves until it aired. While both Mimi and Danny agreed to keep it a surprise, the guilt of having them participate in her lie ate at her.

~

What felt like a few minutes had actually been several hours when Lina woke to find David climbing into their bed a little after two in the morning. Lina was exhausted but determined to make good on her marriage. She slid off her silk bonnet and shifted closer to David's side of the bed, draping her arm around his bare, pale chest.

"How were the kids?" he asked.

"Good. You know, school, after-school activities. Same old routine."

"Miss me?" He pulled her closer so she'd spoon him tighter.

"Yeah." Hope flickered in her chest. She gently ran her toes down the back of his legs. He shuddered, inching them away from hers.

He rolled over and caressed her cheek. "How can you be under the covers and still feel like Frosty the Snowman?"

Lina wrapped a leg around him. "I'm warm where it counts."

He pulled her closer. "I see."

She caught a whiff of something more than toothpaste on his breath. Had he, in fact, been drinking again? She kissed him to taste but was unable to confirm her suspicions. Maybe it had all been in her head.

David's lips trailed down her neck. "Anything new happen?"

Lina moaned. "Just the usual."

"You made chicken again." He inched her panties down. "Think you can make pot roast tomorrow?"

Lina would make any damn thing he wanted just then.

David stopped and glared at her. "Pot roast?"

"Yes, I'll make pot roast, David." She brought her lips to his and kissed him to recapture their moment, but he pulled away, assessing her.

"What's up with the sudden change?" He tugged at the delicate straps on her new negligee. "When did you get this?"

In the moonlight filtering down through their skylight, Lina pushed back the duvet and posed seductively. "You like it?"

"Where did you get it?" His fingers slid across the silky fabric covering her breasts until her nipples hardened.

"Picked it up today." She immediately wanted to take back her answer. Ugh, she'd been too busy trying to seduce him to mind her words.

"I didn't see any new charges when I checked the account earlier." His hands explored her body.

"I used cash, no biggie." Lina leaned in to kiss his neck, but he moved back, clearly not quite finished with his questions.

"You had cash? From where? I didn't notice any ATM withdrawals." He brought his mouth close to her ears. "You make it to the gym today?"

"Yeah."

"Tell me the truth, Lina." He kissed the sensitive patch of skin just behind her ear, making her whimper. "Where'd you get it?"

"Saved up to surprise you."

"Don't lie to me."

"I'm not," she breathed.

"You'd better not be," he said, an edge to his voice. When he made love to her, it felt rushed and forced instead of the way she'd wanted. She'd wanted him to look her in the eyes. She'd wanted him to hold her and make love to her tenderly. She'd wanted to feel special and not like an obligation or an afterthought.

She lay next to her husband minutes later, unfulfilled and frustrated. She reached for him as he settled back into his side of the bed. "Hey, David."

"What is it?" he yawned.

The weight of traveling to Los Angeles for *The Sophia Show* pinned her to the bed; her sleep demon was now clamping her mouth shut, paralyzing her muscles.

David reached for her hand, holding it against his chest. "You know I love you, right?"

She exhaled long and steady, her heart softening. Working long hours in Boston had exhausted him; that was all. They were going to be okay. Her plan to redeem their marriage was working.

He kissed her palm, placed her hand on the bed. "I don't want you going to that gym anymore."

CHAPTER 5

The meteorologist had been all wrong. Instead of flurries and ice, the Henry family woke to snow blanketing every surface in an ivory that sparkled like glitter in the bright sunlight. There was something other-worldly about the delicate flakes drifting through the Atlanta air.

Logs crackled and popped in the blazing outdoor fireplace. Lina sat on their covered deck in her thickest flannel pajamas, nursing a steaming cup of coffee. She'd fought with her bed all night, tossing and turning, searching for a comfortable spot. Unbearable malaise had clung to her flesh, itching and needling her no matter how she'd shifted.

Lina sighed heavily, trying her hardest to remember the breathing techniques from her last therapy appointment eight months ago. All she could remember was having to visualize stress leaving her body. Eyes closed, she inhaled and exhaled slowly, trying her hardest to imagine what stress leaving her body looked like. Soon she found herself fascinated with the puff of air fogging in front of her nose. Was that her stress?

"Morning, gorgeous." David stood in the doorway, a mug of coffee between his hands and a satisfied smile on his face. He looked like he'd stepped out of an old coffee commercial: handsome middle-age man with bright-blue eyes, morning stubble, and dimples. She couldn't help but return the smile. He ducked into the house, returning with a thick knit throw before joining her on the wicker sofa.

"How'd you sleep?" He pulled her close beneath the covers.

"Not so great." She leaned into him, comforted by the familiar way his cheek prickled her forehead. He kissed her and held her for a moment.

"How was everything?"

"Okay. Glad you're home."

"Just okay?" He nibbled her earlobe.

She had to come clean before the kids woke up. "Yeah. Hey, can we talk?"

"Sure." He dug his phone from his robe pocket.

"Um, how was Boston?"

"Exhausting. Still can't believe they promoted Daniella over me. I've been with the firm longer, have landed more clients, and I know for certain I've had a hell of a lot more billable hours." He sipped his coffee, placed it on the glass table. "Feels like a box had to be checked; know what I mean?"

Lina wanted to roll her eyes so badly. David's ills had always been someone else's fault. His start-up investment firm hadn't succeeded because Lina hadn't supported him enough, when, in fact, it'd failed because he'd refused to follow her guidance as a small business strategist. CrossFit hadn't rewarded him with his dream body because the coach hadn't pushed him hard enough, not because David ate like crap. And now a woman had been promoted instead of him because the firm needed to check a box, not because of David's DUI. Lina firmly recalled overhearing a conference call where the partners had issued a stern warning and demotion because they couldn't jeopardize the firm's reputation due to their high-profile clients.

Lina took this as an opportunity to clear one thing off her secret slate. "Maybe I can go back to work, and you can cut back a little." She shifted to look at him. "I've kept in touch with Bev, and you know she'd hire me back without question." That was an understatement. Her boss had been begging her to take on more than the five to seven consulting hours she'd been doing every month. Bev had even dangled an executive position in front of her like a carrot.

David was silent, his shaggy hair covering his eyes and his attention on his phone. She ran a hand through his hair, tangling her fingers in his thick, reddish-brown strands. When he groaned, it reminded her of a time when they'd had a problem keeping their hands off each other. How could she miss him so much when he was right beside her?

Part of her wondered if he'd heard her mention returning to work, but she knew he was ignoring her. She cleared her throat, spoke up. "So what do you think?"

"You're serious?"

She crossed her arms. "Yes, I've been thinking about it a lot. The kids are older and don't need me as much."

"But I need you."

This conversation again? She took a deep breath, trained her eyes. "What about—"

"What about us trying again?" David's hand slid across her belly. A thousand tiny spiders blossomed in its wake and crawled across her skin.

Heat pricked the back of her neck. Despite his hand being warm, a shiver crept from deep within her gut up her spine. Needles, pain, and loss flashed behind her eyelids when she blinked. She stopped his hand from making little circles on her stomach. "You can't be serious."

"Of course I am. You promised we'd try again."

Promises had been made, but any rational person would understand her hesitance given all the rounds of IVF, miscarriages, and . . . Lina couldn't bring herself to say his name. She shook her head, adamant about her decision.

"But we still have some embryos left."

"David, I can't go through that again." She pulled away from him. "I won't."

"Go through what?" Danny asked, making his way over to them in a sleepy shuffle.

"No school, man!" David fist-bumped Danny and opened the throw for the boy to crawl under.

"I know, but my stupid alarm went off anyway," Danny whined, rubbing his eyes. He nuzzled into his father's armpit. "Look at all the snow."

"It was like this in Boston all week. Had to buy another coat," David said. "You planning on making a snowman or something?"

"Yeah. Texted Jacob. Waiting for his lazy butt to get up, and then me and Meems'll probably go hang out down the street." Danny sat up straight. "Crap. I need to start making snowballs."

"Give me a few minutes; then you can go after breakfast. M'kay?" David held him closer. "Haven't seen you all week."

"Morning," Mimi said, climbing into the fold on Lina's lap. Lina was tempted to say something about her being a big baby but decided against it.

"Good morning, Angel." David opened his arms for everyone to lean into him.

Lina held on to her family in that moment and tried her hardest to imagine them like this for the next fifty years. She wanted more than anything for her and David to be surrounded by their grandchildren. She wanted them to be the cute older couple doting on each other. She reached down and held on to David's hand, squeezing it firmly as if she could pour her dreams into him through touch.

He squeezed her hand back and kissed her neck, then whispered into her ear, "I'm going to call Dr. Huang's office so we can get the process going."

She winced. At forty years old, there was absolutely no way she wanted to be pregnant. Why couldn't David understand the mental and physical toll IVF had taken on her? She was content with Danny and Mimi and wanted to go back to work. She opened her mouth to protest, then caught some movement inside the house.

"David, someone's in the house," she whispered, trying to remain calm.

David glanced over his shoulder. "Relax, it's Jules. Picked her up on my way home from the airport."

Twenty-seven years younger than David and technically his half sister by way of his father's third marriage, Jules could've passed for his daughter. She had the same tall, slender body as her brother, same sea-glass-blue eyes, and thin lips. They even shared the hallmark Henry jawline that gave them both edgy-model vibes. If Lina looked hard enough, she could catch the faint outline in Danny's face.

As if summoned, Jules appeared in the doorway, borderline-orange spray tan, pink-streaked hair, short shorts, crop top, and all. Before David could protest, Jules snapped a photo of the family snuggled up on the couch and declared, "Y'all so cute. Hashtag family goals."

"Say hello to your aunt Jules." David clapped the kids' backs.

"Morning, Aunt Jules," the kids said in unison.

"Lina?" David glared.

"Morning, Jules. How did you sleep?"

"Y'all need a new mattress in the guest room." Jules raised her arms and stretched. "And maybe some ambient lighting and a quieter ceiling fan."

"Do they have those in the dorms?"

"Like they would ever pay for anything new in the dorms." She snickered.

"Did your college close, too, Aunt Jules?" Danny asked.

"Yup. No school, boo. When you wanna start on the snowballs?"

"Now!" Danny leaped to his feet and ran inside.

"Wear layers. Brush your teeth. And you have to eat breakfast first," Lina called after him.

"I'll tell him." Mimi pecked her parents' cheeks. "He's so going down today."

"Why didn't you run it by me first?" Lina asked once the kids and Jules cleared out.

"Run what by you? IVF?"

"No. Yes. But I'm talking about Jules."

"You want me to ask if my little sister could stay in our six-bedroom house when her college shuts down because of a snowstorm?" He peeked over his mug at her, taking a long sip of coffee.

Here goes another roller-coaster ride, she thought, wondering if she'd ever get off. "You know we don't get along. She got all up in my face the last time she was here. Don't you remember?"

"She's my baby sister. What do you want me to do?"

"Her parents live twenty minutes away. Why didn't she go home?" Lina asked.

"Because they wouldn't let Carl stay with her."

Lina rubbed the bridge of her nose. "He's, like, thirtysomething and doesn't work or do anything but sit around all day smoking weed and playing video games."

David put his mug down a little too hard. The glass sounded like it was going to shatter. "It's my house. My sister can stay as long as she wants to, and you will be nice to her."

"Why didn't she go to his house?"

"Because I insisted. It's fine."

It's not fine, Lina wanted to say. *You not asking me about Jules when you know we don't get along is not fine,* Lina thought. But she swallowed it all down, knowing pressing it further would lead to an argument. She was just too tired to even start one, and with him bringing up having another baby, she needed to save her outrage for what she knew would be a massive fight. "I would've liked a little heads-up; that's all," Lina said.

"Heads up, they're here." David stood. "And Carl doesn't really need to work. He's one of those trust fund guys. I've helped him with a few investments."

That was news to Lina, but not surprising. David didn't tell her much when it came to business . . . or anything else.

"Speaking of which, I need to log in." David took one more look at the snow and made his way back into the house. After a few minutes, he popped his head out and said, "I love you so much."

47

CHAPTER 6

Their snow day had been uneventful.

While David had busied himself in the basement office, coming up for the occasional baked good, Lina had poured her nervous energy into making dinner and baking bread, cookies, and basically anything with massive amounts of carbs and sugar. She'd needed to take her mind off the billion nauseating, toxic, worst-case scenarios popping in and out of her head as the kids ventured outside. They'd donned their almost-too-small ski clothes from last year's Aspen trip and taken off to play with the neighborhood kids immediately after breakfast. Mimi had sent her occasional pics and videos of them sledding and building snow forts.

In the living room, just off the kitchen, Carl and Jules had occupied themselves watching television. Lina'd heard them laugh every now and then and wished for that sort of simplicity in her marriage. But if she were honest, there'd never been any simplicity in her marriage. Lina and David's relationship had started with a powerful, explosive passion, a furious supernova of desire and need. By their second date, David had declared without an ounce of doubt that she was his soul mate.

They'd been inseparable. He'd swing by her job with flowers or lunch for the entire office, or he'd pick her up from work and drive to the airport instead of taking her home, so they could spend the weekend making love in a bungalow on some island or another. The way he'd doted on her had made her breathless and dizzy. Sure, she'd had boy-friends before, but the assuredness with which David spoke about their future had been both exhilarating and oddly comforting. She'd finally have the stability she'd been missing all her life—she'd found her person, and he'd found his, and they'd spend the rest of their lives together.

All that snow-filled day, Lina'd considered reminding David of how freely they'd used to travel and how they would never be able to pick up and head to the airport as easily with a baby in tow, but she'd received an email inviting her to confirm her appointment with Dr. Huang's office and couldn't say more than a few words to David without curses clogging her throat. *What fucking part of "I don't want to be pregnant again" didn't David understand?*

By that evening, with the sun slowly dripping into the frozen hori-zon, casting its golden-red shadow across the snowy ground, everyone gathered in the kitchen. The kids looked beat but wouldn't stop talking or sharing photos of their snow adventure, with David at the table at the far end of the kitchen. After several minutes of Danny's nonstop, top-of-his-lungs story of how he caught air on a sled going down the hill in his friend's backyard and then won ten bucks in a bet by throwing a yellow-snow snowball at Mimi's friend, Jules and Carl slowly retreated back to the quiet living room, back to the TV.

"This is so good, Mom," Danny mumbled after finishing his story, his mouth full of pot roast. He'd returned home famished and was "hungry enough to eat brussels sprouts voluntarily."

"It is really good, honey," David said, peeking up from his phone.

Lina hadn't quite made it to the table yet. She was still fuming, bubbling over with frenetic energy when her phone sounded with a text message. She almost dropped it onto the counter when she saw it was from Noah.

Noah: Hi Lina! Had a quick thought about your kids' website.

Noah: Hit me up when you get a minute.

"Who's that, Lina?" David asked.

Lina slipped her phone into the pocket on her flannel bottoms and raced through her mind for an answer. How would she tell him it was Noah Attoh? How would he react?

"Lina?" David said.

"OH MY GOSH!" Jules cried. "David! Mimi, you're on TV. Danny! You guys come here!"

Ice ran through Lina's veins until she was both burning up and frozen solid the second she heard Danny's voice playing on the television in the living room. Her stomach lurched. The room spun round and round. The kids both looked at each other and darted into the living room, David clipping on their heels. But she'd had another two weeks to break it to him. Two weeks, not a day. Why were they playing the kids' segment *NOW*?

"Lina." David's voice carried into the kitchen. Lina's feet were lead weights anchoring her to the bamboo flooring.

"Lina!" he snapped.

"Hey, Mom, we're on TV," Mimi said, beside her. She wove her fingers through her mother's and walked with her into the living room.

Dead man walking . . .

Lina was certain she'd vomit as she glanced up to see the rest of the kids' interview on their television screen. The room was deathly silent, save the TV and the occasional squeal from Mimi or giddy laughter from Danny. Lina's face felt like it was on fire from the searing heat of David's glare from across the room.

The segment seemed to go on forever.

When it was over, their living room exploded into laughter and cheering from everyone except David and Lina. She waited for his wrath, digging her nails into her palms until she felt stabs of pain.

The room hushed when David spoke. "That's pretty incredible. Isn't that filmed in another city? New York or LA or something?" he asked.

"You like it?" Danny said. "We worked really hard on the website and all. You think it's cool, don't you? Mom wanted to surprise you. We flew all the way out to Los Angeles, and they gave us fancy food, and we saw everything and swam in the pool on the roof."

"When?" David asked.

"Yesterday," Danny said. "Remember our website, Dad?"

"We flew back yesterday, dork," Mimi added. "We left early Tuesday—"

"When I was in Boston?"

"I'm going to go Snap all my friends." Mimi took off for her room, her phone in her hands.

"Yeah. You like it? Didn't we do a great job?" Danny's eyes were as wide as the sweet smile on his face. He was on his feet now, shifting his weight from one foot to the next like an eager puppy. "Wasn't it awesome, Dad?"

"I'm so proud of y'all. You killed it." Jules fist-bumped Danny, then elbowed her brother. "Didn't they, David?"

David patted Danny's back. "Yeah, how about you get ready for bed. Shower and teeth, m'kay. And tell your sister I want her phone down here tonight."

Danny deflated like a balloon. "Oh, okay, Dad." He shrugged before heading up to his room.

Lina waited on pins and needles for David's reaction, but he walked right past her to the table and resumed eating dinner. Lina shuffled behind him.

"What did you think?"

"You pulled them out of school for that?" David's eyes were trained on his plate. He stabbed a carrot with his fork, held it up, then popped it into his mouth.

"Yeah, their teachers were cool with it."

Shoving a potato around his plate, David cleared a path through the thick brown sauce. The white plate peeked through for a moment only to be covered again. "Why didn't you tell me?"

"I told you about their website and *The Sophia Show* last week, and you were cool with it," Lina stammered. "Wanted to surprise you when it aired."

The fork clinked against the plate as he pierced a small chunk of beef. Gobs of juice dripped while he studied it, turning it from one side to the next.

Drip.

Time seemed to drag on.

Drip.

Lina knew better than to push him.

Drip.

She could sense the chum in the water now.

Drip.

One drop of blood was all it took to attract a predator.

Drip.

She didn't dare move.

"I don't remember having a conversation about any of this," he finally said.

She swallowed, conjured her sweetest voice. "I mentioned it the other night when we were, um, together." She really hoped the kids were not listening to any of this.

"Is that the game you're going to play? You're really going to try to tell me I made a serious decision after sex?"

"Their site is incredible, David. I . . ."

"You what?"

"I didn't want you pulling the same crap you did with their first interview."

"You're the genius who canceled it. I was just asking questions. Anyone with half a brain would do the same thing."

Maybe she'd read too much into it at the time. "I also didn't want you to stop them from having this experience. They worked so hard."

His mouth dropped open. One. Two. Three blinks. When he opened his eyes the final time, he looked at her like she'd grown a second head. "C'mon, baby. I'm not some monster. It sounds like a great opportunity for everyone. I would've liked to have been part of making the decision, you know. They're my kids too. You were all the way across the country. What if something happened?"

Was *that* all he had to say? She waited a few more minutes, biting her bottom lip. Hesitating, she mulled over how she'd expected the conversation to go and how wrong she'd been. She glanced over at David. He winked, checked his phone.

Okay, then, she thought and put the whole thing to bed, hopeful they'd turned a new corner in their marriage. "Thanks for understanding."

He captured the remaining bits of beef and vegetables onto his fork. Before putting it into his mouth, he asked, "Is it making any money?"

Lina shook her head. Truth was she'd used her consulting money for the server space, monthly fees, and professional help for Mimi when she was stuck on coding stuff.

"Did they get my permission to make it and put themselves out in public like that?"

Lina's head dropped between her shoulders, knowing it'd been too good to be true. "No."

"Did you think to ask my opinion on any of the potential legal problems you are opening up this family to?"

"I was—"

"Did you consider asking me to help with a budget or projections?" he asked.

"Well, I—"

"Did you incorporate or anything?"

"It's in—"

"Is it a registered business?"

"I—"

"You know everything, don't you?" David was stabbing the air with his fork now.

"I advised them on the business and legal stuff because you've been so slammed with traveling for work the last few months. It wasn't anything major," Lina said.

David's eyes narrowed. "You and the kids seem to have thought of everything, haven't you?"

Something in her wanted them to have a win for once. Why couldn't he appreciate the incredible work the kids had done? "Listen, I apologize for taking them to LA without telling you, but you've seen them around the house, working on that website since last year. Danny told you about it at least a hundred times, even showed it to you when they were beta testing and then when they went live, but you've been so distracted. You haven't taken any time to listen to them."

David pushed his plate away and rose from the table. "Distracted?" He shook his head, scoffed. "I've been busting my ass trying not to lose my job, trying to smile and keep my cool at work."

The television's volume rose, drowning out her thoughts. Lina wanted to thank Jules but knew she'd done it to look out for her brother.

"You do what? Drive the kids around and cook." David shoved his hands into his pockets, glared at her like she was absolutely nothing. "Get real, Lina. Do you even know what it's like to have some stupid woman get promoted over you? Of course you don't. You don't have any real work experience. You worked for what? Two, three years total until I came along and rescued you?"

"Okay, that's enough. You're the one who made me quit working." She couldn't help herself.

David snarled, his lips tight, thin lines. "You know *exactly why* you had to stop working." Each word came out staccato, their weight crashing down on her like a tidal wave, rolling her over and over, dragging her into its depths until she gave up her last breath.

Fighting against it was no use. Of course he'd blamed her. Had she not gone into work that day . . . Lina couldn't allow herself to go there. She had to end this argument before he said anything else hurtful. "I'm . . . I'm sorry, David. I didn't mean to say you were distracted. You've been distant, but I know it's because you're working so hard."

"A little appreciation would be nice."

"I'll make it up to you."

"You will." He glared at her until she turned her head; then he returned to his office in the basement.

Their conversation played back in her ears like a bad song on loop. She knew the kids had started their website before the corporate shuffle. David made her second-guess her timeline. She very specifically remembered the many times Danny had tried to show his father Mimi's handiwork, but David had brushed him off to play golf with his coworkers or go out with friends, or scroll through something on his phone.

Lina shook her head, hoping to dislodge the uneasy feeling of not being 100 percent certain. She'd gotten in the habit of writing important things down or recording herself to keep from feeling insane after arguing with David. But she hadn't done either with the kids telling him about their site.

Maybe she was, in fact, wrong. She chewed on it for the rest of the night as she cleaned up the kitchen and tucked the kids into bed, hugging them each extra tight, hoping that small motion would trigger a memory—a knowing—to no avail. She replayed the last year in her head as she climbed into bed beside David much later that night— month by month, week by week—but her mind felt sticky and cloudy, uncertain of so many facts she'd once known to be true.

Panic—the subtle, yet terrifying, "Maybe I'm actually losing my mind and should go see a doctor," like the kind that always followed when she lost her car keys or misplaced her cell phone to later find them where she *knew* she'd placed them—met her every time she closed her eyes to sleep. She tossed and turned until David looped his arm around her waist and closed the space between them.

"I love you," he whispered.

Moments later, he was fast asleep while Lina lay there even more confused than she'd been earlier. Was it all over? Were they cool now?

As the temperature warmed the next day, David's temperament thawed along with the snow. He met her on their covered patio once again, this time with a fresh mug of coffee "just the way she liked it." He continued to do little, sweet things like that throughout the day: kneading her shoulders while she read, making lunch for everyone so she could finish her book, drawing her a hot bath after they'd played outside with the kids, bringing her a warm towel fresh from the dryer, and leaving her a bright-yellow sticky note on the mirror that read: *I love you so much.*

When they made love later that night, Lina wondered if she'd imagined their fight just a day earlier.

Was she officially starting to lose her mind?

CHAPTER 7

To the chagrin of the kids, the snow had melted by Sunday, which not only meant they'd have school that week, but they'd all go to church that morning. Normally, the kids would be excited to see their friends, but youth service had been canceled, which meant they had to go to regular church. To soften the blow, Lina had allowed Jules to borrow her car to take the kids to Waffle House for breakfast.

Church was one of those things Lina could do with or without. She hadn't grown up in a church like David had and loved the fact that his family had been going to the same church since he was a kid. She couldn't think of any place, person, or thing she had or did now that she'd had or done in her childhood. It pained her to look through family photos and have only a handful of pictures from her youth, while David's mom had given her three boxes of photos from his childhood. The stability of the concrete building and fifty-year legacy drew her more than anything. She'd hoped to pass it on to their children.

"You should wear that dress I bought instead," David said from the bathroom doorway, adjusting his dark-gray paisley tie. Clean shaven and hair gelled into place, he looked especially handsome in his charcoal Tom Ford suit.

She side-eyed the gray sweater dress draped on the chair beside her, Neiman Marcus tags still attached, and briefly considered changing, but it was still so very cold outside, and she really didn't want to wrestle with tights and knee-high boots. Her dark jeans and pink sweater would do just fine, and since they'd made up and seemed okay, she'd be honest with him. "I really don't want to change."

"Oh." He nodded, blinking. "I see."

She pressed the flat iron down her hair for one more pass. He watched her in the mirror. She watched as well, her soft, curly tresses submitting under the heat and pressure to become acceptable: silky and straight, what David liked.

He rapped his knuckles against the doorframe when she put the flat iron down. "It's time we got on the road."

In the garage, David beelined to his Tesla.

"I can drive if you want. Know you've had a long week traveling and all." She kept her voice light and sweet.

"I'm capable of driving."

Once inside his car, she fastened her seat belt. "We good, right?"

David raised his eyebrows, then tapped the steering wheel.

No, they were not good. She should've worn the dress.

The garage door rose and sunlight flooded in, making Lina squint. She stole a glance at her husband, whose attention was focused on the driveway in front of them now, and decided to let it go. She didn't want to start more drama with him, and his silent treatment kept his mouth shut, so there was that. She'd take full advantage of David's silence, maybe even curl up with a good book after church and have everyone fend for themselves for dinner. The cold leather warmed and molded into her back and thighs when she pressed the button for the seat warmer. She eased back, closing her eyes.

Lina wondered if his silence would extend to her if she brazenly started working. Would he never speak to her again? Was she finally going to have some peace and—

Her body lurched forward and was snatched backward as her seat belt tightened across her chest. David had slammed on the brakes at the gated entrance to their neighborhood.

She searched for a deer or rabbit or some animal or child that had made him stop so abruptly, but there was nothing in front of the car. "What was that about?"

David gave her no response.

Slowly, he turned onto the road. Lina settled back into her seat and peeked over to find him smirking at her. With that, he floored the gas. The engine whined in response, rapidly shifting gears. Soon, David had the car past ninety miles per hour, navigating their winding suburban back roads like a roller coaster.

Lina's heart clambered farther up her throat with each turn. Sharp pins stabbed her wrists, and her palms were stark white from gripping the seat belt. "David, slow down already."

He accelerated, racing through the streets, skidding down secondary roads, swerving between cars. He ran up on slower vehicles to ride their bumpers until they moved and took corners like a wild man, car screeching. Lina prayed to survive if the car flipped or crashed into another vehicle.

By the time David veered into the back parking lot of their church, Lina was a trembling wreck. She'd call an Uber or Lyft to get back home if she had to. There was no way in hell she'd ride back home with David.

"Good morning, Mr. Henry," a stout police officer called out when David opened his door.

"Morning, Billings. I hear congratulations are in order," David said like nothing had happened. He motioned for Lina to join him.

She slipped out of the car and almost kissed the ground. Her legs still shaking, she braced herself, inhaling and exhaling deeply to calm her heartbeat.

"Yes, sir. My wife wanted to thank you for the flowers and gift cards. They've helped so much with the baby and all." Billings clapped him on the back.

"It was nothing." David put his arm around Lina's waist when she stumbled around to the back of his car. She tried to pull away, but he held her close.

"Hoping to have another addition of our own soon." He kissed her tenderly on her forehead.

She felt as though she'd landed in an alternate dimension. She hated it when he made her feel off-center. Hadn't he just been driving like a crazy man? Hadn't he done it to punish her in some way? He rubbed her back gently, winked at her with the most sincere smile. She knew he was putting on an act for everyone else, but still, the sharp change nearly gave her whiplash.

"Keep us in your prayers," David added.

"I'll make sure Jess adds you guys to our prayer list."

"We appreciate it." David threaded his fingers with Lina's and started for the massive church.

Bethel Christian had grown from a small family church of three hundred or so people to well over four thousand members in the time they'd been married. David had been an usher, a parking lot attendant, a greeter, a small group leader, and the pastor's assistant. He was now a board member and had pressed Lina to be more active in the church, but every time she did, he'd complained about how much time it'd taken away from their family.

Eventually, he'd thought it was best she support him in whatever role he took on within the church instead. She played along. It was only one day a week and gave her a chance to wear more than yoga pants, pajamas, and jeans.

"I love you so much, you know," David said softly, the massive steeple covering them in its shadow. "You make me so angry sometimes."

"And you think killing us in a car crash is the answer?" The words escaped Lina's mouth before she could catch them.

David stopped just short of the greeters at the entrance and turned to face her. Lina bit the inside of her cheek, not knowing what to expect. Tenderly, he stroked his thumb across her hand. His eyes reflected the same cloudless blue of the morning sky, and when he tipped her chin to look her square in the eyes, she was sure he'd apologize.

"Lina," he said, his voice wrapping her in a warm blanket. "Nothing would've happened *to me*."

His eyes went from sky to ice in seconds.

"All right, you lovebirds. Service is starting. Save room for Jesus," the greeter called a little too cheerfully.

It was like a switch flicked on. David blinked and a thousand-watt smile shone across his face. "You got me. I can't keep my hands off my wife. Can you blame me, though?" he said, all teeth. All venom gone within the blink of an eye.

Lina wanted to scream and maybe vomit. It was showtime, and David was center stage as they entered the building. Rhythmic bass pumped through the sanctuary doors. Inside, people raised their arms and bounced as the skinny jeans–clad band rocked on electric guitars, keyboards, and drums. Lina blinked to adjust her eyes in the dark, fog-filled arena. It felt more like they were in a concert than a church.

They sliced through the crowd to their seats in the second row. Lina slid across the row and collapsed into her chair beside Mimi, her heart threatening to crack her sternum wide open. She glanced past her kids to see David shaking hands and church hugging people in greeting. It felt like millions of ants were crawling over her skin at the sight. Her lungs protested. Between the dark room, the earsplitting music, the jumping people, the fog, and David, her head swam. The arena walls closed in around her. Each breath was like sucking on a straw. She gasped, gripping the back of the chair in front of her.

"Mom, are you okay?" Mimi yelled over the noise. Lina couldn't answer. Mimi grabbed her arm and led her back through the crowd to the restroom, where all the contents in Lina's stomach came up. She shook, grasping the cold toilet seat.

Mimi wiped the hair from her mother's forehead. "You want me to get you anything?"

"I'm okay," Lina said after a few minutes, washing her hands. "Really, I'm better."

"I'll stay with you." Mimi placed a cold, damp paper towel on the back of her mother's neck.

"I'm good." Lina dragged a metal IKEA chair into the largest stall. "Go back to church. I'm going to stay here." She sat and rested her legs on the toilet paper holder.

Mimi smoothed down her mother's hair, kissed her forehead. "You sure?"

Lina nodded, thankful for the quiet restroom.

"Love you, Mom."

"Love you, too, Meems. Text me when it's over." Lina locked the stall door, exhaling. She'd had panic attacks before, but they seemed to come more frequently now. Eight months was way too long; she needed to return to therapy. Maybe Brenda could help her figure out a way to convince David to join her for a session or two . . . or fifty.

Someone shuffled into the stall beside her. Lina stilled. It felt wrong to listen to someone else pee, but what were her alternatives? Her chest tightened at the thought of returning to the sanctuary just then. She'd take bodily functions over watching David's performance any freaking day.

Lina's phone vibrated with a text. She wavered, picking at the painted blue flower on her phone case. It was probably David wondering where she'd gone and why she hadn't returned yet. She inhaled sharply when instead she saw it was from Noah.

Noah: Hi Lina! I'll be in Atlanta for a few days this week.

Noah: Would you like to have dinner with me again?

The last thing Lina needed was to get caught up in whatever drama someone like Noah Attoh commanded. Drama probably followed him like a shadow, and she needed more of it as much as she needed another round of IVF. What she needed was to ask him about shouting the kids out and delete his phone number.

Lina: While I appreciate the offer, you should know I'm married.

Noah: I can respect that.

Noah: Honestly, I had such a great time the other night. Haven't laughed that much in years.

Noah: It was . . . refreshing.

Lina: Have to admit I had fun too.

Noah: How about friends?

Friends? It'd been years since she'd had anyone to call a friend. David had chased them all away with his suspicions. Nancy, her very best friend since freshman year of college, had been nosy and jealous. Jerica, her closest gym friend, had been too ghetto. India, her mom friend, had been flirting with him all the time and "you know you can't trust her," and Addie, her former neighbor friend, had been a lesbian who was "trying to turn her." The list of ridiculous excuses went on for each and every person Lina had gotten close to until she was an island.

Isolated.

Alone.

Sure, she'd had her PTA "friends" and her church "friends," but they were all empty, surface relationships: friendly smiles and distanced waves. It'd been a long time since she'd had anyone to really talk to. Considering how genuine they'd been with each other when they'd had dinner, it would be an easy friendship. She finished scraping the blue flower from her case and made a decision.

Lina: Friends sounds nice.

Lina: But it feels weird.

Noah: How so?

Lina: You're Noah Attoh.

Noah: Thanks for the reminder.

Lina: Seriously.

Noah: I'm a normal person.

Noah: And now you're friends with a normal person.

Lina: So what's a normal person like you doing right now?

Noah: Laundry.

Noah: What are you doing?

Lina: I don't believe you.

Lina: I'm hiding in the bathroom at church.

Lina wasn't sure why she'd told him the truth about hiding out in the church bathroom. Her phone vibrated with a text, and she shook her head in disbelief at the photo of several piles of laundry spread out across a distressed leather couch.

Noah: Traveling last few weeks. Got home and had to catch up.

Lina: Don't you have people to do that?

Noah: My dirty clothes? No way!

Noah: Now why are you hiding out at church?

Lina didn't really feel like going into details. What was she going to say? How'd she explain her marriage and her panic attacks? How would she describe the terror she'd felt when David had driven her to church? Lina bit her lip, her fingers hovering over the screen as she thought of an answer that wouldn't make her sound crazy.

Noah: It's okay if you don't want to talk about it.

Noah: I have a hard time in crowds sometimes.

Noah: Add that to my confession list.

Lina: Charging it to your therapy bill.

Noah: Ha! Good one!

Lina: Not a joke. I take all forms of payment.

Noah: Including waffles?

Lina: Best form of payment.

Noah: I'll call Mama Tish next time you're in LA.

Lina: It's a deal.

With each text, Lina's nerves relaxed. She found herself working to keep from laughing out loud in the ladies' restroom. Easing back into conversation with Noah was seamless. It was like they'd never left the rooftop restaurant in Los Angeles. They talked about his trip to New York, his indie film, her snow day (minus her fight with David), and the shows on HGTV she liked to watch. It caught her off guard at how interested he was when she brought up her consulting work. He asked tons of questions and stumped her when he finally asked why she didn't return full-time. They talked about everything . . . except for him promoting the kids' site. Lina just couldn't bring herself to ask. It didn't feel right.

Eventually, people trickled into the restroom. As much as she wanted to continue talking to Noah, church was over, and her family would be looking for her soon.

Lina: Hey, I'd better go.

Noah: Hope your day gets better.

She imagined Noah on the other side, laundry in careful piles, and smiled. *It has gotten better, friend.*

CHAPTER 8

It'd taken three weeks for the Henry family to establish a new normal since Mimi and Danny's *Sophia Show* debut. Besides being a little more popular at school, their website had crashed twice from increased traffic. As Lina had anticipated, David had refused to pay for anything having to do with their website. His excuses had ranged from it being "too much money for the kids' silly project" to "we're buckling down now because of another round of IVF." Lina had never been more grateful to have a little money of her own set aside. Without a second thought, she'd purchased a larger hosting package and more server space after he'd fallen asleep late one night. It was her virtual middle finger to her husband.

In addition to demanding having his name added to the business paperwork, David had to know about every interview, every email, and the kids had to work at the kitchen table, where he could monitor them when he was home. He'd said it was so they were all on the same page. Lina'd known there was more to it than simple accountability and had taken her sweet time to carry out his orders. It'd been her way of rebelling since he was forcing her to start IVF again.

No matter how much she'd explained that she did not want to try again, he'd talked and talked and talked for hours, pressing his case, reminding her of her shortcomings and her promises. He'd filibustered until she'd given in just to have a moment of silence before spiraling into madness. He'd had that effect on her. Most times it was easier to comply than to listen to him drone on for hours. Water rushing over rock, his words slowly eroded her resolve.

With David having left for Boston earlier that Monday morning, Lina found herself en route to the gym after she'd dropped the kids off at school. Sure, he hadn't wanted her going back to her gym out of irrational jealousy, but Lina'd simply switched the monthly debit to her secret account. Head down, Adidas hat pulled low over her eyes to block out the world, and earbuds cranking Beyoncé at earsplitting volume, Lina ducked into the large purple building and beelined to the first treadmill in the far corner.

Working out hadn't always been something Lina enjoyed, but it helped clear her head and better manage her anxiety. Since her first IVF appointment was scheduled for later that day, Lina needed to run far and fast. She started slowly, worked her way up to a comfortable gait, pumping her arms and striking the balls of her feet against the rubber belt in sync to the bass beats. After a while, she was Beyoncé at Coachella: hips swaying, legs marching, muscles flexing, booty shaking. Sneezing on beat and making it sick and running the world because she was a girl made her run faster.

A satisfied smile played on her lips when her workout playlist slowed tempo, signaling a cooldown. Sweat beaded on her skin and dampened her shirt. Endorphins surging, she felt better than she'd felt in a long while: strong, capable, competent, healthy. Despite the pull in her thighs, she moved to the weight area, a bounce in her step. Feeling herself, she added extra weight to the machine and carefully positioned herself beneath the cool metal bar. She leaned into her squats, studying her form in the mirrored wall: back straight, knees over her ankles, glutes tight. Heat scorched her quads, but she pressed on.

Down.

Up.

Squeeze.

Down.

Up.

Squeeze.

Down. The day's agenda rushed through her mind: groceries, laundry, run by Costco for the PTA 5K fundraiser snacks.

Up. She thought about what to make for dinner. David was going to be gone for the rest of the week, so it was most likely going to be a variety of sandwiches, tacos, and breakfast for dinner. Brinner was Danny's favorite meal besides pizza, and since they could only have it when David was gone, she'd make it tonight.

Squeeze. She felt like she was missing something.

Down.

The IVF appointment . . . Lina's legs buckled beneath the weight. She fell to the floor. The machine's safety mechanism locked, clanking loudly, stopping the bar from crushing her.

Familiar twisting immediately returned to her gut. She waved off the gym associate who was heading her way.

"I'm okay." She stood, wiped off her legs. "I'm good. Thanks," she said for added measure to get him to turn back around and leave her alone.

"Time to bring the thundah," a familiar voice sounded. She spun to see Noah's face on one of the televisions mounted overhead. Leaning against the squat bar, she sipped from her water bottle while her heart rate returned to normal.

Noah seemed so much larger clad in his black-and-blue, leather-and-spandex Vengeance costume. It was surreal watching him on television and also knowing she'd texted him every day for the last three weeks. She couldn't even see him as someone famous and inaccessible. He was her friend. Needing the distraction from her impending appointment, she snapped a photo and texted him.

Lina: You're stalking me at the gym.

Noah: Of course!

Lina: Not creepy at all.

Noah: Looks like it's the second movie. Those fight scenes were brutal.

Lina: Your tights look brutal. LOL

Noah: Those tights are my archenemy. Takes like, 20 mins to get into a pair. No lie.

Lina: OMG. Did I wake you up?

Noah: No. I'm in NY this week. Same time zone!

Lina smacked her head. They'd texted each other multiple times every day since her panic attack at church weeks earlier. He'd told her about his trip to New York and how nervous he was about it. He was meeting with his distributor to negotiate terms for an indie movie he'd produced last year, only the distributor didn't really want to work with him on this film since it wasn't a big action blockbuster like Noah's *Vengeance* franchise.

Lina: How's it going so far?

Noah: Not great, actually. I'm thankful for the distraction.

Lina: Want to talk about it?

Noah: I'm about to lose a lot on this deal.

Lina: I'm sorry.

Noah: Took a risk on that movie and believed in it so much. Guess not everyone sees it that way.

Lina: Are they the only distributor in the country?

Noah: No, why?

A few guys crowded around the squat machine, waiting for Lina to move. She gathered her stuff and made her way to the stretching area, remembering the games she'd played as a strategist when her clients wanted industry leverage. She thought very carefully about her next words but decided to text them anyway.

Lina: Walk away.

Noah: What?

Lina: Cancel negotiations and tell them you're going with someone else who'll be more equitable and offer a wider range.

Noah: You're serious?

Lina: I mean, you are Noah Attoh.

Lina: Noah?

Noah: Hold on.

Instead of stretching, Lina found herself pacing the matted area, checking her phone every few minutes. Did he think her plan was stupid? Should she have suggested he walk away? Had she put her foot in her mouth again? What if she'd just screwed up his entire career? What if she'd sunk the movie he'd loved so much?

Who was she fooling? Her days of business know-how were long gone. She was just a mom. A wife. Lina . . . nothing more. David had been right all these years. She'd be better if she'd sit quietly and look pretty—that was her job now. That and going through another implantation in David's hopes of one more pregnancy. The thought of walking back into Dr. Huang's 1980s pastel-pink office to start the process of trying to conceive, despite being adamantly opposed, made her want to scream.

Lina darted to the restroom and splashed her face with cold water, gasping. Her phone vibrated. She almost dropped it like a hot potato.

Noah: You there?

Lina: Yes. I'm sorry. I shouldn't have suggested you walk away. I'm pretty sure you pay professionals to take care of your business stuff.

Noah: It worked!

Lina was beside herself.

Noah: I went back into the office. Looked the rep in his eyes and told him the deal is off.

Noah: Actually, I told him I was pulling every movie under my studio since he didn't want to make this work.

Lina sighed, relieved it'd worked out for him. She beamed at her reflection in the mirror, noticing shallow lines of definition around her shoulders. She lifted her shirt, and, sure enough, the work she'd been putting in was finally paying off. Just above her wrinkled, stretch mark–lined mommy pouch was the faint outline of a two-pack.

She had abs! She checked out the rest of her body, noting a new muscle here and less puffiness there. She certainly felt stronger and leaner but had stopped jumping on the scale daily since Brenda had recommended she throw it away altogether.

"But how do *you feel* about it," Brenda had asked, adjusting her glasses, when Lina had lost fifty pounds.

Lina had been thrilled to see the number on the scale and immediately called David. He'd asked her when she was planning to lose the rest of it.

Her extra weight had been the result of multiple cycles of IVF over the years, stress, and postpartum depression after miscarriages at nine weeks and another at sixteen weeks. Losing their last baby in the second trimester a little over two years ago had taken its toll on her—both mentally and physically.

Now, discovering remnants of her former self in the form of abs and a much slimmer frame, she was once again thrilled. Something in her wanted to share her transformation with Noah. Her phone lit up with texts before she could send anything.

Noah: You. Are. Incredible.

Noah: You saved my film.

Noah: My entire legal team, several advisers, managers, and not one of them had the nerve to tell me to walk away.

Noah: Thank you, Lina.

It was as if her soul was smiling. Noah had trusted her and hadn't even known her that long. He'd taken her advice without question or argument. He'd never demanded to know her qualifications. She'd never had to explain herself.

He'd taken her at her word.

She felt capable for the first time in a long while and knew what she had to do next. With a deep breath and a prayer, Lina called Dr. Huang's office and canceled her appointment.

CHAPTER 9

"Uno, losers!" Danny slammed down his last wild card and pumped his fists in the air. It'd been his sixth win, and Lina was finished. She knew the little butthead was cheating but couldn't prove it.

"I'm so done," Mimi sighed, tossing her cards down. "This is not how I planned on spending my Friday night." She checked her phone. "Mom, can I please go hang out with my friends instead of this torture?"

"No, it's family night, for crying out loud. You both agreed to it earlier this week."

"Technically, it's not family night without Dad," Danny said, shuffling the deck.

Lina shot one of her warning looks at him.

"You're such a dork," Mimi added. "I'm out. Want to watch a movie or something?"

"I'm out too. Find something good." Lina rose from the kitchen table and started wrapping up pizza slices from dinner. A smile played on her lips while she listened to Mimi and Danny try to agree on something to watch. Mimi wanted to watch the latest episode of her vampire show, while Danny insisted on watching the last Vengeance movie. *If only they knew . . .*

Maybe she could have them meet him without divulging their friendship. Danny would certainly freak out, and Mimi would probably go full-on fangirl. It would definitely be worth it. Maybe they could even convince him to give them a shout-out themselves. She texted Noah.

Lina: How's it going?

Noah: Heading to Seoul for a week or so.

Lina: Such a regular person.

Noah: Was trying to impress you.

Lina: I'm impressed.

Noah: 12 hr time difference, but I don't mind if you text me. It's totally cool.

Lina: Are you begging?

Noah: Is it that obvious?

Lina: I'd imagine Noah Attoh has hordes of women texting him.

Noah: Nope.

Noah: Just you.

Lina: Sure, friend . . .

Noah: So serious.

Lina: I'll think about it.

Noah: I'll hold my breath.

Lina: Would love to visit Seoul one day.

Noah: Don't try the live octopus.

Lina: You didn't!

Noah: I did. It was a dare and lots of soju was involved.

Noah: Swear I felt it trying to escape all night.

Lina: Gross.

Noah: It was quite funny. How are you?

Lina: I'm good. Just got crushed in Uno.

Lina: Danny is ruthless.

Noah: LOL! Your kids are great. How's their site going?

Lina: Unbelievable since the Sophia Show.

Lina sighed at the low whine of the garage door opening. David was home.

Lina: I've gotta run. Safe travels and stay away from the octopus.

Noah: Thanks. I'll try. Talk later?

Lina: There you go begging me again.

Noah: Guilty.

Lina: Maybe.

Lina quickly deleted the chat and pocketed her phone. The mudroom door squealed open. She turned just in time to see a massive bouquet of pale-yellow roses. There must've been more than a hundred stems in the ornate crystal vase. David gently placed them on the kitchen island and stepped around, beaming like he hadn't seen her in years.

"You look incredible. Where'd you go today?"

"Fundraiser stuff at the school," Lina said, a little confused that he found her mom uniform—a pair of jeans, a shirt, and a cardigan—appealing.

"Come here, baby." He wrapped his arms around her and buried his face in her hair. "I missed you."

She stiffened when he held her, waiting for the punch line. Waiting for the camera crew. Waiting for one of his friends or coworkers or church people to come through the door behind him. She waited . . . but there was nothing else to his random display of affection. Was this something new? Did he really miss her? Did he feel bad for how he'd treated her the last few weeks since the kids' segment aired? Slowly, she brought her arms to his waist and held him, hopeful.

He nibbled her ear, awakening her senses. "You smell so good."

"Gross. Get a room," Mimi said.

Dizziness swirled around Lina when he let her go. What was happening?

"Come here, you." David wrapped his daughter in a giant bear hug and fished out a small Tiffany-blue box from his jacket pocket.

"Sweet sixteen is next week. Happy birthday." He waited for her to open the box.

Mimi was hesitant for a few seconds, then carefully reached for the box and opened it. She held up a delicate gold necklace, a Tiffany key pendant dangling from it. "This is so perfect. Thank you, Daddy."

The glimmer of something more crossed David's face. For a second, he looked like a kid himself. "Think you left something in the box."

Brows knit, Mimi peeled back the cardboard and gasped. "No way! No freaking way!" Her eyes almost fell out of her head as she held up what looked like a car key.

No way, David.

He shrugged. "Where would it be? Can't fit in the box." He glanced over at Lina and winked.

Mimi shrieked, sprinting out of the house. "HOLY CRAP! OHMIGOD! THANK YOU, DADDY!"

Mimi was on her phone, FaceTiming a group of her friends by the time the rest of the family shuffled into the garage. Parked behind Lina's SUV was a brand-new red Jeep.

David stood behind Lina and wrapped his arms around her. "It's perfect, isn't it?"

"Why didn't you tell me?" *Or ask me?*

He kissed her neck. "I couldn't help myself."

"Let's go for a ride, Meems," Danny said, climbing into the car in awe.

"Can we?" Mimi asked.

"No. You don't have your driver's license yet," Lina said.

"But I'm getting it next week. Please, Mom?"

Danny joined in, "Jacob's sister is going to freak out! She was just talking about—"

"Yeah, Jacob's house is, like, two houses away. C'mon, pretty please?"

Lina didn't care what Jacob's sister thought. Rules were rules. She could wait to drive alone if she passed her test next week, which Lina was certain she would. "I don't think it's a good—"

"Two houses up, right?" David said. "I have something for you," he whispered in Lina's ear.

"But—" *Mimi doesn't have a driver's license.*

"They're fine. C'mon."

"No, it's not legal." Lina motioned at the kids. "Out. Go and walk. No driving."

"Mimi, take the car to your friend's house. You know how to drive. It's not like we paid for all those classes for nothing," David said.

"But she still shouldn't—"

"C'mon, Lina. I have something for you." He caressed her arm.

"It's not right, David. What if—"

"Don't ruin this for her. For us. I want some time with you. Just the two of us," he purred in her ear.

Mimi and Danny waited in limbo—half-in, half-out of the car— until David made the final declaration. "Guys, go. Take the car. It's okay. Mimi, I want you back in half an hour or so. And don't leave the neighborhood, okay?"

Lina worried as Mimi shut her door and started the engine. She hated when her husband did this to her. She hated feeling voiceless and powerless in their household. She hated always being the bad cop so David could be the good cop. Like every other time, she sucked it up and went along, this time praying Mimi wouldn't hit anyone or anything.

After watching the red Jeep's brake lights shrink as Mimi's new car drove out of their driveway, David gently held Lina's hand and led her back into the house. He paused in front of the rose bouquet and presented her with a small gift box and a greeting card. "I know I've been difficult recently. I . . . ." He gazed at her like it was his first time seeing her in a long while. "This is my way of apologizing."

Lina's heart softened. This had been what she'd wanted for so long: an apology, a change. She supposed she could forgive the car gaffe if it meant keeping the peace and starting fresh. Mimi *was* one of the most responsible kids she knew, and she'd always worn her seat belt and had driven more than the needed hours for her license and . . .

David's hand slid across hers. "Go ahead. Open it." He guided her fingers, opening it to reveal a diamond bracelet.

She turned to face him, leaning on the granite island at the center of the kitchen. Her fingers glided over the brilliant stones, and she made a wish: *Please let this peace last.*

"I love you." David took the bracelet from the box and fastened it snugly on her wrist.

"It's beautiful, David."

He brought her hand to his mouth, brushing his lips against her skin. "Like you."

"Did you really mean what you said earlier?"

"I did. Forgive me?" David gave her puppy dog eyes, transporting her to all the times he'd returned home with a piece of jewelry and some flowers. Each piece of jewelry filling the custom drawers in her massive walk-in closet held a different apology.

She hesitated. "What's different this time?"

"We are. Our family. Everything."

Before she knew it, his mouth was on hers with a passion and desire she hadn't felt in years. She gasped, coming up for breath. He claimed her mouth again, his lips in total control of her now. He tasted like caramel and a smoky sweetness she couldn't put a finger on. Her senses went into overdrive trying to keep up with the feeling of being wanted. Of being desired again by her husband. It was almost too much.

He pulled her closer and dipped his fingers beneath her shirt.

"The kids." Lina stopped him from unbuttoning her bra.

"They won't be back for a while." His hands went to work unfastening her bra and cupping her breasts. His hot mouth soon followed. A moan escaped her lips. Who was this man, and what had he done to her husband?

Her legs weakened as he explored her. She braced herself on the counter while he awakened every nerve ending in her body. The rational side of her brain tried to figure out what had triggered his change. What had made him want to finally apologize and be the husband she'd wished for? The husband she craved.

The emotional side of her brain wanted her rational side to shut the hell up and enjoy the gift her husband was bestowing on her. She couldn't remember the last time he'd wanted foreplay. Maybe the prayers she'd stopped saying had finally been answered.

Yes. There. Don't stop. She ran her hands through his hair, encouraging him. They both froze at the sound of the garage door rising. *Damn it.* The kids had come back early. Like a pair of busted teenagers, they stumbled around, fixing themselves. Lina almost fell, wriggling back into her bra and unevenly clasping it. David nudged her with his elbow, giggling conspiratorially as the kids entered the house. She couldn't wait to get him alone.

David cleared his throat. "How was it, Mimi?"

"So cool. Thank you so much, Dad. Mom, I can't wait to take my test next week. Think we can practice parallel parking later?"

Lina's heart was still racing. "How about in the morning?"

"That works."

"So"—Danny leaned on the counter and crossed his legs at the ankle—"I should expect something similar when I'm sixteen, right?" He waggled his eyebrows at them. "Right?"

"Boy, go find a movie to watch." Lina ruffled his hair. She and David shared a laugh. It felt so good to have everything cleared up between them; they'd broken through a heavy cloud layer and crested a mountain to see the vastness of their future.

David must've felt it too. He made his way back over to her and held her against his chest for a long while. It was a moment she wanted to live in for the rest of her life.

Tenderly, he brushed her hair out of her face. "Want to clean up and meet me in the room in a bit?"

"Only if you promise to finish what you started."

"And then some." He kissed her forehead. "Gotta check in with work. Was expecting some contracts before my flight earlier."

"Okay." She playfully spanked his backside as he left for the basement. Excitement thrilled in her gut. She shrugged off her cardigan, noticing the light-blue envelope beside the flowers.

Gently, she slid a finger beneath the flap and pulled out an intricate card in the shape of a paper doll, tabs and all. David's handwriting—intentional angles and careful slashes along neat lines, nothing like Lina's sloppy cursive that fell off the page if unguided—spoke to her from the glossy card stock, and she found herself falling for another apology:

To the love of my life,

I love you more today than when I first met you so many years ago. We've both grown so much. Our family is better because of you—you make it home instead of just a place to live. You have made me the luckiest man in the world for putting up with me all these years.

I know I haven't been the easiest person to get along with recently. I will do better. I will be better for you and for the kids.

You are my life.

My only reason to smile after a long day.

Please keep loving me the way you do. I promise we will be better and stronger than ever because that's what I prayed for and you know God's never let us down.

I love you with all my being and more.

Yours forever,

David

CHAPTER 10

"We need to talk," David announced, ascending the stairs.

Lina carefully tucked the paper doll card into its envelope after skimming the last few lines again.

Please keep loving me the way you do. I promise we will be better and stronger than ever because that's what I prayed for and you know God's never let us down.

I love you with all my being and more.

"I didn't expect any talking in the bedroom." She grinned, giddy about all the things he was about to do to her.

"Why did you cancel Dr. Huang's appointment this week?"

Crap.

He pinched the bridge of his nose. "Why, Lina?"

She would not back down this time. She would not let him bully her into something so major. She steeled herself. "I can't go through that again."

"We agreed we'd try one more time. You promised."

"I've had three miscarriages, and you remember what happened with . . ."

"Say his name."

She couldn't say his name. It'd been seventeen years, and she still couldn't say his name.

"Why do you keep lying to me?" David shuffled over to the fridge and reached into the small cabinet above it. He took out a bottle of bourbon.

Lina gawked. "Unbelievable. I knew I wasn't going crazy. You *HAVE* been drinking again."

He scoffed at her and poured himself three fingers, downing it all in one gulp.

"I'm sorry about Dr. Huang, but that's no freaking excuse to break your probation."

"Just like you're sorry about LA and sorry about whoever gave you that nightgown from the gym."

"I'm not doing this again. I told you I bought it."

"I don't know what's true with you, Lina." He poured himself another glass.

"I've told you everything. Can we go talk about this somewhere private? The kids are in the next room."

"All you had to do was go to one appointment, and you couldn't even do that. What did you do instead?" He grabbed her ass and squeezed hard. "Are you seeing someone? Is that why you've wanted it more often?"

"Stop it." She swatted him away. "*I've* never been unfaithful." Her words dripped with enough accusation to make him stagger backward.

Two years ago, he'd had an affair with one of the PTA moms shortly after Lina's last miscarriage. He'd confessed only because the woman had been in the car with him when they were pulled over for reckless driving in another county. Lina'd had to arrange bail for them both—him for driving under the influence and reckless driving, her for drug possession. David had managed to blame his affair on how sad and alone he'd felt after the miscarriage.

Lina glared at him now, knowing he was remembering the same thing.

"Who have you been talking to, because this isn't like you?" He downed the second glass. "Who convinced you that you didn't want to be pregnant again? What friend is it now? Where's your phone?" He pawed at her, slipping her phone from her back pocket.

"No one told me or convinced me of anything. Listen to what I'm saying, David: I don't want to go through IVF again. I don't want to be pregnant again. I'm forty years old, and you're forty-seven, for Christ's sake."

"I'm in the best shape of my life," he muttered, scrolling through her phone.

"Did you hear anything else I said? I don't want to. It's my body." Lina felt like she was talking to a brick wall.

"What's this number here?" He pressed the button to call.

Lina rolled her eyes, sure he was calling one of the sponsors for the school's 5K. She had nothing to hide. There was nothing going on with her and Noah except for friendship, but still, she'd deleted their chats for this very reason. In their house, privacy was an illusion.

David continued thumbing through her phone, calling numbers and asking her about text messages from PTA members until he was satisfied. He poured a third glass, shaking his head. "I can't believe you. I seriously cannot believe you." Glass in hand, he headed toward the garage.

Lina crossed her arms and leaned against the island. It'd taken less than twenty minutes of him being home for the drama to start. When was enough going to be enough? "Where are you going?"

"Wherever the hell I feel like. Isn't that how this works? You do what you want and I do what I want, right?"

"You're being so melodramatic, David."

The glass tumbler slipped from David's hand, shattering. Lina flinched, watching the bourbon splash across the baseboards and puddle on the floor. She immediately wanted to shrink from David's crosshairs when he scowled at her. After marching over to her so close she could smell the liquor on his breath, David leaned down so his mouth was near her ear.

"Do you want me to show you melodrama?" He placed his hands on either side of her, corralling her in.

Lina dared a glance at him.

"You had one job that you couldn't even do right. One appointment." Spittle misted her neck.

"If you didn't want more kids, you should've told me from the start. You made a promise."

Lina pressed her palms against his chest and pushed against him. "I'm going to stop you there. You've made so many promises you don't—"

His fingers clamped around her arms so tightly she winced. He shook her once. Twice. "You don't work. You don't clean. You barely cook." His voice boomed now. "You just started wanting me to fuck you again, and that's mediocre at best, so what good are you, Lina? Why do I even bother?"

"Cut it out." She tried to wriggle free. "That hurts."

"Mom?" Mimi asked from the opposite end of the kitchen.

"Go to bed, Mimi. Your mother and I are talking," David said.

"Are you okay?" Mimi asked.

"Go to bed, Mimi!" David clamped down harder on Lina's arms. Tears welled in her eyes. She blinked them away to keep Mimi from seeing them.

"Mom?" Mimi asked.

"Go to your room right now!"

Mimi started toward them.

"That's it; your car is going back first thing in the morning. Keys. Now."

Mimi hesitated before taking her brand-new key from her pocket. She slammed it down onto the granite and ran to her room, crying.

"See what you made me do? Was that your plan? Turning the kids on me? Is that why you kept their site from me? Is that why you're doing everything without me? You just want it to be you and them?" He was shaking her again now. "Are you trying to take my kids away from me?"

"No. No, I'm not. Stop it already! You're hurting me!"

"I'm hurting you?" His words strung together.

Why couldn't he be a happy drunk instead of a mean one?

"Have you considered how you've hurt me? How you keep twisting and turning the knife you stabbed in my back?" He narrowed his eyes. "You *will* go to your next appointment, if I have to drag you in there myself. Do you understand?" He shook her again. "Do you?"

Lina crumpled to the floor when David released her. He stormed out of the house, a trail of terror in his wake. Moments later, his engine sounded; then the garage door opened and closed.

Another DUI tonight? Or worse, she thought.

CHAPTER 11

Had Lina been wrong for canceling her appointment? She *had* promised David a big family, knowing they'd both grown up as only children.

It was just one more round.

One more pregnancy.

One more potential baby.

Forty wasn't that old nowadays, so what had she been so worried about? And it mattered so much to him. He'd been so happy lately . . .

"Mom?" Danny said softly. "Are you okay?"

Lina rubbed her sore arms, certain shadows of dark bruises would mottle her warm amber skin by morning. "We were just talking. I'm fine."

Without another word, Danny helped her stand, then wrapped his arms around her. Lina rested her head on his shoulder, realizing just how much he'd grown in the last few months.

"I'm okay, Danny." She tried to reassure him, but he held her a little longer.

"I'm going to bed," he finally said, releasing her gently.

"You can stay up longer if you want. It's only nine, and it's Friday, and you don't have anything—"

"I'm tired," he said over his shoulder. "Night."

"Love you."

"I love you, too, Mom. Hope you sleep good."

She hoped she'd sleep tonight instead of worrying about David, their marriage, how he'd treated her, and everything else. The yellow roses David had given her moments earlier now mocked her, their delicate petals sunlight in her stormy house. She grabbed the vase, opened the back door, and lobbed the entire thing over the railing. In the dark night, she heard it land with a soft thump on their lawn instead of the satisfying shatter she so desperately wanted.

The tennis bracelet was next, a hollow apology for their sad state. David could take it back, along with Mimi's car, for all Lina cared. That was usually what his gifts amounted to anyway: tokens given and taken away like Lina and the kids were all Skinner's pets. Only they were David's pets to control. His *things*. It hit her when she picked up the card and returned the bracelet to its box—she was his paper doll. His perfect *thing* to dress up, smile, and look pretty. Everything from her wardrobe to the way she wore her hair—blown out and pressed straight, never full-bodied curls dangling in carefree ringlets—had been by his design, his tastes.

Why hadn't she noticed it before?

Her phone rang. It was the one person she wanted to both ignore and also talk to for hours: her mother. Lina answered her phone this time. "Hello, Celeste."

Lina's mom had been born Jennifer Ewes. Jennifer had shown up late to Lina's wedding in a white formfitting strapless dress. She'd interrupted the best man's toast to announce to everyone she'd decided to change her name, in a gesture of overwhelming kindness, because she loved her daughter so damn much and now her soon-to-be granddaughter could go by Jennifer without any confusion. It'd been a huge sacrifice, Celeste liked to remind Lina every now and then, especially since they'd named their daughter Miriam instead of Jennifer.

"How'd you know it was me? I got a new number." There was so much noise on Celeste's side Lina could hardly hear her.

"Lucky guess." *Also, you always call whenever David and I get into it.* "Mute your TV or turn it down." Lina waited, knowing Celeste had to first find the remote. It was bound to be a long conversation, so Lina grabbed the leftover pizza and a Coke and shuffled to her room, her shoulder pressing the phone to her ear. She'd give the kids some time to themselves and check on them later.

The noise quieted by the time Lina settled herself onto the floor beside her charger. Her phone beeped while her mom attempted to FaceTime her. She wiped the pizza sauce from her mouth and accepted.

"There's my girl." Celeste looked paler and thinner than usual—her round, honeyed face had given way to angles and a cooler pallor. Lina hoped it was due to the bad lighting or the angle at which her mom was holding the phone.

Lina opened her Coke and took a long sip. The fizzy bubbles tickled her throat, making her burp. "You okay?"

"I'm perfect, just as the Universe deems so."

Lina shoved more pizza into her mouth. "So am I going to start or are you?"

"Start what? I was just calling to check on you."

"Cut the crap. You just talked to David, and now you're calling to tell me to be nice." *Like you always do.*

Celeste's eyes went wide at Lina's boldness. "I would never do that. How are you and David, by the way?"

"We're okay."

"Just okay?" She fished for details—details Lina didn't really want to talk about. Instead, Lina wanted to talk about why her mother always chose David's side over hers, no matter what.

Once, when the kids were much younger, Celeste had shown up completely unannounced and unexpected. Nancy had been visiting as well, so she'd answered the door when Celeste had first arrived. Since they'd had some former beef from Lina and Nancy's college days, the women grumbled a greeting, sidestepping each other.

Lina had been seated at the kitchen table. She'd shifted Danny from one breast to the other, wincing as he latched on. Sweet relief had quickly followed as her engorged breast slowly emptied. He'd been fussy, crying nonstop since waking. Between his crying and Mimi's massive diaper blowout earlier, Lina had been sure she was going to lose her mind until Nancy had shown up that morning, a bottle of Prosecco and breakfast burritos in one hand, diapers and teething rings in the other.

Celeste had beelined to Mimi, who'd been perched in her high chair eating dry Cheerios in nothing but her diaper. "It's a little too chilly in here for that baby to be naked." She'd rubbed her manicured hands across Mimi's chubby arms. "Hmph. She's getting darker."

Lina'd sighed heavily.

"Lord, here she goes," Nancy'd mumbled.

Celeste had brushed a hand over Mimi's curly morning Afro, harrumphing like she'd wanted to say more.

"What are you doing here, Celeste?" Lina hadn't had the energy for her mother's particular style of mind games. She hadn't had the energy for much lately, though.

While Celeste had begun picking up Cheerios off the floor, Nancy had opened the Prosecco and rummaged through the refrigerator for orange juice, shooting Lina the "You want me to get rid of her?" face.

"You sounded so stressed when we spoke earlier this week, so I talked to David, and we both agreed you might need a little help," Celeste had said, emptying her handful of Cheerios into the garbage and moving on to the dishes in the sink.

"She has live-in help. His name is David," Nancy had said, pouring mimosas in two small plastic cups.

"Hey, guys, c'mon. David's been . . . he's, um, been busy," Lina'd said, trying her hardest to sound earnest.

"Busy playing golf. Going out. He's at a Falcons game right now and spent the last two weekends in Miami and Vegas, for crying out loud."

Lina had held up a hand to Nancy for her to stop. She'd been right, though. Since the second Mimi had been born, David had disconnected from all domestic tasks. She'd been adamant about not getting pregnant so quickly again but found herself back in Dr. Huang's office a year later and holding Danny another year after that.

Earlier that week and without talking it over with David first, Lina had dropped the kids off at Nancy's, then visited a women's clinic. "One small insert that is undetectable and lasts up to three years" had been all the nurse had to say. Three years had sounded like the perfect reprieve for Lina to regain her bearings while she'd learned how to juggle two young kids. She'd been home before dinner, and David hadn't noticed a thing.

Lina'd waited until the pain in her breast eased, then offered Danny a bottle.

"A bottle?" Celeste had scoffed. "Please tell me you pumped and that's not formula. You know what they put in that—"

"It's formula. I'm weaning him."

"But he's not even a year old yet. You know the doctors say—"

"He's eight months old. Tell the doctors to come and nurse him themselves!" Lina had slammed Danny's bottle onto the table, feeling the front of her shirt soak through with breast milk from her leaking nipples. Everything had hurt, and she couldn't remember the last time she'd slept . . . or showered. She'd wanted to both cry pitifully and rage scream at the same time and couldn't, for the love of God, figure out why her arms had been so itchy and her legs restless. She'd felt like her soul had been trying to slowly crawl out of her skin to get away from the hot mess she'd become.

"Lina, I didn't mean any harm." Celeste had offered to hold the now-crying Danny, but Nancy had beaten her to him, swapping a burrito for the baby.

Celeste had seemed to take that as a cue and scooped Mimi into her arms. "Honey, go and take care of yourself. I think me and Nancy can hold it down awhile. Besides"—she'd poked Mimi's tummy, making her giggle—"this one can use a bath and something done to her hair."

"As much as I'd rather get a Brazilian wax from Edward Scissorhands than agree with your mother, I think she's right. Truce, Sell-esssst?"

Celeste had given her a slight nod, mumbling something that sounded like, "Bitch," before relenting. "A tentative truce sounds needed, but I hope Lina makes better choices when it comes to her friends in the future."

"Guys," Lina'd interjected when she'd noticed Nancy slowly taking off one of her earrings. "Can you really just chill for like an hour? All I need is an hour. Okay?"

"Go, I'll be in the guest room with Danny here." Nancy had managed to coax him into drinking from the bottle. "See, it's all good."

After a quick shower, Lina'd collapsed into her bed. Just before dawn the next morning, she'd woken up to Celeste lying beside her instead of David.

She'd stretched and yawned wide.

"You know you really should find some better friends. Some moms in the area or something," Celeste offered.

"Nancy's the best. Can't help that you guys got into that fight back in the day."

"She actually slapped me. Your own mother."

"She warned you. I warned you. You wouldn't stop." Lina'd risen, slipping on her robe to check on the kids. "You just had to talk about her dad being in prison. She'd told you in confidence, but you used that against her when you didn't get your way."

"I wasn't wrong."

Lina'd noticed how silent and still the house had been for the first time in a week and thanked God and every single angel. "Where's David?"

"I told him to stay out. Didn't realize he'd take it as an invitation for all night." Celeste had gotten up as well. "I'll go check on the kids. Why don't you, I don't know, spend some time doing your hair or nails or something?"

"What do you mean?"

"You know how men are, Lina. They like shiny, pretty things, and with you . . ."

"Me, what?"

"You've put on some weight. A lot of weight and you're not taking care of yourself. I mean, you can't blame him for not wanting to be around. And he told me he's tried to, you know . . ." Celeste had lowered her head and gotten close to Lina. "Sex," she'd whispered.

"No he did not talk to you about our sex life! I can't believe it." Lina'd been mortified.

"Not in so many words, but you guys need to spend more intimate time together, and you're always so tired—according to him, of course."

"You're serious? I'm busting my ass doing everything around here, about to lose my ever-loving mind, and he wants sex? And you're standing up for him, again? Like always?"

Like always . . .

Lina chewed on the memory of how Celeste had defended David back when the kids were much younger. How her mother had defended David after Lina'd caught him sexting a coworker. How her mother had even defended David after he'd blamed her for losing their first child. And now, of course, Celeste was defending him again, after he'd yelled at Lina and grabbed her arms in their kitchen moments earlier. Lina shrank, remembering how scared and small he'd made her feel in that moment.

Why was she hoping for anything else from her mother? Even growing up, it'd always been Celeste first, boyfriend of the week second, Lina last.

Feeling like she needed to try one more time to get Celeste on her side, she said, "David is not the Prince Charming you think he is."

"I'm sure it's not as bad as you're thinking. You always make such a big deal out of everything." Celeste was walking around her house now.

"David wants, no, he needs to control everything. It's getting real hard, Mom." She paused. She hadn't called Celeste "Mom" in seventeen years.

"Every prince is a frog deep down."

"That's not helpful, Celeste."

"What do you want me to say? So what if he's difficult—he's a man. You need him. Look at how you live. Where you live."

"What are you saying? You don't think I'll be able to take care of myself without David? Did you forget I used to work? Remember when I moved to Georgia for college? I can't believe you right now." Why did Lina even bother?

"He's a good man, Lina, and he cares a lot about you and the kids. Maybe try another tactic. You guys go on a vacation or something. Just the two of you. I can come watch the kids."

"Ohmigod, it's like the time you tried to tell me to have sex with him when I was suffering from postpartum depression. He cheated on me after my last miscarriage; did you know that? Did he tell you about that?"

"But I'm sure he apologized and made up for it." Celeste moved her phone to her other hand, and Lina caught sight of a new leather sofa and some Amazon boxes stacked in a corner.

"Where did you get the money for all that?" Lina asked.

"What?"

"You just asked me for money for your bills the other week. Where did all of that stuff come from?"

Celeste's eyes shifted from the boxes to her phone.

"David sent you money, didn't he?"

"What does it matter?" Celeste said with a flourish. "Let's get back to you. Now, tell me what's this nonsense about IVF?"

Lina couldn't with her anymore and ended the call. Only Celeste and David could push all her buttons at once and act like she was imagining it all. Why couldn't they be normal, caring people? Why couldn't they both respect her for the grown-ass woman she was?

Something raw and powerful yelled at her from beneath the pile of horseshit her husband and mother had just unloaded inside her head. She had the right to not want to go through another implantation. She had every right not to want another pregnancy. It was her body—not his. She had the right to want something more for herself than PTA meetings, cooking, cleaning, and being a wife. She could have an entire existence outside the four walls of their house, and there was absolutely nothing wrong with that.

CHAPTER 12

The Henry family's yard sprang forth with life that April. Various hues of greens, yellows, oranges, and every color in between dotted the flower beds outside while the color slowly drained from inside the house.

Lina had been able to pacify David by convincing Dr. Huang she'd needed to take prescription-strength vitamins for a few months before starting the IVF process. She hadn't been quite sure what she'd do after the three-month prescription finished.

After giving Mimi back the keys to her car, along with a long lecture about respecting him, David had retreated back into silent mode, only this time it applied to everyone. He hadn't spoken more than a handful of words to Lina: *Where's dinner? How are the kids? House needs a good cleaning.* He'd stopped sleeping in their bedroom, opting for the couch in his home office. He'd also worked on-site and traveled more. They were lucky to see him every other weekend. She and David had felt more like roommates than spouses, but with the traffic on the kids' site increasing, Lina had been glad for the respite.

She'd busied herself with crafting press releases, managing their blog posts, and helping Mimi with the site. Something deep inside her needed to see them win when she felt like everything she tried failed, especially now that she'd lost her job. It seemed like the only good things she had left were the kids, going to the gym, and talking to Noah daily.

Shortly after learning Lina had canceled her first IVF appointment, David had called Bev, accusing her of filling Lina's head with "nonsense about returning to work." Bev had decided it was in everyone's best interest for Lina to discontinue consulting until she either "divorced or murdered the asshole."

Lina considered Bev's words on restless nights like tonight. Could she ever divorce David? How would the kids feel about it? Would they hate her like she'd resented her mother growing up? Could she really manage life on her own?

Sighing, she rolled over and stared at the moonlight through her bedroom's skylight. She reached for the void on David's side and felt her eyes water. Why was it so hard to be with him?

Her phone buzzed. She scrambled to reach for it on the nightstand, grateful to have Noah to distract her.

Noah: Hey!

Lina: Hey there.

Noah: What are you doing?

Lina: In bed. Can't sleep.

Noah: I'm sorry to hear that.

Lina: I never sleep anyway.

Noah: Vampire?

Lina: Something like that.

Noah: So a trip to Hawaii is out?

Lina: I'll slather on layers of sunscreen. It would be a sacrifice I'd have to make.

Lina: What are you up to?

Noah: I'm in NY.

Lina: Work or play?

Noah: Work. Always work. Press stuff in the morning.

Lina: Yay for the same time zone.

Noah: Can I be honest with you?

Lina: Of course.

Noah: I've been thinking about that conversation we had about my dad.

Noah: I've never told anyone that story about him kicking me out.

Lina: Your secret is safe with me. Made me think about the last time I saw my dad.

Noah: Yeah?

Noah: Is he still alive?

Lina: I think so.

Noah: When did you see him last?

Lina: Ran into him when we were picking up food from a food bank one Christmas.

Lina: Super awkward considering he was volunteering with his wife and kids. I was ten years old.

Noah: Oh, Lina. No.

Lina: That was a fun holiday.

Lina: We moved to another city shortly after Mom met boyfriend #7. Never got another chance to meet his other kids.

Noah: I had no idea. Shouldn't have even brought it up.

Lina: It's okay. Just wish my kids could get the family experience— grandparents, aunts, uncles, cousins. Know what I mean?

Lina: David's parents live close, but they don't really have relationships with our kids. It's weird. And his sister is UGH.

Lina: And don't even get me started on my mother . . .

Noah: I get it. But that explains even more why you're such an incredible mom.

Lina: Maybe I'm fighting my parents' crazy.

Noah: No. I think you're just trying to be everything you didn't have.

Lina: Sounds like you understand.

Noah: More than you know.

Noah: We're a lot alike.

Noah: I've fought a whole hell of a lot to be different from my father.

Noah: It's a struggle.

Lina: Wow . . .

Noah: Yeah, wow.

Noah: Sorry to make it so depressing. Let's switch things up.

Noah: What's your best memory?

Noah: And nothing like kids or wedding or graduation. Something personal.

Lina: You're really making me work at 1:00 am?

Noah: Yup.

Lina: Do I have to?

Noah: Only if you want.

Lina: And I can't mention anything about the kids?

Noah: No. Too easy.

Lina: Give me a sec to think.

Noah: Sure.

Lina sat up in her bed, running through her memories for the perfect one until her best friend's face popped into her head. How could she have lost contact with someone so important to her? She pulled her mouth to the side and nibbled on the inside of her cheek.

Lina: Think I've got it—my best friend all throughout college and beyond was this tall blonde named Nancy.

Lina: If I'm a hot mess, she's a dumpster fire . . . but in a good way.

Lina: Start of senior year at UGA, I discover I've not only received 3, but 5 scholarships and grants for various reasons. I'm basically flush with cash for the first time in my life.

Lina: Like I can eat not only breakfast and dinner, but I can have breakfast, lunch, dinner, and snacks. All I want. And I didn't have to work either.

Noah: Baller.

Lina: Right? So my scholarships and grants cover everything and the kitchen sink, even a stipend. I end up getting a huge overage check in the mail when it's all said and done.

Noah: Following.

Lina: A few weeks into classes, I come home to my dorm room to find Nancy packing because her scholarships got canceled.

Lina: She couldn't even apply for financial aid because it would take too long. She'd have to return the next semester if she returned at all.

Noah: So you paid for your friend?

Lina: Both semesters and I got a job to float the rest. It was worth it.

Lina: She never found out it was me.

Noah: That's amazing. She's lucky to have you.

Lina: Haven't seen her in five years.

Noah: Why?

Lina: Long story.

Noah: You'll have to tell me someday.

Lina: Maybe.

Noah: Or maybe not.

Lina: What about you?

Noah: What about me?

Lina: Happiest moment of your life.

Noah: Easy. When I moved my mother into her own house.

Lina: So cliché.

Noah: You'd think, but it took a whole hell of a lot of convincing for her to finally leave my dad. Sure, he'd stopped beating her by then, but she was still terrified of what he'd do to her.

Lina: I don't know what to say.

Noah: You don't have to say anything. The look of relief and peace on her face that second night has to be my happiest moment.

Noah: Knowing I was able to buy her the first taste of peace she'd had in damn near thirty years is a feeling I can't describe.

Lina: That's . . . I don't have any words.

Noah: She was able to enjoy her new life for a few years. I'm at peace knowing she was finally in a good place.

Lina: Oh Noah ...

She wanted to reach through the phone to hug him. To hold him tight and tell him he was nothing like his father.

Noah: I'm good, really.

Lina: And here I thought you were going to pick something like winning an award or meeting someone at a fancy Hollywood party.

Noah: 10 years ago, I'd probably pick something like that, but I've learned what's important.

Noah: Like this.

Noah: You're very important to me.

He'd become very important to her too.

His comment stirred a longing she'd tried to ignore for some time. Over the last few months, she'd grown to rely on their daily chats. They'd shared every part of their day with each other. She'd usually wake him up; he'd stopped setting his alarm because of her.

By Lina's lunchtime, Noah would give her the rundown of his brutal workout, and she'd usually send him a photo of whatever she'd cooked the night before to tease him into a cheat meal. They'd update each other throughout the day, sharing their hopes, fears, insecurities, silly moments. Nighttime had always been her favorite, though. They'd talk for hours about everything and nothing at all over a few episodes of *Tiny House Hunters* on HGTV. It'd become their thing.

Noah: Hey Lina ...

Lina: I'm here.

Noah: I'm going to be in Atlanta again next week. Would you like to do dinner?

Noah: Or coffee?

She heard footsteps in the house. The kitchen lights flickered on, followed by the sound of water dispensing from the refrigerator. As much as she wanted to, Lina could not meet Noah. She needed to fix whatever was going on with her husband.

Lina: I'd better go. Don't want to keep you up all night.

Noah: My phone is always nearby if you need to talk.

Lina: I'll keep that in mind.

Noah: Good night, Lina.

Lina: Night, Noah.

The hardwood floors were cool when Lina stood. She wrapped a thin microfiber robe around herself and carefully headed to the kitchen to find David rummaging through the fridge, shirtless, his pajama bottoms hanging low on his hips.

"I can heat something up for you, if you'd like," Lina said softly behind him.

He paused. "I'd like that," he said, shifting out of her way. He eyed her as she took out leftover rotisserie chicken.

"Did you just get in?"

He nodded.

"How was Boston?"

"Exhausting." He yawned and suddenly looked ten years older. She felt sorry for him.

"How are the kids?" he asked.

"Busy with school. Testing. Projects . . . you know how the end of the school year gets." She started cutting onions and peppers, then tossed them all into a pan with some spices, adding the chicken shortly after.

"You look good. How have you been?"

Lina took out another pan and heated a few tortillas. "Okay."

The sound of sizzling and popping filled the gaping crevasse between them.

"Smells good," David said after a few minutes.

"Thanks." She plated his fajitas, adding a dollop of sour cream on the side just the way he liked. He caught her hand when she placed it beside him and ran his thumb across her skin.

David's eyes were full. "I miss you."

"I miss you too," she admitted. "Why don't you come to bed after you eat?"

"I'd like that."

"So would I," Lina said and meant it. He was her husband. She wasn't going anywhere. They had to figure things out, and that wasn't going to happen with him banished to the basement. She sat with her husband as he ate.

Moments later, they climbed into their bed. Slowly, he inched over until his body heat warmed her. She exhaled, praying this was yet another new beginning for them. He brushed the hair from her shoulder, placed a tender kiss, and held her close until he drifted off to sleep.

Lina lay there listening to her husband's soft snoring. It'd been over eight weeks since the very hands that were now cradling her had gripped like a vise around her arms. He'd hurt her. She'd had the dark bruises to show. They'd freckled and yellowed before slowly fading away, like her anger and sadness. Time had muted her emotions, quieted her memory of that night until she'd forgiven him . . . again.

When sleep finally claimed her, Lina's dreams were filled with rose petals, paper dolls, and monsters.

CHAPTER 13

David buzzed around happier than he'd been in quite a while that next morning. He'd woken the kids up with chocolate chip waffles and Disney music blaring through every speaker in the house. He'd convinced Lina to stay in bed and brought her a tray of waffles, sausage, and her favorite Tinker Bell cup filled to the brim with a special blend that had hints of cinnamon and cardamom.

As the music changed from "Arabian Nights" to "Be Our Guest," David waltzed into their bedroom. "How was breakfast?" He spun and did something that looked like a pirouette.

Lina giggled, trying her hardest to not spill her coffee. "What's gotten into you?"

He attempted a ballet leap. "Thought we'd try something new."

"Are you going to tell me, or do I need to guess?"

He twirled over to Lina's side of the bed and held out his hand for hers. "Join me."

They danced a horrible and ridiculous-looking waltz for the remainder of the song until Lina was in hysterics over the silliness of it all. What the hell had she put in his fajitas last night? Or what in the world had he taken this morning?

"I like this," he said, slowing as the song changed to something from *The Lion King*. It'd been so long Lina couldn't remember the words.

"*Lion King?*"

He brushed her hair from her face. "No, this. With you."

"Yeah?" Lina felt all flirtatious and hopeful.

"Yeah." He claimed her mouth with his until she was his to command again. One more start. One more hope. One last time. This was it. This had to be it. They were going to be okay.

David's phone buzzed. His eyes lit up when he checked it. "Get dressed. I've got a little surprise. Meet me in the garage in thirty minutes, or you're getting left. Kids already have a head start. First one in the car gets a special surprise." He winked.

"David. What is it? What's going on?"

"You'll see." He slowly backed away from her. Before he closed the bedroom door, he said, "Twenty-nine minutes."

~

Twenty-three minutes later, Lina was showered, dressed, and waiting in the passenger seat of David's Tesla, wondering what he was up to. Moments later, the kids both climbed in, pecked Lina's cheeks, and then got on their phones. David followed shortly after, that same glint of something in his eyes.

"Got your backpacks?" he asked.

"Yes," both Danny and Mimi answered.

"Perfect. Lina, you ready?"

"To take the kids to school? Sure." She'd play along . . . or at least that was what she hoped until curiosity got the better of her when David passed the kids' high school. He shot her a grin.

"Where are you going?" she asked at the stoplight.

"You'll see." He continued onto the interstate and through the city until the airport exit came into view.

"No. Seriously? Where are we going?" She was both annoyed and also excited at his spontaneous venture.

"You'll see in a few minutes." He gave her thigh a reassuring squeeze. Once parked, David hurried to the trunk for the carry-on and handed each of them shiny plastic Mickey ears.

Danny and Mimi both freaked out, excited to miss school to spend a few days at Disney World.

"What do you think?" David asked Lina as they navigated through the airport to their gate after TSA.

"What about school?"

"Sent an email to their teachers. Everything's good."

"I can't believe you did this. When did you plan all of this?"

"I've had the ears for a few months. Got them at a work function but kept them in my office. It all came to me when I woke up this morning. Hold on." He handed Danny the handle to the carry-on rolling bag. "Your turn, man."

Danny gladly held the handle as he skipped down the concourse. He was so excited about Disney Lina was sure he would've done anything just then. She smiled as he took the lead, Mimi following close behind him while she watched something on her phone.

"Hey"—David reached for Lina, letting the kids find their way to the gate ahead of them—"I want this to be okay. I want us to be okay."

Lina gawked. He'd never said anything like that before. "Do you mean it?"

"Of course I do. I'm nothing without you." He held her waist. "You love me still, right?"

"You know I do."

He pulled her close to him. "Tell me you love me, Lina." He kissed her neck.

"David, there are people around."

He ran his hand down to her ass and squeezed. "Tell me or I will scream how much I love you right here. Right now. I may even sing. I don't know. Feeling a little silly right now."

"David, c'mon." Lina swatted him away playfully, still trying to figure this new David out.

"Excuse me, everyone. May I have your attention?" David turned and shouted, his arms raised overhead.

Lina wanted to run and hide. "David, no. Stop."

"Tell me you love me."

"I love you. There."

"Say it and mean it, or I think I'm feeling a song coming on. Michael Jackson? 'Thriller' dance?" David moved into his "Thriller" dance position: his arms bent at the elbows and wrists and his legs bent slightly at the knees. She'd only seen his "Thriller" dance a few times and each time wanted to sue him on behalf of Michael Jackson's estate.

The thought of his horrible MJ rendition made her want to run and hide even more. "I love you. I love you. Now stop." She laughed and he kissed her.

"I love my wife! That's all! Enjoy your flights!" David shouted before Lina pulled him down the concourse to their gate.

At Disney, David was the model husband and father: riding all the rides, singing and dancing along with the parades and character appearances, and sneaking Lina kisses under the fireworks. The Disney magic had struck the Henry family, and Lina's hope grew and multiplied one hundredfold. This was a new David, and they were a new family, for better or worse.

CHAPTER 14

"We're up to forty thousand users!" Danny shouted during breakfast. His plaid shirt was lopsided because he'd buttoned it all wrong, and his hair was a curly nest. But it was a Friday, and Lina could not care less.

It'd been over four months since they'd appeared on *The Sophia Show*, thirteen days since Lina had stopped replying to Noah's texts and blocked his number, and nine days since they'd returned from Disney. Lina could feel the last of the Disney magic fading as they each fell back into their routines. Only one major thing was now missing from Lina's routine: Noah.

When they'd first returned, Lina'd figured she'd try to talk to David like she'd come to depend on Noah's texts, but it hadn't been as easy. She'd started small by texting David silly photos or funny memes. He'd reply with an "lol" or "k" without sending her anything silly in return. Then she'd moved on to texting him updates about her day. He'd asked her to stop after the first few days because it'd interrupted his workday. Begrudgingly, David had agreed to watch HGTV with her one night. He'd complained about his sacrifice for three days afterward. By the second week of trying with David, she'd missed Noah's friendship even more.

"Holy crap, let me see." Mimi pulled Danny's laptop to her side of the table. "Mom! Mom! Did you see this?"

She needed all the good news she could get to keep from succumbing to the Noah-shaped hole in her life. How had she let him grow on her?

"Sure did. Been up the last few nights tweaking the SEO on your site." Lina set plates of pancakes and bacon in front of her kids. "Even sent out a few more press releases for you guys. Plus, if you eat your breakfast, I'll send you the links to all of the bloggers who've promised to review your site."

"I can't believe you did that. I love you, Mom!" Danny hugged her, then ran into the pantry, returning with syrup.

"Hey, save some hugs for me," David said, taking the last few steps up from the basement. He wore a light-pink button-down shirt Lina had picked out when they'd gone shopping in Orlando. It looked incredible on him, despite his protests. He'd bought it to show her he was trying to change by adding a splash of color to his otherwise color-less wardrobe.

"Good morning, you." He wrapped his arms around her waist as she flipped the last few pancakes.

"Morning. Hungry?"

"For you." He nibbled her earlobe.

"I'm gonna vomit," Mimi cried.

"Eeewwww!" Danny said.

"How do you think you guys got here?" David laughed. Both kids hollered like they'd been sprinkled with holy water.

Mimi buried her head in her hands. "I may need counseling."

"Seriously, guys?" Lina loved their light and witty banter, but the ominous feeling of darkness just beneath the surface lingered. While David had been everything she'd hoped for since they'd made up, she couldn't help but feel like she was waiting for the other shoe to drop. For something else to happen . . . for the real David to make an appearance.

David kissed her once more before pouring himself a large glass of water. "What are you guys working on before school?" He swallowed a handful of vitamins.

"Our site is up to forty thousand users," Danny said, turning his laptop for his dad to see.

"But you're not making any money. What's the endgame?" David passed Lina her prenatal vitamins along with a glass of water. "Daily reminder."

Lina sighed, keeping a smile on her face. "Thanks."

"We didn't do it to make money," Danny mumbled, clearly disappointed by his father's tepid response. "A lot of people like our site." He plopped into his seat and slammed his laptop shut.

"You always need to have an endgame. Is it helping with school? Are you getting extra credit? School's almost over, so is it impacting your GPA?"

The kids shook their heads. Danny shot his mother a look.

"What was that?" David asked. "What's going on with your grades?"

"Eat your food, honey," Lina told Danny, wanting to shield her son.

"Lina, I asked him a question. Danny, what's going on with your grades?"

Danny glanced at his mother.

"Danny Elijah Henry! I asked you a question."

"It's English," Danny said, tremors in his voice.

"What about English?"

Danny's bottom lip trembled. The kitchen suddenly felt charged with millions of electric atoms waiting to come together.

"Honey, Danny's been struggling the whole year. English is not his strong—"

"Can you stay out of it and let me talk to my son?"

"I was just—"

"Trying to baby him." David pulled at the collar on his shirt. "It's that damn site, isn't it? You're spending too much time on that nonsense, and now it's the end of the year."

Lina shook her head slightly and shot both kids the "don't say anything" look.

Danny couldn't help himself. "It's not nonsense!"

Lina winced. *Just be quiet, Danny. Play the game.*

"Are you yelling at me?" David closed the space between him and his son. Lightning struck the ominous clouds over their family. "I should put a stop to all this website nonsense."

"You can't do that," Danny cried.

"The hell I can't." He snatched Danny's laptop from the table, rose, and threw it on the counter. It clattered, hitting the stone backsplash. "Your site is canceled until your grades come back up. Do you hear?"

Lina flinched.

"I'm supposed to help Danny do a project this weekend for extra credit," Mimi said and held up a slice of bacon to her father. "Want some of my bacon? You haven't eaten anything yet."

David spun around. "What is this? Gang up on the big bad guy? I can't chastise Danny for screwing up?"

"It's not like that." Lina filled his water glass and went over to him. "You can totally talk about his grades. He's working really hard to pull them up before the year ends. Aren't you, Danny?"

David sipped slowly, his eyes darting between the kids and Lina. "I knew you were turning him soft."

Lina rolled her eyes, instantly regretting her transgression.

"Now you're rolling your goddamn eyes at me?" he asked on cue.

Hello, real David. It was official: the Disney magic was finally gone.

"Absolutely no respect. First, you let them make some site to fill whatever insecurity you have; then you take my kids across the damn country without telling me. You cancel your appointments, lie to me, and do whatever you want, and now you're rolling your eyes at me like I don't have any say in this house?" He raised the hand holding his glass of water to her face. Water sloshed over the sides and dropped onto the hardwood. "I should . . ."

"We should go talk somewhere else."

"Is that so?" David asked, his pupils tiny beacons in the raging sea of his eyes.

"Hey, kids, finish getting ready for school and head out, 'kay?" Lina said.

Without another beat, David splashed his water in her face, emptying the glass. It was sudden and so cold she gasped.

He scrambled for a kitchen towel and began patting her dry. "Look at what you made me do." He ran his hands through his hair. "Why can't you just stay out of it? I'm trying to parent my kids."

She couldn't make eye contact with Mimi and Danny; it was too embarrassing. How would she explain what they'd just witnessed? It wasn't freaking normal. It wasn't acceptable. Water dripped from her hair, spiraling her straightened mane into tight ringlets. Her muscles went rigid when David reached to hug her.

"I didn't mean it, baby." He pecked her cheek, turning to the kids. "We were just messing around, guys. Danny, work on your grades, man." He checked his watch. "I've gotta go into the office for a meeting. Why don't we meet up later for dinner at Keely's? Steak? Those scallops you guys love?"

The kids mumbled something that sounded like, "Okay."

"Sure," Lina said, disappointed he couldn't even last two weeks.

"Great." He kissed her cheek. "Love you guys."

They all stilled as he gathered his things and left for work. It seemed like everyone counted to ten before moving a muscle.

Lina was the first to exhale shakily.

"You okay, Mom?" Mimi asked, rising to help clean up.

"It's just water; I'm fine." She continued dabbing her tank top, clearly shaken up. She was back on the carousel. Up and down. Round and round. It was dizzying. Being married to David was like running on sand—she could take steps toward her destination, but it never felt solid or stable. If she stood still too long, her footing would disappear altogether, swallowed up by the rising tides of his moods.

She couldn't let the kids feel that way. Pulling her damp hair back into a loose bun, she patted the rest of the water from her face and asked, "Are you really helping Danny with an extra-credit project this weekend?"

"No." Mimi shrugged. "But I had to say something."

"I'll call Ms. Bennett after I drop you off, 'kay, Danny?" Lina ruffled his hair, making it even worse than before. "Don't worry about anything. Mama will work her magic with your teachers, and you'll put in the work." Lina's phone rang just then. Was it David? Had he forgotten something? Was he coming back? "Hello?"

"Mrs. Henry?"

"Yes."

"I'm one of the assistant producers at CNN, and we've been passing around your pitch all morning."

Lina winked at the kids. "That's great."

"We had a spot open this morning for the ten-o'clock taping, but we need you guys to be here within the next hour. Think you and the kids can stop by the studio to tape a segment?"

David's threat loomed. They weren't supposed to do anything else with the site until he'd decided. But what if they'd done this earlier? She could say they'd already taped it and she'd forgotten to tell him about it. The kids could easily tape their segment and be back at school by lunchtime. Lina took the phone from her mouth and whispered, "Anyone have sports, tutoring, or anything else this afternoon?"

Danny and Mimi both shook their heads, confused.

"It's CNN, and they want you guys today."

"Yes!" Mimi said.

Lina replaced the phone to her ear, her stomach churning. "Can you email me everything?"

"Sure. I'll send you all of the information, and we'll validate your parking too."

Lina held the phone to her chest, David's voice still in her ears. Was she making the right decision?

"CNN? For real, Mom?" Mimi asked.

"That's not fair!" Danny yelled. "I'm so stupid. I ruined it for you, Mimi."

Lina hated seeing her bright boy dim because of his father's words. No more. She'd make a stand for her kids if she had to. "We'll be there."

"Excellent. Thank you so much. Looking forward to meeting with you guys."

"Listen carefully," Lina said softly after ending her call, afraid somehow David would hear. "Do you guys really want to do CNN today?"

They nodded.

"Go get dressed. We have to be there in the next hour."

"What about Dad?" Mimi asked.

"He's having some work issues. I'll talk to your father, okay?" She hated hearing her lies out loud. They'd sounded a lot better in her head but were still better than the glaring truth: *your dad has some major control and anger issues.*

Danny wrapped his mom in a tight bear hug. She leaned down to kiss his forehead and got a nose full of onions and corn chips.

"Have you showered anytime within the last week?" she asked.

"I'm conserving water."

"Boy, go wash yourself. With soap. And shampoo your hair . . . and you're going to school if you don't slather your pits with deodorant."

CHAPTER 15

An hour (and two smell checks of Danny) later, Lina found herself sitting in a makeup chair sandwiched between Mimi and Danny. She'd insisted on watching the show from the greenroom, but the producers had suggested she receive the glam treatment just in case they'd wanted to loop her in for an interview with the kids.

"Mom, check out my eyes," Mimi said, looking at her mom in the mirror. The makeup artist had been heavy handed, outlining Mimi's eyes in thick black lines. Her eyelids were a mix of greens and blues. On Mimi, it looked fun and perfect for someone her age. Lina was certain no one else could pull it off.

"Slay, chica," she said, stealing one of Mimi's favorite sayings to make her laugh, but Mimi gave her a tight-lipped smile that nearly broke her heart. It was happening—her kids were finally sensing something was definitely wrong with their family. She could see it in their guarded faces and skittish mannerisms.

David's actions loomed before her like a tropical storm warning. Somehow, she knew it'd get worse, strengthen, and grow into a category 5, leaving nothing in its wake. She didn't want to admit it—she couldn't. *What kind of idiot stayed with someone who treated them like crap?*

It made her think back to the stories Noah had shared about his mother. She shook her head. No, Noah's father had done way more than say some awful words and splash her with water. Noah's mother had been abused. Lina was just going through some sort of awful marriage crisis.

Noah.

She sighed and continued thumbing through her Instagram feed and Facebook posts. Her family looked so happy and perfect. Taking another look at the Facebook post of her family Jules had taken from the snow day made her think about everything that had happened since that day. They were anything but happy and perfect.

"Um, Mom?" Mimi said softly.

"Yeah?" Lina answered, still studying the photo of David holding all of them. What could she do to fix her marriage? Was it even salvageable?

"Mo-om." Mimi's voice had a strange tone to it.

Lina glanced up. "What is it?"

She followed Mimi's gaping stare to the doorway and almost spontaneously combusted in her seat when her eyes locked onto Noah's. He was there. He was really there, in person . . . and he was gaping at her. She suddenly felt self-conscious and smoothed her hair down, wondering if she should be the first one to say something.

Noah cleared his throat. "Um, hi. I was told to—"

"Yes, Mr. Attoh. We've been expecting you. Please have a seat." One of the makeup artists patted her chair.

Mimi squeaked.

Lina stole glances of him as he stepped inside the small room. She quickly shook her head and prayed he understood what she meant. She'd never told her kids about their friendship. She'd never told anyone, for that matter.

Noah gave her a quick nod, put his game face on, and flashed an anxious grin in her direction. "Hey, you're the kids who made that workout website, right? I was just telling my friend Jamal about it earlier this morning," Noah said like he was a fan.

Lina nudged her daughter, but girlfriend was a zombie.

"Yes," Lina answered, holding out her hand. "I'm Lina. This is Mimi, and that's Danny."

When Noah took her hand in his, the thousands of text messages they'd sent to each other over the last four and a half months filled her head. Her breath caught in her chest.

"It's great to meet you. I'm—"

"Holy crap, VENGEANCE!" Danny gasped, dropping his phone onto the ground.

"You must be Danny." Noah offered him a fist bump.

"Mm-hmm." Danny nodded like a bobblehead.

Oh geez, kids. He's a regular guy. Have some chill. Lina couldn't with them both fangirling so hard over him.

"Hey, Danny." Lina waved her hand in front of his round face. "Mr. Attoh likes your site. Did you catch that?"

Danny nodded and shook his head to snap himself out of the trance. "Think you can get all of your famous friends to post about it?"

"I like him. He doesn't waste any time," Noah said. "I think I can do something better than that. We just started filming the next Vengeance movie not too far from here. Got the crew setting up for a huge scene as we speak. How would you like to visit my studio after your interview?" He seemed to catch himself. "If it's okay with your mom, of course."

"Mom, please? Please? PLEASE?" they pleaded, then straight up begged. Mimi promised to do dishes for the rest of her life, even when she was married with her own family. Danny promised to take over laundry duties until she died. The kids went back and forth until they started fighting among themselves over who would make the larger promise.

The idea of being around Noah for any longer was overwhelming and a little intimidating. While she wanted to jump at a chance for some more time with him, it probably wasn't a good idea. *Why couldn't decisions be simple, for once?* she wondered.

The AP poked his head through Hair & Makeup's doorway, his eyes brightening when he saw Noah.

"Hey, Noah, your setup's almost done. Shouldn't take more than twenty minutes or so. I meant to ask earlier—wanna grab some lunch afterwards?"

Noah shot a glance in Lina's direction. "Can't. Have to be on set soon."

Jamal nodded. "That's cool, man."

"But I'm good anytime next week." Noah crossed his arms. "But first, you owe me a makeup game."

Jamal sucked his teeth. "I'm still gonna beat you." His phone beeped. "Hey, Imma hit you up later, 'kay?"

"No problem."

"Ready for the Henry kids in five," Jamal said.

"Does that mean you don't need me?" Lina asked, thankful for a chance to escape.

He looked down at his phone and said, "As of now, it's just going to be the kids."

"Guess that means I'll be in the greenroom." Lina wriggled from her perch and kissed each kid on the cheek. "Breathe. Don't panic. I'm so proud of you guys."

"Please, Mom. Please?" Danny begged.

"We'll see. I don't know. It was nice meeting you, Mr. Attoh," Lina said, managing to keep her chill and not walk into a wall or trip on her way out. She exhaled in the hallway. She hadn't expected Noah to have that effect on her. Hell, she hadn't been expecting to ever see him again.

The greenroom was at the end of the hallway, tucked behind a nondescript corner filled with various plastic ficus trees and fake flowers. There was a table set up with snacks and water bottles. A massive television piped in CNN's live feed.

Her kiddos would be on-air any minute. She slipped out her phone, dropped her purse on the couch, and stood in front of the TV, hands on her hips. Her stomach was a mess of nerves. She closed her eyes, took several deep breaths. Once again willing her daughter not to fall, she wondered what she was going to do about Noah. She unblocked him and considered texting him an apology.

"They, um . . . ," Noah said, just inside the room. "They told me to wait in here."

Lina slid from in front of the TV. "Am I in your way?"

"Not at all." He sidled up to her, crossed his arms. She tried her hardest to ignore the war in her head. He was there. He was really there beside her. She crossed her arms, mirroring him. Hints of sandalwood and something clean and crisp swirled around her. It was intoxicating. God, why did he have to smell so damn good?

Lina wanted to say something. They'd grown so close before she'd blocked him. He certainly deserved an apology.

"I'm sor—" they said in unison.

Noah smiled. "You can go first, if you'd like."

No pressure. "I want to . . . no, I owe you an apology." Lina brushed the hair from her face. "I shouldn't have ghosted you like that. I'm sorry."

Noah chuckled, more to himself.

"What was that for?" she asked.

"I was actually going to apologize to you," he said. "I overstepped on our last conversation. I didn't respect the fact that you are married, and for that I am sorry."

She bit her bottom lip, his declaration of her being important to him echoing in her head. "Yeah, um . . ." It wasn't like her own husband respected their marriage. "It's okay. We're, um . . . David and I are . . . my marriage is, um, well . . . it's—"

"It's okay. You don't owe me any explanation." Noah smiled gently. "Please just know that I sincerely apologize."

They watched the kids for a while.

"It's good to see you. I was honestly just telling Jamal about the kids' site because I thought he'd like it. I didn't know he'd go and book you," he said softly.

"Yeah, he probably recognized the kids' stuff from all the press emails I sent last night after you mentioned it this morning. Got the call a few hours ago. Last-minute booking," Lina said over her shoulder. "What are you doing here?"

"Prepping some promo work for a music festival I'm deejaying this fall."

"Deejaying?"

"I've been spinning since I was eight." Noah sounded wistful.

"How did that work with your parents?"

"I deejayed out of necessity when they were too high or drunk to do it themselves. Took some pretty good smacks upside the head when they sobered up and found scratches on their records."

"I'm sorry, Noah. I shouldn't have asked that."

"It's okay. You don't have to apologize for being you. I like that you say what's on your mind. Keeps me on my toes."

That made her smile.

After a few minutes of comfortable silence as they watched the kids' interview, Noah dipped his head closer to hers. "How have you been?"

"Okay." *Lonely.*

"Can I be honest?"

Lina nodded.

"I missed hearing from you."

"Missed your morning wake-up texts?" Lina snorted a laugh.

"You won't believe how many training sessions I was late for." He laughed, and it felt like no time had passed between them.

They both sighed after a while.

Noah ran a hand across his head. "Are you guys doing anything after the show?"

"Homework, most likely."

"I was serious about visiting today. It would be my pleasure. We're doing some pretty incredible fight scenes, and there's going to be a few explosions and everything."

"The kids would love it, I'm sure, but I don't think it's a good idea . . ." She left it at that.

Noah tightened his lips pensively, an understanding rippling across his face. "Just one more day, Lina?"

She wished for a thousand years in that one day. The kids' laughter rose from the TV. They deserved all the happiness she could give them, especially after what they'd experienced at home with their father. One day. One more time. She could do it to make them happy.

"Just today," Lina said and meant it.

CHAPTER 16

Danny had refused to believe his mother was taking them to Noah's studio to see the new Vengeance movie being filmed until they'd followed Noah Attoh's silver Audi through the guard gate.

Mimi squealed, officially at DEFCON 1. Lina doubted her daughter would be capable of simple speech for the rest of the day. She pulled into a parking space beside Noah and cut off her engine. What was she doing?

She had to lay down her rules, needing to make their visit as short as possible.

She turned, making eye contact with both Mimi in the passenger seat and Danny directly behind her. "One: we will not be here for more than an hour. Don't even ask for more time or you'll be grounded." She ticked off her points with her fingers.

"Two: Danny, do not be a smart-ass. Three: Mimi, have some level of chill or I'll leave you in the car. Four: do not touch anything. Five: quick in and out and don't forget to take pics; Instagram and Snap everything for your site. Okay?"

"Yes, ma'am," they said in unison.

"And don't harass Noah, okay?"

"It's Noah now, Li-na?" Mimi raised an eyebrow, finally able to speak.

"Car or studio?" Lina threatened.

Noah tapped on the driver's-side window. "Everything all right?" Lina nodded and opened her door. "Just laying some ground rules." He stood beside her. "Kids, listen to your mother, but the only thing I'll add is to have the most amazing time of your life," he said. "C'mon." He waited for the kids to get out of the car and glanced back at Lina as she slid out of the SUV, her dress inching up higher on her thighs. She caught him blush before he turned his head in the other direction.

Lina adjusted her dress, blushing herself at the fact that she'd caught him checking her out. Flattering as it was, they were just friends. That was all they'd ever be, and after today, they wouldn't even be that anymore. "You might want to tell the kids not to touch anything, and I apologize in advance if something breaks or falls," she said.

"We're good." He waited for Lina to catch up with him. "Hey, guys!" he called to the kids, who were now some distance ahead of them. "I arranged something special for you."

He had her attention.

"Everyone's heard about your site and can't wait to meet you. How would you like to be extras today?"

"Shut up!" Mimi squealed, back at DEFCON 1.

"No way!" Danny ran toward the double doors.

"Are you serious?" Lina asked, wondering why he'd do something so incredible for her kids.

"Called ahead in the car."

"Why did you do that?" She couldn't wrap her head around his generosity.

"Are you upset? Should I have stayed in my lane?" Noah reached for his phone. "I can cancel everything right now."

Lina watched the kids race through the doors. "No. I'm not upset." Her eyes watered. She wiped them with the backs of her hands. "Why?" It was all she could say before choking up. Why had he done anything for her kids? Why had he gone out of his way for Mimi and Danny?

They weren't his kids, and after today, she'd never see him again, so why even bother?

"Hold on." Noah stopped midstride, pressed a few numbers. "Hazel. Good. Perfect. Spoil them. Whatever they want. Did you hear back from Disney? I'll have their mom look it over. Email it to me. I'll be in my trailer. An hour or so. Stay with them. Call me if you have any problems."

"What was all that?"

"My assistant. She'll be with the kids the entire time. Mimi might even get a small speaking role."

If she can even talk.

"Did you bring your laptop? We can join them in a few minutes. I want to show you something first, if it's okay?"

While Lina wanted to see Mimi's and Danny's reactions to being stars for the day, curiosity got the best of her. What was Noah up to? What did Disney have to do with any of this? "Yeah, I have my laptop." She squinted at the afternoon sun, adjusted her bag higher up on her shoulder. "Do you have somewhere to work?"

Noah led her away from the main entrance to a row of trailers between two tall buildings. He entered the largest one, holding the door open for Lina to follow. The set trailer was nicer than some houses Lina had visited. It was decked out with hardwood floors, granite counter-tops, luxurious furniture, and high-tech trimmings. Noah sat at a table near the door and focused on his laptop screen.

"What are we doing?" Lina asked.

He patted the banquette seat for her to sit beside him. "Wi-Fi password is my last name."

"So secure."

"Don't steal my files or identity."

"I'll leave that up to Mimi." Lina smirked, sliding into the cushioned seat beside him. She opened her laptop and entered the Wi-Fi password. "What's going on?"

"Got it. Perfect. What's your email address so I can forward this to you?"

Lina gave him her email address and waited for whatever had made him so excited to land in her in-box.

Her laptop dinged with a new email.

Subject: Henry Kids Disney.

Lina almost fell out of her seat. "Disney Channel?"

Noah beamed like he was handing out Christmas gifts. "Yeah, what do you think?"

Lina read through the email. Noah's production company was going to send footage from today's visit with Mimi and Danny over to the Disney Channel to use in their *Amazing Kids* series. "You've got to be kidding," she said.

"It's as good as done. Set it up in the car. It was Hazel's idea. Her daughter works there. Only need your permission."

First, the extra parts and now Disney Channel? For her kids?

This morning's tirade still fresh in her mind, David's words found their way into her ears: *Is their "little project" even worth all the buzz they were getting, or was it because they're kids?*

Could Mimi and Danny handle something as major as the Disney Channel? Was their site good enough . . . or was Noah doing it to have an excuse to stay in touch after today?

You let them make some site to fill whatever insecurity you have, David's voice reminded her. She felt off-kilter again, like something wasn't quite right. There had to be more at play here.

She cleared her throat. "Why?"

"Why what?" Noah asked.

"Why are you doing this?"

"Their website is brilliant. Hell, wish I would've thought about it first. And Danny is a natural. Like, if he ever wants to try acting, let me know."

Mimi and Danny's own father had never showed this much interest in their site, and they were his own blood. The way Noah had blushed when she'd climbed out of her car popped into her head.

You're important to me, Noah had said.

A creeping feeling washed over Lina. Noah was a man. And in her experience with men, they were interested only in what they could get, not give.

Slowly shaking her head, Lina slid away from Noah and stood. "Look, I'm not sleeping with you over—"

"It's not like that." Noah scooted out of the banquette. "I swear it's nothing like that. I thought this would be good news."

"But what do you want for all of this?" She held her hands close to her sides to keep from trembling.

"I don't want anything but to see you smile. Swear I have no ulterior motives." He reached for her. "And I take our friendship seriously. It means a lot to me."

She flinched away. "Everyone wants something."

"If that's the case, I want your trust." He moved a little closer to her. "I will never manipulate you. Lina, c'mon. You should know me better than that now. We've talked for hours every single day for almost five months. I've told you things I've never told anyone else."

Could she trust him? Could she trust herself to let go when everything around her seemed so unstable? She'd kept her shit together and been strong for everyone else around her for so, so long. "I don't know." No way should she trust him. He was going to be another disappointment. Another person to take advantage of her.

"If you don't want any of this, you don't have to do it. I can email Disney and tell them we won't proceed. It's your choice. I won't be offended. I promise."

Her choice?

She could say no without him being upset? She couldn't believe it. He wasn't the type of person that heard no often. "I don't want Disney," she whispered, tasting the words, testing his reaction.

He nodded. "It's okay."

"No, I don't want Disney," she said a little louder, trembling now, feeling the words sprout roots. "No."

"Hey, it's okay. I'll let them know it's off." His voice was soft, filled with compassion.

"No. I. Don't. Want. Disney."

"It's all good." He took out his phone. Tapped the screen a few times. "It's canceled. Done." He smiled. "See, we're good."

"No!" Its roots sank deeper, sprouted buds in her heart.

"No!" she cried out, feral and raw. Her chest burned, and instead of Noah, she was talking to her husband now, saying the one thing he'd never accept. "No! No! No! No, I don't want . . ." *to be pregnant again. No, I don't want to tiptoe around my house every time you're home. No, I don't want to be afraid of you. No, I don't want to feel powerless.*

The dam of tears she'd kept at bay cracked wide open. David's face blurred through her tears as she sobbed. Without another beat, Noah enveloped her.

"I'm here, Lina. It's okay," he whispered in her hair. "I'm here. It's okay," he repeated as she wept.

She wept for how much of herself she'd lost. She wept for the relationships she'd let David control. She wept for how she hadn't protected her children from David's anger.

After a while, her tears slowed; her breath hitched. She felt empty, wrung out, as if her soul needed to purge everything she'd held back throughout her marriage. Her muscles felt weak. Her legs buckled, but Noah steadied her.

"I've got you. It's okay." He scooped her up and carried her to the couch, where he held her. She felt like a weak child in his lap, but also safe and secure in his strong arms. They sat, foreheads touching while Noah repeated, "It's okay. I've got you," between sleep and wakefulness, a singular breath between them as if he were drawing out her pain.

Sometime later, Noah's phone rang several times before either one of them stirred. Apologetically, he eased her to the sofa and answered it.

"Already?" He stretched. "Tell them to call for a break. I'll be there in ten minutes. How are the kids? I thought so."

"Everything okay?"

"I've got to be on set for my scenes. The kids are having a ball. Hazel said to check out their Instagram when you get a chance."

"I should go." Lina shifted to move but her limbs were lead. "I'm sorry. I didn't mean to stay so long."

Noah brushed the hair from her face, tucking it behind her ear. "Stay. Please stay. I should be back in an hour or so."

Lina was too emotionally spent to argue. "Are you sure?"

He placed a pillow beside her and pulled a throw from the overhead storage. "You're safe here. Please rest," he said softly before exiting the trailer.

~

It was like a dream, all hazy and blurry. One minute Lina was yelling at Noah and the next she was being held in his lap. He hadn't snapped at her for being weak and pathetic. He hadn't been impatient and lashed out at her for sobbing. He hadn't even gotten pissed about her crying all over his shirt. She wasn't sure how long she'd been on his sofa when she slowly opened her eyes to the sound of a shower running. The water cut off. Noah's footsteps went away from her toward the back of the trailer.

Woozy and still emotionally spent, Lina checked her phone. It was a little after five o'clock, and they were due to meet David for dinner at Keely's soon. She fired off a quick text to let him know they were stuck in traffic and would be late.

He didn't respond.

Sitting up felt weird at first. Her muscles ached as though she'd just left the gym. She couldn't remember the last time she'd rested so soundly without prescription-strength help. Pins and needles stabbed her wobbly legs when she stood. "Ooooh!" She stumbled into a wall with a loud thud.

Noah darted from the back room over to her. "Are you okay?"

"I'm good." She straightened, blinking at the sight of him in fitted dark wash jeans and a half-buttoned white shirt. His skin was like chiseled onyx. Was this reality or was she still asleep?

"Oh, I'm sorry." He clumsily buttoned the rest of his shirt. "I was dressing when I heard the noise and—"

"It's okay. It's getting late. I—I need to get the kids and head home," she stammered.

"They did a great job today. I told them you were working on your laptop and had a ton of paperwork since they were extras."

Lina's eyes were greedy. "Did they eat?"

"Thanks to craft services."

"I need to . . ." She staggered backward, trying break the trance, and bumped into the table they'd sat at earlier.

"Gimme a few minutes to get dressed, and we can order dinner. Maybe try some more waffles."

It hurt when she thought about leaving. "I can't. I'm—" She didn't want to say *married* out loud, but Noah seemed to understand. In truth, she didn't want to be anywhere else. She sighed. "You know I can't stay."

"But you want to."

"Wanting means nothing to someone like me. I should go." Her legs refused to carry her away from him. She searched for something to say. "Why the shower?"

"Had to wash off all of the fake blood."

She saw a patch of red behind his right ear just then and reached for it, gently caressing the smooth skin above his neck. "Looks like you missed a spot."

He shuddered at her touch, leaning into her palm. Her heartbeat picked up pace at the way his gaze seared her from the inside out. It was all too much. It was all so very wrong. She noticed the same conflict running across Noah's eyes. After a few tense seconds, they filled with a hunger that stirred a longing deep inside her. She snatched her hand away, clasping it at her waist.

What would happen if they touched again? If they closed the fragments of space between them? Would she burn in hell immediately? She already felt like she was on fire. Her breath quickened. What was she doing? Why wasn't she leaving? Why did she want to touch him again?

Noah dipped his head. "Lina." Her name was a prayer on his tongue. She wanted nothing more than to answer it. To grant his request, cross that deadly line, and pull the pin in their grenade of a friendship. But was it a friendship if they were both attracted to each other? Had she known she'd felt this way about him all along, or was this something new?

She gripped the table's edge, anchoring herself from wrapping her arms around him. A breath separated their lips. She'd lived for everyone else all her life. Didn't she deserve one moment of selfishness? One second of happiness?

"Noah," she answered throatily, tilting her head, wanting nothing more than to press her lips to his. Her nerve endings tingled in anticipation.

Noah laced his fingers with hers and gave them a reassuring squeeze. "I'm here, Lina."

While the thought of him being there for her was comforting, the warmth of his hands on hers and the longing for his lips sent her anxiety into overdrive. Her eyes fluttered wide open. What was about to happen?

She couldn't kiss him.

She pried her fingers from his, wiping them on her dress. "I really have to go. I'm sorry." She clumsily twisted out of his reach and bolted out of his trailer.

CHAPTER 17

While Mimi's and Danny's rooms were on the second floor, David and Lina's Pinterest-perfect bedroom suite was on the first floor, opposite the garage and kitchen. It was decorated like the rest of their house in muted, neutral tones, with abstract photographs dotting the walls.

Lina hadn't had much say in the house's decor when they'd built it ten years earlier. Her task had been to work alongside the interior decorator David hired to make his vision a reality. She sometimes felt as if she lived in a boring art gallery, museum, or mausoleum some days. Tonight felt more like a mausoleum—a beautiful tomb for their marriage.

Everything was in its place, even the three rows of decorative pillows David insisted stay on the bed unless they were sleeping, but she felt out of place. She felt . . . different. She'd felt different for a while, but something about tonight deepened that sense. Did she not belong in the house, or was the house all wrong for her?

Turning the shower to the hottest setting, the shame of almost kissing Noah hours earlier haunted her. How had she let him get so intimate? Why had she trusted him so entirely? She sat on the edge of the bathtub, closed her eyes, and felt the steam rise, shrouding her in its mist.

Noah . . .

It'd taken her and the kids the last two hours to get settled in at home, and now that she was finally alone, her fingers itched to check her phone. She swiped the screen, and sure enough, he'd left several texts for her.

Noah: Lina, I . . .

Noah: Call me later?

She felt her body flush and considered calling him but knew she couldn't. They'd almost kissed. That was as far as they could take it. She deleted his messages, blocked his number for good this time, and stepped into the shower, hoping the water would wash her sins away.

Lina stayed in the shower until it ran cold. What had she done? She couldn't shake the guilt of cheating on her husband. No matter how he'd treated her, they were married, and it was wrong.

The rift in her marriage grew larger by the second, kiss or no kiss. It'd been there for years. What began as a hairline crack shortly after losing their first child prematurely widened and lengthened a little more every day. An inch here and a foot there. Eventually, it felt like she was on one side of the Grand Canyon and David was on the other, with no bridge in sight.

It hurt like hell to admit, but she and David had struggled their entire marriage. They'd argue and she'd get pregnant or David would act like an asshole and she'd forgive him. Time and time again, it'd never truly gotten better.

Still thinking about Noah, Lina dried off, shrugged on panties and her robe, and wrapped her hair in a microfiber towel.

David opened the bathroom door. "I was just about to join you."

Lina decided to tuck her emotions away and gave him a curt nod. She'd deal with her confusion later. She leaned into the bathroom mirror, applied her face serum, and unwrapped her hair to clear it out. It fell in damp, curly waves down her back.

David gently stroked her tendrils. "Haven't seen your hair curly in a long while."

She restrained herself from rolling her eyes at his comment when he'd always suggested she wear her hair straight.

His hand trailed down her back. He met her eyes in the mirror. "Remember when we hiked up Amicalola Falls and got soaked?"

They shared a smile.

"It was, what, our ninth or tenth actual date?" David asked, kissing her neck and looking at her all dreamy and wistful like he was back at the falls eighteen years earlier.

"I fell deeper in love with you that day. Your hair was so straight in these two cute braids, and we climbed for an hour or so; then the sky broke open and poured buckets on us." He held her firmly.

"But you didn't care. You loosened your braids, and your hair became this wet, curly mass by the time we reached the falls. You looked like a siren, dripping wet, hair wild. I wanted you so badly I could hardly focus enough to hike back to the car." He peeled her robe from her shoulders and placed tender kisses on her skin.

She remembered all right, but her version was a little different. It'd been her idea to go for a hike. She'd felt like she needed a wide-open space and some air between them since they'd been together twenty-four seven from their first date months earlier. Even Nancy hadn't believed how inseparable they'd been and had begged for some girl time with her.

Lina remembered wondering if hot and heavy was a good thing and had planned on talking to David about taking their relationship a little slower during their hike, but he'd done all the talking and had interrupted her every time she'd tried to start a new conversation. By the time they'd reached the falls, she'd considered breaking off the whole thing. She'd been pissed about the rain messing up a perfectly good blowout and had taken down her hair because she'd needed something to do with her hands before she strangled him.

"Remember what happened when we got back to my Suburban?" David asked, loosening her robe. His fingers trailed across her nipples. Nausea curdled her stomach.

She'd been resolved to tell David she'd wanted to take a break by the time they'd reached his truck. She'd been tired, hungry, soaking wet, cold, and had wanted nothing more than to get back to her condo and sleep alone in her bed, but David had had other plans. He'd surprised her with a hearty picnic basket and some blankets. Their picnic had ended in the back of his truck with the hottest sex they'd ever had.

To David's joy, two months later, Lina's pregnancy test came back positive, and they'd married months after that.

He'd sold the Suburban after they'd lost the baby.

Lina glanced at David in the bathroom mirror, and her muscles tensed. *Wait*, she wanted to say. *You snapped at me this morning. Why are you trying to have sex with me now?*

"What's wrong?" he asked.

"We can't keep doing this," Lina said.

"You're right," he said, pulling off his shirt and unbuttoning his pants. "Give me a sec."

"No, that's not what I'm talking about." She sidestepped around him, but he continued to disrobe. "David, I need you to listen to me."

Down to his boxers now, he stilled. "Everything all right?"

"No. We're not all right. This isn't working."

"We can go to the bed if you want." The taste of alcohol filled her mouth when he kissed her sloppily.

She pushed him away. "Stop it, David. You've been drinking again." She sighed. "I'm talking about our marriage—it's not working. Hasn't been for a long time and it can't be fixed by another trip to Disney."

He froze.

"I can't keep doing this with you. We need to get some help. You're starting to freak me out." Lina couldn't believe her ears. She was finally telling her husband how she really felt. It was both terrifying and liberating. She considered taking it all back and laughing it off as a joke when she noticed his eyes harden.

"I see." He pulled his lips in and looked off.

"And . . ."

"Where were you earlier?" David asked.

She squinted. "What?"

"Where were you guys?"

"Why?" Lina kept her tone even. Had David found out about her and Noah already? She glanced over at her cell phone, wondering if David had checked it while she was in the shower, but remembered she'd deleted his messages.

"You didn't meet me at Keely's. I couldn't find you or the kids on iCloud. Did you turn your location off? You know I only check to make sure you guys are safe, right?"

She'd not only turned off her location before they'd gone to Noah's studio but made the kids turn theirs off as well.

"What did you do today?" he asked.

"Took the kids to school and got a call from CNN. Ran them down for an interview, grabbed some food, got stuck in traffic, and came home."

David glared at her for a long while. "CNN?" he asked, raising his eyebrows. "For their website?"

She adjusted her robe and fastened it. "Yes, and they were amazing."

"Really?" He closed the space between them and wrapped his arms around her waist. "Okay. Sounds like a busy day."

"You're not upset about CNN?"

"If you thought it was best for the kids, guess I have to be okay with it, right?" He kissed the tip of her nose.

It was time for her to make a stand. "We need to go to counseling, or I'm not sure our marriage is going to last much longer."

"Counseling?" He caressed her, nibbled her earlobes.

"Do you promise to go to counseling, David?" she whispered as his hands cupped her ass. She wrapped her arms around his neck, curling her fingers into the thick hair at his nape.

"Tell me you love me," he said into her hair, walking her backward into their bedroom. Lina went along with it. Sometimes it was easier to play along and have sex to keep the peace. A few minutes of pretend for a few days of calm was an easy trade-off.

David slowly laid her on their bed. "You love me, right?"

When he kissed her, it felt off. Like he was holding something back or his mind was elsewhere. She squeezed her eyes closed, meeting Noah's face. He wore a towel slung low across his waist, and his mouth was on hers. She pulled him closer, wanting nothing more than to open her eyes and actually see Noah's face.

She jerked her eyes open.

No, it was so wrong to think of Noah when her husband had finally promised to go to counseling . . . or had he promised? She couldn't remember. She couldn't get her bearings with his hands all over her and his lips trailing down to her most sensitive areas.

"Promise me you'll go to counseling, David," she managed between breaths. "David," she moaned. All he had to do was promise her he'd try to do better, and she'd give herself to him.

But he didn't respond.

Maybe he hadn't heard her. She fought against the building tension in her body. It was delicious and made her delirious, but she needed an answer. She needed to hear him promise to try to change or this was just going to be another night of empty sex followed by a countdown clock to drama.

"Hold on," she said between breaths. "Stop, wait." She scooted backward, crawling away from him, needing time to collect her thoughts. "David, one minute. I need an answer."

He stalked after her. Grabbing her from behind, he pinned her to the bed with all his weight.

"Stop," she managed to breathe, trying to wriggle free. "David, no," she whimpered, pushing against the bed, but he was too strong as he took her from behind with forceful strokes. She murmured for him to stop, but he pounded harder, his teeth scraping across her skin and his fingernails digging into her flesh. She struggled against him, aching to be free until the room had a fuzzy, hazy feel to it like it wasn't quite real. Like she wasn't quite there.

Piece by piece, their bedroom came apart until she lay motionless in a void.

Paper dolls came to her mind in that moment, two-dimensional, pretty little things with permanent smiles, wide, empty eyes, and the best wardrobe. She could be a paper doll. Maybe she was already one, her two dimensions: wife and mom. She was Lina, the paper doll: wife of David and mother to Mimi and Danny. She existed to please David and raise her kids, nothing more.

The bed jostled when her husband grunted. Air slowly returned to her lungs. She stilled, waiting to make sure it was over.

David brought his head close to hers, panting. She could feel his sweaty, hairy chest against her back.

He stroked her shoulder. "I love you," he said softly. "You know counseling isn't the answer. Just work with me and we'll be fine," he added.

A proper paper doll would have its clothes changed. She ached when she slowly rose from the bed. Her panties fell onto the duvet, and she noticed the sides were destroyed. *Like peeling back the tabs of the paper doll's clothes.* She crept into the bathroom, shrugged off the rest of her robe. Dark-burgundy hickeys blossomed on her shoulders. Sharp pains stabbed her here and there. She was sure to see some bruising in the morning.

David entered the bathroom, winked at her while he washed his hands. "Couldn't help myself. You wanted it so badly."

She cowered when he reached to touch a long scratch across her breasts.

His lips twisted into a smirk as his thumb glided over the mark. "Keep your location on from now on, okay?"

A hollowness she couldn't reconcile settled into her chest—her final transition as a paper doll. Was this what her life had become? She waited for him to leave, carefully watching his movements in the mirror until he left. Would he try something else with her? She felt detached. Disconnected. This couldn't be her reality. Maybe it was her punishment for almost kissing Noah. Or having feelings for him. Maybe she deserved it . . .

No.

"No." Her voice was hoarse and scratchy, but she needed to hear herself say it. She needed to combat the other voice in her head that told her it was her fault, that it was what she deserved, and her husband could do whatever he wanted to her.

"No," she said a little louder. She did not deserve to feel the way David made her feel. She didn't deserve to be choked and scratched, and . . . she couldn't think about how he'd forced himself on her.

Before she could consider the larger implications of his actions, she dug through her cabinet. With trembling fingers, she grasped the smooth medicine bottles. She popped a Xanax and an Ambien, anticipating the numbness that would soon claim her mind. The sweet nothingness. No more hamster wheel of what-ifs, no more feeling, no more hurting, no more being. Just sleep.

When she stepped back into the shower, her tears mingled with the water in long rivulets down her body.

CHAPTER 18

Lina woke late the next morning, groggy and aching all over. She squinted against the sun, wanting to pull the covers over her head and stay in bed all day. She considered taking another round of prescription meds to numb herself from the truth: David would never change.

"Morning," David mumbled, stroking the hair from her face.

Her first instinct was to crawl away from him and lock herself in the bathroom.

He appraised the bruises across her skin. "Makeup sex can be so passionate, right? Didn't want to wake you earlier, so I went for a run. Picked up some pancakes from that trendy place you like. The one with all the fancy syrups."

She was a marble statue when he crawled back into their bed.

He settled into his side without reaching for her again. "I've gotta head to Boston this evening for the next week or so. Daniella can't handle this client, and they keep requesting me."

She exhaled, grateful to hear he was going to be gone, wishing he'd stay gone for good.

"We should plan another vacation. Maybe a week or two. It would be good for us." He yawned. "I'll even let you pick the place this time. Seattle or Puerto Rico." His voice drifted off.

It took mere minutes for snoring to rise from David's side of the bed. Bev's words echoed in Lina's ears: *Call me when you either murder or divorce the asshole.* Careful not to wake him, Lina slid out from the covers. She looked at her husband stretched across the bed, his pale leg peeking out from the embroidered duvet, and his hairy arm hooked around a pillow.

She imagined creeping over to his side of the bed and covering his face with the pillow. Laughing, she'd throw all her weight onto it until he wriggled like a fish gasping for his last breath. But she wouldn't kill him. That would be too good for the son of a bitch. She'd wait until his desperate throes slowed, and as he was on the cusp of death, remove the pillow. She'd stare at him until his eyes widened with fear.

Lina rubbed her hands together. Could she actually do something so sinister? It would be his word against hers. She took a step in his direction and froze when he shifted in the bed. What the hell was she doing? It was like being in an episode of *Snapped*. She couldn't lose her children over this. He wasn't worth it.

Murder or divorce.

Her choices were clear: she needed to get as far away from David as she could. But could she actually go through with it? His sinister smirk from last night made her skin crawl. He'd known exactly what he'd done to her. He'd made her feel like she was losing her mind all the time, and now he was getting comfortable hurting her. She needed to make a decision.

~

"You all right, Mom?" Mimi asked in the car later that afternoon. They'd dropped Danny off at his best friend's house and were heading to Mimi's friend's house. Sure, Mimi could've taken both her and Danny in her Jeep, but Lina wanted to be with her kids for a little while longer. She needed to be with them.

"I'm fine," Lina lied, tightening her grip on the steering wheel. She was anything but fine. The magnitude of her situation was crashing in on her like a tidal wave. Being groggy didn't help. She'd moved from being calm and methodical to rational yet annoyed, and now she was pissed off and wanted to break something with a bat.

She chewed last night over in her head. Why couldn't her life be normal? Why couldn't her husband be normal? Light, purple-blueish lines had marked Lina's shoulders and back when she'd checked herself in the mirror earlier that morning. No excuse in her head would suffice as an explanation if the kids asked, so she'd decided a colorful long-sleeved shirt would be an easier solution.

"I'm okay, you know," Mimi said after a while.

"Are you, Tater Tot?"

"I mean, I'm okay if you decide to leave Dad."

"Mimi—"

"Mom, stop." She sighed. "Me and Danny see and hear everything. EV-ER-Y-THING. We live in the same freaking house. Stop trying to act like everything is perfect. It's not."

There was no more protecting them. No more shielding them by pretending everything was A-OK. She should've known they'd figure it out; they were smart as hell, and Mimi was absolutely right: they lived in the same house. Gone were the days of passing off David's outbursts as just a bad day or excusing his bad temper under the guise of him working too much. They knew, and there was no going back.

Now she had to stop protecting David and finally protect her kids and herself, especially after last night. The curtain had been pulled back and the mighty Oz revealed as a common man, not the flawless hero she'd tried to paint David as. She felt a sadness, her heart breaking over Mimi's and Danny's loss of innocence. She'd failed to guard them the way she should have. But how could she make up for it now?

Her decision had to be for them. For her. For their future.

She ignored the lump that was now forming in her throat. "I can't keep this up with your dad."

"I know," Mimi said softly.

"I'm . . ." Hesitating, she cleared her throat, adjusting the scarf around her neck. Although her throat was sore, she needed to get the words out. "I'm going to leave your father."

"I would, too, with the way you guys always argue," Mimi confessed. "You know Dawn's parents used to fight like you and Dad? Her mom took a bunch of pills and was in the hospital for a week."

"What? Why didn't you tell me? Is she okay?"

"Yeah, she's fine. They're all in therapy, and her parents are separated. Probably going to get a divorce."

"Mimi, I'm so sorry. I didn't know."

"Lots of couples get divorced. Not a big deal, Mom."

But it was a big deal. It was such a big deal. Lina had grown up with divorced parents. Lina never wanted that for her marriage. When she was much older, she'd planned to celebrate her fiftieth wedding anniversary surrounded by her kids and their spouses, tons of grandchildren, and a doting husband.

Lina knew it was a silly fantasy, but on their tenth wedding anniversary she'd bought them companion plots at the Grand Cemetery overlooking a small pond. Of course David had berated her for wasting money on something so macabre. He'd resold the plots to an older couple for twice the money she'd paid.

"Mom!" Mimi braced herself with the dashboard. Lina slammed on the brakes to keep from hitting a kid who'd darted out into the street. The boy hadn't even noticed. He chased after his stupid little red ball and skipped back to his yard, waving innocently at Lina and Mimi.

"Little brat," Lina spat.

"He's, like, four or something. Have some chill."

"I'm sorry." Lina's nerves were shot. She needed sleep and probably another Xanax or two. "You all right?"

"I'm good."

"Has Danny said anything to you about me and your father?"

"No. He's emotionally walled off. I blame you and Dad for that."
Mimi checked her makeup in the visor. "What? I'm taking AP Psych,
remember?"

Lina wasn't sure why, but that made her go into hysterics. She
laughed and laughed and laughed and laughed. She laughed so hard her
sides hurt. Mimi side-eyed her like she'd finally snapped under the pressure. Lina pulled to a stop at Mimi's friend's house, gasping for breath.

"I'll pick you up tomorrow afternoon, 'kay?" she wheezed, tears
streaming down her face.

"O-kay." Mimi kissed Lina's cheek and hopped out of the SUV,
but before closing the door, she added, "And I want to live with you
full-time instead of Dad. Both me and Danny have to come with you."

Lina's laughter dried up instantly. Hell no was she going to give
them an option to live with their emotionally unstable father. Lina
watched her sweet baby girl until she disappeared inside her friend's
house and remembered the sinister look on David's face after he'd had
his way with her.

Her head swam.

The car felt both too small and too big. She gasped for oxygen to fill
her lungs. Fumbling with the buttons on her door until all the windows
rolled down, she gasped. Wind rushed past her face, stealing the little
breath she had and tangling her hair.

Her mind went into overdrive. Would David's rage extend to the
kids next? Had she damaged them by staying with David too long? Was
Danny going to grow up and fall into the same cycle? Was Mimi going
to subconsciously seek out someone like her father? Or vice versa? Why
had it taken so long for Lina to wake up?

Lina's phone buzzed with a text. At the next stop sign, she peeked
at the screen.

David: Was hoping to see you before I left.

David: Where'd you and the kids go? Did you turn your location off again?

David: Should I have Jules stop by to keep you company?

A vicious, wild scream clawed up Lina's throat and out her mouth. She shook with rage, throwing her stupid phone into the passenger seat and striking the steering wheel until her palms hurt. Was this what a mental breakdown looked like? Had David finally won at his twisted game of psychological warfare? Had there been warning signs before the wedding? Probably, but she was six months pregnant and in love.

She also distinctly remembered her premarriage counseling sessions, which encouraged wives to submit to their husbands and that the husband should have the final say in the house. Sitting in church services contemplating leaving David after he'd lashed out at her only perpetuated the whole "submit to your husband" spiel.

He'd blamed her for going into premature labor. She'd forgiven him.

He'd blamed her for losing the baby. She'd forgiven him.

He'd demanded she stopped working at the job she loved. She'd forgiven him.

He'd mentally destroyed her over the laundry piling up, or the babies crying too much, or another miscarriage, or her weight gain, or the house not being up to his standards, or her weak mind when she'd struggled with a dangerous bout of postpartum depression, but she'd forgiven him over and over again, justifying his behavior.

It was a vicious cycle she was finally ready to break.

If leaving her abusive husband was going to send her to hell, she figured she'd already had a reservation because of her feelings for Noah, so why not seal the deal?

It was a drab gray, cloudy late-spring afternoon that matched her emotions well. With nowhere in particular to go, Lina drove aimlessly from one city to the next, stopping for coffee as she contemplated her next moves. She'd have to figure out how to keep the kids in their school, to keep from disrupting their lives too much. Living in an apartment wouldn't be the worst thing in the world. It might be good for them all. And Lina could go back to working for Bev; she knew that much.

She wondered if she'd ever tell Noah about her plans to leave David and decided against it. It wasn't like she was leaving her husband of seventeen years for him or anything. Sure, what they had was nice and all, but Mimi and Danny were her primary focus.

Besides, Noah was a celebrity, and she knew deep down she could never compete with red carpets, premieres, movie love interests, fangirls, and everyone else who wanted a piece of him. For now, it was nice to be wanted and appreciated. His friendship and affection were like a desert oasis, and she'd been lost in the barren Sahara for so long . . . but an oasis is not a traveler's final destination, simply a place to refresh their weary souls.

CHAPTER 19

Hours later, Lina found herself in Athens, Georgia. She wasn't quite sure how she'd ended up in her old college town, but she welcomed the change of scenery. The familiar streets hadn't changed much since she'd walked them so many years before. Sure, neighborhoods had been built, and new stores replaced her old ones, but it was like good plastic surgery: Old Athens, only better. Fresher.

Would she find anyone familiar? Was there anyone left she knew? She parked along the street and walked around campus, stretching her legs. Her old dormitory had received some new paint and an extra wing. Most of the buildings had been repainted or refinished with new stonework or stucco or some other facade. Still, good plastic surgery. So many incredible memories had been made on the campus. They flooded her mind like ghosts, whispering stories of hope, laughter, joy, and foolish simplicity. A part of her wished she could go back.

"Lina? Lina Jacobs Henry? Lina, it's Nancy," the tall blonde woman in a tailored designer suit before her said. She shifted her stack of books to the side and hugged Lina's neck. "I can't believe it's you. You're here?"

"Nance?" Lina recognized the silvery ridge above the woman's right eyebrow. It'd been a horrible accident but made for a hell of a story.

The first week of their freshman year, they'd gone to an off-campus party. Nancy had been crazy drunk, while Lina was tipsy and buzzing by the end of the night. Nancy hadn't been able to walk straight, so Lina'd had a brilliant idea: steal a bike and ride it with Nancy perched on the handlebars.

They hadn't made it two blocks before Nancy's stiletto heel had gotten stuck in the front wheel, and they both had flown off the bike. Seven stitches later had sealed their friendship until five years ago, when David had made a big deal over how much time they'd spent together. It'd been easier for Lina to slowly lose contact with Nancy than to constantly hear David complaining.

Nancy's hug was so tight Lina gasped when she released her. "What are you doing here? How are the kids? I caught a snippet of some show the other week and thought I'd heard them mention teenagers from Atlanta with Henry as a last name. Looked you up, and holy crap, I'm so proud of the kids!"

Nancy's bullshitometer was scientifically calibrated to sense the slightest nonsense. Lina always thought she would've made a brilliant prosecutor or judge, but instead Nancy filled her days teaching college-level psychology. As much as Lina wanted to plaster on a fake smile and give the usual "everything is great" dribble, she knew Nancy would see straight through her and demand to know the truth. Lina wanted her friend to finally know.

"Nance." Lina's hand went to her neck. "It's not so good," Lina started, but that wasn't exactly what she wanted to say. "I'm thinking about leaving David." Sure, she'd told Mimi, but she had to hear herself say it aloud again.

"What's stopping you?"

"I don't know."

"Thinking about it is progress I'll take. It's about damn time."

Nancy had always made Lina feel emboldened, and it *was* about damn time. How much longer was Lina supposed to be miserable? "I missed you."

"Missed you, too, but I figured you had some stuff to work out." Nancy shifted the stack of books to her other hip. "Especially after how David bugged out during our last girls' weekend. I wanted to say something so badly when he showed up at the spa with the kids and demanded you take them since he had to work."

Lina kicked herself for thinking his behavior had been normal this whole time.

"And don't apologize to me; I don't even want to hear it unless it's over some wine. Lots of wine." Nancy smiled when she said it.

It was like they hadn't missed a beat. Nancy was her old Nance: brash, confident, and her friend no matter what. "Wine sounds great. Guess I'm buying, right?"

"Oh yes. You most certainly are, and not that box shit either." Nancy hugged her again, and for a quick second Lina thought she saw Nance's eyes water.

"C'mon." Nancy sniffled. "I was supposed to drop this stuff off at the dean's office an hour ago, but they can wait. You hungry?"

Lina nodded, still in shock from running into her old friend. "You work here?"

"They offered me more cash than Emory; plus I'm tenured. I can do whatever I want, and they won't fire me. Besides, the men are a hell of a lot hotter here." Nancy stuck out her tongue. Lina picked up her pace to keep up with her leggy friend. At the corner bistro, Nancy placed their orders while Lina claimed a table. Moments later, Nancy approached with a very young and adorable barista carrying her tray filled with cappuccinos, cinnamon rolls, and toasted sandwiches.

"Thanks, Kenny." Nancy fluttered her long eyelashes.

The boy's cheeks matched his red hair.

"Doesn't he look like a Ken doll to you?"

"A little."

"So tell me all about this awakening of yours." Nancy took her seat with a flourish.

"He's getting worse," Lina said.

"One minute." Nancy held up a perfectly manicured index finger, tapped out a message on her phone. "Classes are canceled. You're staying with me tonight."

"Thank you." Lina had considered staying at a hotel for the night and was grateful that her friend had offered. Being alone with her thoughts after the night she'd had scared her.

"You need to tell me everything." Nancy sent off another quick message to her students. "I know people," she said softly. "Know what I mean?"

With Nancy's father and brother both having been incarcerated for various violent crimes, Lina knew it was definitely not a joke. "Nance."

"I'm dead serious."

"I know, but that's not an option." Lina sipped her cappuccino. "I feel so stupid for staying as long as I have. Never thought I was one of those women. I mean, let's face it: I'm not some helpless blonde in a Lifetime movie." Lina struck the table, frustrated she hadn't left sooner. "I'm a college-educated Black woman who grew up seeing her mom take all kinds of crap from men."

"You're not to blame. This isn't your fault. He did this to you. He groomed you. Remember how subtle he was at controlling you when you first started dating? He practically had you move into his place the first month. I never really saw you much after that . . . and then you were pregnant and kept getting pregnant." Nancy picked at her cinnamon roll, her lips pulled to the side. It'd always been a sensitive topic since Nancy's abortion sophomore year. She'd tried and tried to conceive all throughout her first marriage, but nothing had worked. Not even IVF. And since Nancy's second husband already had had four children, they hadn't tried. By the time husband number three had happened, Nancy was always either working or traveling. Their marriage had ended after she'd discovered he'd gotten some other woman pregnant.

Lina reached across the table and squeezed her friend's hand, imagining what was going through her head.

Nancy blew out a heavy breath. "Life's shit sometimes, and some people are just shitty."

"I just feel so stupid."

"Love blinds the hell out of people. I should know." Nancy wiggled her ring finger. "Looking for lucky number four."

They shared a smile.

"Hey, David is not your fault. Stop blaming yourself, okay?"

Lina hadn't quite gotten to that place in her head. A tiny part of her still felt like there was more she could've done. She could've been more loving, more patient, lost more weight . . .

"Enough with David. I'm so over him and his craziness. I will come to Atlanta and throw you the biggest divorce party ever, strippers and everything, when this is all over."

"I'll settle for a night out with you."

Nancy took a few bites of her sandwich. "So tell me. You've only been with David this whole time? Like, you never fooled around?"

Lina almost choked on her drink.

"I see." Nancy leaned closer, raised an eyebrow.

Lina looked away.

"Girl, talk."

"Na-ance."

"Lina Nicole Jacobs Henry. As your best friend, even if we haven't been in touch for a while, it will always be besties before testes for life. Don't make me invoke the Gummy Bear Pledge."

Lina winced. Shortly after the bike accident, Lina had declared she and Nancy were bound to be friends for life, and since neither had a sister, they'd also be sisters. They'd been too old to do silly spit shakes like kids, so they'd used what they'd had at hand: gummy bears soaked in vodka. The poor gummy bears had soaked for almost a week and had plumped to twice their normal size. Over a massive bowl of vodka gummies, stale chips, and cold pizza, Lina and Nancy had pledged:

1. To always remain friends,
2. To never allow a lover to come between them,
3. To never name kids or pets after each other,
4. To never cut their own bangs no matter how tough life got,
5. To get tattoos of a bicycle together,
6. To hire strippers for their funerals, and
7. To always tell the truth, especially if the other person mentions gummy bears.

Lina was cornered. She'd have to tell Nancy about Noah. She was a little relieved to have another person know about him, if she was being honest.

"So here's the thing," Lina started. "I can't quite say without you freaking out. Promise me you won't freak out."

"So it's a new woman, I see." Nancy waggled her brows. "I'm not judging. You remember me and Dana freshman year?"

"You're ridiculous! No, it's not like that."

Nancy snorted. "You're trying to distract me. Gummy bears. Gummy bears. Gummy bears."

Lina knew she wasn't playing around. Nancy hadn't even invoked gummy bears when Lina had slowly stopped answering her calls and text messages. She hadn't demanded an answer when she'd texted Lina every year to "wish her bestie a happy birthday because she deserved all the happiness."

"It's something that's happened recently." Lina felt a blush wash across her skin.

"I'm listening." Nancy moved her plate aside. "Really wish they served wine here."

So did Lina. A ridiculously large glass of wine would make the conversation easier. "Where to start? We met in California and have been texting each other practically every day for almost five months."

"That is so not like you." Nancy waved at Kenny to bring a menu.

"He looks at me. Like, he *looks* at me. And he's great with the kids."

"I'll take something a little stronger. How about an espresso? Make it a double," Nancy said to Kenny when he approached their table. Nancy gave Lina her attention once again. "Your superspecial friend sounds like Superman."

Vengeance could totally kick Superman's butt. Lina giggled to herself, remembering Noah in his painted-on Vengeance tights.

"What aren't you telling me?" Nancy asked.

"He's famous."

"We talking Instagram famous, has-been-actor famous, or you'll-see-his-face-everywhere famous?"

Lina took time to get her words straight. "He's everywhere, Nance. At first, it was innocent. We had dinner and hung out after the kids' interview. He was so down to earth and normal. It was a nice change for once; know what I mean?" Lina picked at her cuticles. "We exchanged numbers. I reached out to him about giving the kids a shout-out but couldn't ask. It was weird; I don't know." Lina thought back to that first texting conversation she'd had with Noah. "Then we ended up texting all the time. We were friends, and then it turned into . . ."

Nancy waited a moment as Kenny brought her espresso, gently setting the delicate mug down in front of her. "Thanks, Kenny." She handed him a twenty and told him to keep the rest. After taking a sip, she asked, "So what happened?"

"I almost kissed him yesterday."

"Yesterday? And . . ."

"Promise you won't freak out."

Nancy sipped her espresso, looking over the cup's rim at Lina for her to finish. "Lina, I swear to God I will do something crazy right here if you don't tell me who this guy is in five . . . four . . . three . . . two . . ."

Lina took a deep breath. "Noah Attoh, Nance. Vengeance."

Nancy's double espresso slipped out of her hand. The mug crashed into tiny pieces on the tile floor. Kenny promptly appeared with a broom and mop bucket.

"I'm sorry, Kenny. Felt this sharp stabbing pain creep up my left arm," Nancy said dramatically.

"Do I need to call an ambulance, Professor Jewel?"

"No, honey, it passed. Be a doll and clean this up for me?"

"Let me know if you need anything else, okay?" Kenny said, sweeping up the shards of porcelain.

Nancy pursed her lips and eyed Lina while Kenny cleaned up around them. Once he returned to the counter, she gave Lina a matter-of-fact look, picked at her cinnamon roll. "That is a glimpse of what will happen to your best friend of twenty-plus years and godmother to your children if you stay with David. I will die. I will literally drive two hours to Atlanta, get out of my car, ring your doorbell, have a heart attack, and die on your front porch."

Just being around Nancy made her feel a thousand times better. She felt invincible; nothing David said or did could hurt her. She would definitely leave him; she just had to be ten steps ahead of him.

Nancy's phone rang. "Crap. Gotta take this one."

Lina checked her own phone when Nancy stepped outside. Both kids had texted her to tell her they loved her. David had also sent her a message.

David: Jules says you're not home yet. Where are you?

She bit her bottom lip and replied before he started blowing up her phone with calls.

Lina: Kids had sleepovers so I decided to visit Nancy in Athens.

David: Nancy?

David: I'm at the airport and you're in Athens?

David: I thought we agreed she wasn't a good friend for you ... or our marriage. She's trouble, baby.

David: I'm just trying to look out for you.

Lina: Okay.

David: So you're going back home tonight, right?

Lina: No. I'm spending the night here.

David: But you just agreed with me.

Lina: I did not.

David: You need to be home. What if the kids need you? What's Jules going to do?

Lina: Jules is an adult. The kids are fine.

David: See, Nancy is already making you disrespect me.

Lina: I'm going now. Enjoy Boston.

Once upon a time, David's words had been law. It was as if she'd broken a spell when she'd decided to leave him. She smiled to herself, seeing her screen fill with angry texts from David demanding she return home NOW and that he was going to cancel his trip to restore order in their house. She blocked him, remembering how she'd blocked Noah.

Noah . . .

Without hesitation, she unblocked Noah and texted him.

Lina: Um, hi.

Noah: Hey, you!

Lina: Hey.

Lina: I'm sorry for leaving the way I did yesterday.

Noah: You don't ever have to apologize to me. I know what I'm asking of you. I need to apologize to you. I'm sorry.

Noah: It's just . . .

Lina: Just what?

Noah: I'm not sorry for wanting to kiss you.

Noah: I've never met anyone like you.

Noah: I'm sorry for putting you in this position and understand if you never want to talk to me again.

She couldn't imagine not talking to Noah again. What they had may never end up as anything—she wasn't naive—but it was time to do something for herself.

Lina: I don't want that.

Lina: I wouldn't mind seeing you again.

Noah: Really?

Lina: Yeah.

Noah: Me too.

She considered telling Noah all about her marriage and how David had treated her and started a text message explaining everything. Something didn't feel right about it all. It wasn't his place to know her darkest secret, and when she finally left David, it wouldn't be because of him. She probably wouldn't see him after she left anyway. It would be too much, juggling a toxic ex-husband and a new special friendship / relationship / make-out buddy; she wasn't sure what they were to each other. She deleted the text message.

Noah: Hey, tell me something funny.

Lina: My jokes are awful.

Noah: Bet they're not that bad.

Lina: Knock knock.

Noah: Who's there?

Lina: Amos.

Noah: Amos who?

Lina: A mosquito.

Noah: OMG that was horrible. You're right.

Lina: But you're laughing.

Noah: I'll admit to it.

Lina: Your turn.

Noah: Oh, feeling some pressure here.

Lina: It better be funny.

Noah: What's orange and sounds like a parrot?

Lina: What?

Noah: A carrot.

Lina: I can no longer see you. Your jokes are PAINFUL!

Noah: So we're seeing each other now?

Lina: How's this going to work?

Noah: I don't just play a superhero in the Vengeance movies. I am one, so don't worry.

Lina: Are you on something?

Noah: You make me feel all giddy, like a teenager.

Lina: Obvi fwiw totes feel the same way jsyk #feels LOL QQ

Noah: You just did that.

Lina: Couldn't help myself. I swear I need an interpreter to read Mimi's texts sometimes.

Noah: Would you like to meet for dinner?

Dinner with Noah sounded like a perfect night, but not tonight. Tonight belonged to her and Nancy's friendship, and they were long overdue. Besides, how would she explain the marks on her neck? No, she could not meet him; she wasn't ready for any of that.

Lina: Not tonight. I'm in Athens visiting an old friend.

Noah: Old friends are the best.

Lina: Remember the college friend I told you about?

Noah: Yes!

Lina: I'm visiting Nancy.

Noah: I'm so happy for you. Sounded like you really missed her.

Lina: I did.

Noah: I'm working late tonight, so call or text anytime.

Lina: Begging again?

Noah: Naturally.

Lina: Maybe.

Noah: I'll take a maybe.

Nancy entered the café just then, looking flustered.

"Everything okay?" Lina asked.

"Yeah. First call was from a Tinder hookup begging for seconds. My battery-powered silicone friends last longer. Asked him to delete my number."

"First call?"

Nancy rubbed her temples. "You won't believe who I just got off the phone with."

"Who?"

"Your husband."

"David? Ugh." Lina wanted to act surprised, but she wasn't. David had called her friends before. Her friends, her mother, PTA members. It didn't matter.

"You really need to get the hell out of there."

"So sleepover's canceled?" Lina dared to ask.

"Not on your life. Let him throw all the temper tantrums he wants. My phone is off for the rest of the night, and I keep the guard at my place satisfied."

"Nance."

"I buy him food. Jesus, Lina. I don't hook up with everyone." A mischievous smile crept across Nancy's face, and Lina waited for her to confess.

"So it was once or twice, but he's super cute and massive." Nancy held her hands at a distance for emphasis. "And you know I have needs."

They both whooped and hollered until Lina's stomach hurt. God, she'd missed her friend. With sunset not so far off, Lina's time was dwindling, and she needed as much time with Nancy as she could get. "C'mon," she said, gathering her stuff. "We'd better get going. Need lots of wine for our epic slumber party."

CHAPTER 20

That night, Lina had an epiphany watching the last of the wine puddle where the goblet met the stem: marriage wasn't supposed to be drudgery or painful. She wasn't supposed to check her identity at the wedding altar, blindly exchanging her hopes, dreams, goals, and personhood for scraps of affection, an endless barrage of criticism and condescension and abuse.

Abuse.

There it was.

Admitting it was more painful than David's mind games. More painful than what David had inflicted on her physically. It wasn't like the sharp clawing of his nails from when he'd scratched her, or the way her biceps seared and throbbed from when he'd grabbed her arms too tightly, or even the soreness that'd settled all across her body after he'd had his way with her. No, this was an agony at the very core of who she was, that she'd allowed him to violate her sense of self for so long.

Growing up, she'd known better; that was what she couldn't understand most. Witnessing the way men had used and taken advantage of her mom, she'd vowed to never be one of those stupid women, but here she was . . . one of those stupid women.

It didn't take long for Nancy to pick up on Lina's burgeoning melancholy before she cranked up the music. She pulled Lina to her feet, held her hands, and sung along with the Black Eyed Peas, obnoxiously loud and off-key. Before long, they were jumping around, badly dancing to "I Gotta Feeling." Lina's cares eased by the time the bass dropped. Arms raised, she closed her eyes and let the music carry her. They drank and danced it out until they were both breathless and exhausted. It was like they'd never missed a day together. Much later that night, they finally collapsed on a ton of pillows scattered across Nancy's living room. For the first time in a long while, Lina slept through the entire night.

~

The next morning came too quickly and with it a long, tear-filled hug from Nancy, who'd blamed her watering eyes on the absurd pollen levels. Lina knew better but didn't say anything. Nancy would've denied it anyway. By the time Lina drove out of Nancy's neighborhood, she missed her friend like crazy. She considered turning around and staying another night, but the kids had school, and David was in Boston. Lina was renewed. Refreshed. Ready to return home. Ready to leave David and start her new life.

One week?

Two weeks?

She wasn't quite sure of her timeline. She knew for certain she'd have to secure a place to live, then hire an attorney, which was at the very minimum a $10,000 retainer. And there was the money she'd need until she started working and drawing a full paycheck again. Altogether, she'd have to withdraw at least $20,000.

She bit her nails as she pulled off the exit and into a gas station. How would she either transfer that amount of money or withdraw it from their bank without alerting David? She mulled different scenarios while she started the gas pump. Her brain was in overdrive by the time she went inside to grab a Coke and some chips. Caffeine and salty, fatty goodness would keep her company on her road trip.

"Pump four," she said to the clerk, tossed her chips onto the counter along with her Coke, and inserted her card. She stared hard at the Skittles, knowing she'd eat the entire bag within a few minutes. The card reader made an awful sound.

The clerk picked something from his teeth and spat it into a rag. "Declined."

Lina tried her card again, confused. It declined. She tried a third time unsuccessfully.

"Got another form of payment. That ain't working."

Lina unwound the long Publix receipt from her secret debit card and paid. Unfortunately, her account had been drained by all the kids' website's expenses—the professional developer for Mimi, the monthly server fees, hosting fees, social media ads, etc. She was down to her last few hundred dollars, which wouldn't be enough for a new start. As soon as she was back inside her car, she checked her account.

No! No! No! No!

The account balance was five dollars. Frantically, Lina searched through the last few transactions to find David had transferred the majority of her funds to his account and unlinked her account from the family one. The deal was always that they'd each have separate accounts and one joint account David paid the bills from. David had convinced Lina to add his name to her account. "Just in case of an emergency," was how he'd explained it. Lina had been naive enough to take him at his word when he'd said he'd added her name to his account.

Lina raced back home, picking both kids up in record time. She had to figure out how to go through with her plan to leave David. She pulled at her hair, frustrated that she'd become so dependent on him for everything. She hated herself over it. In an attempt to keep her anxiety at bay, Lina blasted the air conditioner at full speed and took deep breaths. Maybe she could sell Mimi's car and her jewelry for enough to get them through the next few months. Mimi would understand, wouldn't she?

"Mom, you okay?" Mimi asked as they waited for the gate to their neighborhood to open.

"I'm good." *Can I sell your car?* She clenched the steering wheel. "How was your sleepover?"

"It was fun. I'm so tired." She yawned as they pulled into the garage. "Told Dawn I'd pick her up later so we can grab some Froyo for her birthday."

"Guys, grab all of your stuff and clean up, 'kay?" Lina waited for Danny to gather his bags and head into the house. "Meems, give me a sec?"

"Sure. Sup?"

"Don't talk to Danny about me and your dad. I'm still trying to figure it all out. Okay?"

"'Kay."

"And I may need to—"

David knocked on Mimi's window, startling them. "Hey, guys. Coming inside?"

What the hell was he doing home instead of in Boston?

Mimi seemed to think the same thing and shot a glance at her mom before opening the car door and sliding out with her bags. Lina followed, steeling herself for whatever David had up his sleeve.

"Um, hey, Dad."

David patted her shoulder. "How was your sleepover?"

"Good. I'm so tired."

"Sounds like fun. Hungry?"

"Starving."

David smirked at Lina. "Couldn't get them anything on the way home?"

He wants to play this stupid game? She wouldn't give him the satisfaction. "Didn't bother stopping. Is there something I should know?"

David shook his head and led them inside. "Hey, how was CNN Friday? Your mom said you guys were pretty incredible."

Mimi shrugged off her backpack, hesitating. Her eyes flickered from David to Lina and back again. "Yeah. It was, um, cool."

"Yeah? Make up your schoolwork yet?"

Mimi shook her head.

"Didn't think so. Can't do that with only a few more weeks of school left. Why don't you have a seat at the table and check to see what you missed."

Lina was not in the mood for drama today but could sense it was inevitable. She hung her purse on one of the nearby hooks and found something in the kitchen to busy herself with. She wanted to know what David was up to, knowing he was probably still pissed at her for hanging out with Nancy yesterday. "Hey, you want to go talk about Nancy?"

"No need. I'm good." He went over to the kitchen table and studied Mimi's laptop screen.

Danny tromped down the stairs, carrying a canvas shopping bag filled with all his gaming equipment. Various cables and cords stuck out of the bag like a caught octopus. "Here you go." He sniffled.

"Put them in Mimi's car," David said.

"David, seriously? Is this necessary?"

"Mimi's car," he said to Danny, motioning for the boy to keep moving. His face was unreadable.

"What are you doing? What's going on?"

"I told them it was all canceled. They didn't listen to me." David turned to her. "I can't punish you, but they need to learn a lesson."

Just then Jules emerged from the guest room. "Oh, hey, guys. David, I really have to go. Supposed to meet Carl in twenty minutes. You still gonna give me a ride?"

"Better than that." David dug around in his pocket and pulled out some keys.

Lina immediately recognized the smiling unicorn kitty key chain she and Danny had picked out for Mimi one afternoon.

"I know you're trying, and Dad isn't going to get you a car, so it's yours," David added, now dangling the colorful unicorn for everyone to see.

"That's my car!" Mimi shrieked when Jules caught the keys.

"It's *my* car, and now it's Jules's car." He corrected her and smiled wide at Jules. "Enjoy. Better get going."

Mimi rose, marched over to Jules. "You can't have my car. It's mine. I got it for my birthday." She lunged for the keys, but David grabbed her by the waist.

"Go, Jules." He held tight as Mimi bucked and kicked and screamed, tears streaking her cheeks.

Lina ran to Mimi's side, pulling her away from David. How could he crush his little girl like this? David's grip loosened when Jules disappeared out the garage door. Mimi spilled into Lina's arms. Lina held her close as she sobbed. It must've hit Danny just then that his gaming equipment was in Mimi's car—the car Jules was now taking out of the garage. He bolted out the door.

"This place is a madhouse. You see what happens when there's no order? You should've listened to me, Lina. You should've done what I said." David paced, running his hands through his hair. "I didn't want to do any of this, but it's like you force my hand, and now I'm the bad guy again." He crouched near Mimi and Lina. "I'm sorry, Mimi, but you'll understand when you're older. You have to listen to what I say."

The load of bullshit spilling from his mouth made Lina furious. The kids were not to blame. No matter how hard she tried, David would never understand how much work and sweat the kids had put into their website. It was important to them, but like everything else they'd had a passion for, David had to be in control. David was the sun and everyone else trapped in his pull, his will. Lina and the kids delicately orbited around him in their careful, predestined paths—no deviations or course corrections.

Lina shook her head, snorting. He'd had it all planned the second she'd told him about CNN. If he was going to show his hand, so would she. She gently deposited Mimi, rose, and calmly made her way to the kitchen, David close on her heels.

He stroked her back. "See, better? We're going to be okay."

Lina reached for her prenatal vitamins.

"That's it, honey." He kneaded her shoulders. "Mimi, why don't you take your homework and head upstairs?"

Danny returned, red faced and sweaty. *Had he chased after the car?* She wanted to go to her sweet boy, but the way his big round eyes watered then narrowed at her made her reconsider.

"Go shower and get your schoolwork done, Danny." David filled a glass of water, handed it to Lina. "I'm going to work from home the next week or two. We need to work on this house, and I made an appointment with Dr. Huang for Tuesday."

She was trapped with him now. No money. No car to sell. No pull with the kids because she was pretty sure they hated her now since she'd taken them to CNN. She was grateful David never found out about their trip to Noah's studio afterward. Friday had been only two days ago yet felt like months.

Noah.

The sound of both kids' muffled crying and hitched breaths upstairs broke her heart. She felt deflated. He'd finally gotten to them and was going to systematically break them down like he'd done to her. She twisted off the top of her prenatals. "You may think you're hurting me, but those kids will never forget how you just made them feel."

David gently brushed the hair from her face. "You'll see how much better we'll all be without all the distractions."

In one swift move, Lina emptied all her vitamins into the sink and flipped on the garbage disposal. It crunched and ground through the thick pills in a low rumble. She braced herself, waiting for David to unleash his anger. His face erupted, bright red and furious. She stood her ground.

Reaching across her, he slammed off the garbage disposal, fuming. "I can't believe you did that. Why, Lina? Why when all I want is the best for our family?"

"I'm not going to see Dr. Huang again." Lina crossed her arms. "I will not be pregnant again."

David staggered backward, confusion crisscrossing his face. "Why are you so against our family?"

"I'm not against it; it's not working. Can't you see what you're doing is wrong?" She waved her hands around. "This is not right. The way you treat me and the kids is not right. I don't even have access to my own money in the bank."

"You have an account. What are you talking about?"

"Is Nancy why you emptied my bank account?" Lina spat.

"It's pretty obvious you can't be trusted."

"So now you're going to treat me like a child?"

"I'm not treating you like a child; I'm helping you. Keeping you from hurting yourself. You know Nancy is bad news. She's bad for our marriage, and you want to have her around our kids? Our baby?"

"I'm not having any more children."

"See what she did? Now you don't want more kids. We were doing great. We were working on our family, our marriage, and now Nancy turned you against us, again."

The way he twisted everything around was certifiable. No, she'd not allow him to scramble her head again. "David." She raised her voice. "This isn't working. It's just not working." She motioned between them. "This. Isn't. Working."

Arms folded across his chest, he was silent for some time. "You want me to leave?"

The air particles prickled with electricity. She wasn't sure if she should answer him.

"Do you want me to leave my family?" he asked again. He struck the counter, spittle flying from his mouth when he shouted, "Do you want me to leave my family?"

She flinched, her words hiding behind her teeth.

David struck the counter again and again and again, his hair falling across his eyes. "Do you want me to leave my family? Do you want me to leave my family? Do you want me to leave my family? Do you want me to leave my family?"

Her ears rang. She was shaking now, terrified to move as he brought his head close to hers.

"If I leave, you'll be completely on your own. I'll cut all of you off. Do you hear me?"

She gritted her teeth as his threat lingered between them for what felt like an eternity.

"That's what you want," he muttered, taking a few steps backward, his eyes never leaving hers. "I see." Hands in his pockets now, he nodded slowly as understanding blossomed in his eyes. A flash of hurt crossed his face, pinched his lips. He cleared his throat. "Guess I'll, um, go to Boston after all."

CHAPTER 21

David made good on his threat.

By the time Lina'd returned home from dropping the kids off that Monday morning, the electricity had been cut off. She'd had to slink around to the back of the house in her pajamas to retrieve the emergency key hidden in a hollowed-out rock because the garage door wouldn't open. No water flowed from the tap when she'd turned it on for a shower, and the stove had clicked and clicked and clicked, flameless. Everything had been turned off except her phone. Lina had been sure David still wanted to track her movements. He'd probably expected her to call him, crying and begging for him to come back.

Not this time.

With the kids at school, Lina had gathered all her jewelry, except for her wedding ring and band—she hadn't been quite ready to get rid of them—and sold it all at a local pawn shop. The few thousand dollars had been a godsend. She'd been able to turn everything back on and in her name this time. She'd even bought enough groceries to float them a little while, not sure how long David would be willing to play the game.

Despite all his posturing and outbursts, she'd known with everything in her being David would act like he was the victim when she finally asked for a divorce. He'd drag her through hell just for the fun of it. She'd witnessed David ruin people for lesser offenses, and it haunted her now. One particularly spiteful time had been shortly after she and David received news that the latest round of implantations had been successful.

On the way home from Dr. Huang's office, a college student had cut David off on the highway. He'd followed the guy to Target and gotten into a yelling match until the guy punched David. David had pressed various charges against him and ended up petitioning the judge for the harshest punishment. Poor kid had been sentenced to a year in jail, two on probation, and he'd been expelled from college after David had reached out to some of his alumni friends.

Part of her wondered if she could maintain their volatile status quo until the kids left for college. Mimi had two years of high school left, while Danny had three years remaining. Three years of putting up with David's mood swings, manipulative behavior, and abuse? No way she'd survive that. No way she'd want the kids exposed to their toxic relationship for another three years. And there was no way she wanted to put off living and enjoying her life for that long.

It'd taken Lina and the kids a little over three weeks to establish a new normal without David. Not having access to their money had been a temporary inconvenience but worth her small victory—one step closer to taking back control of her life. Afternoons filled with tutoring and extracurricular stuff were quickly replaced by long walks, studying, and movie nights.

Eventually, the cool spring melted into a long, hot, never-ending summer. It felt like the twenty-four-hour days they'd been used to were somewhere dawdling lazily beneath a shade tree. Longer days meant even longer nights and falling asleep on the phone talking to Noah. They'd upgraded from texting to calling and eventually FaceTiming. It'd been a happy accident—Lina butt dialing him during a panic attack the night David left. Noah's excitement over hearing her voice on the other line reassured her that she'd made the right decision.

On nights like tonight, after wrestling with the kids and breaking up their squabbles all day, Lina was relieved to have another adult to talk to. Noah listened intently between baskets of laundry while she blathered about the kids arguing, how messy her house was, how tired she was, and how she wished Bev would hire her full-time instead of part-time. Since Lina hadn't jumped at any of Bev's previous offers, and Bev had to let her go after David's call, she'd hired someone full-time to take Lina's spot.

"Hey, you got quiet on me," Noah said, neatly folding another towel and adding it to the stack on the couch beside him.

Lina stretched and rolled her shoulders. She'd been sitting on the floor beside the electrical socket for hours now because she couldn't find her long charging cord. It wasn't like she could go wake the kids up to ask them where they'd put her charger without them asking tons of questions she wasn't prepared to answer. She didn't even have any answers for herself. All she knew was she liked Noah. She loved talking to him and was looking forward to seeing him again. He made a goofy face into the phone's camera, and she stuck out her tongue at him. "I'm still awake. Butt's numb from sitting on the floor for so long, though."

"You want to talk tomorrow?"

She shifted. "I'm okay. Thanks for letting me complain so long. Felt good to get all of that out. You should've seen the kids today. Swore I had toddlers running wild." Thinking about all the kids' yelling and fighting made her tension headache throb more. *The kids. Disney.* "I forgot to ask you if Disney was still on the table. I mean, if it's not, that's okay."

"It is. One call and they'll run it. But it's up to you. And I'm okay with you saying no."

Lina considered the shitstorm life had handed Danny and Mimi and wanted to make it a little more tolerable. She wanted to give them everything she could to compensate them for the abusive environment in which they'd grown up, for not leaving David sooner. It was her guilt offering.

"No, I want it."

"Are you sure?"

"I am. Would you make it happen?"

"Definitely. Just sign the release forms and send them back to me, and I'll have Hazel make sure her daughter runs it."

"It's that easy?"

"If I could make it easier for you, I would." They gazed at each other for some time.

Lina longed to be with him again so much it hurt. How had they become so intimate without any physical intimacy? The concept was so strange to her, but it worked for them.

"Lina, are you okay?" Noah asked.

She rubbed her temples, her headache still throbbing. "I'm okay. How was your day? And how in the world do you always have so much laundry?"

"Why do you always pick on me about my laundry?"

"I'm still in shock that you actually do your own laundry. Hire someone, man."

"It's therapeutic." He shook out another towel and began folding it. "When you deal with the kind of privileged, entitled people I have to deal with every day, it's good to stay grounded."

Lina liked that about him. He was one of the most famous actors in the entire world and made more money than she could ever imagine, but he did his own laundry, fully aware of his privilege. "Okay, I won't pick on you anymore."

"I was going to say if you mentioned my laundry again, you'd have to meet me for dinner this weekend, so please keep picking on me."

Lina blushed. "This weekend?"

"Flying in late Friday night. Would you like to have dinner with me Saturday, Lina?"

While she'd told Noah about her and David's separation, she hadn't told him about her decision to divorce him yet. Being seen in public with Noah Attoh when she was still married to David was a terrible idea—he'd have a field day with her and the kids again. "I don't think being in public with you is a good idea."

"I understand." He gave her a sheepish look. "Would you like to come to my place for dinner? I'm a pro at ordering food."

"Saturday? This Saturday? Two days from now?" Imagining being alone with Noah again tied her tongue and made her all jittery.

He laughed. "Yes. This Saturday. I'll even show you my linen closet and laundry room."

Lina joined him in laughing. "Saturday, then."

CHAPTER 22

Tonight was Lina's first Saturday night without the kids since she'd spent the weekend at Nancy's a month earlier, and she was on her way to have dinner with Noah. The kids had been all too happy to have sleepovers at their friends' houses. She hoped for many sleepovers during their summer vacation.

Lina's heart thrummed in her chest when the elevator stopped at the penthouse level in the spire of private condos. What was she thinking? Why had she agreed to meet Noah at his place for dinner?

Two steps out of the elevator, the familiar fluttering in her gut began. Why was she so anxious to see Noah? They'd only grown closer over the last month. He'd become a part of her life, and she was certain she'd been part of his, so why was she freaking out so much?

Three more steps and she tugged on the heavy brass knocker hanging on the massive hand-carved door. She ran her fingers across it, feeling the deep notches and intricate details. She snatched her hand back when the bolt clicked. Holding her breath, she anticipated kissing him until her lips were swollen and red. She'd get it out of the way, once and for all.

"Now she's very special. I want you to be super nice to Ms. Lina, okay?" Noah's voice seeped through the door. Lina's legs tensed in expectation. Did he have a puppy? When the door opened, Lina understood.

Standing beside him, in the cutest striped pajamas, was a miniature version of Noah.

Lina crouched down to the boy's height and held out her hand. "Hi. I'm Lina, and I really like your pajamas."

"I just got them," the boy said.

"Yeah? What's your favorite color?"

The little boy's plump hands ran across his round tummy. He pointed at a stripe on his top. "Yellow. I like yellow."

"I like yellow too. Know what it reminds me of?"

"Um . . . the sun!"

"I was thinking of something else," Lina said.

"Bananas!" the boy giggled.

"Nope. Try again."

"Um. I don't know."

"How about lemons?" Lina tickled his tummy. "Know why I like lemons? Because when you eat them"—Lina sucked in her cheeks and made the goofiest face—"they make your lips pucker, and you talk like this!"

The boy laughed heartily. "Daddy, she's silly."

"Lina, this is my son, Edward."

"I like your name, Edward." Lina tapped his nose and stood to face Noah.

"Why don't you go color for a bit before bedtime?" Noah said to his son.

"Story after?" Edward asked.

"Of course. We need to find out what happened to Meg's father. You think we'll see Mrs. Who, Mrs. Whatsit, and Mrs. Which again?"

"I don't know."

"How about you draw me a picture of it, okay?" Noah patted Edward's head and watched the boy teeter off. "I love how you were with Edward," he added, inviting her in.

"Why didn't you tell me about him?" She felt foolish for not internet stalking him after their first dinner.

"I was afraid." He rubbed his head. "I didn't want to make this more complicated."

"Not sure it could get much worse." Lina thought for a second, then stopped abruptly. "Are you with his mother? Like, am I—"

"No. Definitely not. I'm not seeing anyone." His hands found hers. "Except you."

All the blood rushed to her head. There it was again—his declaration of the undeniable force drawing them to each other. She glanced down at her hands in his and remembered the last time they were together.

"How often do you have him?" she asked, too chicken to make good on her plans of kissing him.

"Every other week or so, but this wasn't supposed to be one of those weeks. I got a call from the nanny that she had an emergency and couldn't get ahold of Mariana, Edward's mother."

Lina rolled Mariana's name around in her head, imagining what she looked like. *Mariana.* The woman had to be stunning with a perfect body, most gorgeous smile, and eyes that sparkled with energy. Mariana definitely didn't have a mom uniform. Lina considered her own boring smile, dim eyes, and saggy body. Insecurity rippled through her like a shiver. Noah seemed to notice the change in Lina and ran his thumb across hers.

"I jumped in the car and picked him up without a second thought," he added.

"Does she usually do this?"

"Mariana?"

"Yeah, like leaving him with a nanny and not being available." Lina couldn't even imagine doing that to Danny or Mimi.

Noah seemed to think about it for the first time ever. "She's done it maybe two or three times the last few months."

"What would've happened if you weren't in town?"

Noah's eyebrows knit, and he spoke slowly. "I'm not quite sure."

Lina felt like crap for turning this into something negative. She rubbed his arms and nodded at a stack of aluminum take-out containers at the end of the counter. "Hey, is that dinner?"

That seemed to snap him out of his thoughts. "Concierge just brought it up a few minutes before you arrived."

"Concierge?" She'd never get used to any of this.

"Couldn't leave." Noah lowered his head to hers. "I didn't want to miss you." He kissed her forehead then, tenderly drawing out every trace of insecurity and doubt until all that mattered was that she was in his arms. Eyes closed, they shared a breath. Was this how it felt to be adored?

"How is this so easy?" she whispered.

"I was just thinking the same thing."

"It's unreal."

"No. It's very real. I think that's why it's so different."

Lina's phone rang just then. She gave Noah an apologetic look and answered, "Hello?"

"Hey, Mom," Mimi said.

"Hey, Meems. Everything okay?"

"Yeah, I'm good. Everything is fine."

"Have you heard from Danny?" Lina asked.

"He's good. Just texted him."

"Oh, okay. What's going on Mimi?"

"Nothing major. Just wanted to check on you."

"I'm okay. How's it at Dawn's?"

"It's good. Her mom gave me something for you."

Edward called for Noah to read to him.

"I'd better go read to little man. Don't go," Noah said.

"I won't," Lina mouthed.

"Who's that?" Mimi asked.

"No one. TV's on. I'm perfectly content right now. Miss my Linguini-Mimi and my Danny-Manny."

"Mom, stop. I love you. See you tomorrow."

"Love you too. Night."

Lina texted Danny to check up on him and to remind him to brush his teeth. Danny responded with an immediate, Sure mom. Just whipped Jacob's sorry butt. We're up to almost eighty thousand users! Can you believe it? Love you.

Eighty thousand users?

It was so much it sounded fake. Lina hurried to the couch and checked the figures on her laptop. Sure enough, the kids' site was approaching eighty thousand total users. Eighty thousand users in six months? Did that even happen? Was that normal growth? Lina researched different options on how to expand their viral marketing until Edward's laughter echoed from his room.

Lina smiled, remembering reading *A Wrinkle in Time* to Danny and Mimi when they were Edward's age. Closing her laptop, she started down the long hallway toward the boys' voices.

Edward's room was sky blue with a massive circus mural—minus scary clowns. Balloon-shaped lamps hung from the walls around his "big top" bed and elephant nightstands.

"See you in the morning," Noah said, flicking off the red balloon lamp near the bed. Slowly, he padded toward the door, winking at Lina.

"I remember those days," she said.

"I'm surprised he let me go with one chapter." Noah closed Edward's bedroom door. "Dinner?"

"Sure."

They ate at the counter, shoulders touching, and talked about their days, their plans for the week, and the French cuisine Noah had ordered. He confessed he'd left it up to the concierge and had no idea what it was until he'd opened the containers.

"Would you like a tour?" Noah asked when they'd finished dinner.

"Sure. I've never been in a penthouse before."

"It's all about the views." He reached for her hand, weaving his fingers with hers as if he'd done it a million times. "Had to install heavy-duty blinds in Edward's room because the height freaked him out. Poor kid wouldn't even go in there until I covered the windows." He led her on a tour of his home, starting with his office, a guest bedroom, his linen closet, and finally his bedroom. Lina wasn't quite sure what to think when he guided her through the double doors to his room. It was large and well appointed with a mix of modern and industrial furnishings, but all that was overshadowed by the wall of windows across from the bed.

Noah turned off the lights. "View's better without the reflection."

Lina gazed at the city stretched before her. Lights twinkled. Buildings and patches of green seemed to go on forever. She tried to identify the streets below, but they all seemed so small. "Beautiful."

"I was just thinking the same thing," Noah said. It took a few moments for Lina to realize he'd been gazing at her instead of the view.

Lina bit her bottom lip. "Can I ask you something?"

"Anything. My life is an open book to you."

"What happened with you and Mariana? Why aren't you together?"

"Funny." He snorted. "We weren't exactly together when she got pregnant." Noah shifted his weight. "She was my Realtor when I bought my mother's house." He harrumphed. "My mom liked her at first. See, we got engaged about six years ago, but she kept putting off nailing down a wedding date for procedures. It was a tuck here, an enlargement there. Her nose, her ears, her stomach, her hips, her breasts. I mean, I don't mind if you want something done. It's cool, but she was never satisfied. Mom started to worry she was with me so I could pay for her surgeries." Noah closed his eyes and took a deep breath. "Then I lost my mom and . . ."

"I'm sorry for asking. You don't have to relive all that."

"It's okay." He smirked. "Haven't thought about it in a while. I'm okay, really."

Lina reached for his hand, giving it a reassuring squeeze.

"After Mom passed, Mariana insisted on selling her house, but I wasn't ready. It caused a lot of arguments between us. Then I found out she was trying to rent it out to someone in her family. I couldn't handle it. It felt so wrong, and I don't know." He shook his head. "Ran into her while I was deejaying a year and a half later. We had some drinks and ended up together. Few weeks go by and I get a call that she's pregnant."

"Did you have a paternity test?" Lina asked, a little embarrassed to even suggest it.

"Definitely. He's mine. Took care of her during the pregnancy, but we never got back together. Filed for joint custody the second Edward was born. She can be a handful sometimes, but we work it out for Edward."

"It's good you guys are being adults about the whole thing. I don't even want to think of the fight David will drag me through over the kids." She caught herself and instantly felt stupid for bringing up her husband.

"It's okay. I'm here if you need me." There was an earnestness in his voice that she'd never heard from anyone before.

Lina knew he would be there for her if she asked. She turned slightly and smiled at him. "I know you are, but I have to do this on my own. In my own time."

Gently, he tucked some wayward tendrils behind her ear and caressed her face. He was so vastly different from David. How different would her life have been if she'd met Noah instead of David seventeen years ago? How was Noah able to be so tender and kind to her when her own husband had little regard for her? How had Noah accepted her just the way she was instead of trying to mold and manipulate her?

"I can't seem to get enough of you," Noah whispered. His warm hand on the small of her back radiated throughout the rest of her body.

She knew exactly how he felt. Their daily talks over the last six months were no longer satiating her need to be near him. To touch him. To feel his lips on hers. *Would that even be enough?* she wondered.

Could she be with another man? She hadn't considered it yet. She'd been with only David over the last eighteen years. Would she be good enough for someone else? She felt herself shrink as David's words haunted her: *You don't work. You don't clean. You barely cook. You just started wanting me to fuck you again, and that's mediocre at best, so what good are you, Lina?*

What good was she? Why was she getting her hopes up? She staggered backward a few steps, David's words stealing her breath. Noah seemed to pick up on her sudden change and held her close to his chest.

So what good are you, Lina? David's voice trilled in her ears. Squeezing her eyes, she fought back. Boldness stirred in her chest, reminding her that she'd managed just fine without David so far. The harder she warred with the David in her mind, the firmer Noah held her. In that moment, she glanced up at Noah and slowly brought his mouth to hers. She needed to show herself that David didn't control her, that she wasn't his little paper doll.

Her heart thrashed with excitement and terror when her lips brushed Noah's. He seemed to be taken aback, like he hadn't been expecting it, and that only made her want to kiss him even more. She closed the space between them, exhaling when they finally kissed.

Noah's house phone rang. "Not happening," he mumbled against her mouth and pulled her in closer, his hands firm on her waist. He was gentle with her, applying the softest pressure to her lips, asking for permission. She permitted, parting them with a breath. Slowly and methodically, he explored her lips with his, her tongue with his until every nerve ending in Lina's body fired simultaneously.

Six months of wanting, and their eager exploring escalated to an insatiable burning. Lina wasn't sure where her body ended and Noah's began in their tangle of limbs. Noah's house phone rang again. And again. And eventually his house phone and cell phone were both ringing.

"You've got to be kidding."

"You'd better get that," Lina panted.

He reached in his pocket, frowning, and answered it. "Are you serious?" he breathed. "Right now?" His features pinched with agony when he looked at her. "Okay, fine. I'll take care of it."

"Everything all right?" Lina asked when the call ended.

"That was the concierge. Mariana is here. She's causing a scene downstairs because the nanny had me pick Edward up." He clasped his hands over his head and sighed. "She's on her way up right now."

CHAPTER 23

A part of Lina wanted to see Mariana. What did the woman who'd been engaged to Noah look like? How did Lina compare?

Noah had begged Lina to stay in his room "just like that," adding, "Do not move an inch." He'd promised he was going to talk to Mariana in the hallway, and it would take only a minute or two. But ten minutes had passed, and Lina wanted to take advantage of the break to freshen up and get something to drink. She splashed her face, gargled with mouthwash, and finger combed her hair into a messy ponytail. This was her: fresh faced, natural, and messy. For the first time in a long while, she was okay with the woman in the mirror.

Curious to see what was taking Noah so long, Lina padded to the kitchen for some water. She lingered near the door for a while but gave up when she couldn't hear anything. Before she could return to Noah's room, the front door opened and a tall, photoshopped-in-real-life woman stormed in, her stilettos clicking against the marble floors. Lina blinked several times at the woman's proportions. Her waist was unnaturally narrow, and her hips looked like she'd had a permanent reaction to a bee sting.

"Oh . . . hello," Mariana said, slowly appraising Lina.

Lina froze. How could she ever measure up to someone like her? Now she understood why they'd been engaged, and she was pretty sure

Noah was reconsidering being with her as he watched both women in the same room.

Mariana flipped her long blonde hair from her shoulder. "And you are?"

Noah crossed the living room and put his arm around Lina's waist. "This is my girlfriend, Lina."

Lina blushed at her new title. *Girlfriend.* Did people their age even use that word? It sounded so foreign. Maybe they could settle on another term. Lady friend? Significant other? Special friend? Lover?

Mariana raised an eyebrow. "That's nice, but I thought we decided not to have random hookups around *our* son."

"I'm standing right here," Lina said.

"I'm not going there with you, Mariana, and like you said, he's *our* son, so I'm perfectly capable of protecting Edward."

"All I'm saying is I don't think introducing *our* son to every woman you're with is good. It might be confusing to him. Besides, it's my week. He shouldn't be here."

"I don't need your permission. And you're right, Mariana. This is not my week. As you can see, I had plans." He held Lina tighter. "You were unavailable for hours, so Anisa called me because she had an emergency and couldn't wait any longer."

"She could've called one of the other nannies or taken him with her. That's what they always do," Mariana said flippantly.

"They always do? Taken him with her? What does that mean?" Noah's hand clenched at Lina's side. "Do you leave him with the nannies all the time?"

"Well, they're well paid for a reason." Mariana threw a hand to her hip. "Edward! Come on. We're going home."

"No, he's not. He's sleeping, and you will not wake him up." Noah leveled his gaze at her.

"We'll see what the judge has to say."

Noah's entire body tensed. "You're not going to threaten me in my home. It's time for you to leave."

Mariana started toward Edward's room. "Not without my son."

Noah hurried after her.

Lina had to de-escalate the situation. "Hey, Mariana. I bet the judge would be interested in talking to the nannies about how often you're unavailable."

Mariana and Noah both turned toward Lina—Mariana clearly annoyed, Noah grinning.

"I think I'll call my attorney first thing in the morning," Noah added.

"Then bring Edward back home tomorrow," Mariana said after a few beats.

"I'll think about it after I talk to my attorney."

"Good night, Mariana," Lina said.

Noah beamed. "Yes. Good night, Mariana."

Without another word, Mariana gave them both the stank eye and exited Noah's condo.

Lina and Noah burst into laughter after a few minutes.

"What was that even?" Noah asked, kissing her forehead.

"I have no idea; you looked like you needed to phone a friend, and I really didn't want her to wake Edward up." Lina was pleased with herself. She grabbed two water bottles from the fridge, popped one open, and drank.

"That's what I was talking about." Noah was looking at her in awe and wonder. "You're incredible."

She handed him a water bottle. "What was all that about a judge? Is everything okay?"

"She asks for an increase in child support every six months or so. It's starting to get old. We have a hearing coming up soon."

"Are you serious?"

"Unfortunately." He sipped some water.

"Are you really going to call your attorney about what she said?"

"I don't know." Noah scratched his head.

"She just admitted to leaving Edward with the nannies all the time."

"Like I'm going to do any better. I work sixteen, eighteen hours most days. My travel schedule is insane. How am I going to be any different from Mariana?"

"So you just want to say you have a kid without the sacrifices it takes to raise him?" She didn't mean to come across as judgy. All she could think about was Edward being alone.

"What do you want me to do?"

"All I'm saying is I wouldn't be okay with nannies raising my son."

Noah pinched the bridge of his nose. "I'm not okay with it at all. I just don't have the solution right now."

"Daddy?" Edward called.

"I'll be there in a few minutes, son."

"But he's so young," Lina said, her heart going out to the little boy. How could Noah not want to fight for him?

Noah took another quick sip from his water bottle, placed it on the counter. "I have no idea what I'm doing most of the time, and between the both of us, I'm surprised I've been able to do what little I have." Noah sighed. "It would be better if I left things the way they were."

He didn't want to be inconvenienced. That was all she needed to know. It said so much about his character—the real Noah behind the cute texts and stolen kisses. Maybe that was why he was okay with being with a married woman. He didn't want any sort of commitment. She was just going to be another conquest. Another check mark. She couldn't look at Noah without feeling heartbroken and disappointed in herself.

"I should probably head home," she said, hoping he'd stop her, hoping he'd show her he wasn't like David.

"Lina—"

"Daddy." Edward came from around the corner just then, doing a soggy-bottomed waddle, dragging his well-loved T. rex by one of its stubby arms. "I had an accident."

"Oh, buddy, you're soaking wet." Noah plucked a blanket from the couch, then wrapped Edward tightly and picked him up. "I think this calls for a bath."

"Bubbles!"

"How many bubbles do you want?"

Edward quirked his mouth to the side in thought and said, "A bajillion."

"Deal." Noah deposited Edward in a nearby chair. "Just one minute. I need to talk to Lina."

"Okay, Daddy." Edward held his dinosaur and put his thumb in his mouth.

"Lina," Noah said in her direction. "Please don't go."

"Look, I'm sorry for getting involved in your business. It's your life and your kid and I shouldn't have said anything about it at all."

"But that's what I like about you. You tell me what I need to hear, not what I want to hear. You're the only person who's straightforward with me." He lowered his head, spoke softly. "It's not that I don't want my son. I wish I never had to let him go to Mariana's. It's just the thought of raising Edward on my own terrifies me. No, it scares the hell out of me that I'll end up just like my father"—he looked away—"or worse." He exhaled. "If you really want to leave, I get it, but please don't leave upset at me."

He actually cared what she thought about him? No, he wasn't anything like David. What was she thinking? And why had she been so quick to want to walk away from him? Going home to an empty house wasn't what she needed; being there with Noah was.

"Lina?" Noah begged.

"I'll be here when you're done with his bath."

He kissed her. "Thank you. Really didn't want to pack Edward in the car and go to your house with sappy love songs blasting while I beg for forgiveness."

"Okay, so now I'm leaving, just to see that."

He slid his phone from his pocket and tapped on the screen, then closed the space between them, his lips brushing against hers. "I'm sorry. You're right. Just texted my lawyer."

"Say that again?" she teased, wanting his lips to lay claim to hers.

"After bath time. I'll say it as many times as you want."

A swarm of butterflies fluttered in her stomach while Noah carried Edward away for a quick bath. She kicked off her Tieks and curled up on the couch with her laptop to do some research on how to best market the kids' site.

"Hey! Get back here!"

Lina heard the sound of wet feet slapping the floor as Edward ran toward her ten minutes later. He jumped onto the couch in only his Batman underwear.

"Daddy said he likes you," Edward sang.

Noah chased after him. "Hey, that was guy talk."

Lina winked at Edward. "Thanks for letting me know."

"Daddy said I could watch cartoons."

"Did he? What do you like to watch?" Lina asked.

"*Scooby-Doo*."

"It's on his Netflix account." Noah peeled a soft cashmere throw from a nearby chair. "Come here, you," he said, wrapping Edward tightly and plopping down onto the couch. He pressed a few buttons on the remote until an episode of *Scooby-Doo* played. With Edward burrito wrapped on his lap and fully enthralled, Noah smiled at Lina and patted the couch for her to sit closer to them.

She deposited her laptop on the reclaimed-wood-and-metal coffee table and slid closer to the boys until she was nestled in Noah's arm.

"Thank you for being honest with me." He kissed her forehead. "You're right. I can't have the nannies raise my son. It's not fair to him."

"Look at him." Lina motioned to the way Edward rested on Noah's chest, perfectly at peace and fighting heavy eyelids. "Did your father ever hold you like that?"

"No," he whispered, swallowing a boulder.

"Then you're already a better parent than he ever was."

Noah sniffled, his eyes glistening. After a few moments, he leaned over slightly and kissed her with the weight of a thousand words.

CHAPTER 24

Lina hadn't been sure if it was the snoring or the *Scooby-Doo* theme song that'd woken her early the next morning. Somehow, they'd all managed to shift throughout the night. The couch's back pillows had been scattered across the floor, and Noah had stretched out on the sofa, Edward on one side of him and Lina on the other.

Gathering her stuff, she'd slipped on her shoes and left Noah and his sweet little boy fast asleep.

Hours later, spicy cinnamon and sweet chocolate scents wafted through the Henry house. Clouds had given way to thunderstorms by that Sunday afternoon. Soft jazz played, infusing every room with a sense of tranquility. Lina and her kids cuddled under layers of warm blankets in her plush bed, eating freshly baked chocolate chip cookies and drinking tea.

They each read a different book and occasionally looked up from the pages to smile at each other. This was Lina's idea of a perfect Sunday. The only thing that would make it better was Noah reading beside her, sandwiched between her and the kids. Noah seemed to make everything better. She'd imagined him beside her as she and Mimi stirred the cookie dough. She'd felt a ghost of his hand warming the small of her back as she'd helped Danny pick a book. He'd even been there when she scrolled through her playlist for some music. She had it bad for him and wasn't quite sure how to handle it.

After a while, Danny rolled over to his side and prattled on about what he'd just read. "Mom, are you listening?" he asked after some time. "Snape is good. Like, he's really a good guy. He's not a Death Eater."

"Mom is so zoned out it's ridiculous," Mimi said, slightly lifting her head from Lina's leg. "Just look at her."

"Mom?" Danny said.

"I'm listening to you both. Snape is good. Not a Death Eater. Got it."

"What's gotten into you recently, Mom?" Mimi asked.

"What do you mean?" Lina knew full well what her daughter meant. "I've got a lot on my mind; that's all."

"Mm-hmm." Mimi shot her an accusatory look.

"What does that mean?"

"Nothing. Nothing at all, Li-na."

"Read your book," Lina said, and her phone buzzed with a text.

Noah: FaceTime?

She wanted to be in two places at the same time: there in her bed with the kids and wherever Noah was, in his arms.

Lina: A few mins.

"You guys want some sandwiches or anything?" Lina asked, scooting from under her kids. They were each using a part of her as a pillow: Danny's head was on her stomach, Mimi's head on her thigh.

"Sandwich, please," Danny said. "Turkey."

"How about you, Linguini?" Lina asked.

"Sure. Turkey works. Thanks, Mom."

Phone in hand, Lina darted into the kitchen, where she quickly fixed her hair and put on lip gloss in the double oven's shiny stainless steel surface. She popped in her earbuds and FaceTimed Noah. He answered on the first ring, shirtless and lying in his bed.

"Hey, beautiful," Noah said.

"Hey, you."

"How's it going?" he asked.

"Having a lazy day, reading with the kids in my bed."

"Sounds like a great afternoon."

"The best." Lina changed her phone camera's direction to show him her kitchen.

"Nice place."

"Thanks, but I was showing you what's left of the cookies I baked with Mimi."

"Woman, you cook?" He pulled a sad face. "What must I do to get some home-cooked food around here?"

"You are so silly."

"That's what you like about me so much," Noah said.

"I'm sure I can think of a few other things."

"Yeah?"

Lina felt her entire body blush. She cleared her throat. "Where's Edward?"

Noah shifted his camera to show Edward lying beside him, playing a game on his tablet. "Say hi to Miss Lina."

Edward looked up and gave her a toothy smile. "Hi, Miss Lina." He waved. "When are you coming back?"

"I was just about to ask her. You beat me to it," Noah said.

"I'm not sure. What's the deal with Edward? Not taking him back to Mariana's?"

"My attorney strongly suggested I build a case against her first. He said I needed to play nice, so one of the nannies is coming soon."

"I'm sorry."

"Me too, but you made me really start to think about what's best for my son. I'm going to move some things around to make it work."

"Like what?"

"I'd like to do more behind-the-scenes work. Producing, directing. That sort of stuff. I love acting. I'll always love acting, but the more I think about it, the more I'm okay with taking a small step back. Maybe I'll only commit to one movie every year or something."

"Are you sure? I don't want you to regret anything, or God forbid end up hating me over this. I was just making a suggestion. It's your life."

"I'm making some room in my life for important people like him." Noah gazed into the camera at her. "And you."

Lina rested against the kitchen counter, not sure what to say to that.

"And I just made it awkward." Noah rubbed the back of his neck.

"It's okay. I'm not used to any of this."

"Hey, who's that?" Mimi asked as she entered the kitchen. She plucked the last cookie from the tray and picked at it.

Startled, Lina snatched out one of her earbuds. "Oh, hey. It's Nancy. You remember Auntie Nance, don't you?"

Mimi's eyebrows knit tightly. "Isn't she white?"

"Yes, but she was letting me talk to her boyfriend, um, Fred."

"No way do I look like a Fred, Lina." Noah snickered in the other earbud. He was finding this whole scenario funny.

"Um, okay, Li-na," Mimi said, something strange in her voice. She flicked a crumb off her finger and left the kitchen.

Lina held her phone up so Noah could see her face. "Fred, I've gotta run. Give my best to Nancy, okay?"

"No way. I'm saving my best for you." Noah laughed. "Mimi is a clever one. You might want to go talk to her."

Panic settled in Lina's chest. "You think she knows?"

"You're absolutely gorgeous when you're flustered, but the nanny just rang from downstairs. I've gotta run."

"Okay. Bye, Fred."

"Bye, Lina."

Oh crap, had Mimi pieced it all together? Was Lina going to have to come clean before she was ready? Could she? They were close, so maybe if she told Mimi, Mimi would help her ease the news to Danny. That would make life a little easier for them all, in theory. She wouldn't have to lie to her kids anymore . . . just her husband.

Lina pocketed her phone into her pajama pants and called for Mimi.

"Sup, Mom?" Mimi said a few minutes later. "Need help with the sandwiches?"

"Um, not really." Lina went to her daughter and swept some of her curly hair from her face. "How was your sleepover?"

"Good."

"Yeah? And your friends?"

"Good."

"And, um . . ."

"Mom, what's going on? How's Auntie Nance?" Mimi crossed her arms. "You're being weirder than usual. She okay?"

"Nancy is fine. Better than fine. She's at UGA in Athens. Might come see us next weekend."

"Sweet. I haven't seen her in forever."

Lina put her hands on her daughter's shoulders. "I need to talk to you about something. Something important."

"About time," Mimi said, and they both started at the sound of David's garage bay opening.

Damn it. He had to come home tonight? Lina thought.

"Maybe later. Go tell Danny your father is home. You guys clean up my room super fast, 'kay?"

Mimi nodded and hurried to Lina's bedroom. Lina moved quickly to clean up the kitchen and wipe off the counters, her ears ringing. What kind of mood would David be in when he walked through the door?

Moments later, the door leading to the garage opened, hitting the wall. David glanced at Lina and scoffed. "Pajamas?"

Jules entered on his heels. She reminded Lina of a stilt walker: long, lanky legs dotted by a stubby torso. Only, Jules's superskinny black jeggings and skintight tank top made her look skeletal today.

"Hey, Lina," Jules said in a singsong. "How have you been?"

"Hey, Jules. Good," Lina said, trying to figure out what her sister-in-law was up to.

"Yeah? So Carl swore he saw you downtown during his run this morning."

"Yeah?"

David's attention turned to their conversation. "You were downtown this morning?"

"Yeah. Church—" Lina said.

"You went to Bethel without me?"

"No. No, I didn't go to your church. I—"

"My church? So now it's 'my church'?" David made air quotes.

Jules folded her arms across her chest with a satisfied smirk.

"I didn't mean—"

"You talk to Pastor Nathan and tell him all of our family business? Was that it? The whole counseling thing again?"

Lina slammed her hand on the counter, not interested in David's drama. "Look, I didn't go to Bethel. I went to an early service downtown to get a few programs for Mimi's summer reading project at the library." Lina glared at Jules.

"What's with the attitude?" David asked, rubbing his temple. "Did you make dinner?"

"I didn't make anything—you haven't been home in a month, and I had no idea you'd be back tonight. You're free to help yourself to a sandwich." Lina turned her back to him and started out of the kitchen.

"Why did I even marry you?"

"I've been asking myself the same thing. You're welcome to a divorce," she said over her shoulder on her way to their bedroom, feeling herself a little too much.

CHAPTER 25

Minutes later, she heard David's bag crash to the floor and his heavy feet stomp after her. Mimi and Danny both leaped to their feet, gathering their stuff.

"You, you." David pointed at each kid from the bedroom doorway. "Out. Your rooms better be clean when I come upstairs."

"You could at least say hello to them; it's been a month. Maybe ask how school went." What was with Lina's mouth today? She bit her tongue to stop talking, but a righteous indignation rose. "You cut all the utilities off and didn't even call to check up on them."

David shuttled the kids toward the open bedroom door, eventually pushing Danny into Mimi to usher them out. He slammed the door closed and turned to Lina. "Why did you have to do that in front of my sister? Why are you always trying to embarrass me?"

"No one is trying to embarrass you. You're embarrassing yourself. You come home slamming doors and demanding answers like a dictator or something. Normal people don't do that. Normal marriages aren't like this, David. Normal husbands don't abandon their family."

"Is this about counseling again?"

"No. What are you even doing home?"

"I live here. This is my house. What did you have to do to get the money to turn everything back on?"

"I'm going to stop you there. You will respect me."

"Respect?" David blinked several times. "It doesn't take much skill to get the kids up and to school. Or to pick them up."

"Seriously? Stop it already. You've been home less than five minutes and we're doing this. It's not healthy." Lina crossed her arms. "I think we need to consider separation."

"Separation? You mean a divorce?" David's eyes glinted with cruelty. "You're going to blame all this on me. Somehow I'm the bad guy when you sit around all day, getting fatter. You don't try to look decent. You don't try to be sexy or anything. All I want to do is enjoy my wife, but you look like this all the time." He rolled his eyes. "I get back in town after busting my ass for a month, and my sister says she heard you were downtown early this morning. What am I supposed to think?"

"Whatever you want to think. I already explained myself," Lina said, waving him away.

"Are you screwing around on me?" He stalked over to her, eclipsing her body. She shrank beneath his glare.

"Let's face it; you're nothing more than someone's pity fuck. That's all you'll ever be. No one else will ever want to be with you. I'm the only person who'll put up with you. I'm the only person that'll love you."

As hard as she tried to be Teflon, his words stuck to her. She heard the soft ripping sound of being torn into tiny pieces.

"I let you drive my car, live in my house, eat my food, use my money, wear my clothes." He yanked on her pajama top. "Least you can do is have dinner ready when I come home."

Fear claimed her breath when David grabbed her arms.

"Instead you give me lip and tell me to make my own damn sandwich."

All Lina could think about was the last time they'd been together and how he'd had his way with her. She turned to stone. "I'll make you a sandwich," she whispered.

He shook her. "I don't want a fucking sandwich. Do I do all this for a sandwich? Do you know how hard I've been working while you . . . you do whatever?"

Had he really been working that hard in Boston? Had she been the one in the wrong, cheating with Noah? Could she lose more weight and maybe do something to be more attractive? Tears lodged in her throat. "I—I'm sorry," Lina said softly.

"Damn right you're sorry. I give you everything you want. You needed space, so I left and lived in a hotel for a month without so much as a call or text from you or the kids. I can't believe I let this go on for so long . . ." David ranted, first complaining about Lina breaking her promise about having a large family, then about how difficult his job had become because Daniella didn't know much, and finally about how maybe Lina should be more like Daniella and let him teach her a few things.

David droned on and on as the sun set, casting them in shadows. Each word bore itself into her head. She felt discombobulated, like someone had put her on a circus carousel for hours. Up and down, round and round. The faint sound of a band organ rang in her ears like a bad case of tinnitus, its waltz offbeat and out of tune. Had she finally gone mad?

"You really want a divorce?" he asked slowly, a dangerous edge to his voice.

Lina wasn't sure if she should answer his question. Of course she wanted a divorce. She'd meant it moments earlier but couldn't bring herself to say it again.

"Even though it'll rip my heart out, you're free to leave. I'm not holding you here."

The sound of the circus music teetered off.

"But," he said, "I'll be damned if you take my kids, and you will never get one dime of my money." He sneered. "I'll make sure your mom doesn't help you either. I've been paying her rent for years. Did you know that? The two of you can fend for yourselves."

"David, you can't be—"

"Don't try me, Lina. You can pack one bag right now and call someone to pick you up, if you want a divorce. But those kids and all this is mine. Do you hear me?" He slowly paced. "I gave you all this and you want to leave me? You want to take my kids and my money? I've supported you this entire time. You and your mother too. No way in hell am I going to work like crazy while you sit on your fat ass and get half of my income, my retirement, my everything. You don't deserve it."

Paper Doll Lina was now in shreds.

"I made you who you are." He looked unhinged when he snatched her arm. She winced at the pain. "You'd be nothing without me."

Fear rooted her feet to the notched wooden floor planks.

"I've gotta make some work calls. I need you to take Jules to pick up her car from the shop—I already paid for it. And since it's over by Keely's, bring back some dinner while you're there." He leaned on the bed and scrolled through his phone.

She was diving in murky water and couldn't find her way to the surface. She'd done a hundred cartwheels, and the earth wouldn't stop spinning. She didn't know anything anymore. He'd managed to do it to her again—make her feel like she'd lost her mind.

David peeked up from his phone. "You gonna take Jules to pick up her car and get dinner, right?"

Lina skittered out of the room.

"You okay, Mom?" Mimi asked, meeting her in the living room.

"Yeah. Yeah, I've gotta take Jules back and grab your father some dinner. How about you make sure everything is nice and clean upstairs and keep it quiet while he naps. 'Kay, honey?"

"Are you going to change? You're still in your pajamas."

"No. I'm just going to run in super fast," Lina said, terrified to go back into her room to change. "Jules, you ready?"

"Yeah. Gimme a few minutes."

Lina went out to the garage. She waited for the door to roll up and took a few steps outside. The rain had stopped, leaving stifling humidity. She gasped for air and tried to piece herself back together again. What went where? How were her pieces going to stay together? How was she supposed to figure it out when she could barely remember her name?

Her phone buzzed with a text.

Noah: FaceTime?

Lina: No.

Noah: What are you doing?

Lina: Heading to Keely's to pick up dinner.

Noah: Oh . . .

Noah: Are you okay?

Lina: No.

Noah: Lina?

Lina: I've gotta go.

"Ready?" Jules called and climbed into Lina's car.

Cars flew past them on the interstate, honking. Lina kept her hands at ten and two and refused to glance over at her sister-in-law. Not that it mattered a bit. Jules spent the entire ride posting selfies and answering her Snapchat streaks.

You're nothing without me. I made you.

You can leave, but not with my kids.

The bright-neon lights of Keely's sign came faster than she'd expected. She jerked the steering wheel hard, wheels screeching, to turn into the restaurant's parking area. Cars honked at her. Lina slammed on the brakes near the rear of the building. Jules's seat belt locked, snatching her backward into the seat before her head hit the dashboard.

"What the hell, Lina?"

Lina shook her head, snapping out of a trance. She wasn't sure how she'd managed to get to the restaurant. It was like she'd been driving blindfolded. She wiped her sweaty palms on her pajama pants, her legs shaking in the seat.

Jules unbuckled her seat belt and leaped from the car. "You need to handle your business better," she said before sauntering off to the red Jeep waiting in the adjacent parking lot. The sight of Jules climbing into and driving away with Mimi's car was infuriating, but Lina had no more fight left. David had taken it all away.

She waited awhile, eased her head back on the headrest, and covered her eyes, wishing she didn't have to go back home. She considered waiting three years until Danny was out of high school. It was her breaking point. If she could just hold on until Danny graduated, then she'd leave David and not ask him for a red cent as long as he took care of the kids and their college expenses. She'd live on the streets if she had to.

Three years . . .

It seemed like a lifetime. Could she survive that long?

The sound of a car pulling into the parking space beside her made her come back to herself. There were many open parking spaces closer to the building, and some idiot had to park next to her? All she wanted was a few more minutes alone. Was that asking too much?

She peeled her hands from her eyes, wiping them, and glanced at the car beside her, hoping to guilt them into reparking farther away. Slowly, the dark-tinted window rolled down until she saw Noah.

CHAPTER 26

The smile on Noah's face vanished the instant he saw her. Lina was sure her eyes were red and swollen from crying. She turned away from him, not wanting him to see her like that. Why was he even there? Couldn't she have her crisis in peace?

Within seconds, Noah was out of his car and opening her door. His hands cupped her face.

"Are you okay?"

"No." Lina wiped her eyes.

"What happened?"

"David's home."

"Has he hurt you?"

A dry chuckle escaped her lips. "Do you want me to say yes so you can feel like a hero and go beat him up? Are damsels in distress your thing?"

"Don't do that."

"Do what? Be honest? My husband is an asshole. There's my big secret. He's a horrible, abusive pig who wants nothing more than to see me lose my mind." Her fingers itched for something to do—a wayward string to pull, a lock of hair to twirl, some nail polish to pick. "Maybe he has some huge life insurance policy on me, and it's part of his grand scheme."

"Can we get out of here?" Noah asked, glancing over his shoulder. "I have to be back home soon."

His jaw tensed. "Scoot over. You don't seem like you should be driving."

That was an understatement, Lina thought while she climbed over the center console to the passenger seat. She fastened her seat belt. Noah started her car and drove off, his hand resting on her thigh. His lips pursed tightly as the sun slowly dipped into the horizon. Moments later, they stopped at a nearby park. Lina leaned her head on the window and stared off at empty swings swaying hauntingly in the gentle breeze. The rhythmic squealing of the rusty metal links echoed.

"How are the kids?" Noah asked, turning to her.

"They're okay." Lina's throat felt raw and scratchy.

"Did they have fun at their friends' houses?"

"Yeah."

"That's good." Noah fidgeted with the keys. "Want to get some air?"

Lina nodded.

Noah slipped his hand around hers as they walked. It was warm and sturdy. She wished she could crawl up into it and never leave, but that wasn't reality. Her reality didn't include anything sturdy or stable. Reality for Lina meant having to tiptoe through the minefield of her marriage to a cruel and vindictive spouse for at least the next three years. She was fooling herself by leading Noah on. It'd be best to end whatever they had now and forget he even existed. Noah made her feel soft and open when she needed to be a hard shell, or David would break her down into dust. That would be the only way she'd survive.

Thinking about breaking it off left a void in her chest, but she didn't see any other option. She sat in the swing, trying to figure out how to go about telling him they couldn't see each other anymore. Noah stood behind her, his body heat comforting. She leaned against him, remnants of her heart shredding into a million pieces. If he spoke just then, she'd shatter. But he didn't. Instead, he gently pushed her on the swing.

Lina pumped her legs to move the swing along. Higher and higher she went, soaring into the dark sky. She closed her eyes and loosened her messy bun to feel the air on her scalp. Her hair fell in tangled waves down her back and over her shoulders. Higher. Faster. Harder. Noah kept her in the air until she felt weightless. The world went past in a blurry streak.

Growing up, Lina had a massive phoenix kite. On windy days, she'd escape outside whenever her mom and her mom's boyfriend of the month had gotten into arguments. For hours, she'd watch her kite sail and slice through the sky and imagine herself that free. Unbound. Limitless.

In the air now, Lina was a kite as the wind rushed past her face. Could she ever be far enough from David and his oppressive toxicity? Could she ever be free enough to soar all day? Leaning back slightly, she closed her eyes and focused on the rusty chains' squealing. David faded away. His words silenced in her head. His threats ceased to exist for the time. Nothing else existed except Noah's hands on her back and the wind's cool fingers tangling through her hair.

You're nothing without me.

You've never been anything.

Lina flinched at David's voice in her head. Her hands slipped from the cool chains, and she lost her balance in the black rubber seat. She fell backward.

"I've got you. I've got you," Noah whispered, catching her. He held her close to his chest. "I've got you. I've got you, Lina." He said it over and over again as if willing it into her heart.

"I've got you," he breathed against her mouth, their foreheads resting against the other.

"Why?" Lina said, sniffling.

"Remember when you asked how I knew your name when we first met?" Noah's arms circled her waist. "It was written on some sheet for the show."

"Sort of. What are you talking about?"

"The show's APs wouldn't stop talking about your kids, and my agent, who was with me at the time, said he ran into you earlier and that I needed to meet you."

Lina scoffed. What was he getting at, and would it make it harder to end things between them?

"He had one of the interns dig up your video call with the booking people. I couldn't take my eyes off you. The way you talked about your kids. The way you smiled and just you—you had so much life, and it spilled out from the laptop screen. I had to meet you."

He kissed her forehead.

"I was in a really low place—my agent and I had just argued about how I wasn't landing the major roles anymore. I was struggling to connect with Edward. I felt like such a huge failure, and everyone around me seemed to want something from me."

Lina shivered despite the balmy night. Noah shrugged off his jacket and wrapped her in it, holding her close.

"And then I met you in that tiny room. You were everything and more . . . and so real. You had me stumbling over my words."

Lina was taken aback by his honesty when she looked into his eyes.

"Then you just happened to be at the pool. When you showed up, I watched you for a while, trying to build up enough courage to speak to you. When that jerk started bothering you, something rose up inside of me." He dipped his head. "I've never met anyone like you."

She was breathless, his words glue and tape. She just needed to believe them and patch Paper Doll Lina back together.

"And then you helped me with my distributor that time you had me walk out. Who the hell would've done that? Who would've told me to do something so insane? But you were so confident. So sure of yourself." He ran a hand over her hair, tucking some tendrils behind her ear. "I mean it when I say I can't get enough of you." When he kissed her again, it was as if he was claiming her as his own. He wasn't gentle like before; instead there was a greediness to his mouth that begged her for more.

She wasn't sure she could give him more, especially with the threat of having to stay in her war zone of a marriage for another three years. She stiffened, imagining waiting years to be with him.

"What's wrong?" Noah asked.

"What do you mean?"

"What's going on up there?"

"The thought just crossed my mind about staying with David until the kids graduate so I don't have to fight him for them."

Noah bristled at her statement. "But Danny—"

"Three more years till graduation," Lina said.

Noah blinked. "Why would you do that?"

"You wanted to know what I was thinking. I don't know what I'm going to do."

"I may not know David, but I know you're terrified of him." Noah took a step back. "A little part of me died when I saw you earlier."

"You don't know my situation or David."

"Three years? I can't imagine not being able to tell the world about you for three years." Noah started pacing.

"You knew I was married. You've known all along and—"

"I didn't know I'd fall in love with you, Lina."

They both froze at his confession. Did she love him back? She'd been dead inside for so long it was an unfamiliar emotion. Was that what she felt every time she thought about him?

He closed the space between them, piercing her with his intensity.

"There it is," Noah said. "All of my cards are on the table. I genuinely wanted to get to know you early on. I was so sure the texting and calling would get old, but there was a simplicity and sincerity I've never experienced. You didn't want anything from me. There were no expectations." He entwined his fingers with hers, kissing one hand, then the other. "Every day I heard from you was like Christmas."

"I don't know what to say," Lina said.

"You don't have to say anything. I am in love with you, Lina."

"I . . ."

"What do you want? I will do whatever you want."

"I want my children. I'm not willing to give them up to be with you. That's something my mom would do—had done many times for different guys. Hell, why do you think I ended up in Georgia for college? Because it was far away from her. Would you ever want me to ask you to choose between me and Edward?"

"I'm not asking you to make that choice. I will never ask you to do that."

"That's what it sounds like. If I leave David, he's going to find a way to get custody of the kids. He'll turn them against me. I know this with every fiber of my being. He's that kind of person. You don't know him, Noah. You don't. This is not a cut-and-dried situation. This is my life. Real life with real stakes. I will lose Mimi and Danny, and I can't live with that."

"And I can't sit back and watch him systematically destroy you. Let me help you," Noah said.

No one could help her now. David knew too many people. Noah's out-of-town money couldn't compare to how well connected David was. She wanted to kick herself for not actively participating when they'd gone to civic events, church fundraisers, or citywide galas. She'd get all dressed up only to spend most of the night hiding away in the bathroom while David networked and charmed everyone he met. Everyone knew him. No one knew her. There was no use in even hoping anymore. She was a prisoner, and the sooner she realized it, the better she'd be. She slipped Noah's jacket off, handed it back to him. "I've got to get home."

"That's what you're going to do right now? Shut down?" Noah ran his hands over his head. "Please don't shut me out."

"I'd better go." Lina started toward her car. Arguing with him wasn't going to change her situation or her mind.

The tension was suffocating as they sat in her car. She placed the order for David's dinner and drove back to Keely's.

"Guess this is my cue," Noah said when she parked.

Take me with you. Help me fight David for the kids. I don't want to be without you. The words filled Lina's head, but she couldn't say any of them. "Noah . . ." *Don't go.*

"I know." He squeezed her hand. "Listen, I'll be in Toronto for a week or so. Sounds like you can use a little space right now. Text me when you're ready to talk." When they kissed, it felt like a last kiss, full of goodbyes and unspoken words.

CHAPTER 27

Monday:
    Wake up.
    Make breakfast.
    Find something to occupy the kids.
    Go to gym.
    Clean house.
    Do a load of laundry.
    Make dinner.
    Clean up after dinner.
    Lie in bed, alone, checking phone.
    Take Ambien to finally sleep.

Tuesday:
    Wake up.
    Make breakfast.
    Find something to occupy the kids.
    Go to gym.
    Clean house.
    Do a load of laundry.

Make dinner.
Clean up after dinner.
Lie in bed, alone, checking phone.
Take Ambien to finally sleep.

Wednesday:
Wake up.
Make breakfast.
Find something to occupy the kids.
Go to gym.
Clean house.
Do a load of laundry.
Make dinner.
Clean up after dinner.
Lie in bed, alone, checking phone.
Take Ambien to finally sleep.

Thursday:
Wake up.
Make breakfast.
Find something to occupy the kids.
Go to gym.
Clean house.
Do a load of laundry.
Make dinner.
Clean up after dinner.
Lie in bed, alone, checking phone.
Take Ambien to finally sleep.

Friday:

    Wake up.

    Make breakfast.

    Find something to occupy the kids.

    Go to gym.

    Clean house.

    Do a load of laundry.

    Make dinner.

    Clean up after dinner.

    Lie in bed, alone, checking phone.

    Take Ambien to finally sleep.

Saturday:

    Hide under the covers after letting the kids go to their friends' houses.

    Make dinner.

    Clean up after dinner.

    Lie in bed, alone, checking phone.

    Take Ambien to finally sleep.

Sunday:

    Hide in bathroom at church.

    Make dinner.

    Clean up after dinner.

    Lie in bed, alone, checking phone.

    Take Ambien to finally sleep.

Week two: repeat.

CHAPTER 28

Sounds like you can use some space.

Lina's schedule over the next two weeks looked the same as it had over the last six months, with one thing missing: she hadn't heard from Noah. He hadn't texted or attempted to FaceTime her since leaving her car when she'd broken the news about possibly staying with David another three years.

Three more years.

An empty, soulless feeling had crept in when she'd finally accepted her fate. She'd been on autopilot for most of their marriage. What was another three years? With David back home, their cycle had restarted: pretend to be a happy family, tiptoe around the house, set David off, deal with his explosion, pick up the pieces, and start all over again.

I'm in love with you, Lina.

Noah's words wrapped around her like a scratchy blanket, over and over again, suffocating her with an ultimatum: him or her children. She lay in her bed, awaiting the sunrise, gutted, pulled apart. Maybe that was why she hadn't heard from him—he knew he couldn't compete with her maternal love. Lina would never ask him to make a decision like that over Edward. It was wrong, and they both knew it. Maybe it'd finally hit him that this thing between them was never going to fully happen.

"Hey, Mom, you okay?" Mimi asked when she rolled over. The kids had crashed in her bedroom the night before—Mimi in her bed and Danny on a pallet on the floor—after they'd stayed up watching some creepy movie on Netflix.

"I'm okay," Lina said, brushing back the matted curls from Mimi's face.

"Are you really?"

Lina shook her head, unable to hide her lie, and pulled her daughter in for a big hug.

"Dawn's parents are doing better now. Her dad was so chill when we went to dinner the other night."

Lina worried her bottom lip. "Dawn's parents got divorced last year, right?"

"Yeah. Dawn has a therapist, and her whole family goes in once a month."

Lina imagined being amicable with David one day and laughed dryly—he'd never push down his pride enough to be friendly with her if she ever left him.

Mimi hid her face under the covers. "Dawn's mom gave me her lawyer's number for you. Said it's all confidential and she'd never tell anyone anything." She slowly peeked out and looked up at Lina with the most innocent, round face. "I saved it in my phone if you want it."

Was this lawyer any good? Could she trust her not to give David any information? Could this lawyer actually help her get away from David with her kids? "Thank you, Meems."

"It's okay."

"What if I dated someone else or got remarried?"

"Seriously, Mom?" Mimi rolled her eyes. "Daddy doesn't love you. You don't love him. Why wouldn't you want to be with someone who loved you?"

"It's not that simple, Meems. I don't want you to think giving up on a marriage is like changing your socks. Marriage is a forever thing.

I wanted to grow old with your daddy. I dreamed of us doting on our grandkids. Everyone goes through hard times. Maybe we'll—"

"But you and Daddy's hard times never end. And I . . ." Mimi glanced around, lowered her voice to a whisper. "I'm kind of scared of him now. I've been scared of him for a while. Like, he's not like how he used to be. I don't think he loves us anymore. Me and Danny disappoint him or something." Tears welled in her sweet baby girl's eyes, and Lina held her tight.

"You haven't done anything to make your dad like this. I don't know what's going on with him, but it's not your fault. You hear me? You and Danny are the reason I wake up every morning. You guys are why I smile when I feel like I can't go on. I can't imagine my world without you, and if I didn't marry your dad, I wouldn't have the two of you, so there's that."

Danny stirred, and his head popped up near the foot of the bed. "What's wrong, Meems?"

"Nothing, honey. She had a bad dream," Lina said and patted the empty space beside her. "Come here. I need some Danny snuggles."

A bright smile spread across Danny's face. He flicked on the TV and crawled under the duvet until he was in his mother's arms. Lina pecked his forehead and spent the rest of the morning and well into the afternoon holding her children tightly as they watched cartoons and ate cold pizza. It was the perfect Band-Aid for her broken spirit.

With Mimi's confession still fresh in her head, Lina wriggled free from her children to shower and change just in time to catch the sound of the doorbell chiming. Nancy was finally here! Lina and the kids ran to the door, pushing each other out of the way.

"There's plenty of me, guys," Nancy said and placed her hands on either side of Mimi's face. "Gorgeous. Absolutely gorgeous. I can't believe you're a young lady now."

"I missed you, Auntie Nance," Mimi said.

"Me too, Sweet Potato. Danny!" she shrieked. "How the hell are you almost eye to eye with me? Come here, you handsome boy." She gave Danny a bear hug and winked at Lina. "What are you feeding this kid?"

Lina parted the kids so she could get a hug in. "I'm glad you came."

"And I brought gifts!" She tossed her keys to Danny. "Want to get them out of my trunk?"

Danny took off through the front door and returned minutes later, bags hanging from both arms.

"You didn't have to."

"Lina, don't start. I haven't seen my babies in damn near five years. I owe them. Mimi—Victoria's Secret, Tom Ford, and Neiman Marcus bags are yours."

Mimi's mouth went slack.

"Danny, baby, you get the one from the Apple Store." Nancy leaned over to him and whispered, "There's a shit ton of gift cards in there too."

Danny dropped the bags and hugged Nancy. "Thank you so much!"

"Thanks, Auntie Nance," Mimi added, and the two flitted off to their rooms with their loot.

Lina hooked her arm with Nancy's and led her to the living room. "You didn't have to do all of that. Like, seriously, it's a bit much, isn't it?"

"Let's face it; they're the closest I'll ever get to children of my own. It's all part of my evil plan for them to take care of me when I'm ancient."

"Thank you, Nancy," Lina said after a few minutes. "Thank you so much for everything."

"Where's David?"

Lina shrugged. "Haven't seen him since Tuesday."

"You know he's cheating on you again, not that it matters or anything."

"Probably, but I don't really care. I just wish he'd leave for good."

Nancy sat on a stool at the kitchen counter. "How's Vengeance?"

"David came home week before last and blew up when I mentioned a divorce. Said he'd find a way to get custody of the kids."

"And you told Noah?"

"It sort of came out."

Nancy fished in her trouser pocket and produced a business card. "Put this number in your phone right now. Use a different name just in case Asshat goes through your phone."

Lina turned the divorce attorney's card over in her hands:

Ashish Singh, I will fight for you. Your safety and financial security are my priorities.

"My gift to you. I already paid the retainer and filled him in on the details."

"Nancy, you didn't."

"I sure as hell did. Think about it as a down payment on your divorce party."

"I don't know if I'll be able to pay you back—"

"No need and I'm serious." Nancy smiled. "I owe you from senior year anyway."

"How'd you find out?"

"Remember the guy with really bad foot odor but really great lips?"

Lina nodded.

"His work study was in the financial aid office."

"And you never told me you'd found out?"

"Call Ashish and we're even; deal?"

"Does Ashish know David, by any chance?"

"He hates David. Turns out your husband screwed over his brother with a few bad investments. This is payback for Ashish." Nancy folded her fingers over the attorney's card in Lina's hand. "Call him as soon as you can. He's waiting to hear from you."

"I'll do it right—" Lina started as she heard the soft whine of David's garage bay door and tucked the attorney's card into her bra. *He just had to come home today.* "Let me handle him, Nance."

Nancy rolled her eyes. "Got anything to drink? I'm going to need something stronger than red wine."

"Above the fridge. Glasses are over there." Lina's stomach churned when she heard David's voice. *Must be on his phone.*

Sure enough, David entered the house, messenger bag in one hand and phone in the other, holding it to his ear. The skin around David's eyes crinkled as he laughed, an unfamiliar sound.

"Yes, we can do that. Whatever you need. No. No, it's our job. It's my job. I don't mind at all. Uh-huh. Uh-huh. Mm-hmm. Sure. Yeah. Yeah. Yeah. It's all good. Drinks are on me next time. Sure. All right. All the best. Send me the files when you can. Then I'll await your email. Of course, I'll be in Denver next month. It's a deal. Okay, I'd better go."

David's telephone persona switched off as soon as his call ended. His eyes narrowed at Lina when he caught sight of Nancy pouring three fingers of his bourbon into a frosted tumbler. "Nancy, haven't seen you in a while."

"David." Nancy fake smiled. "About five years. Missed my girl. Had to come see her."

"Did you now?"

"The kids are so big. They're doing amazing with their site. Caught them on *The Sophia Show* months ago." Nancy took a sip of her drink. "Lina sure as hell taught them how to kick ass and take names."

David sneered. "Their little project is over. Expected them to get bored and move on to something else, just like their mother."

Nancy raised her glass. "Here's to them being amazing." She drank. "This bourbon is great. Where'd you get it?"

"Glad you're helping yourself to my brand-new bottle," David said. "Lina, dinner?"

"I was just—"

"We're ordering pizza. What kind do you want?" Nancy said, pouring another glass. "Something good and salty like pepperoni and ham or maybe anchovies and black olives, right?"

"Actually, just came to check on the house and pack for Boston."

"You're working for the Fourth of July?" Lina asked.

His jaw clenched. "Straight through, till late next week. Is that a problem?"

"Not at all."

David thumbed through the stack of mail on the counter. "When are you leaving, Nancy?"

"Tomorrow."

He grumbled something, glared at Lina.

"And it's been so great seeing your amazing kids and this gorgeous chick right here." Nancy downed the remainder of her glass.

Lina pulled her lips in to stifle a laugh.

"Better watch that liver, Nancy," David said.

"Liver's fine."

David knocked on the granite counter. "It was good seeing you, but don't take that as a future invitation. Lina, I'd better hurry."

"Yeah, sure, David." Lina watched her husband retreat to their room and mentally high-fived her best friend. How had she survived so long without Nancy in her corner?

The attorney's card weighed heavy with promise, safely tucked inside her bra. She paced the kitchen, waiting for David to pack and leave. All she wanted to do was go outside and call Ashish. Nancy made small talk, shifting her weight from one foot to the next, Lina's nervous energy rubbing off on her.

Thirty minutes later, David pecked each kid on the forehead, kissed Lina sloppily, and rolled his luggage out to the garage. She waited a bit to make sure he wouldn't circle back around.

"Hey, think you can watch the kids? I'm going to pick up the pizza and call Ashish," Lina asked.

"Sure, as long as you're making soup tomorrow. It's like the only reason I visited."

"Will send you back with a bucket of soup," Lina said.

"Go. I've got them. I'll get Danny all set up to do some online shopping with his gift cards."

"You spoil them."

"With pleasure. Tell Ash I said he owes me a drink," Nancy said with a wink.

Lina put her hand on her hip. "It's Ash now?"

"Girl, wait till you meet him. I think husband number four might be an attorney." Nancy laughed. "Go. Go. Go. Go. I've got some time to spend with the kids," she said, shooing Lina out the door.

Energy surged through Lina's legs as she sprinted toward her car. It chirped when she unlocked it. She climbed in, locked the doors, started the engine, and took a deep breath before dialing Ashish Singh's cell phone number.

"Hi, Lina, I've been waiting for your call. I'm excited to begin fighting for you," he said.

"Um . . ."

"Nancy made me enter your number in my contacts. Don't worry about a thing."

"Oh, okay," Lina said, pulling out of her neighborhood.

"So, Nancy gave me the gist of your case, but I'd like to hear from you. What do you want me to do?"

"I want my kids. That's all I care about right now."

"Understandable," Ashish said.

Lina bit her bottom lip. "Is it a long shot? David knows a lot of people and has a lot of pull around here."

"Not a long shot, but we've got to be smart here. I've had dealings with your husband before. He's a crafty son of a bitch, so we're going to have to stay ten steps ahead of him now until the kids are eighteen."

Hope gurgled from her gut like a spring and she took a long drink. "I'll do anything to get out of this marriage with my sanity and children. We can't live like this anymore."

"Can you write down a few things?"

215

"Not right now, I'm driving. Hold on." Lina cut in front of another car and pulled into a parking space at the local Publix. Her fingers tingled with excitement. She searched through the car for something to write with, finally finding a pen and some old receipts. "I'm ready."

"I need you to get a new email. Use Gmail or something similar that you can access anywhere."

"Email. Got it."

"Next, you've gotta start tracking his outbursts—anytime he's violent, note it in the calendar app on your phone. Make sure it's backed up to the cloud. Also, it'll be a thousand times better if you can get evidence of his verbal abuse. Get a tiny voice recorder and keep it with you at all times."

"Okay," Lina said, imagining herself recording David's outbursts. She bit her lip, worried how he'd react if he ever caught her.

"I'd like to do a face-to-face when you get the chance, to better assess your level of safety. I'll take my time compiling your case before we take the step to have him served. If you can, secure a safe place just in case. I've seen some men completely snap when they're served. It doesn't end well for the wife or kids. I want you to seriously consider it."

"Can I stay with Nance?"

"Does he know where she lives?"

"I don't think so."

"Find another place, just in case. Remember: ten steps ahead of him at all times."

Could she really go through with all this?

Ashish cleared his throat. "And finally, get your hands on every piece of financial information you can: past bank statements, tax forms, 401(k), stocks, bonds, everything and anything. Take photos with your phone and send them to me if you can't physically take any documents. I know it seems like a lot of work, but if we keep our cards close to our chest, it'll be worth it. Shoot me an email from your new email as soon as you can."

"I'll do it tonight. Thank you so much."

"Thank you for trusting me, Lina." Ashish ended the call.

Lina paused to take in the moment, holding her phone to her chest. So much had changed for her within mere hours. Was the sudden lightness she felt hope?

The pieces of Lina's independent woman puzzle were falling into place. She had the support of her best friend, an attorney who had it out for David, and now a fighting chance at getting custody of her kids. But regret taunted her. Despite everything coming together for once in her life, there was still that Noah-size puzzle piece that needed resolution. She decided to text him one last time. If he didn't respond by the end of the day, she'd block his number for good and move on with her new life.

Hands shaking against the steering wheel, Lina texted Noah for the last time: Hey . . .

Lina: So, I guess you're over me and all. It's okay.

Lina: Well, it's not okay, but I'll be okay. I actually appreciate you not making me choose between you and my kids.

Lina: You know it's something I can never do.

With a silent goodbye, she closed the door of her heart to Noah and turned the ignition. Slowly, she pulled out of the parking space. Her phone sounded with text after text after text. She parked in another space and checked her phone.

Noah: LINA!

Noah: LINA ARE YOU THERE?

Noah: Lina? I swear to God, I'm just NOW getting your text messages. My cell service was a nightmare.

Noah: Finally landed in Vancouver. I turn on my phone and . . .

Noah: Are you there?

She hesitated for a few seconds.

Lina: Hi.

Noah: Forgot how much I hate remote location work. I'm exhausted. Worked 21-hr days.

Noah: Had to use SAT phones.

Noah: Haven't slept in weeks.

Noah: Finally wrapped. Think it's time to hang up my tights.

Noah: I miss you.

She read his texts several times, smiling like a damn fool in the Publix parking lot.

Lina: I miss you too.

Lina: Tried to see how long I could last without thinking about you.

Lina: Made it five minutes.

Noah: Five minutes longer than me. That's what took us so long to shoot.

Noah: I was so unfocused.

Noah: I was so off.

Noah: I'm not the same without you.

Noah: I need you in my life.

Noah: We'll figure everything else out.

Lina: ...

Noah: What's wrong?

Lina: No one has ever told me that before.

Noah: I will tell you every day.

Noah: Don't go anywhere. Need to get off the plane.

Lina: I won't.

Clenching her phone, Lina exhaled, marveling at how perfect her puzzle was coming together. She could make out a clear image of her future without David. She could feel the peace of not having to live with constant drama. She could see the kids healing and developing healthy relationships.

Noah: In car.

Noah: What are you doing?

Lina: Waiting to pick up pizza for dinner.

Noah: I've existed on protein shakes because I've been sick.

Noah: PIZZA.

Noah: I will do anything to eat pizza right now.

Lina: Anything?

Noah: What do you have in mind?

Lina: If you come back to Atlanta tonight I'll save you a slice.

Noah: Wish I could.

Lina: Me too.

Noah: Should be home by Wednesday.

Lina: Sorry you're not feeling well.

Noah: Thought I was going to die the other day.

Noah: Dr cleared me. No pneumonia. No flu. Antibiotics and steroid shot just in case.

Noah: How are the kids?

Lina: They're okay.

Noah: And you?

Lina: Better.

Noah: Glad to hear it.

Noah: FaceTime later?

Lina: Sure. Give me some time to get home and get the kids settled.

Noah: Will do.

Noah: Hey, Lina?

Lina: Yeah?

Noah: I'm in love with you.

Noah: Just thought you should know.

CHAPTER 29

The Henry family lived in two houses at the same address: a dark and silent one-room dwelling where everyone tiptoed around with bated breath when David was home, and a sunny twelve-room, three-story traditional where laughter and happiness reigned in David's absence.

With David off to Boston, Mimi's and Danny's sweet laughter floated downstairs, a precious song to Lina's heart as she cleaned up the kitchen. They'd stuffed themselves full of pizza and brownies and were now contentedly online shopping in Danny's room. She could listen to them all day when they weren't fighting.

Still buzzing from her conversations with Ashish and Noah, Lina grinned to herself as she knocked on the guest room door. "Hey, Nance, just checking on you. Need anything?"

"Come on in. I need to properly talk about Ash with you."

When Lina pried open the door, Nancy was lying across the pale-blue duvet with her phone propped against a pillow. "Say hi to Ashish." Nancy held out her phone, Ashish on FaceTime. With his dark hair grazing his shoulders, he raised a full wineglass. Between his deep, velvety voice and Bollywood looks, Lina understood why Nancy was hoping he'd be husband number four. Not that Nancy had a type. She'd dated men, women, all races and ethnicities, super wealthy, bitterly poor—it'd never mattered. It usually boiled down to how they made her feel about herself, and based on the way Nancy was beaming, he made her feel very good about herself.

"Hi, Lina." Ashish waved and pushed his glasses up. "Got your emails. Thanks."

"Um, hi. Sorry for interrupting. I'll come back later." Lina slowly backed out of the room.

"You're not interrupting anything." Nancy patted the bed for Lina to sit. "I was reminding Ashish he owed me a drink, and he called to tease me. He's such a tease." Nancy pouted.

"I told you to come over, and we'll have that drink." Ashish gazed into the camera with his sultry bedroom eyes as he brought the glass to his mouth.

Lina felt like she'd interrupted a very private conversation and slowly rose to leave.

"Besties before testes." Nancy blew him a kiss. "Sorry, Ash, my girl needs me. Another time, 'kay?"

"You kill me, Nancy." Ashish playfully pounded his chest. "You're going to say yes to me one day, and when you do, you won't regret it."

"We'll see. Bye, love." Nancy ended the call. "Don't judge me. He is freaking hot, and he's my age."

"No judgies. Not one."

"Good. Are the kids asleep?"

"They're still shopping. I hope David doesn't lose it when the packages arrive," Lina said.

"I showed Danny how to send things to Amazon lockers."

"Thanks."

Nancy flicked something from her manicured nails. "How is Noah Attoh? Is he as incredibly sexy in real life as he is on TV?"

"I've got to FaceTime him later." Lina grinned. "And yes, he's sexy in real life."

"Do I get to meet him? Are you going to FaceTime him now?"

Lina shook her head. "No. No. Not happening. It's too late, anyway."

"Bet he's up waiting to hear from you."

"He's been traveling. I'm sure he's asleep."

"Okay. Text him. If he answers, you've got to FaceTime him with me in the room. If he doesn't, no worries."

Lina fidgeted with her phone. It felt like they were nineteen years old again about to do a three-way call to a crush with one of them silent in the background. "Okay. One text."

Lina: Hey!

"That's it? Girl . . . ," Nancy teased.

The friends waited a few minutes—Lina happy she didn't have to make good on her word and Nancy perusing photos of Noah online, nodding and mm-hmming—until the phone buzzed with a message. Lina's heart danced.

Noah: Hey beautiful! Was going over this contract thinking about you.

Lina: Not sleeping?

Noah: No. Manager met me at the hotel with a stack of contracts.

Lina: Sounds like a good thing.

Noah: All good, but lots of work.

Lina: Then I'll let you go.

Noah: No way. You promised me some LinaTime.

Lina: Is that what you're calling it now?

Noah: Has a nice ring, no?

Lina: Okay. Give me a few minutes.

Noah: Anything to see you tonight.

Nancy squealed as she read the messages. "He's so into you."

"Used the L-word the other day, Nance," Lina confessed, not sure of her feelings for him. *Love?*

"Wow. How do you feel about that?"

"I don't know. With David and all—"

Nancy draped an arm around her friend's shoulder. "I get it. Been there with husband number three. Asshole made me feel like I was less than gum on the bottom of his shoes. It'd gotten so bad that I felt like I was in a constant fog. Bastard did a real mind job on me. Took me a long while to figure out what I wanted."

"Sorry I wasn't there for you, Nance."

"I know." She side hugged her. "Don't be pressured into telling Noah you love him back if you're not sure. It's like your emotions are shell-shocked. They'll eventually catch up."

Lina loved the way Nancy phrased how she felt. It was as if her emotions were dysfunctional because they'd been suppressed for so many years. "I'm not sure about love, but I really do like him. He makes me feel things I haven't felt in ages, and when he kisses me, Nance." Lina thought back to how every nerve ending exploded when he kissed her. She paused. "But how do I know he's not going to be like David?"

"Oh, honey." Nancy smoothed Lina's mass of curly hair. "How long did you guys talk before anything physical?"

"Five months."

"And do you really feel like he was being honest, or was he trying to get into your pants?"

"We actually became friends."

"There's your answer. David was trying to get into your pants from day one—granted, you did give him the goodies by, like, day two, but—"

"Nance."

"Be honest with yourself. You knew you didn't really want to be with David, but you got knocked up. You have a choice with Noah." Nancy elbowed her. "That's my after-school special. Now call Noah."

"I missed you so much."

"Missed you too. Stop stalling."

"Promise me you'll have some chill," Lina said.

Nancy attempted the sign of the cross over her chest. "Promise, but you're not calling him like that, are you?" Nancy plucked the phone from her hands and propped it up at an angle against the television. "Do it like this, so you don't get any weird up-nose shots or double chins or anything." She rummaged through her bag, passed Lina a gold tank top. "Oh, and put this on super fast."

Before Lina could decline her offer, Nancy was pulling the tank top over her head. Lina peeled off her PTA T-shirt, slipped her arms through the tank top, and smoothed it down. It was a little tight on her, but the color popped against her skin and gave her cleavage. She smeared on some of Nancy's lip gloss. "Ready?" Lina opened her phone, FaceTimed Noah.

He answered immediately. "Hey!"

"Hey." Lina blushed at the way Noah gaped at her.

"You're so beautiful," he said, his voice hoarse.

"Thanks. You sound horrible."

"I—um . . ."

"I've never seen you speechless before. It's cute." Lina pulled up her fallen strap. "I want to introduce you to someone very special to me." Lina motioned for Nancy to sit beside her. "Remember the college friend I told you about?"

"Nancy, right?"

"Yes. She came to visit me this weekend. Nancy, Noah Attoh. Noah, this is my Nance."

"Hi, Nancy. Glad to finally meet you. I've heard a lot of incredible things," Noah said without taking his eyes off Lina.

"It really is Noah Attoh," Nancy stammered.

"You thought I was lying?" Lina asked.

"I thought maybe he *looked* like Noah Attoh, but he's—this—he's actually—Noah. Freaking. Attoh!" Nancy's face reddened, and her voice went up several octaves. "Oh my God, Noah, it's so cool to meet you. Well, not meet you, but see you. Not really see you, because holy shit, my best freaking friend is seeing you. Like, *seeing you* seeing you. Lina, you were not lying. I'm not making any sense here. This doesn't happen to me often. I'm going to go now because I can't process this all. I love you, Noah. I love you, Lina. I'm leaving now because I just made this next-level awkward." Nancy slipped out of the room before Lina could stop her.

Lina's mouth dropped at Nancy's word vomit. She had not been expecting her friend to freak out. She'd never seen Nancy tongue-tied—not during their sophomore year when Nancy had learned of her pregnancy, not when Lina had told her she was marrying David, not even when Nancy had recognized her brother being arrested on an episode of *COPS*.

Noah cleared his throat. "Nancy seems pretty cool. I'm happy for you."

"Can't believe she fangirled so hard. I'm never going to let her live that down. How are you?"

Noah switched the camera to show her the stack of paperwork on the round table before him. "I've been better."

"What are you working on?"

"Sifting through sponsorship and endorsement stuff. I'm supposed to shoot a commercial tomorrow, but I sound like crap and feel even worse."

"I'm sorry."

"It's okay. You're making me feel better already, especially since you're wearing that."

Lina ran a hand across her body, careful not to pull the tank any lower and flash him. "This old thing?"

"Hold still. Just like that."

"Did you screenshot me?" Lina asked.

"Guilty. You're the medicine I need. Are you going to do this every time I travel? It's absolute torture."

"You're giving me ideas."

"And you are giving me so many ideas." Noah coughed. "Wish I was there with you."

"Me too." Lina held her phone and lay on the bed to get comfortable.

Noah rubbed his eyes with the heels of his palms.

"You really don't look good. Sure it's not the flu?" she asked.

"Yeah. Just a cold."

"I'm supposed to make chicken soup for Nance tomorrow. If you're back by then, I'll bring you a bowl."

"I might take you up on that." He coughed again. "I'd better go finish this so I can hit the sack."

"Good night then."

"Good night, Lina."

Nancy opened the door with a sheepish look. "Thought I'd give you guys some privacy."

"Mm-hmm. Had nothing to do with you being starstruck?"

"Okay, maybe a little. He's really . . . you guys are really . . ." Nancy plopped down on the bed with a heavy sigh. "This whole thing just got real to me. Like, you need to get out of this house before you get caught. Everyone has smartphones nowadays, and let's be honest: David isn't sane. He's the poster boy for narcissism."

"I know." Something Noah had said made her think. "Give me a sec on David. Do you know anything about sponsorships and how they work?"

"A little. Sat through a course on it last year when I considered going into private practice."

"You think I can find sponsors for the kids' site? Like, companies who'd want to slap their names and logos on it and cut us a check?" Lina tried to figure out how it would work.

"That. Is. Brilliant."

"Under Armour. Nike. Exercise companies and stuff." Lina paced. "I can send emails to their marketing teams. Maybe cc some higher-ups.

They're at almost one hundred thousand users. We need more. Bigger numbers to make them salivate."

"You're a genius; you know this, right?" Nancy said. "Make sure everything is locked tightly in the kids' names so David can't touch any of it."

Lina turned to her friend. "Better yet, how about your name? I can set it up. You'll be the owner. The kids and I can be shareholders or something."

"Are you sure you want to do that?"

"Nance, I trust you with my life. Literally, this would be our lives. Would you do it?"

"Anything you need."

Lina's phone chirped just then.

"Is that him?" Nancy peeked over her shoulder.

Noah: I've looked at your picture a hundred times now.

Noah: My battery is probably going to die soon.

Noah: You are absolutely stunning.

Lina: I'm blushing.

Noah: I'm taking your offer.

Noah: On the way to the airport.

Noah: Should be home in a few hours.

Lina: I'll stop by with some soup later.

Noah: Just come up whenever you can. I'll leave the key with the concierge under your name.

Lina: I'll see you tomorrow then.

Nancy squealed with delight. "I'm taking the kids shopping or something. May even take them back to Athens with me. Looks like you need some *alone time* with Vengeance."

CHAPTER 30

It was a mild Sunday evening—a perfect day to be outdoors hiking up Stone Mountain or riding bikes at the park with the kids. Guilt gnawed at Lina for not being with them now, but Nancy had insisted on taking them shopping. Lina was to meet up with them later.

No matter how much time Lina spent with her kids, it never felt like it was quite enough. There was always a nagging guilt whenever she'd done things for herself. The feeling now overwhelmed her because she was headed to see Noah. It almost felt illegal, as though she were breaking some cosmic maternal law for not being with her children 100 percent of the time.

Might as well add it to my list of other sins, Lina thought, feeling the cool air blow across her shoulders and back while she waited for the elevator to reach Noah's floor.

She'd planned to wear jeans and a regular T-shirt until she saw the adorable green halter dress hanging in her closet. It was knee length and flared at her waist, making it look tiny, while the halter gave her just enough cleavage and support to go braless. She'd bought it on a whim during a family vacation and had never worn it because David didn't like the bright color.

The elevator dinged at Noah's floor. A part of Lina wanted to return to the garage and drive back home before the magic in their fledgling relationship disappeared. Who was she kidding? He was Noah Attoh, and she was just . . . Lina.

The elevator sounded again, signaling the door would soon be closing and returning to the lobby. She held her hand out to keep it open, shuffling into the foyer. Noah's key sounded against her wedding band. The thick platinum band mocked her in David's voice: *You're so stupid. You'll never be anything without me. You're such a failure. I won't even entertain the idea of a divorce.*

Why had she even slipped it on her finger this morning? Had it become nothing more than a habit? Something to finish off her outfit? *She wasn't quite dressed without the suffocating reminder of the vows she was breaking.*

A wave of nausea rolled over her, and she steadied herself against the wall, inhaling and exhaling deeply, trying to force David's words out of her head. She turned her ring and tugged until it slipped off her finger. It plinked against her phone when she dropped it into her purse. She took a minute, adjusted her hair, and smoothed out her dress.

Just do it. Key in lock. Push door open. Get out of your head, Lina. She listened to her inner voice, following the directions like a robot until she was inside Noah's house.

"Hey, beautiful." Noah coughed. He was lying on the couch, covered in blankets. "I thought you'd changed your mind or something." One pitiful smile from him eased her mind.

"I come bearing gifts." She raised the bags, depositing them on the kitchen counter. "Forgot to ask if you were allergic to anything."

"Nothing at all." His voice was weak. Lina wanted to go to him and hold him until he felt better. Instead, she ladled warm soup into a large bowl. "I'm glad you came home. You look like hell."

"And you look like a dream." He ran a finger down her bare back, making her shiver. "I really like this dress on you."

"Thanks. How you holding up?"

"Better now. I really appreciate all of this," he said, accepting the bowl. "What kind of plans did you have for the Fourth?"

Lina sat on the edge of the couch and slipped off her shoes. "Nothing much. Nancy took the kids shopping and was going to sleep over tonight to watch them."

"So . . . ," he said sheepishly, "you're mine for the rest of the day?"

"Day and night." Lina blushed. "And I didn't bring any extra clothes because I didn't want to be presumptuous or anything."

"You have my permission to be as presumptuous as you want."

Lina bit her bottom lip. "I haven't done this in a long time."

"You don't have to do anything that makes you uncomfortable."

"I know." Lina couldn't imagine Noah making her uncomfortable. She bumped his leg with hers. "What do you think about the soup?"

His face melted into a look of bliss after several spoonfuls. "You made this from scratch? Homemade?"

"Yeah, that's what took me so long to get over here. Brought you some chocolate chip banana walnut bread too."

"You also baked?"

"Promised Nance, so I made a few extra loaves for when you get better."

"You win. I'll do anything you want."

"Anything, Noah Attoh?"

"Anything, Lina Henry."

Plucking the bowl from his hands, she held up a spoon to his mouth. "I want you to finish your soup and get better."

Noah held her waist, gazing at her as she spooned chunks of chicken, celery, onions, potatoes, and garlicky broth into his mouth. His palms warmed her sides through her thin dress.

"Don't expect this every time you have a man cold."

"I was considering volunteering at the hospital in hopes of catching something next week." Noah held her waist tighter and brushed his thumb gently beneath her breast. "Forgot to tell you Disney is going to air the kids' episode tomorrow night."

"Seriously? Already?"

"Got the email yesterday."

"The kids are going to freak out." Lina laughed, imagining their reactions.

"Wish I could be there."

"I'll FaceTime you, but only if you're better by then." She spooned more soup into his mouth.

"I could really get used to this."

In that moment, Lina remembered how many times she'd nursed David back to health whenever he'd been ill. He'd caught the flu a few years earlier and ended up in the hospital for a little over a week. That had been how she'd learned of another affair.

"What are you thinking about?" Noah asked.

"How I helped David when he had the flu," she said without thinking.

"Oh . . . this is weird." Noah swung his legs around.

Lina reached for him.

He rose to his feet, bracing himself against the couch. "I know we're in a difficult situation, but that was—"

"It wasn't like that."

"What was it like, then?" His lips pressed tightly to prevent a yawn from erupting fully.

"It's going to sound stupid."

"I'm trying my hardest to understand."

"I don't know. The thought just ran through my head. I'm here with you and you're sick. Somehow I remembered the last time David was sick," Lina said.

Noah gaped at her.

She held out her arms to explain. "He ended up in the hospital for a week. I left my phone one night, circled around, and caught him cheating on me with some chick from his office."

"I'm so uncomfortable with this." Noah pinched the bridge of his nose. "I'm telling you my feelings, and you're thinking about your husband cheating on you." He said each word slowly, punctuating them with slicing hand motions. "Are you using me to get back at him?"

"No."

"I—I just can't if you're—"

"If I'm what? Hoping to make David jealous?" Lina reached for Noah, but he stepped back, hurt and betrayal scrunching his face. "Can you hear me out for one second?"

Noah nodded.

"When I was a little girl, I saw guys come and go—my dad, my stepdad, my mother's boyfriends. Eventually I lost count. I promised myself I'd only get married once and it would last 'till death do us part.'" Lina touched the empty space on her ring finger. "I wanted the fifty-year anniversary and the big seventy-five-year gala. I wanted forever. And don't think I'm playing the victim. I haven't been a perfect wife or anything, but I took my vows seriously, even when my husband didn't."

"What are you saying, Lina? You want to stay with him? You want to make it work?"

"No, Noah. Not at all . . . I have a lawyer, and I'm going to go forward with legally ending my marriage, but part of it feels so wrong, like I'm betraying a promise I made to myself."

Noah looked like it was Christmas morning and he'd just unwrapped his favorite toy. "You have an attorney? You're going to go ahead with it?"

"Yes, and now I'm never going to get that fifty-year anniversary or seventy-five-year gala." Lina shook her head. "I don't know; it's stupid. Thinking of catching him cheating again made me realize that he's always been like this, and it's not my fault."

Noah closed the space between them. "So tell me about this lawyer. Are you going to be okay until it's all over?"

"I think I'll be okay. Trying to stay ahead of him. I should be out of there before he's served."

Noah grinned. "You're really doing it then? So I can—"

"I don't want anything from you. And I'm not expecting anything at all. I had to do it for me and the kids. We just can't—"

"Lina—"

"I'm working part-time, and the kids' site is doing really great."

"Lina, hold on."

"I think I'm going to offer it up for sponsorship opportunities as soon as we get more users, so the Disney spot will help a lot."

Noah reached for her, threading his fingers with hers. He gently kissed the top of her hand. "You surprise me every day. Just when I think I know what you're going to do, you change it up and leave me speechless." He caressed her cheek, and she wanted to melt into his hand. She wanted him to hold her and never let go. She wanted . . . him.

Without a second thought, she tilted her head, her lips brushing his. "I'm full of surprises, Noah Attoh."

"I see, Lina Henry," he whispered, his gaze so intense it stole her breath. It was as though he was daring her to look away, to break the magic between them. She hooked her arms around his neck and brought her lips to his, tasting the soup on his mouth. It didn't matter; she needed more of him, and by the way Noah's hands slid down her back and gripped her ass, he had the same need. A soft moan escaped her mouth when he lifted her. She couldn't help but wrap her legs around his hips and kiss him deeper. How was he able to bring out this part of her? How was he able to be so gentle and patient with her?

They kissed clumsily as he carried her down the hallway and into his bedroom. Her stomach fluttered with anticipation and nerves when he gently laid her on his bed. *Oh dear God, yes. Please, yes,* Lina thought. Noah slowly eased onto her like he was trying to make sure she could handle his weight. He felt perfect, their bodies complementing the other. Two perfect halves of one whole.

He carefully brushed the hair from her face and took her all in with a content smile. "I want to make love to you all night."

Was he talking now? Why was he talking now? Lina was out of her mind with lust. "Noah." Lina hardly recognized her voice. It was low and rough, almost feral sounding. "Do you have condoms?" While she'd experienced fertility issues, she'd rather be safe than sorry.

"Bathroom," he mumbled, coming up for breath between kisses. His hands were everywhere: her breasts, her legs, her hips, her ass, her panties. She needed his pants off. Her fingers dipped into the waistline of his sweatpants, making him close his eyes and groan. He pressed against her, and she almost lost her mind.

Condom. Need. Condom. Condom, Lina. One of you has to get it.

She groaned, knowing Noah was too far gone to run to the bathroom. A quick bathroom break would probably be best for her anyway. She could freshen up before reaching pure bliss for the rest of the night. Noah hooked his fingers around the waistband of her lace panties and began sliding them down her hips.

Now or never, Lina. Condoms. Condoms. Condoms. Condoms. Condoms. Condoms. Condoms. Condoms. Condoms.

"CONDOMS!" Lina yelled as if she'd struck bingo. "I'll get them. I'm going now. Like, I'm getting up right now. Right this minute. See, I'm moving." She scooted away from him, fell off the bed, and awkwardly popped back to her feet. "I'll, um . . . I'll be right back."

Noah laughed, shaking his head, seeming to understand her desperation. "We can take it slower when you get back." He pulled off his shirt and dived under the covers. "I'll be here when you're ready."

When I'm ready? I'm so ready. Vengeance is about to bring the thundah . . . Lina was giddy by the time she stumbled across the bathroom's imported tiles. Her hands shook as she searched through drawers and cabinets for condoms.

Condoms.

Sex.

She was about to have sex. She hadn't been with anyone besides David in twenty years. Against her will, her mind drifted to the last argument they'd had.

I'm the only person that'll ever love you.

Her skin prickled and warmed as she remembered how helpless he'd made her feel.

You sit around all day getting fatter.

David's words bit.

I'm the only one who will ever want to be with you.

Lina clutched the sink as tears welled in her eyes. And now she was crying. God, she was crying. She was such a hot mess, and she was taking too long. Noah was probably not used to women making him wait. He was probably also used to being with women with incredible bodies, not saggy, soft, chunky bodies like hers. She thought back to his last movie, where he'd had a love scene with supermodel Heidi Flass. How the hell could Lina compare to HER?! *Even if he likes me, he hasn't seen me naked.*

You could lose some more weight. She heard David's voice and looked at herself in the mirror. Her face wasn't as thin as she'd thought, and she noticed a shadow of acne on her jaw. She pulled up her dress and wanted to vomit at the cellulite dimpling her thighs and her puffy stomach.

You know you're nothing more than someone's pity fuck. That's all you'll ever be, David's voice reminded her.

Did Noah pity her because of her situation? Tears slid down her cheeks, hitting the floor like raindrops, only nothing was going to sprout from her salty tears. They'd just evaporate into nothing . . . like her.

You'd be nothing without me.

A thousand Davids now encircled her in the small bathroom, each one spitting an insult. Each one looking at her with disgust. Each one cutting away at her, taking pieces of Paper Doll Lina and crumbling them.

You sit around all day, getting fatter. You don't try to look decent. You don't try to be sexy or anything. You're nothing without me. You're so stupid. Why did I even marry you? You're so worthless.

You've never been anything.

You're getting the kids' hopes up.

You've failed at everything.

She wanted to be with Noah. She wanted him to make love to her. She wanted to feel beautiful and sexy and sensual, but David's words were a cage. Every hate-filled phrase was another bar in her imprisonment; his disdain for her, chains; and the way he'd rejected her, the lock.

"No," Lina whimpered, covering her ears. "No." It was all she could say to combat David's taunts.

You'll never be anything without me.

Lina sank into the depths of David's many insults. Each hurtful word pulling her farther and farther away from herself, from the new, free life she imagined, from her rekindled friendship with Nancy, from her children, from possibly being loved by Noah.

I'm in love with you, Lina. Noah's declaration shifted something within her.

I'm hiring you because you more than know your stuff, Bev had said. Lina stopped her descent.

I'm scared of him. Mimi's confession made her fight against the sinking current.

You're absolutely brilliant. Nancy's confidence in her buoyed Lina to the surface.

Surrounded by the words of her loved ones, she felt herself break through David's assault.

"I am something, you bastard." Lina was looking into the mirror now, only she saw David's pale face in her reflection. "You can't do this to me anymore."

He'll never love you. You'll be a weight around his neck. You're nothing.

"It doesn't matter. I love me, and there's nothing you can do about it. I'm so much more than your little paper doll, and that terrifies you." Lina stilled, waiting for his taunts. She listened more intently.

All she heard was the soft whine of water running from the sink, the low electrical hum of a house, and . . . snoring. *Snoring?*

Lina tiptoed back to Noah's bedroom to find him nestled in the covers, fast asleep.

CHAPTER 31

Hours later, Lina's eyes fluttered open. She hadn't meant to fall asleep, and yet here she was, comfortably resting on Noah's chest. His hand was carefully tucked into the back of her dress. She listened to the gentle galumph, galumph, galumph of his heartbeat and wondered if hers matched his rhythm. They seemed to match in so many other areas. It still amazed her at how intimately they trusted each other without having been intimate. *Yet.*

They'd been so close last night. Lina shuddered at the thought. She wasn't ready. She wasn't ready for him to see her and all of her imperfections: her stretch marks, her puffy stomach, her sagging breasts. She wasn't sure if she'd ever be ready. Sighing heavily, she carefully slipped from his embrace. It was time for her to go back home.

~

After a quick shower, Lina made a massive breakfast, knowing the smells of smoky bacon and delicate blueberry muffins would trigger her kids' primal sense of survival. Within minutes, Mimi and Danny both slumped downstairs, sleep still in their eyes. Nancy joined them when Lina started the coffeepot, her KISS ME AND BRING ME COFFEE zebra-print eye mask now a headband holding back her bangs. It took the kids a few minutes and a couple of slices of bacon to fully wake up before they shared what Nancy had bought them and about their adventures at the mall. Lina was bursting with excitement about Disney and could hardly wait to tell them. She gave them a few more minutes to clear their plates and gulp down their juice so they wouldn't choke from excitement.

"Hey, guys, got some news." Lina took off her apron and hung it on the back of her chair.

"Good or bad?" Danny eyed the bacon on Lina's plate.

"Have at it. Good news. Only good news."

Danny snatched the crispy strips, beating out Mimi, then gave her one.

"What is it?" Mimi asked, splitting the last of her muffin with Danny.

Should she have made more food?

"Lina, spill the beans, woman." Nancy tapped the table. "You owe me deets, by the way, but we'll talk later." She wriggled her brows.

"Mom?" Mimi asked.

"Okay, don't freak out." Lina held her mug in both hands. "Remember when we visited Noah's set? For the Vengeance movie?" She cleared her throat, put her mug down, and said quickly, "Mr. Noah Attoh, you know?"

The kids nodded slowly, following along.

"Well, remember how I wasn't with you guys? I was filling out a ton of paperwork because he was filming you guys for, get this, Disney Channel! You guys are going to be on their *Amazing Kids* show tonight!"

Nancy clapped. "That's so incredible."

But the kids both just sat, their little faces unreadable.

"Isn't that great news?" Lina waited for a reaction. "Disney Channel TONIGHT. You guys?"

"What about Dad?" Danny asked timidly. "Won't he . . . won't he be . . ." Danny looked down at his lap, fingered the edge of his shirt.

Mimi picked on the remnants of her muffin. "That's great, Mom," she said tepidly.

Lina reached for both of their hands. "Hey, do you guys want to keep doing your site? I'm totally okay if you're done with it."

"But Mimi worked so hard on it," Danny said.

"And Danny likes to do the interviews," Mimi added.

Danny dipped his head. "Mimi's teaching me how to code so I can help her with some updates."

"You are?" Lina asked, impressed.

"Just the basics." Mimi played with the ends of her hair. "I haven't been able to sleep recently, and neither has Danny, so—" She shrugged. "It's nothing major."

"Honey, it is something you should be proud of." Nancy reached for her hand and winked at Danny. "Both of you are such an inspiration to so many people. Hell, I'm proud of you, and you're not my kids."

"Look at me." Lina waited until she had their attention. "I will take care of your father. C'mon, you guys deserve this. You worked your butts off. Don't let him take it away from you, okay?"

They nodded slowly.

"Okay, guys?" Lina squeezed their hands. "This is only good news. Be excited. Call all of your friends. It's major. Chins up."

"You sure, Mom?" Danny asked.

"Positive. Your dad isn't even coming home until next week, and you know he doesn't bother with TV or social media or anything." She waited until excitement returned to their eyes. "I know you guys want to call your friends. Go ahead. Don't forget to post about it. Maybe make a video or two. I'll clean this up."

They darted off, phones in their hands and already texting. Lina spent the rest of the morning telling Nancy about her night or lack of a night with Noah. They talked and laughed until Nancy got a call from a plumber. She'd forgotten she'd made the appointment, and it'd been the only time they could fit her in with a holiday weekend and all. Lina

convinced her to go back home and gave her extra soup and banana bread, then crashed for a quick nap before the kids' Disney appearance.

～

The television in the living room was so loud Lina could hardly think. The kids' excitement rivaled the electric-manic feeling of a packed football stadium. Five more minutes and the kids were going to be on Disney Channel talking about their site. Five more minutes and her children were going to be broadcast nationally on Disney Channel. Five more minutes and their lives were going to change, whether they were ready for it or not. Lina's phone chirped.

Noah: Ready for my LinaTime.

Noah: Guess I'm always ready for LinaTime.

Noah: I love seeing your face.

Noah: BTW, I left a key with the concierge for you from now on, just in case.

Lina: So I can roll up on you anytime?

Noah: Anytime. Go through my stuff. Read my mail. I don't care.

Lina: Already went through your stuff when you were Sleeping Beauty the other night.

Lina: You're like a wizard—you fold the fitted sheets.

Lina: WHO folds fitted sheets so perfectly?

Lina: No judgies. But I might bring my laundry for you to fold.

Noah: You bake. I fold.

She popped in her earbuds to FaceTime Noah. Her heart quickened when he answered.

"Hey, you," she said, making sure to hold her phone at a decent angle.

"There's my smile." It looked like he was sitting at the desk in his home office. He rested his head on his hand. "I keep looking at your picture and thinking I'm such a lucky man."

A blush ran across her entire body.

"Are you nervous?"

"Not really. The kids are freaking out. Had to hide in my room for some peace and quiet."

"I can't wait to see their faces. Hope you guys like our production cut."

"I'm sure it'll be perfect. You ready to do this?"

Noah nodded and rubbed his hands together. "Man, I wish I was there with you."

"Me too. I've got, like, five loads of laundry to fold."

"All depends on what you're cooking." He laughed.

"Mom!" Danny banged on her bedroom door. "Mom! It's about to start!"

"Okay, coming now." Lina took out one of her earbuds and went into the living room. She propped her phone against a family photo beside the TV.

"That's perfect. I can see everything." Noah's voice was smooth in her wireless earbud.

"Hey, Mom, what are you doing?" Mimi asked.

"I'm going to try to record your reactions."

"Ohmigod, it's on! It's on!" Danny jumped up and down in front of the TV as the *Amazing Kids* theme music played.

"I can't believe this is happening," Lina said, more for Noah than the kids.

"It's all for that smile of yours," Noah said.

"Mom, are you paying attention?" Mimi asked.

"Of course, hush. It's on."

Mimi's face popped up on the television screen along with Danny holding a basketball. "Our next amazing kids are a pair of siblings who are taking over the tech industry. Mimi and Danny Henry are teens from Atlanta who've created . . ."

Mimi and Danny were statues. Lina wondered if the magnitude of their website's reach was finally hitting them. Was that why they were so still and serious instead of crying and squealing?

Lina stopped watching Disney and instead watched her kids. Mimi's knees bounced as she gnawed on her nails, her eyes laser focused on the screen. It was as if she'd grown into a mini-adult over the past six months. Danny, on the other hand, sat on the edge of the sofa, leaning on his elbows, ready to leap into action. His eyes were wide in astonishment, a dream realized.

The show cut from the kids and the Vengeance cast to Noah in costume. He was doing push-ups, his laptop open on the ground beneath him. He winked at the camera and leaped to his feet. "I can't imagine keeping in shape when I'm traveling without this site. Mimi and Danny are definitely amazing kids."

An endorsement from Vengeance? Lina glanced up at her phone, her eyes nearly popping out of her head. She had no idea he'd gone that extra mile for her kids.

The TV screen changed to an outtake of Noah's fight scene and the kids in the background pointing and snapping pics of him. As the voice-over began, the lens slowly closed in on Mimi and Danny. They were in the clothes they'd worn to CNN that morning, perched in set chairs. The Vengeance cast surrounded them while they demonstrated how to use their site. It was an intimate shot of her children, a candid moment of them being themselves: confident, carefree, creative. Was that how Noah saw her kids?

"Well, you heard it from the mouth of Vengeance himself. Keep your eyes out for good things to come from Mimi and Danny. We're so proud of these amazing kids!"

A still silence settled in the air over them when the credits ran.

"Oh. My. God! Vengeance!" Mimi was the first to say it out loud. "NOAH ATTOH JUST TOLD THE WHOLE WORLD HE LOVED OUR SITE!"

Danny stood then. "We're going to have, like, a million users soon!"

"Mom, did you know about this?" Mimi asked.

Lina shook her head. "Not at all. I had no idea Noah was going to do that."

The kids shouted and jumped. Danny took off running full speed around the house, screaming, "The whole world saw Vengeance talking about our site!"

Mimi got on her phone, rambling a thousand miles an hour at DEFCON 2.

Lina's laptop dinged with several emails. *Today* show producers had watched the segment and wanted the kids on first thing in the morning.

"Noah . . ." Lina stared into her phone's camera.

"It was worth this reaction." He chuckled.

"This is serious. Thank you."

"You're welcome. I'm glad the kids liked it."

"Liked it is an understatement."

Lina answered the producers and fired off several emails to sports companies along with the sponsorship package she'd worked on. This was all coming together better than she'd planned. She just needed the kids to rock their interview in the morning and follow up with the sports companies later that day, and their fresh start without David would be firmly established.

Danny was now FaceTiming his friend, screaming incoherently, and Mimi was officially at DEFCON 1, her speech reduced to "Ohmigod, ohmigod, ohmigod."

"I—I—I don't even know what to say," Lina said.

"Say you'll see me later this week. It doesn't have to be my place, if that'll make you more comfortable. My studio has a movie theater. We can do something simple like watch a movie and eat popcorn. You're pretty great at snuggling."

"Your legs are perfect for warming icy toes."

"It's a date, then," Noah said.

"As long as I get some Twizzlers."

"Twizzlers are all yours as long as you let me douse the popcorn with butter."

"It's not movie theater worthy unless it's swimming in fake, oily, butter-flavored poison. Total no-brainer."

"I'll set it all up. The first of many, many dates," Noah said. A life with him flitted across her mind. It was a beautiful life, filled with lots of laughter and love. She saw herself curled up in his arms, watching Mimi and Danny play with Edward like a little brother. Her breath caught.

"I might bake you a little something-something, if you behave." Lina rose and started toward the kitchen to get a banana loaf to tease him with. The house was so noisy and the kids so rambunctious Lina hadn't heard the garage. She froze as the door opened and David stormed in.

"I am going to be an absolute angel. I promise," Noah said.

Lina snatched out her earbud and tucked it with the other in the pocket of her skinny jeans. *Please hang up, Noah,* she prayed. The image of her and Noah's new little family faded behind David's scowl.

CHAPTER 32

"What's up with all the noise?" David hung his keys on the nearby hook.

"The kids—I . . . um." How was Lina going to tell him about Disney Channel without him asking a thousand questions and freaking out? She'd promised the kids he wouldn't even be home until next week. Why was he home now?

He headed into the living room. "Why's the TV so loud?" He found the remote and cut it off.

"Oh, um . . . we were just watching—"

"Disney Channel, Dad!" Danny bounded around the corner with the thousand-watt smile she loved so much. Now she wished he'd tuck it into his pocket before his father wiped it from his face with his cruel words. "We were on Disney Channel!"

Poor kid couldn't help himself.

"Hey, you want some dinner? I made chicken soup the other day. Didn't know you were coming home tonight. Thought you'd be home next week." Lina hoped to lead him away from Danny's comment.

"Plans changed." David's hands went to his hips. "What is this Disney Channel thing you're talking about?"

"Vengeance just endorsed our site on TV," Danny said. Lina wished he'd stop talking.

"You probably misunderstood him. There's no way he even knows about your stupid little site. It's not good enough for someone like him." David seemed to catch himself. "And isn't it supposed to be shut down by now?"

Red shaded Danny's sweet face, and Lina heard his teeth grind. He flipped the TV back on and replayed the *Amazing Kids* segment from their DVR. David wore his poker face as he watched the kids and Noah, his arms firmly crossed.

Danny paused the show just after Noah's endorsement, with a satisfied "take that, you bastard" grin. "See, Vengeance endorsed the site that *we made.*"

With Noah's smiling face paused on the screen, Lina inhaled deeply; she and Danny had navigated poorly through a minefield, and now they were trapped. One step to the left or right and they'd be blown into pieces. She braced herself, hoping Noah wasn't still on FaceTime to witness her family drama. "Hey, Danny, why don't you go clean up your room?"

"No, wait." David folded his arms across his chest. "Mimi! Get down here!"

"It was really an amazing segment for the kids. Don't make a big deal out of this." Lina eased herself between Danny and his father.

"First of all, how the hell did they get that footage? Second, where were you guys? And why would someone like him endorse their site? Did you get paid? Did the kids get any sort of reimbursement? How about a contract? Did you sign a contract without me looking it over?"

Mimi nervously walked into the room. "Um, hey, Dad."

"When did you do this?" He motioned at the TV.

"After CNN the other day." Mimi picked at her cuticles without looking up at him. "Noah Attoh had heard about our site and asked us to visit his studio," she said softly.

"We got to be extras in the next Vengeance movie!" Danny added.

David scowled. "Lina?"

"I met him when we were in LA for *The Sophia Show*. It was a brief meeting, nothing to write home about. We just happened to run into him at CNN."

David's jaw tensed. "That seems . . . convenient." He was silent a few beats. "What did you have *to do* to get him to endorse their site?"

"It wasn't like that," Lina said.

David stalked toward her, his eyes narrowing. "Tell me how it was then. What did you have to do for him to get his endorsement, Lina?" David grabbed her ass. "Did he pay you afterward?"

"Cut it out." She slapped his hand away and mentally prepared herself for another argument. Why had he come home today of all days?

Realization hit him with a glower. He held her chin so she'd look at him. "That's why I couldn't find you on iCloud. That was the same day, wasn't it? Wasn't it? CNN and traffic, my ass. You keep lying to me, Lina." His voice was raised now. "Keep fucking lying to me."

Lina tried to push him away from her. She caught him glancing over at the kids. "Mimi, take Danny to Jacob's house. Now!" No way would she have him take his anger out on them again.

"Let them stay and watch what kind of mom they really have. Actually, Mimi, get over here and—"

"Go!" Lina yelled. Mimi grabbed Danny and darted out the front door. It closed with a heavy crash, rattling the house.

"I don't know why I even trusted you to tell me the truth."

Lina wriggled free. "You're making a big deal out of nothing."

"Really? Show me the contract, if there even was one."

Lina scooped up her laptop from the coffee table and opened it for David to read the contract. "See? It's from Noah's production company. Pretty straightforward."

"*Noah's* production company?" David scoffed. She watched him scroll through the contract, which was a standard media release. He seemed satisfied for a second, then clicked on the original email Noah had sent her.

Lina tried to take the laptop away from him, remembering the email had been more than an attachment. *Shit.*

His grip tightened on the laptop. "What's this? *'Hey Lina, hope this brings a smile to your face.'* Why would he care if you're smiling or not?"

Lina made some room between them.

"And *my wife* replied, 'This means a lot to me. Thank you for everything. Ex. Oh. Ex. Oh.'" He was shaking now, anger roiling off him. "Hugs and kisses? Why do you need to thank him for everything? What *everything* has he done for you?"

Lina forced herself not to glance at her phone beside the TV. "It wasn't even like that, David."

"That where you got the lingerie? That was around the same time, wasn't it? I knew it," he sneered. "I knew it."

"David, I already told you I bought it myself. Can I please have my laptop?"

"You want your laptop?" David held it out to her, balancing it on his open palm, studying her.

"Yes. May I please have it?" Lina sucked her teeth. "C'mon, just give it to me already."

Lina reached for her laptop, but he snatched his hand back, tsking her.

"Ex. Oh. Ex. Oh." David glowered at her. "Hugs. And. Kisses."

"David, it's not—"

"Hugs and fucking kisses, right under my nose when I give you everything you could ever want. When I do nothing but love you and pray for you." He glanced down at her laptop, still in his hands. His lips tightened and his nostrils flared. "Hugs. And. Kisses." With all his might, he hurled her laptop at the fireplace. It struck the stone, shattering the screen.

"What is wrong with you?" Lina scrambled to pick up the pieces.

David shoved her with his knee. She fell to the floor beside her broken laptop.

"Hugs and kisses?" He hovered over her, his hands balled in tight fists at his sides.

"David, stop."

He kicked the laptop, striking her leg.

Lina cried out in pain.

"Why do you make me do this? It's like you don't give me a choice."

"You've had so many affairs," she spat.

"So that's it then? You can't cover me like a good wife? You've got to be a whore to get back at me?"

Still on the floor, trying to collect the pieces of her laptop, Lina muttered, "Divorce me already."

"What did I tell you earlier?" David spun on his heels, the blacks of his pupils crowding out the blue in his eyes. "You're *my* wife. I love you!" Lina didn't have enough time to get away from him. He lunged, his hands clamping down on her arms.

Lina screamed, fought back against him.

He jerked her and began dragging her across the floor while she kicked and struggled.

"Stop it, David. No!" Lina couldn't help how her eyes filled with tears.

"You want a divorce? I'll show you what I want."

"No, no, no," she cried out, fighting against his hold, bucking her body and twisting away from him, but nothing seemed to work. She screamed and shouted at David to release her, but her husband was no longer behind his vacant eyes.

The doorbell chimed.

"Help!" Lina cried.

The doorbell chimed several more times, followed by thunderous bangs against the front door.

CHAPTER 33

In the split second it took David to turn his attention toward the door, Lina twisted and bolted away from him. She crashed into the mahogany door. Her fingers were clumsy. She scratched and pawed at the handle with her sweaty hands. "Help me!" She banged on the door, David almost beside her now. When she finally managed to turn the damn knob and swing open the door, two police officers greeted her.

"Mrs. Henry?" the female officer asked, her hat in her hands. VERES stamped on her name tag, she had a young, kind face.

"Yes." Lina panted, grateful to see law enforcement. *How'd they know? Mimi? Danny? Did something happen to them? Did they tell?*

"Is everything okay?" the other officer asked, peeking over Veres's shoulder. His name tag read BILLINGS, and he was a short, stocky man with a plump face and porn mustache. Lina recognized him from their church.

"Yes." Lina caught herself. "No. Not at all." An icy finger trailed down her spine as she heard David's footsteps approaching behind her.

"Evening, Officers," he said, a sickening-sweet charm in his voice. He'd smoothed his hair back into place and tucked his shirt back in. She flinched when he placed a gentle hand on her shoulder.

"Mr. Henry," Veres started. "My chief received a call from a concerned citizen about a possible domestic disturbance. We'd like to come in and check everything out."

David applied pressure to Lina's shoulder. "Everything is fine, just had a little accident earlier."

"Mind if we come in?" Veres asked, already taking several steps around Lina to enter their home.

"David, sorry, we've got to follow protocol."

"It's okay, Billings. Come on in. How's the baby?"

The officers filed into the house. "Growing like a sprout. Been up at the lake recently?"

"I wish. Haven't had a chance to take my boat out from winter storage." David paused, folded his arms, rubbed his chin. "Hey, you feel like taking it out for a weekend or two?"

Billings's eyes disappeared into his cheeks when he smiled.

"Come to think of it, how about for the rest of the summer? Doubt I'm going to get an opportunity with my workload and all. I'd hate for the old girl not to get any action this season."

"You sure?"

"I've got the keys around here somewhere."

Veres came to an abrupt halt when they arrived in the living room. "What happened here?" she asked before snapping several photos of Lina's broken laptop.

"Accident," David said.

"Yeah. David accidentally threw it at the fireplace before he grabbed me and dragged me across the room." She'd had enough for one night. Carefully, she pulled up her sleeve. Angry purplish-red bruises dappled her biceps.

"Is this true, David?" Billings asked.

"It dropped. I've given her everything she could ever want, but she'd rather be with some guy who does this to her."

"Mrs. Henry?"

"He's lying. I told him I wanted a divorce, and he went all psycho."

"David?"

"Seriously, Billings? I've got an amazing house, a high-paying job, two great kids, and an amazing life. I pray to be a God-fearing husband every day." David covered his face with his hands, sniffling. "I just found out about her infidelity and had forgiven her so we could work it all out. I'll keep forgiving her like Hosea forgave Gomer in the Bible. I love my wife and can't imagine a life without her."

Lina's mouth dropped wide open. He deserved an Oscar.

"I'll take it from here, Veres. How about you head to the car and start on the report so we can go home early tonight?"

"I don't think—"

"*Sergeant* Veres," Billings's voice boomed. "I think it's best for you to start on that report."

Veres's fingers clenched around the belt at her waistline.

Lina gaped at their silent standoff. *No freaking way should Veres return to any car. She's the only one listening to me,* Lina wanted to shout. Instead, she held her breath, waiting for Veres to stand up to Billings. To stand up for her.

Billings cleared his throat. "Ve-res?"

"Yes, Lieutenant," Veres said after a moment. Lina felt her world deflate. She shot Lina an apologetic glance before retreating to the front door.

"So are you going to arrest him?" Lina asked Billings. "Are you going to file this as domestic abuse or whatever? He hurt me."

"I'm sorry, Mrs. Henry." Billings glanced over at David. "I don't see any signs of a domestic disturbance. I think you should be grateful to your husband for forgiving you and loving you the way he does."

Lina stumbled backward. "Are you serious? It'll be worse when you leave."

Billings turned to David and sighed. "How about you pack a little bag and crash at a hotel for a few nights? Give her a chance to calm down so you can work it out with level heads? Maybe invite Pastor Nathan over later this week?"

"That's a great idea. What do you say, honey?" David asked with a satisfied grin. Lina was sure she'd fallen into the Twilight Zone.

"No! Hell no! That's not going to work." Lina pulled at the crown of her head. "You're going to let him off because you know him from church and he's letting you use his boat? What kind of insanity is this? He did this to me, no one else."

"Ma'am, please calm down."

"I'm not calming down."

Billings's hand moved to the black gun at his belt. "Mrs. Henry, please—"

"Hell no!"

"Mrs. Henry, I advise you to watch your language."

"Watch my language? He goes nuts and I'm supposed to watch my damn language?"

"It is in your best interest to calm down right now."

Lina started toward the officer. "Do your fucking job!"

He unfastened the holster with his index finger and wrapped his hand around the gun's handle.

Lina froze, her hands raised to her shoulders, hyperaware of the color of her skin and the fact that she'd never taken the time to butter him up like David had. To Billings, she was just another angry Black woman.

"Mrs. Henry, do not take another step forward. David, please gather your things and follow me outside."

She watched David disappear into their bedroom and reappear moments later with a small bag. He ducked into the kitchen, tossing Billings a set of keys, and lingered near Lina's purse at the end of the counter.

"Billings, would it be okay if I took the credit cards from her wallet? They're joint accounts, and I really don't want her to do anything vindictive like take the kids anywhere while I'm gone."

"No. You can't go through my stuff."

Billings pocketed the boat keys. "I don't see anything wrong with that."

"Say, how's your sister? She's what, a judge now, right?"

"Sure is. Family judge in the area and my older brother was just named special prosecutor."

"You guys must be really proud. You should take them out on the boat for me."

"They'd love that. Thanks, David. You almost done?"

"A few more minutes."

Billings glanced at Lina. "He's a good, godly man, you know. Just wants his family; that's all. Can't blame him for that. My wife and I will pray you guys can work everything out."

Lina was seven years old holding her mother's hand, watching in disbelief as their possessions were removed from their apartment and tossed onto the sidewalk. She was ten years old, pleading with her mother's boyfriend to release her mom from a choke hold. She was sixteen years old, begging her principal to punish the guys who took pictures of her in the locker room. She was eighteen years old, frozen with fear, as her professor put his hand up her skirt and threatened to fail her if she told anyone.

Insignificant.

Pitiful.

Powerless.

Helpless.

Watching David rifle through her purse as Billings fingered the boat keys in his pocket made all those feelings come crashing down on her tenfold. If the police wouldn't protect her, who would? What would happen to her when she left David? How would she be safe? How would she keep the kids safe from him?

Had all her efforts been for nothing?

Lina slumped against the back of the couch, drained. Billings flinched, his hand back on his gun.

"Let's go, David," he said.

David tapped the thick stack of debit and credit cards from Lina's wallet against the counter and tucked them in his pocket. "I'm ready. See you in a few days, honey. I love you." He pecked the top of her head on the way out of the house, Billings stumbling closely behind him.

It felt like all the air in the house had been sucked out when Lina heard the front door close. Her chest burned, but she waited, listening to make sure she was alone. She gasped, deep and harsh, an unnatural stillness settling into the house.

Her laptop lay in several pieces scattered across the floor. It looked like her life: a piece here, a piece there, broken, shattered, nothing making sense, nothing cohesive and complete. David had tried his hardest to destroy her over the course of their marriage, but he'd never been as close to his goal until now. Now that he'd shown her how far his influence and power reached. A skillful poker player, his hand was open and he had a full house, only instead of kings and queens, he had cops and prosecutors.

What did she have? What powerful people did she know beside Noah and Ashish?

Crap, was Noah still on FaceTime?

She shuffled to her phone and exhaled at the dead, black screen. At least this way she wouldn't have to text Noah to find out how much of her family drama he'd witnessed. After plugging her phone in to charge, Lina got out the broom and dustpan to clean up her laptop before the kids came home. What would she tell them? *Daddy snapped, kids. He's officially batshit crazy, and I'm probably stuck here with him. We're all stuck.*

The sharp edges and clumsy pieces tumbled into the dustpan. Could she salvage her information?

Today *show. New York City.*

Mimi and Danny had worked too hard on their site to throw it all away now. Lina had worked too hard to put together a sponsorship package to ignore it now. Maybe that was what this final assault was about. Maybe David was like a shark and smelled chum in the water, sensing her decision to finally leave him. She had to keep the promise to herself.

She darted over to her purse and searched her wallet for the secret credit card she kept tucked away for emergencies. It was still there. David hadn't found it wrapped in a Publix receipt in her wallet's change pocket. He wouldn't win this round.

Lina powered up her phone, logged in to her email account, and replied to the producer, confirming the kids' appearance in the morning. Moments later, the producer replied with three electronic plane tickets and hotel arrangements for the night. They'd just have to make the flight within the next few hours. With time running out, she packed an overnight bag for her and the kids and called an Uber.

CHAPTER 34

Being in another greenroom with a gut full of nerves somehow comforted Lina. It was another rectangular room with contemporary couches and chairs. A strange déjà vu washed over her as she watched Mimi and Danny get miked up before their segment like they'd done this a hundred times already.

Hair & Makeup had done a fabulous job covering the dark patches under their eyes to make them look more awake and alert. Poor kids had been up all night asking Lina if she'd been okay and worrying about how epic their father's freak-out would be when they returned home. Guilt gnawed at her like a ferocious lion. Was she pushing them too hard? Was this turning into something Lina wanted more than the kids? Would they wind up hating her in the long run?

But if she didn't push them to promote the site and increase their users, they wouldn't be able to find sponsors and become financially independent from David. It was a double-edged sword.

Nancy's place was looking better as the seconds passed. Maybe she could hole up there until she got a full-time job or until the site sponsors rolled in. She hated herself for being so financially dependent on David. How had she let him talk her out of working? How had she allowed him to have so much financial power over her?

She could beat herself up all day over her stupid decisions, but when she looked at Mimi and Danny on the greenroom television, two things happened:

One: she was grateful for the time she'd gotten to spend with her kids—the classroom visits, lunch dates at school, field trips, class reading time, volunteering for the PTA, even being home when they were sick.

Two: her purpose and motivation to make their site successful was renewed. She was going to land a huge sponsor that would help her leave David and set the kids up for the rest of their lives.

Using Mimi's laptop, Lina logged in to her email and fired off several more sponsorship offers to sports and health companies. She figured someone had to reply eventually, but as she read through the names of potential sponsors, she second-guessed herself. Was she aiming too high?

The sound of a door closing made her turn around.

"I don't have a lot of time," Noah said, rushing over to her. "Producers reached out to my agent late last night and wanted me to surprise the kids in a double segment. I just landed. Been looking for you."

Lina stood, a mixture of emotions spinning through her head. She was in disbelief that he was right there in front of her, embarrassed that he'd probably witnessed everything last night, and horrified that her nasty secret was out in the open.

Noah cradled her face gently in his hands. "Are you okay?"

She nodded, still trying to process her feelings.

"I saw . . . I—I couldn't." He blinked. "When he started to get angry and then you told the kids to go to their friends' house"—he swallowed a brick—"I knew it was going to go bad. I had to call—" He cleared his throat, his eyes reddening. "He grabbed you and I couldn't . . . by the time I got to your house, you were gone. I didn't know where you were or what happened." His voice wavered. "I wasn't there for you. I couldn't be there for you. I couldn't stop him." Noah's stoic mask cracked wide open. He crashed to his knees, hiding his face in her stomach, weeping softly.

She'd broken a superhero.

She wasn't quite sure what to do. No man in her life had ever been as vulnerable and transparent as Noah. She'd never seen any of them cry or show weakness. David had never once cried in front of her—not when they'd lost the baby and not after any of her miscarriages.

And here Noah was, crying at the thought of *her* being hurt.

An unspoken need encompassed them. Lina held Noah close, caressing his head against her as tightly as she could. He wrapped his arms around her waist, matching her firm embrace as he sobbed into her dress.

"I'm sorry. I am so sorry," he said after a few minutes.

"Thank you for calling the police." She sank to her knees and held his face. "Look at me, Noah. I'm okay. I'm not going back. I can't put the kids back in that situation." She wiped his tears with her thumbs. "I'm going to Nancy's for a while until Ashish gets everything together."

"You can stay with me."

"I can't do that. Not with the kids. I need my own place."

"I can—"

"I know, but I think it's best I stay with Nancy when we fly back to Georgia."

"I'm here if you need anything," Noah kissed her palm, and her stomach fluttered. Even with his eyes red with tears, she was helpless against him. She brought her lips to his, kissing him with uncharacteristic ferocity, which he met with a soft groan. She'd never get enough of this.

Noah's cell phone buzzed, and they parted, both panting. "Told my agent to text me when it was time."

"He's here?"

"Flew out from LA on a red-eye 'cause he was worried about me last night. I wasn't in a good place when I couldn't find you."

His phone buzzed again. "I'd better go before someone comes in here looking for me." He kissed her, stood, and helped her to her feet. "Stick around after I finish the kids' segment. I'd like to give you guys the VIP experience around New York."

"We're supposed to fly back around noon." She imagined letting the kids get to know him while they hung out in New York. "But we can go home tonight."

He beamed, kissing her once more before sprinting to the door. She closed her eyes, tasting him on her lips, feeling his warm tears on her dress, and hearing the heartbreaking sound of him sobbing. She didn't want to be without him. She texted Ashish.

Lina: How is everything going with my case?

Ashish: Finally had a breakthrough with the bank statements you sent over.

Lina: Really?

Ashish: They were a few years old, but I have my ways. Found lots of interesting stuff.

Lina: Going to share?

Ashish: Your name is still on all of the accounts.

Lina: Oh.

Ashish: It gets better. Your husband has a condo in Buckhead.

Ashish: Also, does the name David Jr. ring a bell?

Something about reading her son's name breathed life into him again. She could almost smell the ICU, that sterile, permanently sanitized scent with hints of both grief and hope.

Lina: Yes. He was our first child. We lost him at 28 weeks.

Ashish: I don't know how he was able to do it, but there are quite a few investment accounts in David Henry Jr.'s name.

Ashish: I thought it was a little weird because Jr.'s birthday is almost a year before Mimi's.

Lina: That's him, then. David wanted to try immediately. I wasn't ready.

Ashish: I can't imagine.

Lina: I wasn't allowed to work or do much afterward.

Ashish: Let me guess, David got worse after you lost him, right?

Lina: Yeah. He always wanted a huge family.

Ashish: You'd be surprised to know how often I hear this. I'm sorry, Lina.

Lina: When can I leave him for good? I'm in NYC now with the kids and I'm planning to visit Nance for a while. I can't go home to him.

Ashish: Something happen?

Lina: He attacked me last night. Cops were called.

Ashish: Did you get a report?

Lina: Ha! Good one. David knows good ole Officer Billings, who said there were no signs of domestic violence but still asked David to leave for a few days.

Ashish: Damn. Was there another officer present? SOP is to send 2 officers when domestic violence is suspected.

Lina: Yes. Her name was Veres. She seemed to want to do her job. Shocking. But she still left the house when Billings told her to . . .

Ashish: Veres. She a county officer?

Lina: I think, why?

Ashish: I'll reach out to her. Might be helpful.

Lina: Okay. Whatever you think. So do I have to go back home?

Ashish: Tough one. I'd suggest you do, if you can. You don't want him to start moving things around or closing accounts or anything. You don't want him on the defensive. Keep him in the dark as long as you can.

Ashish: Give me another few weeks and we'll be ready to serve him.

Ashish: You need to definitely be gone by then.

Ashish: Not Nancy's place either. Look into some shelters, if you must.

Lina: Shelters?

Ashish: I've seen things go badly when husbands like this are served. It triggers something in them.

Ashish: Lost my first client because she decided to stick around after her husband was served papers.

Lina: I don't know what to say.

Ashish: Promise me you'll get the hell out of there when I say.

Lina: I will.

Ashish: Excellent. I'll keep working on my end.

Lina: Thank you.

Ashish: Enjoy NY!

Lina: I'm planning to.

CHAPTER 35

There are moments in life that are simply perfect: a glorious sunset casting brilliant rays on a thicket of grass when a deer stops to graze in the backyard, coming across a pod of dolphins while snorkeling in crystal clear cerulean water in the Caribbean, all the firsts—first kiss, first dance, first crush, first love, first baby smile.

Sitting in the plush, burgundy seats of the Rodgers Theatre, watching Mimi and Danny totally enthralled by the actors in *Hamilton*, was one of those moments. Lina wanted to press pause and tuck it away in her memory box.

The kids hadn't believed her when she'd told them they were going to a Broadway musical with Noah. They hadn't believed her when they were all whisked away in a dark-tinted SUV that stopped at the theater entrance. They still hadn't believed her when they took their seats just as the theater darkened and the orchestra played.

Both Lina and Noah thought it best that they sit separately. A packed theater meant hundreds of people with cameras. Evidence of Vengeance hanging out with the mother of the kids he endorsed was the last thing Lina needed. David wouldn't just snap like he had last night; he'd use it against her, probably even use her infidelity to build a case to get custody of Mimi and Danny.

The kids sat in the front two seats of the rear mezzanine section. Lina sat behind them. Noah sat behind her, a baseball cap pulled low across his eyes. The second act had just started, and it was driving her nuts to be so close to Noah without being able to talk to him or touch him. She felt his breath on her neck every time he leaned forward. She was beginning to think he was messing with her now as he held on to the back of her seat to rise, his fingers lightly brushing her neck. She watched from the corner of her eyes as he exited.

"I'll be right back. Want anything?" she asked the kids. They shook their heads and shushed her. She rose, squeezed through the aisle, and followed in Noah's steps. He was at the bottom stair and starting down another set of stairs when she pushed through the thick curtain from the theater. By the time she reached the end of the staircase near the restrooms, Noah was nowhere in sight. Maybe she'd misread his body language.

"Hey, you." Noah beamed, leaning against the wall near the door.

"Hey, you," Lina said.

"Enjoying the play?"

"I love it. I don't think the kids will ever forget this experience. Thank you so much."

"You're welcome." He closed the space between them and held her hands. "I want to do something for you."

"You've done enough."

"C'mon, the kids would love it. Just one night and we can fly back tomorrow."

"Depends on what it is."

"I was thinking a private dinner and getting the kids their own rooms."

"Um."

"Oh, not like that." Noah laughed. "I used to love staying in hotels when I was a kid. It was a treat. We didn't get to do it often, but when we did, it was awesome."

"Okay."

"So I was thinking Mimi and Danny can get their very own rooms and order all the room service they want. Hazel said the concierge will personalize each of their rooms—all the gaming stuff Danny can handle and a stylist with a wardrobe for Mimi."

"I'm not really comfortable with them in their own rooms, especially after what happened last night."

"I didn't even think about that. You're right. How about adjoining rooms, then?"

"That may work. I just don't want them to be too far or anything."

He nodded. "No explanation needed. I get it."

"Are you sure you want to do all of this?"

"Yes. Absolutely positive. They deserve it. I was so proud of them this morning. Danny had me in stitches; he's a natural comedian. And Mimi, what can I say about Mimi? She's going to be president one day. Your kids are amazing. I hope Edward grows up like them."

"I guess they're okay," Lina teased. "So what about my sleeping arrangements?"

"I've got something special planned for you."

"So I don't get to know what it is until I agree to it all?"

"Precisely." He kissed the tip of her nose.

"Can we nix the private dinner? They're working on only a few hours of sleep."

"Of course. It's done then. Let me call Hazel and set it up." Noah slipped out his phone and spoke in rapid fire. He was more excited than Lina; it was adorable. "It's done. Will have everything set up in two hours. We can have the car drive around to give the kids a tour."

"You're unbelievable." Lina stretched her arms around his neck and slipped off his hat. "Don't try to sneak up to my room, Noah Attoh."

"I'm turning off my phone tonight and having the staff lock me in."

Lina pouted. "Too bad. I was looking forward to a big bubble bath and climbing into bed to feel the sheets on my skin."

"Lina," he whispered and kissed her until she was breathless and dizzy. Lina jerked at the sound of people heading their way and tugged Noah's hat on over his head.

~

Their tour took the entire two hours. They were driven from the Rodgers Theatre to the Battery, where the kids got out to look at the Statue of Liberty, and back up to the Plaza Hotel near Central Park. The Plaza was a grand hotel with crystal chandeliers and delicate pastel hues. It felt regal, like a castle had been dropped at the very end of Central Park.

Noah had taken another car service directly to the hotel to make sure everything was perfect for their arrival. He met them in the lobby, a wide grin across his face. "Hope you guys enjoyed the brief tour of the city."

"Um, yeah, it was cool," Mimi said, looking between her mom and Noah suspiciously.

"I didn't know you were going to be here." Danny gave his mother the same face.

"Promised the producers that I'd take good care of you guys. Had some special arrangements made because I believe in you and your site. It really is amazing, and I'm so proud of your hard work," Noah said.

Danny's face lit up. "So you really, like seriously, like our site?"

Noah crossed his heart. "Really, like seriously, like it."

"You don't think it's stupid or badly coded?" Danny picked at the skin around his nail.

"Not at all. I think the idea is brilliant, and I really like how simple the sign-up is. Only took me a minute or two. I haven't posted any videos yet, but I've left a lot of comments."

Danny squealed with delight. "You have an account? You use our site?"

"VengeanceIsMine404. Try to log in every single day. I seriously love it."

"Mom, did you hear that?"

Lina ruffled his hair. "I did and I totally agree. I love your site."

"Are you staying here, too, Mr. Attoh?" Mimi asked, looking more at her mom than Noah.

"I am, but I'm on an entirely different floor from you guys, which, by the way, if your mother doesn't mind picking up your keys, I'll personally see you to your suite."

Lina bit her lips to keep from smiling. She couldn't give their relationship away so soon. What would her kids think? She claimed several room keys and slowly walked toward Noah and the kids. Mimi was seated in a tufted chair, her legs crossed as Noah and Danny faced off in an epic battle of rock paper scissors. Noah's and Danny's eyes were locked as they counted off and shot their hands forward. Noah played rock. Danny played rock. They counted off again and shot. Noah played paper. Danny played paper. Another round found Noah playing scissors and Danny matching his scissors.

Lina casually strode over to them and leaned on the arm of Mimi's chair.

"They've been at it forever. I'm so hungry. Can one of you just quit already?" Mimi said.

"Never surrender, Danny." Noah shot a rock.

"You are so going down," Danny answered, shooting a rock as well.

They counted down and shot their hands out again. This time Noah shot paper and Danny shot scissors.

"Ha! Take that, Vengeance!" Danny leaped and clapped.

"Can we eat now?" Mimi whined.

"I'll count my losses. Good game, Danny." He ruffled Danny's hair. "How are you at Uno?"

"Bring your wallet," Danny said, adjusting the collar of his Polo shirt like a boss.

"It's like that, kid?"

"Prepare to go down, Vengeance."

Noah turned to Lina. "I'm officially terrified of your son. His trash-talk game is intimidating."

Lina laughed. "We'd better go to our room, then."

"To your rooms, milady." Noah bowed and motioned for Lina to walk ahead of him.

Nineteen floors up, Lina and the kids entered their massive suite of connected hotel rooms. Danny dashed past the living area and through the connecting door and shouted, "Yes! Yes! Yes! Mom, look!"

His elegant suite included a sitting area, king-size bed, massive bathroom, and a huge flat-screen television decked out with every gaming system he could imagine. Danny flew over to a black podlike seat and donned a headset.

"Mom! Mom! Mom! It's a VR game system," he said. "Mom! Virtual reality!"

"You like it?" Noah asked.

Danny yanked off the headset. "Do I like air? Or food?"

"I think that's a yes. Hey, can I see my room?" Mimi asked.

"Rules first," Lina said, looking at Noah. "What are the rules?"

Noah scratched his head. "Um, order all the room service you want, but if you vomit, it's on you." He pointed at Danny. "And no alcoholic beverages. I had the minibar stocked with water and Gatorade."

"*Anything* from room service?"

"Anything at all, just don't eat yourself into a coma," Noah said. "Mimi, are you ready for your room?"

Lina hugged Danny and gave him a huge kiss on his cheek. "I love you. I'm right on the other side of the door if you need me. Try to get some sleep, okay?"

Noah turned on his heels and clapped his hands. "Sorry to have to do this to you, but I had it set up so everything shuts off at one o'clock in the morning."

Lina was impressed he'd considered a bedtime for her son. He'd actually studied them and knew what they'd like. Her heart skipped a beat when she thought about how much he genuinely cared for her children.

"Mom, my turn," Mimi called from Danny's open door, making her way back through the connecting suite to her room on the opposite side.

Lina gave her son one more kiss and followed Noah to Mimi's room. Mimi opened her door and almost fainted. Her room was identical to Danny's, except where Danny had a TV and gaming equipment, Mimi's room contained three gleaming racks of clothes and a salon chair near the bathroom. Mimi's mouth hung open as she ran her hands across the clothes.

"My assistant had a stylist handpick those for you based on this morning's show. You get to keep whatever you want."

"No way, Noah," Lina said. "That is too much. We can't accept that."

"Please let me do this for her, Lina?"

"Mom?" Mimi's eyebrows rose and knit at the same time. "Please?"

Noah turned to Lina with his hands folded. "Yeah, please, Mom? Please?"

"Are you sure it's okay?" Lina asked.

"Positive. There should be a suitcase around here somewhere as well, so pack what you want."

Mimi squealed. "Ohmigod-Mom-I-can't-believe-this-I-love-you-so-much-thank-you-Mr.-Attoh-AHHHHHHHHH!!!!!" DEFCON 1 was achieved. Lina and Noah looked at each other and slowly backed out of Mimi's room as she ran from rack to rack, screaming and holding clothes up to her body.

Noah offered Lina his arm after they'd closed Mimi's adjoining door to the main suite. "This is all yours."

It was a full suite, complete with a fireplace in the sitting parlor, a huge king-size bed, and a massage table. Her breath caught. No way was this all real. She'd wake up eventually.

He checked his watch. "I'd better get going because about eight people from the spa are heading up this way."

"Are you serious?" Lina half expected him to try to sleep with her the second they were alone, not that she'd complain. But to have him set everything up for her the way he had, with full knowledge of the hell she'd gone through, made her want to be with him even more. He'd cared about *her*.

"I told them to give you everything you want. Facial, hot stones, pedicure. Anything and everything."

"Oh, wow. Thank you."

"You deserve it." He tilted her chin up. "You deserve so much more. I want to give you the world."

"I'll settle for you," Lina said.

"You already have me."

"Then that's all I need."

CHAPTER 36

Velvet. No, suede. No, flower petals.

Lina ran her hands across her skin, mesmerized at how soft and smooth she felt. What kind of sorcery had the aestheticians used on her? She shivered as she slipped on the delicate silk nightgown the spa staff had left on her bed. It was rose gold with thin spaghetti straps, a low neckline, and a hem that stopped right above her knees, clinging to her every curve. She had the growing suspicion that Noah had picked it out and had half a mind to text him a picture.

It was almost eleven o'clock, and Lina wanted to check on the kids. She donned one of the two plush robes hanging in the closet and padded over to Danny's room first. It took the poor kid a few minutes to even realize she was inside his room, even after she'd called his name several times.

He slid off the VR headset. "I only have a few more hours before it turns off."

"Did you eat?"

"A little." He gave her a devious grin, pointing to the four completely ravished room service carts.

"What did you order?"

"A few pizzas and wings and fries and one of each dessert."

"You didn't, Danny."

"I'm growing." He grinned from ear to ear. "Mom, the chocolate mousse was so good. I could eat an entire bathtub full of that stuff. You should order some!"

Lina snorted a laugh. "I can't believe you. Are you okay?"

"What do you mean?"

"With all of this—all the stuff with your site and the interviews and traveling and all. Do you regret it?"

Danny twisted his mouth to the side, slightly biting the inside of his lower lip. It was a gesture David had done countless times. While Lina thought it was adorable on Danny, it'd usually made her anxious when David had done it, and it'd always preceded a condescending remark.

"Danny Bear?" She held her breath. Was Danny unhappy with everything? Had she read him all wrong and messed up big-time?

"I'm okay with everything. Like, I love the interviews and really love everything we built. There are so many people that use it, and it freaks me out sometimes—but in a good way, you know? And don't tell Mimi, but I really love coding."

Lina exhaled. "Yeah, your website is beyond incredible. It blows my mind when I see you guys on TV still. I think: Are these really MY kids?"

"We're pretty awesome, I know."

"You're okay, I guess."

They shared a laugh.

"Hey, are you okay with Mr. Attoh hanging out with us and whatnot?"

Danny narrowed his eyes. "Why, Mom?"

"Just asking. He's a pretty cool guy, isn't he?"

Danny shrugged. "He's okay. Goofier than I thought he'd be."

"But you like him, right?"

"Why?" Danny reached for his headset. "I don't want to talk about this. I need to get back to my game."

"Okay. I need to check on Mimi, anyway." Lina kissed his cheek, but he tugged away from her hug. "I love you. Good night."

"Bye, Mom," Danny said, and pulled the headset over his eyes.

Lina sighed, glancing back at him before leaving. Moments later, she heard the adjoining door close, then lock. She sighed. Danny had to know they couldn't stay with David, right? Shrugging, she visited Mimi's room next. She took one look at her daughter from the connecting doorway and laughed until she couldn't breathe. All the racks had been cleared, with empty hangers dangling precariously. Mimi was sitting on top of a large suitcase, tongue between her teeth, trying to close the zipper.

"If I had my phone, I'd take a picture of you right now."

"Can you help me please, Mom?" Mimi huffed.

"Do they all fit?" Lina lent her weight, pushing down on the top.

"Perfectly. I cannot believe Mr. Attoh did all of this for me and Danny. Mom, he's so cool and down to earth." The zipper finally caught and zzzzzzzzzzziiiiippppppped all the way around. Mimi slid to the floor.

"So you like him?" Lina asked.

"He's cool . . . um, do you like him?"

Lina blushed. "Who doesn't like Vengeance?"

Mimi looked hurt. "Oh, okay. Yeah, Vengeance is great."

"What's the matter with my Linguini?"

"Nothing. I'm okay. Did you have fun today?"

"The most." Lina slipped her robe from her arms. "Feel how soft my skin is."

Mimi ran her small hand up one of Lina's arms and down the other, stopping at the purplish-green bruise on her biceps. Lina jerked her robe back on.

Mimi rose from the floor and pulled the suitcase over to the door. She plucked a bowl from the room service cart. "Have you eaten yet?"

"I had a little sandwich. Not that hungry." Lina joined her daughter on the couch.

"You should try this soup; it's amazing." Mimi held a spoon to her mother's mouth.

"What is that?"

"Lobster bisque on steroids. It's so good. I've had two bowls already." Mimi pulled up her shirt and patted her stomach. "My food baby is back."

"Seriously, Mimi?"

She slapped her gut. "Don't bad-mouth Gigi."

"Okay, stop. What are you doing for the rest of the night?" Lina took the bowl and ate some more soup.

"I don't know. I'm exhausted. Probably marathon something on Netflix until I pass out." Mimi reclaimed her bowl. "Maybe order some dessert."

Lina pecked her forehead. "Try to get some sleep; we've got to fly back tomorrow. I think Noah booked us on an afternoon flight."

"He's flying back with us?"

"He lives in Atlanta. Isn't that cool?"

Mimi smirked. "How convenient."

"Is there something you'd like to say?" Mimi was a smart kid and had probably already figured out there was something going on between her and Noah. Lina bit her bottom lip. "Meems."

"Yeah, Mom?" Mimi looked at her in anticipation, hopeful.

"I really like . . . I, um, have been . . . What would you think if I . . ." Lina couldn't bring herself to tell her—her bright, sometimes shy, sometimes garish, all the time loving and patient daughter. Maybe it was because she favored David so much. She had his eyes, and to have them looking at her the way Mimi was right now racked Lina with guilt. "I really like the clothes."

Mimi's shoulders sank. "Can I ask you something?"

"Anything." Lina hoped she'd ask about Noah so she could just come out and admit to it.

"Were you happy yesterday when Dad was home?"

"Why?"

"You seem so happy today. I like it when you're happy."

"I am very happy. Had the best day with you and Danny."

"And Mr. Attoh, right?"

"Yes. He's fun."

Mimi smiled and hugged her mom, walking her to the adjoining door. "I love you."

"Love you, too, Meems."

"Is it okay if I lock this tonight?" Mimi shrugged. "Just need some space."

Lina nodded. "It's okay, honey." She was 90 percent sure Mimi had picked up on something between her and Noah. She'd have to have a serious talk with her at Nancy's. Maybe the two of them would go get their nails done, and she'd tell her about Noah, or maybe she'd let Mimi meet Edward first and then tell her about their relationship. She'd definitely need Mimi's help breaking the news to Danny when it was time.

Back in her room, Lina threw herself onto the bed, feeling the cool bedding against her smooth legs. She peeled off her robe and rolled around in the empty bed, knocking her phone to the floor. Feeling sexy, she snapped a few selfies and texted them to Noah for him to see in the morning. Her phone immediately buzzed with a message.

Noah: CAN'T UNSEE THAT.

Lina: Thought you were going to turn off your phone.

Noah: I was in another hour or so.

Noah: Just finished my last meeting. Studio manager needed some info.

Lina: All work and no play makes Noah a dull boy.

Lina: Couldn't help it. Love that movie!

Noah: The Shining is a classic.

Noah: Work is done. I can play now.

Lina: How about a movie? Both kids have locked me out, so I'm all alone.

Noah: Sounds good. Have you had dinner yet?

Lina: A little. You?

Noah: Not yet. Can you order me something? I'll be up in 10 mins.

Lina: Sure. What do you feel like?

Noah: Anything. I'm starving.

Lina: Okay.

Noah: 10 mins. Don't change.

Lina: Changing in 9 mins 45 secs.

~

There was a light rap on the door eight minutes later. Noah's mouth was on hers as soon as the door opened.

"Mmmm," he said moments later, unhooking her arms from around his neck and flopping onto the sofa. "That's for the pictures earlier."

Lina was left breathless and cold.

"Come here, you." Noah patted the cushion beside him. "How'd you enjoy your spa day?"

Two could play that game. "My skin feels amazing." She slowly dragged his hands over her legs. "My entire body feels that smooth."

"Does it?" He leaned over to kiss her, but she moved her head away, teasing him.

"How was your meeting?" she asked, bringing her mouth close to his, only to move away when he tried to kiss her again.

He tickled her sides, making her buck and wriggle away. "Shhhh." He laughed, refusing to let go until she was on her back on the couch, and he was on top of her. "Meeting was good. We're expanding the space, and I had to approve the final plans." He tried to kiss her, but she moved her head, so he tickled her more.

"This is torture in some countries," Lina whispered.

"Only in Greenland, I believe."

"Are you ticklish?" Her fingers went to work under his arms. He cringed and fell off the couch, onto the floor. She landed on him, her fingers still tickling his armpits.

"Okay, okay. I surrender," he panted. "You win, Lina." He gripped his stomach, grinning. "You win."

"What do I win, Noah?" She raised an eyebrow and quirked her mouth to the side, knowing all too well what she wanted in that moment. Noah sat up to meet her, his hands cradling her head, his mouth on hers. He was everything she wanted and more. She peeled off his shirt and tossed it across the room.

Noah pulled her closer, his hands warm on her ass. She settled her legs around him, exhaling at how right it felt. In time, his kisses changed from need to adoration. He trailed his lips from her mouth to her jaw and down her neck. He stopped at her breasts, his fingers gliding over the smooth silk at her nipples, in awe at how her body reacted to him.

She wanted him to see her then. To see how her breasts drooped from nursing two babies. To see the saggy pouch left over on her stomach from her weight loss. To see the stretch marks crisscrossing her skin from three pregnancies. She wasn't perfect, but for the first time in forever, she was perfectly content with who she was.

Slowly, she eased her nightgown up over her head and onto the floor. It was suddenly ten degrees cooler and a hundred degrees hotter in her suite.

"You're beautiful," Noah whispered, his gaze almost reverential. He opened his mouth to say something but instead softly brought his lips to her neck. Every kiss he placed on her body seemed to have meaning: a prayer, a hope, a secret being told, a gift, a desire, a wanting, a needing, until he reached the delicate skin around her nipples. The rough prickles of his beard were soothed by his mouth, making her quiver.

"Are you okay?" he asked, a sweet tenderness in his voice.

"Do you have condoms?" Lina flushed when she heard the desperation in her husky voice.

He fished in his pocket and produced an entire box. "Because last time . . ."

"I'm glad you have them." Lina stood, covering her breasts with her hands, feeling very exposed.

Noah followed suit, holding her close to his bare chest and exhaling. "I love you, Lina."

She stood on her tiptoes and whispered, "Show me." He scooped her up and carried her to the bedroom, closing and locking the door behind them.

In one swift move, his pants were on the ground. At the sight of his underwear, a silent giggle sprouted and worked its way through her. She covered her mouth to keep from bursting out, but when she took another look at Noah's Superman sports boxers, she honestly couldn't help it. She laughed so hard she snorted.

"I like Superman," Noah said sheepishly.

Lina was now in hysterics. "I just never." She snorted. "I never expected Vengeance to wear Superman underwear." She coughed, trying to control her laughter. "I love it. Like, I seriously do."

Noah jumped onto the bed and began tickling her sides. "You laughing at my Superman underwear?"

"No." She snorted again. "I'm not. I had this whole"—she gasped for air—"this whole thing played out in my head and never thought you'd wear Superman underwear."

He kissed her stomach. "You've imagined this?"

"You haven't?"

He shot her an "Are you crazy?" look, making her smile.

"Are you sure?" he asked.

"Definitely, but we've gotta talk about your Superman undies."

"I'll get you some Supergirl ones so we can match."

"Yes! I will totally wear them." Talking about anything other than sex put her at ease that she'd made the right decision. He hadn't balked at her body when she'd taken off her clothes. His face hadn't changed, not even for one second. Knowing that he, in fact, wanted all of her made her crave him even more. She pulled his head down to hers and kissed him. "What other ones do you have?"

He caressed her cheek, gazing at her as if he'd won a priceless painting. "Every superhero imaginable," he said softly, gently brushing some hair from her face.

Noah settled on her, kissing her with everything he had. He ground his hardness against her, drawing out a moan. That was all the encouragement he needed. He carved a path with his tongue from her neck to her stomach. Lina could barely hold herself together when he nibbled at her panties.

"Noah," she pleaded.

He found her hands and entwined his fingers with hers. "I'm here."

She wrapped her arms around him, amazed at how perfectly their bodies fit together. It'd been so long since she'd been appreciated and wanted. And he wanted her.

CHAPTER 37

A delicious soreness had settled into Lina's body by the time she blinked her eyes open that next morning. Sunlight peeked in where the heavy damask curtains met the wallpaper.

"I finally get to wake up to your beautiful face," Noah said, lying on his side, smiling at her.

"Guess you earned it," Lina said groggily. It was early enough for a little more time together before the kids were up, and Lina planned to enjoy every minute.

Noah brushed some hair from her face. "We should stay another few nights. Or better yet, how about we fly to Italy. Have the kids been to Italy yet? They'd love it. I mean, it's their summer vacation, and I only have to be in the studio for a few weeks; maybe we can hit up Cannes or the beaches in Kenya. I bet I could even bring Edward. He'd probably be Danny's little shadow and drive him nuts, but he'd love it. Or we could do something cliché like Disney. How does Disney Hong Kong sound?"

"Slow down. I'm going to have to give you a rain check." She faced him, her hands on his chest. "I need to talk to them about us before we do anything like that. I don't even know how this is going to go because you're Noah Attoh. You know how crazy it can get. Let's just take baby steps and enjoy what we have now."

"What do you have in mind?" He ran his hand down her back to her ass, pulling her closer to him.

"I don't know. Maybe breaking it to them when we're at Nancy's? She has a way with words, and they look up to her."

"I can meet you in Athens next weekend, if you want." He kissed her shoulder, and every nerve ending sparked. Could she last a week without being this close to him?

"That might work." Her hands explored him, needing more of him.

Noah groaned into her hair. "Jesus, Lina," he whispered before making love to her again.

Sometime later, Lina found herself back in Noah's arms, marveling at how perfect this all was.

"Breakfast?" he asked, kissing her forehead.

Lina's stomach growled on cue. "Mmmm. Food."

After a quick bathroom break and a shower, Lina crawled into Noah's arms and pulled the covers around them. He kissed her forehead. "I could do this forever," he said, trailing his fingers up and down her arm.

"I bet you could."

"Not this, but this. Me and you."

Lina's heart skittered, imagining a forever with Noah. A life together with all their children.

"You went quiet on me, Lina. Am I frightening you?"

"No. You're not frightening me. I think I'm just frightened; that's all."

Noah glanced at her. "Of me?"

"Of dreaming."

"It doesn't have to be a dream."

"What are we going to do? Go from my divorce court proceedings to file a marriage license and pray like hell David doesn't do something ridiculous or the paparazzi doesn't terrorize us?" Lina leaned on her elbows to better see him. "Let's just enjoy right now. Baby steps."

"You're everything I've ever wanted and more. I think of going home and it's wherever you are. We can build something together. Something powerful and solid. Something that lasts." He held her face. "I can see myself making love to you every night. I imagine watching Mimi and Danny and Edward grow up together." He kissed her. "I'd like to fold your fitted sheets, woman."

"I want you to fold my fitted sheets, you wizard, you."

"I'm serious here, Lina."

Noah's words had been a balm to her open wounds this whole time; she could see it now. She wasn't the same woman he'd met over six months ago; she was more, so much more. Little by little, she'd been able to take back the torn and crumbled bits and pieces of herself. It was up to her to breathe life back into Paper Doll Lina. To transform herself from David's two-dimensional puppet to something better . . . greater.

She inhaled deeply like it was her first breath and exhaled, pushing out her fears and inadequacies, pushing out every lash from David's mouth, feeling reborn. Strength infused her bones. Courage surged through her ligaments and muscles. She was alive. Whole. Capable of living her dreams. Capable of going after what she wanted.

Lina felt the declaration bubbling up, winding its way from her heart to her mouth. "I . . ." She could do it. "I want to be with you, Noah," she said and felt life spring from her gut.

"You want to be with me?"

She smiled. "I do, Noah Attoh."

"You like me?" He traced letters on her arms. "You love me? Circle yes or no."

"You're being silly now."

He had a greediness in his eyes just then. "I'm going to make you scream my name until it's time to go." He reached for her, but Lina scooted out of his way, laughing.

"I'm starving," she teased, wrapping herself in a sheet, wanting him to chase her, to make her feel wanted and needed. Wanting him to catch her.

"Come here, you." He chased her around the bedroom.

Lina yelped, trying her hardest to keep her restraint, when he caught her near the door. She wrapped her arms around his neck and kissed him till her lips felt swollen. He walked her backward until she crashed into the door.

"I will never make fun of your superhero underwear again," she said.

"You just wait till I get you matching ones." He tickled her sides. "I'm thinking Supergirl, Batgirl, Wonder Woman." He kept tickling with each new character name.

They both laughed and shushed each other, then laughed again until they heard knocking.

"Hope you're hungry." He smiled, reaching for the knob.

"Noah!" She gestured at his naked body.

He paused for a few seconds and grabbed a towel, wrapping it around his waist. "That was close."

Lina held the sheet tightly and wrapped her arms around Noah's waist, in complete bliss. Her mouth watered for fluffy pancakes, cheesy eggs, and a strong cup of coffee to top it all off. Could her morning be any more perfect? Was this really how the rest of her life would be? He kissed her one last time before opening the bedroom door. They took a few steps in tandem and froze as the door connecting her suite to Mimi's flew open.

There Mimi stood, phone in her hands and her face streaked with tears. "I'm sorry," she sobbed, her eyes red. "I'm so sorry, Mom. He made me. I had to." Mimi turned her phone around to show them she was on FaceTime with David.

CHAPTER 38

"Hello, Lina," David said, a smug grin curling the sides of his thin lips. Lina immediately recognized the various framed degrees and civic accolades dotting the wall behind his desk at home. She rolled her eyes at his Volunteer of the Year Award for "exemplary character." He leaned back in his chair and clasped his hands behind his head, eyeing her.

What was he doing? Why had Mimi FaceTimed him and come to her room? She saw the raw hatred in Noah's eyes as he glared at the phone but she couldn't think of anything to say. Lina's skin crawled, sure she was going to be sick. How long had Mimi been outside her door? How could she ever face her daughter after this?

"Got some pretty interesting screenshots of you two, so unless you want me to release them online, we're going to have a little chat," David said.

Lina stumbled backward, careful not to trip on the sheet she'd wrapped around herself.

This wasn't supposed to be happening. She was supposed to be eating breakfast with Noah now, not being threatened and humiliated by David. Her fingers itched to reach for Noah, but an overwhelming shame hung over her like a heavy cloud when she took one look at Mimi.

Noah stood beside her, locking his fingers with hers. "What do you want?" he asked David, staring squarely into the phone's camera, his jaw tensing.

"I'd like to talk to my wife," David spat.

Lina nodded at Noah. "It's okay. Mimi."

Still in tears, Mimi handed her mom the phone. Lina motioned for her to come in and wanted to do nothing more than hug her sweet girl and tell her it was going to be okay, but Lina couldn't. She didn't know if it was going to be okay herself.

Lina held the phone in one hand and wrestled with the sheet in the other while Noah helped Mimi over to sit in a chair beside her mom. He went to the closet for the two robes, donning one of them, and brought the other to Lina, gently sliding it over her shoulders.

"What do you want, David?" Lina asked.

"I didn't believe Jules." He tittered. "I honestly didn't believe my sister when she said she saw your face on *TMZ* this morning. 'Mystery woman kissing Vengeance.' Looks like a lot more than kissing. Bet they'd pay a pretty penny for what I have. I mean, I'm seeing you two with my own eyes, and I still can't believe it."

"What do you mean *TMZ*?"

"Guess you've been busy . . ." David looked off. "How could you, Lina, after I've given you the world and more?"

"What do you want, David?"

"I want you to come back home."

"Are you serious?"

"Yes. I want you back home."

"No."

"Damn it, Lina. You make me do stuff like this. You think I like being this way with you? All you had to do was listen to me. I told you to shut down the site. I told you to stop all of this madness with the kids. I told you not to take them anywhere. I'm their father, not him."

"I'm not coming back. You need help."

That wiped the grin off his face. He sat up, his chair squeaking. "Look, I'm sorry about the other night. You just make me . . . you just make me so damn crazy, and I've been under a lot of stress. Come home, baby. I'll do better. I love you so much, and you're breaking my heart right now."

"No, David. I'm not coming back for more drama." She was starting to sound like a broken record.

He struck his desk, making his image wobble. "You're MY wife. MY wife. I can look past this. Everyone makes mistakes."

"It's not happening, David."

"I just said I'm willing to forgive you, for Christ's sake. I'll go to counseling. We can see Pastor Nathan for marriage counseling."

The thought of being condescended to by Pastor Nathan made Lina scoff. "You don't love me. Why do you want me home?"

David stood, his face reddening. "I DO love you."

"Just let me and the kids go. You can be with Daniella or whoever."

He bared his teeth. "I'll do whatever the hell I want with Daniella and anyone else. But I'll be damned if I let you take my kids and everything I've worked so hard for."

"Keep it all. I don't want anything from you. Just the kids."

David cackled. "You think you're all set because you had a one-night stand with Noah Attoh, don't you? What's going to happen when he moves on to someone hotter and younger? You'll come crawling back, trying to get spousal support, child support, everything else. I told you, you weren't anything more than someone's pity fuck. You're embarrassing yourself."

"There's the real David."

"What sob story did she tell you, Noah? I can call you Noah, right? I mean, now that you're screwing my wife and all?"

Noah sneered. "She told me enough."

"Bet she played the victim card, didn't she? Poor Lina, always a victim. Always painting everyone else as her villains instead of taking responsibility. She tell you how she lost my first son?"

"David, don't," Lina pleaded.

"She tell you how she refused to stop working even when doctors put her on bed rest?"

"That isn't fair, David. It was one meeting."

"You couldn't say no to one meeting? It was always one more meeting. One more email. One more conference call. Junior didn't have time for one more anything. You drove to the office and sat through meeting after meeting instead of going to the hospital."

How had she been expected to know the baby's movements were a cry for help? "I didn't realize I was in labor. I was only twenty-eight weeks along." Her voice cracked, remembering how tiny her baby had been when she'd pressed his pale face to her chest, praying for a miracle.

"How could you not have realized he was in distress? There was so much blood when I met you in the ER *at the end of the day*." He stood, narrowing his eyes at her. "The end of the fucking day. After you had to work."

"I didn't—"

"He was my son! You didn't want him anyway. You hated the idea of being pregnant."

David wasn't incorrect. She hadn't wanted to be pregnant. She'd felt trapped, all her choices taken away. But something had clicked in her head during her ultrasound. She'd wanted her son and had been devastated when she'd lost him.

Lina leveled her gaze at David and set her jaw. No way in hell was she going to allow him to tear her to pieces again. "You ever wonder if all the stress you put me through—the yelling, the crying, the cheating, the daily emotional roller coaster, the isolation, the drama—factored into why I went into labor at twenty-eight weeks or contributed to every miscarriage?"

"See, always the victim," he said. "You knew I wanted a big family. You chose your job over me, your mom over me, your friends over me, and now this website over me. Over our family."

"It's over, David."

"It's over when I say it's over." Spittle flew onto the camera. "You hear me? It's not over! You're not leaving me. You will never leave me. You will never take my kids away from me. I won't let you go." The vein in his forehead throbbed.

"Goodbye, David."

"You asked for it."

"You can't threaten me anymore."

"I didn't want to do this, but you're making me. If you're not home by the end of the day, I'm pressing kidnapping charges against you for taking my children out of the state without my permission."

"You can't do that."

"Like hell I can't. I've already reached out to Billings, and he witnessed me telling you not to take the kids during our domestic dispute."

Lina thought about all of Ashish's hard work going up in flames. She'd never get custody of Mimi and Danny with a kidnapping charge.

"You can't do that, David. I don't want to be with you. I want a divorce. You can't force me to stay."

"I'm not forcing you to do anything, but if you want to be with the kids, you'll come home and act like a grateful wife."

"You son of a—"

"Noah, I'd worry more about my reputation right now if I were you. Screwing around with a married woman. The mother of the kids you just endorsed, nonetheless. Not the best optics for you, my friend," David said a little too happily.

Lina shook her head, trying to stop David's words from worming their way back in. "I hate you."

"I'll take that. Come back and hate me in person. Don't think I won't make good on my threat. I've got Billings on speed dial. End of the day today."

Lina shook with rage as the screen blackened.

He'd won.

The bastard had won, and it was all her fault. All she'd had to do was take her flight back to Georgia after the *Today* show. She'd be at Nancy's by now with a chance of keeping her kids and getting out of her marriage. But no, she had to get distracted and lustful. Nausea clawed at her gut as her prison sentence hit her. She'd have to survive another three years with David if she was going to protect the kids—there was no way he'd believe they hadn't known about her and Noah the whole time and punish them for it. If he got custody, he'd take it out on them every single day. He'd make them suffer if he couldn't take it out on her. She opened her mouth to take in more air but couldn't. Her head spun and everything turned fuzzy.

Three years . . .

"Mom?" Mimi called, snatching Lina from her downward spiral.

Lina gasped, forcing herself to stay in the room and not drift off, imagining the hellscape awaiting her.

"Mom, I'm sorry. I didn't want to."

Lina held open her arms, and Mimi crashed into her chest, sobbing.

"I—I—I'm so sorry, Mom."

Lina stroked her hair. "It's not your fault. I'm so sorry you had to hear all that." Lina held her close.

Mimi's breath hitched. "He—he told me he'd make my life a living hell when I got back home if I didn't do it. He said it would be worse than the time he gave Aunt Jules my car." She sniffled. "I'm so sorry, Mom. I never meant to—"

"Mom? Meems?"

Lina glanced up to see Danny filling the hall doorway, his furry brows tightly knit as his gaze shifted from Lina to Noah to Lina to Noah and finally settling on Lina.

"Why don't you come over here and we'll talk?" Lina said.

Danny hesitated, shuffled a few steps, and hesitated again, looking from Noah to Lina. Understanding spread across his face, pinching his lips into thin lines and flaring his nostrils like an angry bull.

"Give me a second to explain everything."

Noah stood, reaching for him. "I never—"

"He was right," Danny said softly.

"Come here, Danny," Lina said.

Danny snarled at her. "It *is* all your fault!"

Lina recoiled.

Danny shook his head. "He treats you the way he does because you're with him." Danny pointed at Noah. "He treats us all like that because of you."

"It's not like that. Your dad—"

"You make Dad the way he is. He'd be nicer if you were a better person."

"No, Danny. He's—"

"He's right. He's been right this whole time. You don't care about our family. About Dad. About us. I hate you, Mom! I hate you!" Danny yelled and ran back into his room, slamming and locking the door.

CHAPTER 39

Noah returned minutes later, shaking his head. "He won't open his door."

"I'll talk to him. It's not your fault."

"It's not your fault either." He sighed heavily, taking a seat beside her on the sofa. He threaded his fingers with hers and brought them to his mouth. "I never meant for any of this to happen."

"I know; neither did I." Lina glanced at Mimi. "I'm sorry for not telling you about us sooner."

"I sort of figured it out a while ago. You were"—Mimi paused, seeming to taste her words—"happier after we visited his studio." Mimi sniffled, wiping her nose with the back of her hand. "And I saw you FaceTiming him that day in the kitchen. I'm okay with it."

"Are you sure?"

Mimi nodded. "I like him. I like that he likes you. You're not as tense as you are with Dad."

Noah's bottom lip trembled. "I love your mother very much, Mimi. We wanted you to find out differently."

Mimi tapped a few buttons on her phone and held it up, showing them a photo of the time Lina and Noah had kissed at the Rodgers Theatre. "It's out now."

Noah's phone vibrated until it fell off the side table.

"Better see who that is." Lina sighed, knowing she'd have to check her phone as soon as possible.

"You going to be all right for a few minutes?"

"Yeah."

He slowly released her hand and ducked into the bathroom to make his call.

"Hey, why don't you go to your room and get ready to go?" Lina said to Mimi.

Mimi hugged her. "Love you, Mom. I'm going to see if the housekeeper has any of those little soaps Danny likes; then I'll try to talk to him."

"Love you too. See you in a bit."

Room service was at the door when Lina opened it. Mimi slid past the rolling cart. The attendant blushed as Lina took the cart's handle and yanked it into her room. Had everyone found out about them by now?

The sweet, sticky smell of pancakes and syrup turned Lina's stomach. How could she even think about eating when her entire world was crashing down? Noah's voice rose from the bathroom. She couldn't make any of the words out, but she was pretty sure she'd just single-handedly ruined his career.

She pulled her robe tighter around her shoulders, wishing it was an invisibility cloak large enough for her and the kids to hide beneath.

I hate you, Mom.

Tears pricked her eyes as she thought about what Danny had said. None of the words sounded like anything he'd actually say; they sounded more like David. *He'd already started turning the kids against me. How long had he been manipulating them?*

Noah exited the bathroom, wearing the trousers and shirt he'd had on when he'd visited her last night. She was too embarrassed and afraid to look him in the eyes. She picked at her nails, waiting for him to leave and never want to see her again.

"Hey, I'm going—"

"I know." Lina tried her hardest not to break down.

Noah folded his arms across his chest and tilted his head slightly at her. "Do you?"

"Yeah. I think it's best anyway."

"Really?"

"It was fun." Her voice cracked. "You don't owe me an explanation."

He crossed the room. "Why do you do that?"

"Do what?"

"Shut down?" He closed the space between them and held her tenderly. "I'm not going anywhere, Lina. That was my manager. Told her to get ahead of this because you mean everything to me, and I can't lose you."

"David isn't going to stop."

"Neither are you. I know that with everything in me." He kissed her forehead. "I've got to run down to my room, but I'll be back in fifteen minutes or so. Hazel pushed up the flight, so we've got to be downstairs in thirty minutes."

"You're still flying back with us?"

"Of course. Pretty sure the lobby is teeming with reporters. Bet it'll be worse in Atlanta. I refuse to throw you to the wolves right now."

"This is really happening?"

"It is, but we'll get through it." Noah's phone rang. "It's Hazel; she's having some sunglasses and hats sent to your room. I'll be right back."

Sunglasses. Hats. Reporters. Kissing on *TMZ*. They'd really screwed things up, but sitting in her robe about to have a pity party wasn't going to help her out of this mess. She watched Noah leave and called Ashish. He picked up on the first ring.

"Please give me some good news," Lina said.

"Got in touch with Veres. She was apprehensive but very sympathetic to your situation. I'm working on her. We can't file for custody without concrete evidence of abuse."

"What about my arm?"

"How does the judge know you didn't do it to yourself? What if Noah Attoh did it to you?"

"You know?"

"Everyone does. How long has this been going on?"

Lina bit her lip. "Almost seven months."

"Oh, wow. Not going to lie, infidelity sure as hell doesn't help right now."

"David has had affairs throughout our marriage."

"Listen, Lina, none of that matters. Has David contacted you?" Ashish asked.

"Yes. He forced Mimi to FaceTime him while me and Noah were together. He took some screenshots and threatened to press kidnapping charges for taking the kids up here. Can he even do that?"

"Not really, but if he can convince a judge you're going to take them again, he might try to file an emergency injunction for custody. We definitely don't want that."

"He wants me to come back home. What should I do?" Lina asked, picking up her clothes.

"Hmmm. Bet there are a ton of paparazzi and news station crews heading to your house soon. He won't do anything to you while they're around; he's smarter than that. Let him think he's won. Can you give me a few weeks?"

A few weeks was definitely better than three years, but it was still a few weeks. Would she crack in that short amount of time? Would David hurt her or the kids again? "A few weeks?"

"Two weeks. Three weeks, max."

Two or three weeks, she could do. Three years, definitely not. Lina exhaled, closing her eyes. "I trust you."

"You'll have to. I'd better run. Play it up for the cameras and be super sweet to David. Make him think he's won."

"I'll try. Thanks, Ashish."

"You're welcome. Give Nancy a call; she's been freaking out all morning."

"Will do."

Lina's phone buzzed with a text message.

Mimi: Mom look!

Lina followed the text message link to a gossip website. A grainy screenshot of Noah in a white towel with Lina wrapping her arms around his waist was plastered on the home page with the caption:

VENGEANCE BROUGHT THE THUNDAH . . . BUSTED WITH MARRIED BAE

Bastard sent it anyway. Lina looked at the photo again, remembering the earth-shattering time she'd spent making love to Noah. It hadn't been planned. She'd actually wanted to wait a lot longer, but it just felt right. He felt right. Everything about him had felt right. A shiver rippled through her. While he may have felt right, it may not have been the right thing.

The faint tan line encircling her ring finger taunted her. Truth was she was married. Sure, she was working on divorcing David, but she was still married nonetheless. She sighed heavily, feeling like a trapped animal. Nervous energy and the desire for freedom surged through her, but she could move only two steps in every direction before hitting a wall in the dollhouse David had put her in. Her palms itched for a sledgehammer—something solid and fearless to destroy her prison.

She could almost see it striking the wall, cracking the drywall and tearing into the insulation, shredding the fluffy pink batting. Another strike and the thick wood beams would splinter and weaken. A few more strikes and the wood would break away. With the support beams out of the way, the brick and mortar would crumble, letting streaks of light into her cell. She wouldn't wait for the sledgehammer to work then; she'd kick and punch and push her way through until she was basking in the sunlight, surrounded by life.

Lina glanced back at the photo on her phone, wanting to bash David's head with a sledgehammer. Before she could close the screen, user comments populated the space below her photo:

> I'd do Vengeance and I'm married.

> She's such a ho.

> Skank.

> Doesn't he already have a baby mama? Not watching his crap movies no more.

> Why he gotta hook up with someone so ugly?

> Thought he was dating some model?

> She's cute. I'd do her.

> "You shall not commit adultery" Exodus 20:14.

> There are so many single ladies who'd want him to bring the thundah. Hell, I'm one of those. Hey, Noah Attoh, call me.

> Dang, he thick AF.

> They so messy.

They look so happy, why you guys hating on them so hard?

Dumbass, SHE'S MARRIED WITH 2 KIDS!!!

Wish them all the happiness. They look so cute together.

People don't need to be married anyway. Monogamy is something the government uses to control us.

You dumb.

Married or not, he'll get it whenever he wants. She looks like she could put it on a brotha, for real. Those quiet ones are like that.

Ew, he could do so much better.

Ask me how you can make up to $2500 a week working from home!

I thought he was into white chicks?

Lord, my ovaries cannot handle him shirtless.

I give them a Hollywood minute—2 weeks tops.

Hope it's worth it to give up your family for some man.

They both going to hell.

I wish them the best. They're super cute together.

Can't remember the last time I saw him with a chick. Thought he was gay.

Get it, honey! I ain't mad at her. I'd forget I was married too if he came along.

CHAPTER 40

It was as though the magic privacy bubble surrounding them burst the instant the elevator doors opened at the hotel lobby. Bright flashes of light went off in quick succession. Lina squinted and donned her sunglasses.

Security guards tried to manage the mob, but the throng of people pressed against the four of them, shouting questions and snapping photos. Danny was the first one to cry and duck under his mother's arms. Mimi quickly followed, tears heavy in her eyes. They'd both refused the hat and sunglasses from Noah, so Lina did her best to shield them from the reporters and paparazzi.

"How long have you been seeing each other?"

"Are you leaving your husband?"

"Smile for the camera, honey."

"What do the kids think?"

"Noah, was this what prompted you to endorse the kids' site?"

"What happens now?"

"Is that a baby bump?"

"Is it true your husband wants to reconcile?"

"Noah, what about your baby mama? Aren't you still with her?"

Holding the kids close to her chest, Lina dipped her head and followed Noah to the SUV waiting at the curb. She climbed in, sitting between the kids. Mimi and Danny clung to her like terrified cubs. This was really happening.

"It's going to be okay," she lied, stroking their heads. It was not going to be okay. Nothing would ever be the same for any of them. By the time the driver turned the corner, Lina glanced up to catch the terror and sadness in Noah's eyes, confident they mirrored her very own.

What had they done?

Why hadn't she just returned to Georgia immediately after the show?

Why hadn't she said no to dinner with him so many months ago?

But that wouldn't have made her feel any better. Meeting Noah and being with him had taught her so much about herself. Allowing him to love her and reciprocate that love to him opened doors that had been closed to her for so long. She wasn't just a submissive wife and mom when she was with him; she was a capable, sensual woman with emotions and desires and feelings. She was so much more.

Her phone buzzed.

David: Still with him, I see.

David: I don't want my kids around him.

David: They are MY KIDS. Not his.

David: Be grateful when you come back to my house.

Lina clenched her teeth so hard they hurt. She'd barely survive the next few weeks with David's mind games and insults, but she had to go through with it to keep her kids. She was a knotted rope with the kids on one end and Noah at the other.

~

Her first private jet ride should've been an awe-inspiring experience. She should've put up her feet and relaxed in the supple leather seats. The kids should've enjoyed their fill of the rich, gourmet dishes flight attendants served with white-glove attention. They should've all rested comfortably as the jet sliced through the clouds from New York to

Atlanta . . . but after David's morning surprise and being swarmed by paparazzi at the hotel, reality had set in, and it wasn't pretty.

Reality was: nothing Lina or her kids did would ever be private again.

Reality was: her marriage and life were being picked apart with a fine-tooth comb.

Reality was: Mimi and Danny's website's success would be scrutinized.

Reality was: this scandal could ruin Noah's career.

Reality was: Lina wasn't sure their new relationship could withstand the pressure cooker.

Despite having ample seating in the jet, Mimi, Danny, and Lina huddled at the rear of the plane, while Noah sat alone near the cockpit in the seats facing them. She hadn't said more than a handful of words to him since the hotel hours earlier. How could she? What was there to say? *Thanks for the amazing sex; it should last me another three years or so if my attorney can't get me the hell out of my marriage. Noah, please don't hate me for ruining your stellar reputation. Um, so . . . how are you doing besides having to deal with my psychotic husband? Noah, remember when you said you had me? Well, what do you think now?*

Her stomach took a massive nosedive when the plane descended toward Atlanta. *Please hurry, Ashish,* she prayed and braced herself for whatever games David had planned.

"Um, Mom," Mimi said, yawning from her catnap. She held out her cell phone, motioning toward Noah. "You might want to show him this."

What is it now? Lina sighed, holding Mimi's phone to see Mariana's unnaturally perfect face on the screen.

"Lina?" Noah asked from across the plane. "Everything okay?"

Lina shook her head, feeling bile rise. She'd not only jeopardized getting custody of her children, but she'd totally screwed up Noah's chances of getting Edward now. She glanced back at Mariana's face and saw the caption beneath the video: **Vengeance's Girl Breaks Her Silence**. *Ugh.* Lina unbuckled her seat belt and went over to the empty seat beside Noah.

"That bad?"

"Didn't think it could get any worse." She held up the phone to show him the video. "I was wrong."

Noah bit the insides of his cheeks as the video buffered, then played.

"We were engaged for a while," Mariana said to the reporter. "He broke it off when he found out I was pregnant. Sure, he supports us, but he's never there for our son. I mean, look at him. He's with her and her kids all the time. My poor baby is an afterthought. We were working on getting back together to be a family and whatnot, but then I showed up at his place, and she was there."

"How long ago was that?"

"Few months ago. She was so nasty toward me and my son. I'm so heartbroken over this. I just wanted us to be a family." Mariana sobbed into a tissue.

Lina's mouth dropped open.

Noah leaned forward, resting his head in his hands. "I can't believe she did this," he whispered through clenched teeth.

"Think I'm going to be sick." Lina closed her eyes, pinching the bridge of her nose. What was she supposed to say about Mariana's accusations? How could she salvage anything after that nuclear bomb? None of it was true, but that didn't matter. Noah's squeaky-clean image was now sullied. He'd abandoned his son to be with another woman, and Lina was a home-wrecker. That was how the media would portray them from now on.

"I can't lose Edward."

His declaration made the hairs on her arms stand to attention. Was he putting all the blame on her? "I know. I can't lose Mimi and Danny."

"I've done everything these last few years to be better than my father, and she goes and . . . and pulls this stunt."

"You are a great father, Noah."

He shook his head. "A great father would've put his kid first. I shouldn't have—" He pulled his lips between his teeth, his eyes glistening with pain.

He shouldn't have been with her. Lina knew what he meant. She'd felt the same regret. The beige leather squeaked when she leaned back in the seat and sighed.

The jet shook slightly as it touched down on the runway with a bump. That was it, then. Vacation from reality was over. Their time together was coming to a close. The memory of the love they'd made would eventually fade. It would be like trying to remember a dream after waking, fuzzy bits and pieces here and there until her imagination filled in the holes with lies. That was what the last seven months felt like to Lina as the plane rolled to a stop—a dream. Noah Attoh had loved her and she'd loved him. That was what she'd hold on to if she had to survive another three years with David.

Tears pricked the back of Lina's eyes when she felt Noah's palm warm her back. She'd come to adore that gesture from him.

"Can you give me a few minutes before you leave?" he asked softly as flight attendants opened the door and fussed over the kids and their bags.

Lina sniffled. "Sure."

Noah stood as a wiry flight attendant strode past. "Justin, did we get the hangar?"

"Sure did, Mr. Attoh. The two cars you requested are waiting as well."

"Perfect. They're in the Explorer. Can you help them settle in and give us some time?"

Danny grumbled, glaring at his mom. He snatched his bag from Justin and shoved past Noah to exit the plane.

"Mom, you okay?" Mimi asked, fastening her purse.

"Yeah, honey. Go ahead with Justin. I'll join you in a bit."

"Um, okay." Mimi hiked her purse higher on her shoulder. "Well, thanks for everything, Mr. Attoh." She held out her hand.

"Thank you, Mimi. And if it's okay with your mom, please call me Noah."

"It's fine," Lina said.

"Um, well, thanks, Noah." Mimi smiled. "I'll go talk to Danny. Take your time."

Lina stood and handed Mimi back her phone. "You've got a ton of messages. I won't be long."

Noah waited until they were alone, then sat back down and reached for her hand. He kissed where their fingers met. "For the first time here, I'm not sure what we should do."

It hurt so damn much Lina wasn't sure she'd be able to speak. She cleared her throat, feeling tears rush back to close it. "Me neither. Mariana made a pretty compelling argument."

"She's lying."

"Doesn't matter. You're about to go through a nasty custody battle for Edward and a smear campaign. This is the last thing either of us need."

He glanced down at their entwined hands. "This is what we need."

Lina shook her head and peeled her hand from his. "It doesn't work like that. We're not in one of your movies where everything works out at the end. This is real, with real consequences. Look at what David said. I have to go home to him until my attorney can find a loophole. You were there. You heard everything. I can't lose Mimi and Danny, and you can't lose Edward because of this."

His Adam's apple bobbed as he swallowed. "So that's it then?"

Lina stood, afraid if she stayed near Noah any longer she'd change her mind. "It's all I've got." She ran her hand over his head lovingly. "It's all we've got."

Noah pulled her to him, burying his face in her chest. "I love you, Lina." His breath hitched after a few moments. "That will never change."

"I know." She kissed the top of his head and slowly separated herself from him. "I'd better go." She forced her legs to take one step, then another, and another until she was near the door.

CHAPTER 41

There had been a news report a few years back chronicling the emotional toll soldiers suffer when returning to war zones. While the stress and terror was familiar as a recurring nightmare, there was also the unexplained excitement that accompanied returning to a familiar place. Lina felt it now. The bundle of nerves in her stomach knotted as the driver rounded the corner and turned into her gated neighborhood. The kids shifted nervously, probably feeling the same apprehension and anticipation. What was David planning for them all? What new ways would he find to torment her and belittle the kids?

Lina's phone buzzed.

Noah: Call me.

Noah: I was wrong. We can fight this together.

Noah: You don't have to go back to him.

Noah: Please don't go back.

She blocked his number and turned off her phone before receiving another message. It was too painful to hope for a future with him. Even if she won against David and got full custody of her children, even if his career was okay and he won custody of Edward, they'd never be able to pick up and move on from this public shaming. She and Noah would be hounded and harassed about her infidelity and Mariana's accusations. Noah had to finally face it: their beautiful seedling of a relationship had been plucked before it had the chance to grow roots and bloom into something beautiful. Lina's chest hurt at the realization. It was really over.

"Ohmigod," Mimi whispered, gazing through the dark-tinted windows.

"Damn," Lina muttered as the crowd of people swarmed their SUV. Reporters held microphones at the ready. Paparazzi aimed their cameras at the windows, preparing for the perfect shot. Neighbors gathered along the street with their cell phones out; some were even talking to reporters. The driver slowly eased through the mass of people and stopped in Lina's driveway.

"Why isn't Daddy opening the garage door for us?" Danny asked, gripping his backpack tightly.

Because he wanted her to suffer as much public humiliation as possible. "I'm not quite sure. I don't want you guys out in all this."

Mimi pointed at the front door. "Look, there he is."

"What is he—" Lina knew all too well what he was doing.

He wore dark-gray trousers, a white button-down shirt with his sleeves rolled up to the elbows, and one of the blue ties the kids had given him for Christmas the year before. David ran toward the vehicle with a cheesy smile on his face. He opened the door and helped the kids out one by one, hugging them with big, excited motions. Not wanting to be part of the fake circus, Lina scooted away from the open door.

David ducked his head into the car. "My firm has rallied around me over this. The free PR alone has made me invaluable, so don't even think about it."

"Mr. Henry, how do you feel about your wife and Noah Attoh?" someone shouted.

"I've got Billings on speed dial. Play nice, and get your ass over here." He held his hand out to Lina, helping her out of the back seat, and plastered a somber look on his long face. Holding Lina around her waist, he said, "The last twenty-four hours have been very difficult, but we're choosing to do what's best for our children. If anything, this has taught me that I need to be more present for my beautiful wife." He kissed her forehead.

She shuddered.

"We are committed to repairing our marriage."

Lina was 1,000 percent sure she'd vomit all over his polished shoes. He'd never been committed to their family.

"Mrs. Henry, is there anything you'd like to say to Mr. Attoh?" someone else asked.

"Not sure what you mean by that."

"You and Mr. Attoh were seen together this morning."

"I think I left my scarlet letter in the car. Would you get higher ratings if I wore it?" Lina cringed as David's fingers dug into her side and he leaned in close. "Noah had nothing to do with all this. I told him I was separated when we initially met." She remembered how comforting and safe Noah's warm palm had felt on the small of her back at *The Sophia Show* so many months ago. Something deep within her broke. Her knees buckled, and within seconds Lina's eyes were watery traitors.

"Are you planning on seeing him again?" the same reporter asked.

"No." Her voice cracked. "He didn't know I was married."

"I'm sorry; my family has been through a lot today. That's all for now," David said and ushered her to the house, stroking her hair, bearing her weight, and holding her tenderly. He was the model of a caring husband. As soon as they were inside and the door was locked, he shoved her away. She almost fell to the floor.

Scowling, he shook his head. "Can't believe you're standing up for him. You better get on Team Henry or everything I have will be released online. You hear me? This is not about you anymore. My firm is going to make me partner over this. Partner." He clapped. "I should've pimped you out years ago."

Lina wiped her eyes. "I can't stand you."

He stalked up to her, his shadow long from the sunset peeking through the thick plantation shutters in their formal dining room. "You don't have to like me, but you will respect me from now on if you want to be with the kids."

"You bastard." She struck at his chest with all her strength and immediately hated herself. Now David was turning her into a version of himself—using rage and violence instead of words like an adult.

He caught her arm with a twisted curling of his lips and squeezed until she whimpered in pain. "That's not showing me respect." With his other hand, he took out his phone. "Hey, Siri," he said, staring at Lina. "Call Billings."

"Hey, David!" Billings said through the speakerphone after the first ring. "Was just heading your way. Everything all right?"

"Everything is good on my end. Wanted to remind you to send over your sister's phone number—the one who's the county family court magistrate." David punctuated each word with a sickly smile directed at Lina.

"She gave me a business card for you with her personal contact information. Said something about an injunction."

"Yeah. I'd like to make sure she's on the same page just in case I've got to file an emergency injunction for custody with all of this craziness. You remember how worried I was when I got home last night and didn't know where my children were."

Lina snatched her arm from him, wanting to hit him again but knowing that wasn't right, no matter how much she hated him. She refused to sink to his level. She had to stick to her plan and pray like hell Ashish knew what he was up against. Shaking her head at David, she tamped down the building rage and went to the living room to check up on the kids.

"Hey, where's Meems?"

"Room," Danny said without looking up from his phone as he sat cross-legged on the sofa.

"Oh, okay. Can I get you anything?"

Danny gave her no response.

"Danny, do you want anything?" she asked again, but he was silent.

"Hey, Dad," Danny said when his father entered the living room. "Did you catch our segment on the *Today* show the other day?"

"Why would I?"

Danny bit his lip. "Um . . ."

"And I need everything for that little site of yours gone. Party is over and I mean it." David struck the back of the sofa where Danny sat.

"But me and Mimi worked really hard on it. Please? Can we keep it?"

Lina's heart broke for Danny.

He gave the boy a swift cuff to his head. "What did I say?"

"C'mon, David. You made your point. Don't take it away from the kids," Lina said.

"Danny, look at me, son." His hands were on his hips as he stood over the boy. "Your mother should've never let you get your hopes up. Your site is shit; everyone knows it. Turns out your mother screwed a lot of people to get you on all of those shows."

"Jesus, David, I'm not doing this craziness with you. I may be here, but I will not let you do this," Lina said, putting herself between him and Danny. "Deleting the site wasn't part of the deal. I'm here. You've got me. I'm trapped with you until whenever. It's my prison sentence for trying to be happy for once in the last eighteen years of this miserable marriage."

"The site goes if I say it does. This is my house. You are my wife. They are my kids."

Lina sighed heavily. "Danny, go to your room and delete everything from the server."

"But Mom—"

"Just go, honey. Everything is on the Weasley server. Please delete it all." Lina waited a beat until Danny's brows relaxed when he recognized the name they'd given the test server. She winked at him when David wasn't looking. *Play along.*

"Okay, Mom." Danny shot her a puppy dog look. He frowned at his father before heading upstairs to his room.

"About damn time you back me up. This house could use some order for once."

The doorbell sounded, echoing throughout the house.

David clapped. "Perfect timing. That should be Billings to check on everything."

"I'm going to bed," Lina said.

"You'll go when I say so. Wait here for Billings." David sprinted to the door and returned to the living room minutes later with the officer. Lina rolled her eyes.

"Evening, Mrs. Henry," Billings said, hooking his thumbs through his belt loops.

Lina bared her teeth, wanting to curse him out for being such a self-serving person. David crossed the room, draped his arm across her shoulders.

"Thanks for stopping by, Billings," David said. "How's the boat? Had a chance to take her out yet?"

"Not yet, was planning to take the family out this weekend when I'm off."

"It's supposed to be a beautiful weekend for it."

"Good to see you, Mrs. Henry. Glad you guys are working it out. Y'all have such a beautiful family, and the Lord is all about reconciliation . . . and forgiveness."

"I've got a migraine; I'm heading to bed," Lina mumbled and shuffled toward the guest room.

"Okay, then, hope you feel better."

"I'll check on you in a bit, honey," David called and picked up the conversation with Billings about the damn boat.

Was this going to be her life for the next few weeks or even years? She closed and locked the guest bedroom door behind herself in time to hear laughter rising from the living room. Billings's guttural hee-haw rose above David's glib I'm-better-than-you-but-you're-too-dumb-to-recognize snigger. Lina leaned against the door and closed her eyes. Hate was too kind a word for them.

She slid down the door and sat on the double-padded carpet. Maybe wherever she landed after all this craziness would be as soft. She couldn't get over how much control she'd ceded to David over the years. No money. No credit. She had nothing to show from the last eighteen years besides Mimi and Danny and buckets of tears.

How had she dealt with David for so long?

Turning her phone back on, Lina decided to reach out to Ashish. As soon as it powered on, her phone buzzed with several messages.

Nancy: I saw. I'm here for you. Call me when you're ready. Love you, girl.

Nancy: Good one. I just bought you a scarlet letter.

Nancy: I know some people. Some unscrupulous people, if you KWIM.

Nancy: I'm your alibi. Xoxoxo

Ashish: Play the role. I'm trying my hardest to get Veres to come around.

Ashish: She's very loyal to her job.

Ashish: Call Nancy, she's worried.

Mimi: Went to bed. Needed some time alone.

Mimi: I love you, Mom. I don't want you to be sad again.

Mimi: I'll talk to Danny tonight.

Danny: Thanks, Mom.

Danny: I don't hate you.

Celeste: Hi honey, it's Mom.

Celeste: Why didn't you tell me when we last spoke?

Celeste: Is the Noah Attoh thing true?

Celeste: You know it won't last, so get everything you can.

Celeste: David is an asshole. He's always been one. But look at how you live. You don't want to risk your stability. Remember what it was like for us when you were younger?

Celeste: Go and apologize. Make it up to him.

Celeste: I can come watch the kids if you 2 need to get away.

Celeste: Love and light.

Lina frowned at her mother's message and remembered her mother's one motivation: money. It was all about money with her.

He's going to take good care of you; don't let him get away.

It was just one time, Lina. He won't cheat on you again.

Look at the Tiffany necklace David bought for me when he was in town. He's such a sweetheart.

I don't see a mark.

It wasn't that hard. Stop being so dramatic.

Tell your husband I owe him a home-cooked dinner next time he's up here for business. It's all I can do for the car, but it'll be from my heart.

Go easy on him; you're the one who lost the baby. Not like he was carrying it.

Forgive him. I'm sure he didn't mean anything by it.

Is it worth losing everything you have? Don't be so melodramatic.

CHAPTER 42

Lina turned her phone back off, not wanting to respond to anyone. Sitting in silence was all she needed. Sometime later, she realized how quiet the house had gotten. She listened closer. David had probably had enough of Billings and wrapped up his visit. Relieved, she rose to check on the kids.

The door squealed when she opened it slightly to peek out into the living room. It was empty and dark. She flipped on a light on her way to the kitchen to make a few sandwiches and snacks to take upstairs for the kids. Gathering everything from the fridge, she closed it with her foot and flinched, dropping the deli meat when she saw David standing on the other side.

"I don't want sandwiches for dinner," he said.

"Good, these aren't for you."

David glanced down at his phone. "Let's see; Billings's sister never got married, so her last name would naturally be Billings. But what did I save it under?"

"Cut it out, David. You're as pathetic as the kid who pays people to be their friend." She couldn't believe he was having fun at her expense. "I don't love you. I will never want to be with you."

"But you'll do anything for the kids."

"What sick game are you playing here?" She slammed everything on the counter and spun around to him. "Tell me so at least I know what I'm up against."

"Game? You cheated on me."

Lina scoffed. "You've had so many affairs; I'm not stupid. You're probably screwing around with Daniella. Let's be honest here; you can't deal with the fact that I was happy for once."

David crossed his arms as if she was amusing him.

"Your little male ego is offended. Want a Band-Aid for your owie?" she said in a singsong. "Come to think of it, you're so butt hurt because you know I really cared for him. Because I gave myself to him in ways you'd only imagine. Do you want me to describe how my body reacted to him when he—"

He slapped her so hard she almost fell. Her cheek stung like it'd been bitten by a thousand angry fire ants. Lina ran her tongue across her teeth and tasted pennies. Something feral in her rose up, ready to claw his eyeballs out.

Murder or divorce.

Slowly, she regained her footing. She wiped her mouth with the sleeve of her shirt. "Did that make you feel like a man?" She glared at him. "Get the other side so they match for the cameras outside, you coward."

"You make me like this."

"No I don't. You're like this because you choose to be."

"But you—"

"Stop making excuses for being an abusive pig, David. Blame it on your father, your mother, anyone else, except for me."

David grabbed her arms. "You watch your mouth before I—" They both froze at the sudden commotion from outside. He knit his brows at her.

"Another one of your guests? Let me guess—another police officer? Or maybe the magistrate herself?" Lina shrugged away from him.

He grimaced. "Wasn't expecting anyone else tonight."

The noise grew, and the camera flashes brightened the dark front side of the house. Who was paying them a visit at this time of the night? Lina started toward the door, David following her.

"Let me get it," he said, shoving her aside and opening the door.

Lina blinked.

David clucked. "Unbelievable."

"Noah?" she whispered, shielding her eyes from the blinding camera lights that flashed and glared brightly. What was he doing here? Did he know how awful this looked? Did he even think about how his visit would further damage his reputation? What would David do to her because of this?

David held her back. "Gotta give it to you. You've got some major balls coming here like this."

Noah glanced at Lina and took a few steps toward her. "Are you okay?"

David pushed Noah's chest. "The hell you think you're doing?"

"I need to see Lina." Noah squared his shoulders.

David took a step closer to him, pushing him backward this time. Noah pushed him back so hard he slammed into the doorframe. The sound of camera shutters clicking was all Lina heard as she scrambled to stop them.

"Cut it out already." She held David's arm before he could throw a punch. "What would your firm say about this? Look at the cameras."

David was like a bull about to charge. She'd seen him like that before: spine hunched, body tight.

"Imagine how great you'd look if you shook his hand and let him in the house. People are watching." Lina's voice was barely above a whisper now. "Your firm will be watching."

The tension in David's shoulders slowly released.

"Shake his hand and smile, because that is what a partner would do in this situation." Lina was unable to keep her eyes off Noah as he gaped at her. "Noah, offer your hand and smile at him. You're an actor, for Christ's sake."

Noah stuck out his hand and mechanically shook David's.

"Can both of you smile and get in the damn house, please?" Lina sighed. Both men followed her directions, faking smiles and entering the house cordially.

"What are you doing here, Noah?" Lina asked when David shut the door.

"I needed to see you."

"You see her. Now go." David drew himself up to Noah's height. He went over to Lina and draped his arm around her shoulders.

She couldn't break the invisible strand connecting her to Noah. He was really there, in her house, still wanting to be with her despite all the drama. "David, can you just give us a few minutes?"

"Hell no."

"Either you go somewhere and let me talk to him in private, or I will walk straight out that door and let all of those reporters see the bruise that's forming on my cheek."

Noah curled his lips in a vicious sneer at David.

Lina shrugged David's arm from her shoulders and started toward the door.

"Fine," David said after a moment. "I need a drink anyway."

"Noah, why did you come here?" Lina asked when David was out of earshot. The way he looked at her made every cell tingle. She wanted to touch him to make sure he was real.

He caressed her cheek with the slightest touch, his eyes glistening.

"It's not as bad as it looks," Lina said, leaning into his warm hand. "Lina."

She eventually rested her forehead against his, sharing his breath, his worries, his desires, his dreams, his love. "Noah."

They stood like that for a long while until Noah said, "Please leave with me. A part of me is dying knowing that you're here with him."

"You know I can't do that without Mimi and Danny. Ashish is so close to gathering everything for the courts."

"Let me help you fight him. I'll hire the best lawyers I can."

"I can't let you do that."

Noah straightened, his eyes murky pools. "What can I do?"

"You have to trust me." She made a pocket of space between them. He reached for her hand, sighing. "I trust you."

"Promise me you'll fight like hell to get custody of Edward."

"I promise."

"And promise me you won't ruin your career on my account. You've come so far."

Noah's bottom lip trembled. He swallowed. "Why does this feel like goodbye?"

Because it is. She couldn't meet his eyes. "I'm . . . I'm not sure." The dam of tears broke in Lina's eyes then. With it came the most excruciating, soul-rending pain she'd ever experienced. "You'd better go."

He seemed to understand her internal torture, judging by his own pained expression.

CHAPTER 43

For the first time since painting Mimi's room, Lina was grateful her daughter had picked a dark color. The rich charcoal walls matched her mood perfectly. With the shades tightly drawn, she was able to block out the entire world beneath Mimi's weighted comforter.

The house was a hollow shell without the kids.

Lina had made the mistake of downing several glasses of David's bourbon with her Xanax and an Ambien—one to make her temporarily forget her misery, the other to make her sleep—after she'd broken it off with Noah. By the time she'd woken late the next day, David and the kids were gone.

He'd taken them to a sleepaway camp in Tennessee. It'd been her punishment, his way of reminding her that he was still in control. He'd taunted her the first few days afterward by refusing to tell her where he'd taken the kids. He'd even suggested sending Mimi and Danny to boarding school in the fall to keep them away from her.

If losing Noah had broken her, losing contact with her children destroyed what was left. Without Mimi's knowing smile and Danny's warm hugs, she felt like she wasn't anchored to herself anymore. She was floating aimlessly in a sorrow-filled void.

With the covers secure over her head, she rolled to her side, wincing. Days of sobbing had left her raw and tender everywhere. David had succeeded in putting her back into her dollhouse. Her cage. Her prison. He had total control once again, and she'd wept for the Lina she'd become these last few months. The living, breathing, multidimensional, competent woman she'd rediscovered was going to soon be replaced by a smiling, empty paper doll.

She'd reclaimed so much of herself to have it all snatched away like a thief in the night.

I love you no matter what happens. Noah's voice whispered from the pillow, and a fresh wave of tears rolled over her. She grasped whatever was solid, grabbing handfuls of the pillow, bringing it as close to her chest as possible. Shuddering, the tears fell, dotting the pillowcase with wet spots. They'd both given each other pieces of themselves and were now left with open, gaping wounds. When would she ever recover from losing him?

Lina stilled as the doorbell rang. *Someone else for David,* she thought, remembering the stream of visitors David had received over the past week. They'd been difficult to ignore since Mimi's room was at the front of the house. There were his coworkers who came to console him, a few HR people with paperwork to make his partnership official, pastors to pray with him and over her, and some prayer-team people who stood outside Mimi's bedroom door and offered prayers on behalf of Lina when she'd refused to unlock the door.

She buried her head in the pillow as the doorbell rang again. *Just go away, already.*

David's footsteps thumped against the hardwood floors to the front door. Several clicks and a squeal later, David's muffled voice sounded. "Oh, what do you want?"

"Play nice for the cameras, David."

Lina's eyes opened wide at Nancy's voice. *Ugh.* She'd forgotten to text her after Noah had left.

"Lina isn't available," David said.

"I'll determine that."

"Okay, enough with the niceties. I don't want you in my home."

"Oh, so we're finally being honest with each other? I don't want you to put another hand on my friend. Let me in now, or I will go directly to those cameras and tell them everything I know about the poor husband whose wife couldn't resist Noah Attoh's prowess. Come to think of it, I'm sure I have some photos of her bruises somewhere on my phone."

Lina held her breath, waiting to hear more of the conversation below.

"Bitch."

"Asshole."

The door closed, and now there were two sets of footsteps in the house. Lina wasn't sure why, but her eyes watered at the thought of seeing Nancy.

"She's upstairs in Mimi's room," David said.

"Where are the kids?"

"Camp. I'm going back to work. Make it fast. I'm expecting to finalize some paperwork today."

"I'll take as long as I want," Nancy said, her bangles jangling against the stair's handrail. Moments later, Mimi's room filled with floral and citrus scents as Nancy entered the room and plopped on the bed beside Lina. She peeled back the covers.

"You look like hell," Nancy said.

Lina was crying again now. "It hurts so much, Nance."

"Oh, honey." Nancy curled up beside her friend and held her. "Let it out. I'm here." She stroked hair from Lina's face as ragged sobs eventually gave way to hitched breaths for what felt like hours.

The doorbell rang again, and David darted to the door. He spoke excitedly about finally being a partner and how honored he was to fully contribute to the firm in such a capacity. Lina rolled her eyes. He'd won and she'd lost everything. How was any of this even possible?

"He's gonna get everything he deserves one day," Nancy muttered. "Have you spoken to Ashish?"

Lina shook her head.

"You really should talk to him. He's finally gotten through to that female officer. She's supposed to do a deposition on your behalf soon."

"Really?" Lina was hoarse, her throat dry like the desert. It was too much to hope for.

"Yes. Ashish is amazing, which is why you can't hide from the world right now. I know what it's like to lose someone you love, but you're so close to getting out of this shitty situation."

"It's all too much, Nance. I had so much hope for a different life for me and the kids. And Noah—" Lina felt her throat begin to close.

"Come here." Nancy held her friend tighter. "I'm sure he's hurting too."

Lina sniffled. "And the kids are gone, and David won't add me as a guardian to pick them up."

"It's probably for the best that they're gone. You don't want them in the middle of all this."

"I lost everything and it's all my fault."

"Don't do that to yourself. Seriously, don't. You have no idea what'll happen months or even years from now. You remember junior year when I dated that frat boy, Hudson, and he'd gotten all serious and started talking about marriage?" Nancy nudged her. "Remember when I thought I actually wanted to be with him like that? How I'd started planning a life with him, and I even met his parents in Rhode Island over summer break?"

Lina remembered, all right. Nancy had been crazy in love with Hudson. He'd treated her like a princess, spoiled her with all his attention, indulged her. Lina'd been shocked when Nancy had returned from Rhode Island with an engagement ring. Hudson had wanted to marry shortly after they'd graduated. Everything had seemed so perfect until Nancy had asked him to push the wedding off until she finished her master's degree.

Hudson wouldn't hear it because his mother had already started the wedding planning at their country club, so Nancy had broken it off right before the start of their senior year, hoping to show him how serious she'd been. Hudson's family had been so offended at her slight, and since his father had been both a trustee and a powerful alumni, all Nancy's scholarships had been revoked.

"What did you say to me?" Nancy asked. "What did you say when I thought my life was ruined?"

Lina sighed, remembering exactly what she'd said.

"You told me everything would work out. You said he'd get what he deserves in the end, right?" Nancy nudged her shoulder a little harder this time. "What happened a month before graduation?"

A small grin cracked Lina's lips.

"Hudson's father had been indicted on federal racketeering charges, and poor Hudson got expelled after that hazing incident where those drunk frat boys almost drowned in Herty Fountain after they poured bottles of dish liquid in it." Nancy snickered. "It all worked out. You literally dragged me out of my bed and forced me into a cold shower when I thought I'd lost. You want me to do that?"

She hated her friend sometimes.

Nancy sniffed her hair. "By the way, a shower wouldn't be a bad idea." She moved to get out of the bed. "How long have you been in this bed?"

"Not sure."

"Have you been here since Noah visited?"

Lina nodded.

"That was five days ago, Lina. Five days. Have you eaten anything?"

Lina pointed at the small mountain of chocolate wrappers and empty potato chip bags on the nightstand.

"Salty and sweet. Major food groups covered, but have you eaten any actual food?"

Lina shook her head.

Nancy jerked back the covers. "Get up and take a shower, and then we're going to get some food. Real food. Maybe even a few drinks."

"I can't."

"Why the hell not?"

"All of the cameras and reporters. I—I just can't right now."

"You can and you will. This isn't going to break the Lina I know. Besides, I brought your scarlet letter." Nancy stuck out her tongue, her nose scrunching.

Lina knew Nance was right. She knew it in her head, but her heart wanted to lie in the dark beneath the thick comforter until it withered away. She imagined the openmouthed gawking she'd get if she actually wore a scarlet letter in public. It couldn't be any more obnoxious than how people were going to react to her anyway, now that her secret relationship with Noah Attoh was public knowledge.

Nancy helped her sit up. "Have you checked your email since you sent out the sponsorship packages?"

Lina stretched, feeling pins and needles prick her everywhere. "Not yet."

"Where's your laptop?"

"David broke it."

Nancy twisted her mouth to the side. "Danny's?"

Lina shrugged. "Probably in his room. David didn't let them take any technology to camp. He demanded the kids delete everything for the site."

Nancy stood, straightening her maxi dress. "Get up. Go shower. I'm going to try to find Danny's laptop." She looked at her watch. "You've got twenty minutes or I'm coming to drag you out of the shower." Nancy adjusted her cleavage in Mimi's mirror. "Pity party's over, sister. Time to get to work."

~

Lina returned to Mimi's bedroom to find Nancy hovered over Danny's laptop, worrying her lip.

"Able to get in?" Lina asked, the images of her and Noah flitting from her head. She really had to pull it together. Nancy was right: it wasn't over for her yet.

Nancy looked her up and down. "Own anything other than pajamas, woman?"

Lina shoved her hands deep into the flowered pajama bottoms, feeling the soft microfiber against her skin. "They get me on a spiritual level. Don't judge."

"I'm judging. I am so judging you right now, but I'll let it go because I just ordered us some food"—she tapped several keys on Danny's laptop—"and I'm in." Nancy donned her reading glasses, adjusting them on her thin nose. She leaned closer to the laptop screen. "Holy shit, Lina," she said after several moments.

"What? What is it?" Lina hurried to Nancy's side. Her mouth dropped to the floor when she saw all the email replies to the sponsorship package proposals she'd sent out.

"I cannot believe you were having a pity party, and these were sitting in your in-box," Nancy said. "I'm going to forgive you only because I totally understand how you feel, but I'm also going to shake you if you don't start sifting through these offers. You're about to have a bidding war." Nancy giggled. "A freaking bidding war and you were lying in bed."

Lina counted eleven offers from major companies like Nike, Under Armour, Reebok, and a few drug companies she hadn't even pitched. "This is happening, Nance," Lina said.

"It is! I've already set up the company legally so David can't get anything." Nancy faced the laptop in Lina's direction. "Do your thing. I'm going to get us food . . . and wine. We need wine. We need all the wine tonight."

"Thanks, Nance."

Nancy pecked a kiss on Lina's forehead. "I love you, girl. I'm so proud of you. You did this; you realize that?"

"Yeah." Lina nodded, her eyes wide in amazement at how much her life was about to change. "I'm beginning to realize it."

She worked over the next few hours, reading over contracts, creating counteroffers, checking site stats. Nancy returned with wine and food sometime later. Lina picked over dinner, still deep in concentration, the satisfied hum of working fueling her.

She could survive without David. She knew this without a trace of doubt now. She was talented and capable—that had been what had attracted David and also validated his insecurity. He'd tried so hard to discourage this part of her. He'd almost succeeded.

She glanced over at Nancy, who was now fast asleep in Mimi's bed, and remembered to contact Ashish. She sent him a quick text message. He replied immediately.

Ashish: Nancy told me about your offers. Congratulations!

Lina: Thanks.

Ashish: Send me any contracts if you need a legal eye.

Lina: Will do. Waiting for a few more offers to come in.

Ashish: Do you feel safe?

Lina: Yes. We still have a yard full of cameras.

Ashish: There's a rumor Noah visited.

Lina: Nancy told me he was spotted with his son at a resort in Kenya.

Ashish: I imagine he needed to get out of crazy town.

Lina: I don't blame him.

Ashish: Are you sure you feel 100% safe at home?

Lina: Yes. Why?

Ashish: I'm ready to have David served.

Ashish: Officer Veres finally came around.

Ashish: Can we meet so you can sign the documents?

Lina: I think so.

Lina: I have an idea how to serve him.

Ashish: Are you sure you want to be around when it happens?

Lina: Definitely. I'll tell you what I'm thinking when we meet up.

CHAPTER 44

"That's the second time you've gone running this morning."

"It's a free country, David," Jules said, checking out her backside in the huge federal mirror in their formal dining room. "Hey, Lina, shirt or no shirt?" Jules held a hot-pink crop top up to the neon-green sports bra covering her flat chest.

"Why don't you go naked? I'm sure you'd get some attention then," Lina mumbled, pulling the miniquiches from the oven. Her sister-in-law had shown up on their doorstep days earlier in hopes of getting famous over Lina and her family troubles. Jules had given interviews about how she "supported whatever decision her brother made" and how she "was praying for her family to get through this rough patch, because family is everything." She'd even cried her eyes out on camera when asked to recall how she'd felt when she'd received the news about Lina's affair. The entire charade sickened Lina, but she played nice with Jules's trifling ass to keep the peace.

It'd been a week since Nancy's visit, and Lina had to tamp her excitement down since Ashish was finalizing the sponsorship bidding contracts. The interested companies had less than seventy-two hours left to submit their best offers. Hope prickled at Lina's chest when she thought about how different her life would be in three days.

"Why isn't the table set?" David asked.

"It's nice outside, so I set the table on the deck," Lina said sweetly, glancing at the tall living room windows to the glass-and-wicker table on their covered deck. It was a cloudy July morning and much cooler than normal due to a hurricane threatening the Gulf. It made perfect weather for brunch. She'd been up since sunrise preparing the house for Pastor Nathan's marriage counseling visit. It'd been part of the game she'd had to play in order to get David to submit her name as a legal guardian to the kids' summer camp.

"What about the bugs?" Jules asked, now in the kitchen picking at a quiche she'd stolen. Lina glared at the vacant space on the fancy silver tray.

"Lit those citronella candles David bought last summer," Lina said. She plucked several glasses from the shelf and balanced them on a tray alongside a frosted pitcher of her homemade lemonade.

"Don't embarrass me in front of Pastor Nathan, you hear me?" David said, heading toward them, rolling up the sleeves of his shirt.

"What would I do to embarrass you?"

He glared at her for a few minutes. "I can easily remove your name from the camp, and the kids will stay there until I pick them up."

"I wouldn't piss him off if I were you," Jules said, plucking another quiche from the tray. "These are really good."

Lina plastered on a saccharine-sweet smile. "Thanks, Jules. Hey, David, I've been thinking . . ." She approached him and began tying his tie. "I'm glad we're doing counseling. Think it'll be good for us."

"For you." He tapped the tip of her nose with his index finger.

Jules chortled.

Lina forced herself to remain calm.

"And I'm sorry." She looked up at him innocently, her hands on his chest. "Can you please forgive me?"

David tilted his head slightly, appraising her. "Jules, can you shut the hell up for a few seconds? And go put on some clothes."

"Think I'll go for that run now," Jules said before taking another quiche.

Lina finished with David's tie and moved on to straightening his folded cuffs. When she glanced back up, his gaze softened.

"You look really nice," he said.

"Thank you for the dress. It's beautiful." She turned around for him, the delicate fabric swishing as she did. It'd appeared on Mimi's door late last night, with a note on the dress bag: *Wear this tomorrow. Remember the kids.* The pale blue complemented his dark-navy trousers and paisley tie, and she wanted nothing more than to rip the dress off and burn it.

David tenderly brushed her hair from her shoulder. "You know I'm only doing all this because I love you, right? There's no me without you."

A part of Lina wanted to believe him—had believed him time and time and time again, but this Lina, this powerful and fully formed Lina, let his empty words fall to the ground. She had to look out for Mimi and Danny—they could no longer be pawns in David's sick game. She had to do what she had to do.

"I know, David." Lina stood on her bare tiptoes and kissed him softly on his cheek.

He trailed a finger down her arm. "Maybe after this we can—"

The doorbell rang, interrupting whatever lame offer David was proposing.

"I'll get it," Jules said.

"You think Pastor Nathan'll want more than just the quiche I made?"

"Maybe. You got any of that banana loaf left?" David asked.

Something stabbed at her chest as she remembered how much Noah had loved her banana loaf. "Freezer. Get him all settled, and I'll be out in a few minutes. Gotta pop the loaf in the microwave." She bit the insides of her cheeks, turning away from David's gaze. She leaned

329

on the counter, taking several deep breaths to compose herself. Her gut tightened at the sound of Pastor Nathan's heavy southern drawl.

"Haven't seen you in church, young lady," he said.

"I'll be there this Sunday. I promise," Jules said.

"I'll hold you to it."

"Good morning, Pastor Nathan," David said as Jules and the pastor entered the living room.

"Heard congratulations are in order," Pastor Nathan said. "Partner suits you."

"Daniella tell you? It was her suggestion."

Lina's ears pricked up at the mention of Daniella's name.

"You know my niece can't keep much to herself. She sends her regards."

So the woman from his job was Pastor Nathan's niece? Was this all part of his plan? Play the victim. Become partner. Use Pastor Nathan so word gets back to his firm that he's trying to work on his marriage? The chess pieces were starting to make sense to Lina now. She was no more than a pawn on his board. Another piece to conquer to get what he wanted. Could she pull off her moves without him noticing?

"Beautiful house. How're y'all dealing with all of those people outside?" he asked.

"It's been difficult for the kids, so Lina and I decided it was best to send them away to summer camp for a few weeks."

"How have you two been?"

"I won't lie; it's been rough." David paused and glanced over at Lina. "But we're glad you're here. We're ready to put the work in."

"And how are you, Lina?" Pastor Nathan asked, shifting his Bible and notepad from one hand to the next before pushing his thick glasses farther up his bulbous nose.

"I—" She pulled her lips to the side. "I've been better." The microwave dinged.

"That smells amazing." Pastor Nathan rubbed his round belly. Lina bit back a smile, imagining the pastor in a Santa Claus costume.

"Thanks," she said, slicing into the loaf. Ribbons of steam curled into the air. She had half a mind to open the kitchen window and send the spicy cinnamon and nutmeg scents to beckon Noah old cartoon–style. She shook the image from her head. Noah was gone. Their relationship was over. Getting away from David sane and with her kids was all that mattered. "I'll join you guys on the deck in a bit. The caramel pecan sauce won't take long."

Pastor Nathan licked his lips. "We're scheduling a counseling session every week, right?"

"Maybe twice a week." David clapped his back. "C'mon, deck's this way."

Lina watched David lead the pastor through the french doors to the covered deck. She caught David scoff when Pastor Nathan went to the edge of the deck to check out their hilltop view. Once the caramel pecan sauce was at a full boil, she pulled the pan from the stove, gave it a quick stir, and carefully drizzled the sauce over the warm bread.

"I'll do the dishes if you leave me a little plate," Jules said, leaning against the counter.

"You know you won't do the dishes."

"I might." Jules shrugged.

Lina piled some food onto one of the small plates and slid it across the counter. "I'd better go." Her phone buzzed with a text.

Ashish: You can do this.

Ashish: You have to do this.

Pocketing her phone, she knew he was right. She knew it with everything in her. She gathered the tray and went out to the deck, her pulse pounding in her ears.

"Pastor Nathan, will you do us the honor?" David asked.

Pastor Nathan bowed his head and gave a quick blessing over the food and the preparer. His hands reached for the delicate china dessert plates before he'd even said, "Amen." Lina was glad to have someone appreciate her time in the kitchen.

She sat beside her husband at the round table and scooped a few miniquiches onto her plate alongside some plump strawberries. *The kids would've loved a morning picnic outside,* she thought, her heart aching to see Mimi's delicate face and to feel Danny's strong arms around her waist. *What kind of monster would keep his children away from their mother?*

"Since this is our first meeting, I'd like to hear what's on your mind. David, how about we begin with you?" Pastor Nathan took a dainty bite.

David slid his hand over hers. "I love my wife. I adore my children. I'm trying to be a better husband in light of recent revelations."

"And you, Lina?"

She slipped her hand from David's and put it in her lap. "I, um, cheated on my loving husband, but I will do anything for my children."

Another forkful. "Sounds like you both want to do whatever you can to repair this mistake and strengthen your marriage. David, as the husband—"

Lina smirked, catching sunlight glinting off something in their wooded backyard. *Here it goes.*

Pastor Nathan tilted his head slightly at her. "Why the look?"

Busted. "I don't know."

"I want you to be honest. This is a safe place."

"Well," Lina said, biting her bottom lip. *Screw it.* "I'm just waiting for the whole 'Lina, you're going to hell. You need to submit to your husband no matter what. He's the leader of the family. Shut up and smile.'" She felt David's body go rigid beside her. Now she'd done it.

Pastor Nathan stared at her for a few moments, his face pinched. "I get it," he said, leaning back in his chair. His features relaxed, and his eyes shone with compassion. "Humans are imperfect; that's why we have faith. Bette and I struggled early on in our marriage, and now we're about to celebrate our thirty-fifth anniversary."

Jealousy nipped at Lina like an annoying mosquito at the pastor's thirty-five-year marriage.

"If she'd have just listened to me about that site and the kids, this would've never have happened. I keep telling her—"

"Well, hold on, David," Pastor Nathan said. "Look at all the good your kids have done."

"But they were all supposed to listen to me. To submit to me."

"Submission is a two-way street."

Lina sat up a little higher. This was new and unexpected.

"Huh?" David mumbled.

"Nowhere does it say women should submit blindly."

"But I'm still the head of the house, and she needs to do what I say."

"Yes and no."

"What does that even mean?"

"Think of your marriage as a partnership. Where she's weaker, you're stronger and vice versa. You need her like she needs you. Husbands aren't bosses. It doesn't work like that."

Vindication swelled in her chest until she thought she'd pop. Maybe she'd been wrong about the good ole pastor all these years. "That's enlightening."

Pastor Nathan brought his folded hands to his lips for a brief second. "I'm sensing a little tension here. Mind if I try a different approach?"

"Sure," David said, monotone.

"Has there been a lot of harsh words and criticism in the relationship?"

"Yes," Lina said.

"No," David said at the same time.

"I see."

"The only thing you see is that my wife has a crappy memory."

"Well, how about any times where either of you have felt pressured into agreeing or going along with the other to keep the peace?" Pastor Nathan asked.

"Never," David said before Lina could answer. His hand dipped below the table and pinched the tender skin on her thigh. She wriggled against the pain.

"And you, Lina? Have you ever felt pressured into agreeing to keep the peace with your husband?"

David's fingers now dug into her flesh. *How the hell were his hands so damn strong?*

"I fail to see what these questions have to do with my wife's infidelity," David said, the vein in his forehead thick and pronounced. "She's the one who broke our marriage vows. She's the one who did all this."

The sound of the doorbell was faint. Lina turned around to see Jules hurrying to answer it.

"How about any physical violence? Has there been any—"

"He's out here." Jules's voice and approaching footsteps cut through the tension on the deck.

David squinted at Lina, but she shrugged. "I'm not expecting anyone," she said, her heartbeat quickening.

David stood as Jules stepped onto the deck, a rail-thin older woman on her heels.

"Mr. Henry?" the woman said, producing a thick manila envelope and clipboard from her canvas bag.

"Yes. What can I do for you?"

Lina rose, making space between herself and David.

"I'm a process server. Need you to sign for this," the woman said.

"Process server?" David asked, then bared his teeth at Lina. "Am I being served?"

"Yes, sir. Sign here and here."

Lina slinked along the house to get away from her husband, feeling the rough bricks snag her dress. David snarled from across the deck as he slashed the pen across the various documents. He snatched the envelope, ripping it open.

"Thank you, sir. Have a good day."

Pastor Nathan sat quietly, his mouth dropping as David studied the petition for divorce.

"Full custody?" he roared. "Spousal support? Child support?" David leered. "I can't believe you did this."

Pastor Nathan stood. "Now, David, I'm sure—"

"I'm sorry, but I think we're going to have to postpone this session, Pastor Nathan." David waved him off. "Jules! Come show him out. Now!"

Please don't go. Please don't go. Please don't go.

The pastor gave them both apologetic looks. "I'll be praying for you both. Don't hesitate to reach out when you're ready."

David stared poisonous darts at Lina while the pastor gathered his things and left with Jules.

"I cannot believe you chose to serve me in front of Pastor Nathan," David said slowly, his jaw firmly clenched. "His niece is a partner. What do you think he's going to tell her the second he steps foot outside? I needed to make it look like we were trying to fix this." He paced. "I told you I'd never grant you a divorce. This"—he motioned to the house—"all belongs to me and me alone. You haven't worked a day in the last seventeen years."

"We can't keep this up anymore, David," Lina said, stepping backward until she bumped into the railing.

"I can do this all day."

"I can't; don't you understand?"

"The respondent, without cause or provocation by the petitioner"—David read the divorce petition out loud—"has been guilty of extreme and repeated mental and emotional cruelty toward the petitioner." David's eyes narrowed. "You're really going to put all of our business out there, aren't you?"

"We can't keep doing this."

"You begged and begged for counseling, and now that I'm doing it, you file for divorce?"

"David, it's too late. You frighten me."

He stalked toward her. "Always the victim."

"David, please—"

"This about Noah?"

"Noah doesn't have anything to do with this."

"You'd rather be with him than me. You'd rather be with that man than be a mother to your kids. Selfish bitch." He jerked a fist at her, slamming it against the deck railing.

Lina flinched.

"Can you be rational for once in your life? This isn't about Noah. Do I want to be with him? Yes, but that's not even an option. All I know is I can't be with you." She needed to poke the sleeping bear. "You're abusive."

"I'm abusive?" He laughed. "You serve me in front of my pastor and I'm abusive? You lie all the time, cheat on me, make me feel unappreciated, and I'm abusive? You've hurt me in so many, many ways." He ran a hand through his hair. "You'd better be glad I was able to gain some leverage from this, or you would've been so damn sorry. I mean, you didn't even have the decency to be neat about your little affair, like everyone else. Did you even think of how embarrassing it would be for me? Did you stop and think, gee, maybe I shouldn't be caught kissing this guy or it'll be on every news station, shaming my husband as though he's not enough for me. Is that what you wanted? To embarrass me? To ridicule me?" He threw the divorce package at her. "Is that what this is about? Are you trying to humiliate me?"

"No. The kids—"

"You're not taking my kids and leaving me for him. I don't care how many papers you file."

"I have to leave. This is not—" Her cheekbone felt like it exploded when the back of David's hand came up across her face, sending her into the railing.

"You'll leave when I say so."

"I'm leaving today, and I'm going to go pick the kids up."

"The hell you are." He struck her again with such force she lost her balance and fell to her knees on the deck.

"David, stop!"

"You ungrateful bitch!" David was gone, his Dr. Jekyll fully giving way to Mr. Hyde. "I gave you everything! Every last piece of me and you want to leave me?"

She tried to scramble away from him, but he was on her within seconds.

"You're not leaving me." He struck her again and the world was muffled. His hands found purchase around her neck.

"Help!" she squeaked, her chest burning. She kicked and pushed, but he was too strong.

"You'll never leave me. You'll never see the kids again. You will never leave this house."

"David, st—" She gasped. Dark specks clouded her vision. She searched for someone to help her. Anyone.

"You are mine, you hear me? Everything here is mine!"

David's hands were a noose crushing her airway. Exhaustion claimed her muscles. Dizziness swirled in her head.

Mimi.

Danny.

Her heart cried out for her children. She imagined snuggling with them on one of their epic Sunday pajama days. She felt tears slide into her hair as everything around her slowly faded into black.

Goodbye, Noah.

CHAPTER 45

She couldn't feel anything.

One minute her body was riddled with excruciating pain, the next she was numb and weightless, as if floating across a placid lake. Now she felt heavy and weighed down all over, like her arms and legs were hundred-pound sandbags, with several hundred pounds resting atop her chest. No matter how hard she fought, she couldn't budge.

Stillness had claimed her body.

Darkness had claimed her sight.

It made no sense. She drifted between sleep and wakefulness, spending all her energy trying to get her fingers or toes to move.

Her efforts were futile.

Faint sounds came in spotty waves. A beep here. Voices there.

"Unresponsive."

"Close call."

"Intubated."

"Mom?"

"Lina."

"Come on."

"Fight."

After some time, Lina figured she was in the hospital in some sort of unconscious state, and soon she grew to hear everything. She mentally ticked off the beeps she heard, imagining them as music beats. Little by little, voices became recognizable, and the needles went from slight pressure to a sharp stab when they pierced her flesh.

Nancy's was the first real voice she recognized and understood. She tried her hardest to respond. She wanted Nancy to know she was okay and that she was still in there.

"Take it easy, Lina," Nancy said, sniffling. "Don't fight it. Rest, so you can heal. The kids need you." She cried for some time, holding Lina's hand. "Gummy bears, Lina: you're the only sister I have. You have to get through this. I need you."

Lina's eyes felt dry and sticky, despite the prickling sense of urgent tears.

"Nancy?"

Lina knew that voice.

She wanted to yell for Noah to help her. For him to reach down and pull her out of the void in which she was trapped.

"Yeah? Shit! It's you! You're here!" Nancy said.

"I came as soon as I could," he said.

"You think it's a good idea to be here?"

"I don't care anymore. How is she?"

"She's okay. She's going to be all right."

Lina listened intently, grateful she had a positive prognosis.

"Mimi and Danny? How are they?" Noah asked. Lina wanted to know as well. Where were they?

"Ashish got an emergency injunction before David was bonded. They're at my place right now with Ashish. I told him not to let them see the footage, but at this point it's everywhere."

Lina wondered why David had been bonded. Had he been arrested? What footage?

"I know. I can't get it out of my head," Noah said. "What are the doctors saying?"

"There's no permanent damage, so far, but she *has* to wake up soon."

Lina wondered why she was at risk for permanent damage. From what? What had happened to her? She raked her memories and came up blank.

"That's good news. I'll take it," Noah said.

"Here. Never took you for a crier."

"Thanks. I've never been one until recently. She has this effect on me."

"You really do love her, don't you?"

I love you, too, Noah, Lina thought.

"More than words. She's . . . she is the most amazing woman I've ever met," Noah said.

"I wish things were different for you guys."

"Me too. Can I have just one minute with her? Promise I won't be long."

"I don't think you should be here. It doesn't look good."

"I'm so tired of trying to make everything look good. I wasn't there for her. I wasn't there like I should've been, and he did this."

"Nothing you said would've stopped her," Nancy said.

"What do you mean?"

"This was all her idea."

My idea?

"Her idea? I don't get it," Noah said. Lina shared in his confusion.

"She set it up. She orchestrated having David served. The paparazzi in the backyard. The police officer. Everything. It was all Lina's idea. She knew it was the only way to get the authorities to believe her so she could finally get the hell out of there with the kids, especially with David having a judge in his pocket. No one expected it to go so badly," Nancy said.

"What happened?"

What happened? Police? Paparazzi?

"Cop didn't have a warrant. David's idiot sister wouldn't let her in the house. Cop had to be textbook so the charges stuck. Lina expected David to slap her or rough her up or something. He'd done that much already. She was ready for it, but . . ."

David. His hands. Panic rose in Lina's chest at the memories of David on top of her, his hands around her throat.

"But she wasn't expecting him to damn near kill her," Noah said. Lina's neck felt like it was on fire.

"Nail on head. She wasn't breathing by the time the officer got to her. Took two people to get David off her."

"That's what she meant when she asked me to trust her?"

"I don't know, but she felt this was her only option. Ashish tried to talk her out of it, but she was adamant. David was not going to let her go easily. Her back was against a wall with him," Nancy said.

"Lina?"

She felt Noah's hand on hers and willed her body to snap out of it just then.

"I'm here. I'm here now. Part of me understands why you let this happen. The other part wants to kill him. We should've never left your room at the Plaza. I should've been stronger. I will spend the rest of my life trying to make it up to you, if you let me."

"Seriously, you've got to go before someone sees you," Nancy said.

"I'll fold your fitted sheets. Hell, I'll fold all of your laundry if you want me to. Just open your eyes and give me one of your smiles."

"I'm so serious. You've got to go before someone sees you. I can't have a circus here like the one at her house," Nancy said.

His hand left Lina's. "Here's my number. Can you let me know when she wakes up?"

"I don't think that's a good idea. I mean, she's going to have a lot of stuff to work through. Both her and the kids . . . but I'll leave it up to her when she wakes up."

"I understand."

"I'm sorry."

"It was good to meet you in person, Nancy. I see why you mean so much to her."

"Yeah? Well, the last few years without her were a living nightmare. Think I need her more than she needs me."

CHAPTER 46

"Hey, guys! Can you hurry up? Nance will be here any minute now. Danny, don't forget those socks. Mimi, c'mon, get off your phone and straighten up the pillows," Lina called from her small kitchen before pulling three blueberry loaves from the oven. The fruity, sweet doughy scent wrapped around her like an old friend. It'd been a while since she'd baked anything. The kitchen in her condo was much smaller than the one from her house with David, but it was clean, peaceful, safe, and all hers.

It had been four months since David's attack.

She'd ended up spending a little over a week in the hospital; then she and the kids had spent the rest of the summer and most of the fall with Nancy in Athens while Ashish filed the protective orders and petitioned the courts for full custody. It'd been a much-needed respite for all of them since her affair and abuse had been so public.

Their long summer days had been filled with swimming, reading, and relaxing, followed by homework and after-school activities when school resumed. Lina had insisted on weekly family therapy sessions for her and the kids, in addition to individual sessions every other week.

While she bore no external scars, she still had occasional throat pain and difficulty swallowing every now and then. Not to mention how her pulse raced and her head swam whenever she imagined seeing David when they were out. He'd almost killed her. Technically, he *had* killed her. She'd been close to never seeing Mimi and Danny again.

She leaned against the counter, hand at her neck, and thought about that day. She remembered how unnaturally cool it'd been that morning. She remembered changing her mind about Pastor Nathan. She even remembered the rage crisscrossing David's face when he'd been served, but she couldn't remember much after the first slap. She'd been expecting it. She'd made sure she was near the deck railing so the photographer in the backyard could get a clear shot of the attack, but everything after that was muddled and confusing, like trying to watch a movie from the bottom of a filthy pool.

Maybe it was a good thing she was unable to remember the assault. She'd woken up in the hospital with pain surging through her limbs, throbbing in her head, and her eyes bloodshot. Talking had been excruciating, so the doctors had suggested she give it a week or two before trying, and when she had, it'd felt like a sharp knife was slicing her throat open.

The house phone rang, making Lina jerk. She almost knocked a warm blueberry loaf into the sink. Mimi answered it, shooting her a concerned look.

"Yes. Please let her in," Mimi said to the security guard and disarmed the alarm near the front door. A smile settled on Lina's face, and relief flooded her chest, warming it. Nance was finally here. Knowing her best friend would soon be in her house made her feel less alone, despite having her children there. Being used to having another adult in the house and now not having one was such a strange feeling.

"There's my handsome boy," Nance said and wrapped Danny in a massive bear hug when he answered the door. "I missed you so much. How's school? Any girlfriends yet?"

"It's only been a few weeks, Auntie Nance."

Lina couldn't help but smile. She'd missed her friend. It'd been three weeks since they'd packed up and moved back to Atlanta to resume their lives.

Mimi hugged Nancy. "I might have a boyfriend."

"Oh really, chica?" Nancy elbowed her. "Tell me all about him later, and we'll stalk his online accounts."

"Definitely." Mimi locked the front door and armed the nearby alarm system.

"How's she been holding up?"

"I'm fine. I'm right here, Nance," Lina said. "Keep it up and you're not getting any food."

"Full of sunshine and roses, I see." Nancy held open her arms. "Where's my hug, woman?"

Lina embraced her. "Thanks for coming."

"Place looks amazing." Nancy sniffed. "And what is that? Ohmigod, blueberries? You didn't."

"I did. Tacos and homemade blueberry loaf."

"Marry me?"

That made Lina laugh until her sides hurt. "You're too much. Besides, I think Ashish would have a problem with that. How is he?"

"Said he'd stop by later. You got enough food, right?"

"Of course." After pulling some plates from the cabinet, Lina rummaged through a box labeled "kitchen junk" in the pantry, searching for the set of taco holders. Lodged between the hard plastic holders was the last card she'd received from David—the paper doll:

To the love of my life,

I love you more today than when I first met you so many years ago. We've both grown so much. Our family is better because of you—you make it home instead of just a place to live. You have made me the luckiest man in the world for putting up with me all these years.

I know I haven't been the easiest person to get along with recently. I will do better. I will be better for you and for the kids.

You are my life.

My only reason to smile after a long day.

Please keep loving me the way you do. I promise we will be better and stronger than ever because that's what I prayed for and you know God's never let us down.

I love you with all my being and more.

Yours forever,
David

She dropped it. When she knelt to pick it back up, the cool tile reassured her she was in a different house now, with a much different life. A safe, peaceful, quiet life. One of her own choosing.

She returned to the counter with the taco holders and tossed the card into the garbage. She was no longer a paper doll, and she'd never be one again. She turned back to Nancy, feeling renewed. Whole. "You want to wait, or are you hungry now?"

"Feed me now. That drive was no joke." Nancy deposited her Louis Vuitton on a barstool near the counter and ran a hand through her hair. "Anything new about you-know-who?"

"Hey, guys, turn off the TV and go wash your hands for dinner. Mimi, put up your homework and grab the taco shells from the pantry when you get a chance."

Nancy leaned on the counter. "I take that as a no."

Lina nodded, sighing. "His sister finally stopped calling, but I think I saw his father in the grocery store last week."

"Still in therapy?"

Lina dipped a chip in queso. "Of course."

"At least the deal with Nike went through. I still can't wrap my mind around how you managed to negotiate like a boss when you couldn't even speak. Three hundred fifty thousand dollars." Nancy shook her head slowly. "It's un-fucking-real. Unreal. I mean, I saw the money in the bank, but it still hasn't hit me."

"Me neither." Lina leaned in close to Nancy. "Can I be honest?"

"Of course, what's wrong?"

"I'm still waiting for something to happen. Like, this can't be my life. I don't win. David doesn't just give up and go away. I've never . . . I don't know." Lina felt stupid hearing her word vomit, but she couldn't deny the constant rumble of nerves in her gut.

Nancy held her hands. "It's over. This is your life now. You and the kids and that cash in the bank. You've won. Relax. Live."

"I guess you're right. The ink is dry on the sponsorship package. David is too proud to break the protective order and end up in jail again," Lina reassured herself. Soon her divorce would be finalized, and she'd be free to move on with her life. She wondered how Noah had spent the last four months of his life. Had he won custody of Edward? She'd considered calling him when she first woke from her coma, but talking had been excruciating, and no one really knew the extent of the damage she'd suffered. Last thing she'd wanted was to be a burden and have him as her caretaker.

Days had turned into weeks and then months, and eventually Lina had become too afraid to call him or even google him for that matter.

What if he'd moved on with his life and was now dating some supergorgeous model? Or even worse, what if his reputation never recovered and he regretted being with her?

Maybe walking away from each other had been the best option. Besides, what would she ask: Do you still like me? Circle yes or no?

"Can we eat tacos now?" Nancy knocked on the counter.

"It's not called Taco Tuesday for nothing." Lina faked a smile. What was wrong with her? She should be content. Hell, she should be over-the-moon happy with her life right now. So why was she so lifeless? So zombielike about her situation? Had David been right about her never being happy? She shook her head, not allowing his voice to penetrate her mind. *No. Never again.* His opinion didn't matter. She'd just fake it until she was fully content.

They all huddled around the coffee table in the living room, eating tacos and playing a fierce game of Uno. Of course, Danny talked the most smack and beat everyone with bravado. His prize: the remote control to the television for the rest of the night. Mimi scrolled through her phone while Danny flipped the channels in search of something to watch. There was a certain joy in the cacophony of voices, television murmur, dishwasher rumble, and electronic whir from the various appliances.

Lina's heart warmed. Her place was finally starting to feel like a home.

"Mom, you okay?" Mimi asked, looking up from her phone.

"Yeah. I'm good."

"You sure?"

Lina nodded, opened her mouth to ask Mimi about her potential boyfriend when a familiar voice caught her attention.

Noah's face filled the screen. Everyone froze as the news played.

"Can you tell us what charity you're supporting tonight?" the reporter asked. Lina's heart hammered in her chest.

"Diana's House. It's a charity that is very close to my heart." He cleared his throat. "Diana's provides emergency and ongoing services to abused women. I'm currently working to renovate my mother's house to be used as additional housing for their program graduates."

"You've been silent about your childhood experiences with abuse until recently. Would you attribute your recent public relationship to this sudden change?"

Noah's Adam's apple bobbed, and he blinked uncomfortably. Lina's palms itched to reach for him. "It changed a lot of things in my life for the good, and I don't regret a single second." He gazed into the camera for what felt like a millennium. "I'd do it all over again."

"But we're here to invite people out to tonight's event, so can you give us the details one more time?"

"Sure. I'm guest deejaying at Frenetic tonight. You can purchase tickets online or at the event. I am personally matching all proceeds, and they go directly to Diana's House, just in time for the holidays."

"Thank you so much, Mr. Attoh. You heard it here. Get those tickets while you can. This is Jenny Nolan for Channel Three News."

Was he happy? She couldn't read him from the small snippet of an interview. Had he wanted her to come out tonight? Had he been trying to send her a sign by supporting Diana's House?

"You know you have to go, right, Mom?" Danny said.

"He's right. You're going. No questions asked," Nancy said.

"I can't. I don't have anything to wear. I don't know if I—"

"Mom, we're okay. I'm okay if you want to go," Danny said.

"Me too," Mimi added. "I really think you should at least try. I mean, you did get a new phone and a new phone number."

"You don't even know if he tried to call you," Danny said.

"And I know we promised not to google anything about him, but he hasn't even been in the country this whole time," Mimi admitted.

Danny got all excited. "Yeah, he's been in Kenya and then France—"

"UK, derp. And I'm sure he really wants to see you. I mean, he like posts these cute pics with his son all the time on Instagram now."

"And likes all my comments and one time replied with rock, paper, and scissors emojis."

"He always likes everything I post, and last week when I posted the pics me and you took on that hike, he commented with a big red heart," Mimi added to top Danny.

"Hold on. You guys have been in contact with him this whole time?" Nancy asked.

The kids looked at each other and nodded.

"I'm sorry, Mom. I didn't know if you wanted—"

A smile played on her lips, knowing he'd kept in touch with the kids this whole time. "It's okay, Mimi. I'm glad you didn't tell me. Maybe it's for the best. I mean, the doctors weren't sure about my recovery, and I don't know. I didn't want to call him because I was so embarrassed. And adults change." Lina fished for excuses to cover up her fear. What if she misread him just now and he was simply deejaying for a charity with no hopes of ever seeing her again?

Lina's phone buzzed with a text.

"That's the VIP ticket I just bought for you," Nancy said.

The kids squealed with delight.

"I'm sure Ashish and I can handle things here."

"So you're going, right?" Mimi asked.

"C'mon, Mom," Danny added.

They were all too much. But what if they were right? What if Noah keeping in touch with the kids was a sign that he wanted to keep in touch with her? She'd never know unless she asked him. "Yes."

CHAPTER 47

The event had started earlier that evening, but Lina's nerves had been a mess, and she was now entering the club hours late. Frenetic was a two-story monstrosity. The black walls were splattered in fluorescents that came to life under roving black lights. Her shredded skinny jeans hugged her curves, and her pale-pink sweater gave her just enough cleavage. She adjusted her top self-consciously, sure she was showing a little too much.

The strappy black stilettos Mimi and Nancy had forced Lina to wear were pinching her toes and scraping the backs of her heels, but the discomfort subsided the second she spotted Noah in the deejay booth. With a set of bulky headphones up to his ear, he waved a hand at the crowd and nodded his head along to the beat. Lina stared at him in awe. He was in his element, entertaining the people and making them dance to his mixes.

As part of her VIP ticket, she was given special access to the second floor. It was more elaborately decorated than the first level and included an open bar. She ordered a red wine to have something for her hands to do.

Black lights rolled across murals on the walls like a moving picture. While she tried to keep track of Noah, the paintings quickly caught her attention. There was an eagle taking flight in a star-filled sky. Its path, illuminated by the black lights, made it seem to soar across the walls and over the crowd below. Lina followed it from one wall to the next, up to the ceiling, and over to the opposite end of the club, where it exploded into a million flecks of light.

It was then she noticed the music had changed. She focused her attention back to the deejay booth, but Noah was nowhere to be found. She scanned the crowd below, searching each face for Noah's.

No.

Had she missed him?

She darted over to the nearest bouncer. "Do you know where Mr. Attoh went?" she asked as innocently as possible.

"I think his set was up. He's probably about to leave."

"Is there any way I can meet him?"

"Every chick's been asking that tonight. I'm sorry, but I don't think that's possible."

Lina's heart sank. "Are you sure he's about to leave? Can you double-check or something?"

"Ma'am, his set is over. He was only contracted to be here for a certain amount of time. His time is up, so he's leaving. Hell, he probably already left. People like him always bounce the second they're done."

Her knees buckled. She'd missed her chance, watching some stupid painting. "Um, okay. Thanks." That was it then. She'd accepted their breakup months earlier, but seeing him again and hoping to reconnect was like opening a scabbed-over wound. She missed him so much; it wasn't fair.

The blaring music was the perfect noise to drown out her thoughts and pitiful sobs. She shuffled over to the railing to steady herself and looked down at all the joyous revelers below. She had been that happy once. The night they'd shared in New York was something she'd never forget. Inhaling deeply, she wiped her eyes with the heels of her palms, sure she was smearing her makeup. Thankfully, she had her children to go home to. She'd snuggle them and leech from their happiness for a while.

Someone's shadow hovered near her. She really didn't want to be bothered, so she ignored them and pretended to be focused on the crowd below.

A palm warmed the small of her back, and she smiled.

"Hoped you'd show up tonight," Noah said, his head near hers.

She sniffled. "I have a ton of fitted sheets I can't fold."

"Well, I've been told I'm a wizard."

ACKNOWLEDGMENTS

I am so grateful to all the wonderful, talented people at Lake Union, with special thanks to Alicia Clancy for believing in this book and for sharing my vision.

Thank you to my Ambassador of Quan (inside joke) and agent extraordinaire Kat Kerr, for championing my book when it was just a Twitter pitch. Your patience, guidance, and overall badassery have been instrumental.

A writer may write all their words themselves, but to complete a novel, it takes family, friends, support groups, Facebook writing groups, daily text messages, panicked calls, and socially distanced hugs. I am forever grateful to everyone who has supported me through this journey.

Thank you to my parents, Gloria and Robert—look, guys, I wrote a book! A special thanks to my sisters, my children, my extended children (Sumer, Jacqueline, Dawn, JJ, and McKenzie—promised Dawn I'd add this), my incredible friends for your encouragement through my darkest times, and to Jae, thanks for being you!

I can't leave out my writing community for making me a better writer and for your unflinching support: Genn/Gennifer/Jennifer for your relentlessness, ATL Writers (Gilly, Kim, Vicky, Connie, Jo, Nic, Nicole, Rachael, and Gina), WrAHMs, Tamara Mataya, Write Club (Melissa B, Melissa H, and Jessica), Nathan Bransford and the

Bransforums!, Beth Phelan and #DVPIT, and Dede for your daily text check-ins.

In the end, this novel was written by me but tells the story of so many women caught in the cross fire of their significant other's words. Domestic violence isn't always physical. Verbal and emotional abuse is a death by a thousand tiny cuts to your soul. Don't let anyone turn you into a paper doll. And if you are a paper doll, talk to someone. Get help. You are not alone.

BOOK CLUB DISCUSSION QUESTIONS

1. At the beginning of the book, we learn Lina has been withholding information from David, her husband. She never expressly told him about traveling with their children, she had a secret bank account, and, despite David's request, she continued to work throughout their marriage. Is there ever a reason to keep information from a significant other, or is it best to always share everything? What does keeping information from one's spouse say about the relationship?

2. We learn Lina is lonely and has no friends, so given how natural their conversation during dinner was, Lina thinks a friendship with Noah is a good idea. Do you think members of the opposite sex can have platonic friendships? Do the same rules apply to married couples?

3. David makes it a habit to check Lina's and the kids' locations and to constantly monitor their bank accounts. How would you handle this situation? Do you think it appropriate to check your significant other's location and bank account?

4. When Lina returns home from Noah's studio, David wistfully remembers a time when they dated, and he wants to sleep with his wife. Does consent apply to marriage?

5. There are many instances in the novel where Lina purposefully uses her "sweet voice" when talking to her husband. Have you ever had to use your "sweet voice"? What do you think consistently using a "sweet voice" to keep one's significant other from lashing out says about that relationship?

6. We see the violence slowly increasing from verbal to emotional to physical until Lina's life is threatened. Does verbal abuse always lead to physical violence? Are there warning signs?

7. Throughout the book, David pits himself against Lina as the good cop versus the bad cop. Is there ever an appropriate time for one parent to be the "good" one versus the "bad" one?

8. Mimi tells Lina that she and Danny "see and hear everything" in their house. Do adults tend to underestimate how much kids pick up on within the household?

ABOUT THE AUTHOR

After finding her way to Atlanta, Georgia, by way of Hawaii, USVI, Miami, and South Carolina, Robyn Lucas developed a successful career in communications and marketing. Her background came in handy when her teenagers created an award-winning mental health app. But living the fabulous life is tough, so Robyn grounds herself with piles of laundry, managing busy teenpreneurs, and writing women's fiction because it's cheaper than therapy. When Robyn is not writing (with a spreadsheet filled with plot bunnies for countless novels), she enjoys traveling, spending time with her teens, marathoning (TV shows, not running), reading, and snuggling with her dog, Trooper. For more information, visit www.robynlucas.com.